DAWN

Borgo Press Books by S. Fowler Wright

Arresting Delia: An Inspector Cleveland Classic Crime Novel
The Attic Murder: An Inspector Combridge & Mr. Jellipot Classic Crime Novel
The Bell Street Murders: An Inspector Combridge & Mr. Jellipot Classic Crime Novel
Beyond the Rim: A Lost Race Fantasy
Black Widow: A Classic Crime Novel
The Capone Caper: Mr. Jellipot vs. the King of Crime: A Classic Crime Novel
Crime & Co.: An Inspector Cleveland Classic Crime Novel
Dawn: A Novel of Global Warming
Dead by Saturday: An Inspector Cleveland Classic Crime Novel
Dream; or, The Simian Maid: A Fantasy of Prehistory (Marguerite Cranleigh #1)
Elfwin: An Historical Novel
The End of the Mildew Gang: An Inspector Cauldron Classic Crime Novel (Mildew Gang #3)
Four Callers in Razor Street: An Inspector Combridge & Mr. Jellipot Classic Crime Novel
The Hanging of Constance Hillier: An Inspector Cleveland Classic Crime Novel
The Hidden Tribe: A Lost Race Fantasy
The Jordans Murder: An Inspector Combridge & Mr. Jellipot Classic Crime Novel
The King Against Anne Bickerton: A Classic Crime Novel
The Mildew Gang: An Inspector Cauldron Classic Crime Novel (Mildew Gang #1)
Murder in Bethnal Square: An Inspector Combridge & Mr. Jellipot Classic Crime Novel
The Police and the Public
Post-Mortem Evidence: An Inspector Combridge & Mr. Jellipot Classic Crime Novel
The Return of the Mildew Gang: An Inspector Cauldron Classic Crime Novel (Mildew Gang #2)
The Rissole Mystery: An Inspector Combridge & Mr. Jellipot Classic Crime Novel
The Screaming Lake: A Lost Race Novel
The Secret of the Screen: An Inspector Combridge & Mr. Jellipot Classic Crime Novel
Spiders' War: A Novel of the Far Future (Marguerite Cranleigh #3)
Three Witnesses: A Classic Crime Novel
Too Much for Mr. Jellipot: An Inspector Combridge & Mr. Jellipot Classic Crime Novel
The Vengeance of Gwa: A Fantasy of Prehistory (Marguerite Cranleigh #2)
Was Murder Done? A Classic Crime Novel
Who Murdered Reynard? A Classic Crime Novel
The Wills of Jane Kanwhistle: An Inspector Combridge & Mr. Jellipot Classic Crime Novel
With Cause Enough?: An Inspector Combridge & Mr. Jellipot Classic Crime Novel

DAWN

A Novel of Global Warming

by

S. FOWLER WRIGHT

THE BORGO PRESS

An Imprint of Wildside Press LLC

MMIX

AUTHOR'S NOTE

This book is complete in itself, but is a sequel to *Deluge* in the sense that some of the characters are the same, and the latter part of the book continues the narrative of *Deluge* beyond the point at which that book closes.

ABOUT THE AUTHOR

SYDNEY FOWLER WRIGHT (1874-1965) penned over seventy volumes of science fiction, fantasy, classic mysteries, historical novels, poetry, and non-fiction, many of them being published by the Borgo Press Imprint of Wildside Press.

No abstract doctrine is more false and mischievous than that of the natural quality of men.

—Sir James Fraser, *The Scope of Social Anthropology*

DAWN

BOOK ONE

CHAPTER ONE

THE May sun shone through the unblinded window of Muriel Temple's bedroom, and a warm wind lifted the curtains. A moving shaft of light fell on her face, and she stirred and wakened to a sense of impending evil. For a moment she could not recall the nature of the trouble which had overshadowed her mind. "*To be with Christ, which is far better*"—the words which had brought sleep came back, and with them she remembered. Six months, the specialist had said, or it might be twelve, or eighteen, but it was not likely to be so long. He could not recommend an operation. He had been very kind, but quite definite. There would be more pain later, he admitted, but much could be done to deaden it. She hesitated about that. It might be better to endure the pain, if it were God's will. She was not afraid. She would want to be conscious of death when it came. "*To be with Christ, which is far better*." She did not doubt it.

She had been urged to rest this morning, and had reluctantly promised. She knew that her days of active service were over. She tired so easily. And now that her voice had gone.... But she would far rather have risen for the Sunday morning service as usual.

She had hoped that another operation might have been possible, and followed by some degree of recovered activity, though she knew that she would never see South Africa again. But that hope was over now. If God had decided that He did not need her further, she must not be faithless and defiant. He could build the new mission church at Nizetsi, on which her heart had been set, without her aid should He will it. She knew that; but she did not think that it was His will, or He would not have sent her this summons to lay aside the work she was doing. Perhaps, had she made better use of the time she had...

It was twenty years since she had sailed from Southampton for her first station in Basutoland. Life had seemed long then, and now.... *"The night cometh, when no man can work."*

The night had come.

Her thought paused as the bells of Sterrington Church commenced their summons for the early Communion. She did not like the Anglican service. She knew it to be full of superstitions and laxities. Sinners should be converted, not confirmed. But she had a wide charity of mind, and today she would gladly have knelt in any place that was dedicated to her Master's service, however blindly.

She thought of dawn moving over the earth, and of a world that waked to worship.

> *Fast as the light of morning broke*
> *On island, continent, and deep,*
> *Thy far-spread family awoke,*
> *Sabbath all round the world to keep.*

She remembered how she had used that great conception of James Montgomery to move a Zulu audience. She did not think of it as James Montgomery's hymn. She did not know or care who had written it. She had no literary sense, but she had imagination, if only she were approached on the one side on which her mind was open, and she had a gift of clear and musical speech which could take an audience with her—till her throat had failed. Even in the harsh Zulu gutturals. "She who speaks as we speak," so they had called her.

> *Thy poor have all been freely fed,*
> *Thy chastened sons have kissed the rod,*
> *Thy mourners have been comforted,*
> *Thy pure in heart have seen their God.*

The familiar words brought comfort. God was so very near to those who sought Him. She reached out for the Bible on her bedside table. She would read the usual morning chapter. As she did so Mrs. Wilkes knocked timidly, and, being answered, brought in her breakfast.

Mrs. Wilkes brought some gillies also. She knew that Muriel loved flowers. It was a world full of kindness, even for those for whom Death was waiting impatiently. Death might be near, but God was always nearer.

CHAPTER TWO

MURIEL'S mind wandered from selfish considerations, which it was unusual to indulge, to an incident of the previous afternoon, when she had gained the frightened confidence of Lena Atkins, a girl whose parents lived at the farther end of the village.

She was employed as a factory hand at the Larkshill Iron Works, four miles way, and had been lodging with a girl friend in Larkshill during the week, and coming home each Saturday.

She had contracted a foolish intimacy with the girl's brother, the result of which could be concealed no longer, either at home or factory, and she had a terrified anticipation of the contempt and wrath of her parents, and of dismissal from her employment, as the first consequences of the folly which she had committed.

Muriel was not entirely free from the subconscious bitterness or jealousy which is commonly felt by the childless woman who has maintained her maidenhood toward those of less circumspect experiences, but she was controlled by the larger charity of her Master's teaching, and she had sufficient knowledge of life, and of the human nature of two continents, to be aware that the girl's condition was evidence of a comparative innocence rather than of exceptional vice.

She had already met the head forewoman, and the welfare worker, who were perfunctorily responsible for the conditions prevailing among the three hundred girls and women employed at the Larkshill Works. She knew that devilish contrivances to enable them to lose their chastity and their self-respect, without experiencing the condoning mystery of procreation, were openly sold at the factory gates, and that it was a thriving traffic. She knew that many of the girl's companions, who would be contemptuous of an illegitimate child, would excuse abortion. She knew that immediately the girl's condition should become known among her acquaintances she would be exposed to tempting whispers, advising her of the ease and safety with which she could destroy her child through the agency of noxious drugs, or with the aid of some repulsive hag who made a living by that unnatural wickedness. She knew that a large part even of the medical profession had surrendered to a vice so popular and so profitable, and that it was not only in the cottage or the slums that a doctor would look hard at a woman who suggested the probability of a third or fourth child, and ask if she felt she were strong enough; or did she *really* want it?

But this knowledge did not deflect the rigidity of her mind in its recognition of what is honourable and decent living, whether in a savage kraal or amidst the recondite vices of a dying civilization. Nor had she that perversion of mind, not uncommon among professional exponents of righteousness, which imagines a universal degradation among a population that does not give much attention to the teaching they offer.

She did not doubt that there were many happy and natural marriages among the eight hundred workpeople employed by the Larkshill Iron Works, in spite of the squalid lives to which their boasted civilization had brought them: many clean engagements of unsoiled romance: many integrities, both of men and women, which lived aloof and undegraded....

She had heard the tale with a ready sympathy, and with the occasional helping word or the well-judged silence that made it easy to tell. She had heard so many like it before!

Her thoughts wandered to a kindred trouble in a Zulu kraal, where a girl who had crouched stolidly in expectation of death had waked to a trembling terror at the knowledge that the white woman had interposed, and might, or might not, persuade her husband to pardon her infidelity.

In the end she had said what she had thought it right to say, and the girl had listened sullenly. She was not thinking of any trouble which she might cause to God, but of what the discovery might cause to her. Muriel had been resolved to help her practically as well as spiritually, but they differed as to the relative importance of the two parts of the programme.

Muriel had asked Mrs. Wilkes on returning if her husband would drive her over to Larkshill in his market-cart that evening. She had felt that she lacked the strength to walk such a distance, but she was not used to delay when dealing with anything that she had undertaken. She wished to see Tom Butler, the alleged cause of the trouble, and perhaps others.

Mrs. Wilkes had agreed, as she would have agreed to almost anything that her lodger had asked, but she felt that Mr. Wilkes might look at the matter somewhat differently. It is a natural consequence of such habits of thought as Muriel Temple cultivated that they are apt to be as exacting to others as to themselves. Mrs. Wilkes may never have had a lodger who caused her more trouble in proportion to the remuneration she offered. But Mrs. Wilkes served her gladly.

"Perhaps, Miss Temple, if you asked him…. He might do it for you," she said doubtfully.

Muriel had asked him. He was busy earthing up his potatoes, and in no mood to leave them. Opportunities were few, and the growth of weeds unceasing. He meant to have the whole garden straight before the short Whitsun holidays should be over. He had compromised at last by saying that he'd see how he got on, and she could ask him again come Monday.

He felt that he was doomed as he said it. Miss Temple would have her way. Probably she felt a corresponding confidence. Unless something very unforeseen should happen…. As, in fact, it did.

* * * * * *

Muriel lay till late, as she had reluctantly promised her doctor, and rested in the garden during the afternoon, half asleep in the sunlight.

Unused to leisure, her mind wandered backward in reminiscences that were sometimes sad, and sometimes pleasant to recall.

She had had much happiness, she decided, and also many mercies.

The sky was comparatively clear, its smoke-laden atmosphere having been unrecruited since the previous noon, and the June sun was warm and bright. Sterrington, though on the edge of one of England's invented hells, was clear of mine or foundry for twenty miles on its north-western side, from which the winds of that time and place most commonly blew.

Muriel felt that it was a fair world, and a kind one. It was sad to think that it might be the last earthly summer that she would see She did not feel ill when she lay quietly, only weak if she tried to do too much.

In the evening she felt the need of joining in the acts of worship in which her life so largely consisted. There was a little Unitarian chapel in the village, but that was impossible. Unitarians, Muriel knew, are not Christians at all. There was nothing else but the Anglican church, and there she went (borrowing a prayer-book from Mrs. Wilkes) to hear a sermon from a text in the one hundred and seventh Psalm, "He turneth the wilderness into a standing water," which wandered into abstract considerations of the methods of the Divine control of the cosmos, the antiquity of geologic records—the

Rector was an enthusiast in geology—and introduced, rather awkwardly, the newest theories as to the rather numerous occasions on which Great Britain had been separated from or reunited to Western Europe, with allusions to the "Carboniferous Limestone Sea," the "deltaic apron of the Hercynian Mountains," and the "confluent deltas of the Millstone Grit," which may have featured prominently in his reading of the previous week, but were unlikely to be received with any intelligent interest by his evening audience.

To Miss Temple's thinking it was not a sermon at all.

CHAPTER THREE

MURIEL went to bed at once when she returned from the evening service. She had done a good deal during the day, and she was physically tired and mentally somewhat depressed. She tired so easily now. She remembered when.... But she supposed that, for good or evil, her work was done. It had never been anything to boast of. It was all as God willed it.

> *I would not have the restless will*
> *That hurries to and fro,*
> *Seeking for some great thing to do,*
> *Or secret thing to know.*

She had had ambitions once; dreams, as we all have. But they were faded now. Besides, she was not her own, and the regret was an infidelity. "Thine be the glory." Tears came as she thought how little glory she had brought to God. And now His message had come that she was no longer needed. She must just rest and die.

Her thoughts wandered to the Rector to whom she had listened that evening. His personality had attracted her. A somewhat ascetic face, with a weary look in the eyes. She was not uncharitable. She supposed he served God in his own way, though it was not hers. "He who is not against us is of our part." She wondered vaguely as to the nature of the work he did—so different from what hers had been among the Zulu kraals. Probably he was tired and dispirited also. The empty pews.... But what use was there in telling people about geological changes, which, if they were true at all, had no meaning today? The flood was past. That was part of the old dispensation. Now there were only the troubles of the last days for the world to endure before the glory of the millennium dawn. "There shall be wars, and rumours of wars, and earthquakes in divers places….." The last days might be very near….

She went to sleep at last; and while she slept the earth's crust sank slightly and very gently in the northern hemisphere, and lifted slightly further toward the equator.

It was a trivial change. Not enough to make it falter in its settled course through the heavens, scarcely enough to change the axis on which it spun. There would be some space of bare land, steaming in tomorrow's sun, which the tropic ocean had covered: some space of water where the land had been. That was all.

Muriel dreamed that she stood with the Rector on a bare plain. It was black night, and the wind was terrible. They were lost in the night. He said he knew the way, but she did not believe him. He was leading her into a pit where they would drown together. And there was a voice that cried through the night—a voice she knew—a voice that cried in an agony of terror, "Miss Temple, wake up! I think the roof's a-falling!"

Muriel was awake now. By the light of a candle which she was holding she saw the comfortable face of her landlady, now white with fear. She heard the noise of a steady rush of air, which did not pause nor vary. She heard the rumble of a falling wall. She heard the woman's frightened voice protesting. "I'm scairt to death, Miss Temple. It's got such a queer sound. It's not an ornary storm."

No, it was not an ordinary storm. Muriel realized that, as she reassured her companion with a cheerful word, and began to dress quickly, for the cottage might really prove unsafe if this wind continued.

It was fortunate that her dressing was soon done, for she had scarcely finished when the window blew in, extinguishing the flickering light of the candle, and the next moment, through the darkness, there came a rattle of falling tiles at the farther end of the room, where the cottage roof was descending upon them.

Muriel stood uncertainly. There was a sound behind her in the darkness like the snapping of wood, and then a heavy gliding of something, and then a fall. But these noises, however loud and near, seemed confused and distanced by the sound of a wind which never ceased nor varied as it rushed southward to fill the void from which the land had fallen. But she knew nothing of that. She was concerned—though still with something of the serenity of those whose minds are trained to self-discipline—with the triviality of her own environment. She was aware that part at least of the roof was gone, that something struck her on the shoulder, causing her to lose her footing. She stumbled over the body of Mrs. Wilkes and came to her knees across her. She spoke to her, but there was no answer. She knew that their safety lay in flight down the narrow stairs if they could reach them, but she could not stir, and would not leave her. She tried to drag the inert body, but its bulk among the fallen rubble of the roof was too much for her strength. As she made this effort she was aware of something warm and wet that was flowing over her hand. She knew that it was blood. Perhaps she could staunch…. She had not lived for twenty years in savage Africa to be strange to the results of accident, or any form of violence. Feeling upward, she learnt the uselessness of her efforts. The woman's head was half severed from her body

Knowing this, she lost no further time in attempting her own security. She crawled on hands and knees to the place where she supposed the door to be, raising her hands continually to feel for any fallen obstacle that might confront her, or for the guidance of the wall. Her eyes were adjusted to the darkness, and she began to see a little way ahead She found the door, and then the stairs.

Soon she was in the open air. Rain was falling heavily now—or scarcely *falling*—stinging rain that was carried almost level on the steady force of the wind. Rain that struck her face like hail. She turned sideways to the wind. She covered her face with her hands. She knew the way to the garden gate, and she feared at every moment that the cottage would collapse toward her.

But she could not make much headway. She tried to keep straight, and found that ridges of soft soil were beneath her feet. She must have been blown on to the potato-bed which she had observed Mr. Wilkes to be hoeing on Saturday. She wondered where he could be now. It seemed impossible that he could be asleep in the battered cottage. Yet perhaps she ought to try to go back to warn or find him?

As she tried to turn she was seized in sudden arms that caught and whirled her forward for ten or fifteen yards and then dropped her breathless. It was a great bough with many smaller branches from the cherry-tree in the hedge that the wind had severed. She knew that she had been scratched and torn, and her clothing shredded by the unconscious violence of this fellow-victim of the elemental fury around her. She was in the rhubarb-bed now. She could feel the broken stems beneath her hands as she lay.

The noise of the falling walls, as the cottage flattened to the wind, roused her to a momentary further effort. She rose with difficulty, made two stumbling steps, and fell to her knees. Then she lay flat again on the wet earth that seemed the only stable thing remaining in a world of ruin. She did not doubt the earth.

She lay there for an hour or more, while the wind blew over her. As, she did so her body recovered a measure of its strength from the violent ordeal it had endured. She had a natural desire to find some place of rest and shelter. She did not think that any of the cottages in the lane could offer such a haven, even if they had stood more solidly than the one from which she had fled.

Perhaps the Rectory, which she had scarcely seen, but which she knew lay in the hollow of the hill behind the church, not more than three or four hundred yards away, might give her rest and shelter.

As she lay face downward, half sunk in the rain-soaked soil, and among the stems and litter of the rhubarb-bed, torn and beaten and motionless, she might have seemed dead already to anyone who could have seen her in the darkness. But her mind, courageous, practical, tenacious, was already planning the way to the safety of which she had thought. She must find the back gate, and avoid the well; the lower lane would be a little longer, but it would be so much easier to follow its curving hollow and not to face the wind. She tried to remember, to construct the way which she must take before making any effort to commence the journey. Then she rose on her knees, and was surprised to find how well she could see among the surrounding shadows. But they were strange, confusing shadows. The contours of familiar things were changed and flailed and flattened. Yet she could see the gap of the back-lane gate in the low hawthorn hedge that still stood stoutly. But the walls and roof of the well must have fallen in.

An uprooted plum-tree, dragging at intervals farther across the garden, lengthened her progress, but she found the gate at last, or, rather, the gap where the gate had been, and scrambled down the three stone steps to the lower level of the lane.

After that progress was easier.

CHAPTER FOUR

THE lane was very deep and narrow. Its width was just sufficient to allow two farm-carts to pass each other, with one wheel in the gutter, or tilted somewhat on the bank-side. These sides rose steeply for thirty feet to the level of the ploughed lands. Trees grew thickly from the steep slopes of the banks, and lined the edges, which were fenced with hedges of untrimmed hawthorn—untrimmed because the countryside had been deserted of all but the most inevitable labour, and those who remained to do it were old men whose ancient habit still enabled them to overcome the reluctance of stiffened muscles and the vagueness of failing sight; and such of the younger generation as lacked the restless energy of a race more virile than were those who led it.

The lane was older than any record of the lives of men: older than those straight and narrow ways that the Romans cut blindly through the midland swamps and forests. The wild strawberries on its banks had an ancestry of possession that outdated the flood of Genesis.

There was an old oak on the northern bank. Its roots went deep in the sloping side. They projected also where the feet of climbing children had kicked away the soil that had once sustained them. Its branches spread, broad and low, over the narrow lane, and stretched across the field above, from which the wheat was springing.

The storm struck it, but it felt no fear. It had fought with storms for three centuries. There was no lightning, and it was only lightning it hated. A half-dead branch on its western side, and a weal down its wrinkled trunk, showed how nearly it had met disaster eighty years ago. But that was when the elms on the farther side had been too small to shade it.

If it thrilled to the first impact of the wind through all its sap-fed fibres, it was not with fear, but with the pleasure of a sport it knew, and to which it knew itself to be equal.

It did not meet the wind's assault as do the palms of tropic lands with a slim bole that could bend over, at the worst, without snapping, and with a feathery crest of a similar flexibility—the elms had tried the idea of the straight bole, and a poor job they made of it. Nor did it grow to a full and equal amplitude, as did the ash, as in pretence of a perpetual calm, or in mere contempt of the wind's power to harm it. The ash was a tree of good repute, not to be contemned by any neighbour. It would not snap and show a rotten heart, as the elm may, when it looks most confident. But yet the oak, its clutching claws deep in the rocky soil, its short, thick arms jutting awkwardly from its squat and stubborn trunk, knew that it might still be there when the ash's children had perished.

It met the early fury of the storm with a joyous quickening of tenacious life in nerves that were alert and vivid with the youth of spring, and veins in which the sap pulsed strongly, despite the centuries which it carried.

But the storm did not strike with the sudden and interrupted violences of the tempests which it had known so often. It struck once, and the blow endured and continued, a relentless pressure. And the hours passed, and it did not slacken, and the stubborn strength endured it, and would not fear, though the joy of strife was gone, and every fibre ached and quivered; and the time came when the aching of the boughs was in the deep roots also, clutching, in terror now, to the hard rock which they had riven deeper for centuries The aching of the great east limb, which stretched horizontally across the path of the unceasing wind, became an increasing pain, and when it snapped at last, as a twig snaps, through its eight-foot girth, the stunned tree scarcely felt the pain of its parting. When the storm paused for a moment, and then struck with a fresh force, that bore the great tree bodily, with all its roots, and a hundred tons of the rock it gripped, into the hollow of the lane, it was scarcely conscious of the calamity that had overthrown it: it leaned, still half-erect, conscious, as in a dream, of the cessation of that intolerable strain, and falling into the heavy sleep from which it must wake at last to be aware of its ruin.

* * * * * * *

Muriel made her way up the deep lane with comparatively little difficulty, till she came to the place at which the oak had fallen. Here she found herself wading in loose soil, and sinking deeper at every step, till she fell over a projecting root of the fallen giant, that had held its position almost upright as it slid into the hollow.

To surmount this impediment would have been difficult in the daylight for one of her physical limitations. It was impossible in the darkness. But she was of the kind that does not easily turn from any purpose when once it has been undertaken. The bank rose steeply, its surface hidden by the overhanging shadows of bush and tree, and coated with a heavy undergrowth of weed and bramble. But she tried it, after an interval of rest—fortunately, in the blind chance of the darkness, selecting the opposite side from that on which the oak had grown, and in which it had left a gaping pit as far as its roots had spread beneath the surface level.

Actually, it was not as difficult as might be thought for one who had ceased to regard the scratching of face and arms or the tearing of sodden garments. Bush and tree gave support as well as hindrance to slipping feet, and aid as well as obstacle to hands that groped vaguely upward.

The time came when she felt the wind on the level field, and having struggled against it for a hundred difficult yards was glad to take to the bank again, and descend as best she might into the shelter of the narrow lane.

Having surmounted this obstacle, she might have had some difficulty in finding the hillside path that left the lane and straggled vaguely toward the Rectory and the church, with no evidence of where it forked in mid-field which she could have observed in the darkness, but that there was now a measure of light around her, of which she became conscious as soon as she had outflanked the obstacle of the fallen oak.

By this light she found her way round the hill as easily as the storm permitted, and learnt its cause as the Rectory came into sight. It was burning fiercely. Whether from the fire itself, or from the earlier action of the storm, its main structure, old and timber-built, had collapsed entirely. It showed now like a huge bonfire, from which a long trail of flame and smoke held down by the pressure of the wind, lay almost horizontally upon an ancient orchard, finding fresh fuel in its uprooted trees, and stretching on across a farther field, till it formed a hot and choking barrier to any who might attempt to struggle along the road that led to the shelter of the church from the eastern end of the village. For the church stood. It showed no lights, for its northern windows had fallen in, and its southern ones blown outward, and it would have been impossible to keep its candles or its ancient lamps alight in the tempest of wind and rain which blew through it.

But the walls remained, and the squat tower that was itself scarcely as high as the swell of land upon its northern side. And in the darkness, half lit by the flickering glow of the burning house, the Rector's household, and about thirty others of the four hundred inhabitants of Sterrington village, crouched and sobbed and whimpered, or spoke confident words to others, as their natures led them.

The Rector stood in the shelter of the east porch, looking out in hesitation as Muriel reached it. He had just quietened an injured, frantic woman who had lost one of her children in the darkness as they had made their way to the church by promising that he would himself go to its rescue.

It was not a promise that he would lightly break. Yet what could he do till the wind should slacken and there be some light to guide him! The glare of the burning Rectory shone in his eyes, and made the howling darkness blacker. It would be difficult, he thought, on such a night, to find familiar paths, but now, when all landmarks were flattening, and the air was perilous with flying boughs and falling timber, and the ground was strewn with ruin... And what cries could reach him through the screaming storm?

The firelight glowed up suddenly as Muriel approached, and shone directly upon her; yet at the first glance he did not recognize who she was.

Her sodden clothes were torn from her left shoulder and arm, and were otherwise filthed and shredded. Her face was smeared with soil and streaked with blood and rain and her hair was a wild disorder above it. He could see from her stumbling walk that she was in the last stage of exhaustion.

"Miss Temple! Are you hurt?" he said fatuously as he drew her on to the seat within the porch that gave some shelter from the wind.

She could not answer for some time, but leaned back, breathing with difficulty. There was the dreaded pain in her side. He was aware that she had fainted.

What could he do but wait beside, supporting her lest she should slip from the narrow bench.

After a time she revived.

"I think I'm all right now," she said. "You mustn't stay with me. There must be so much to do."

The words reminded him of the errand on which he had been starting.

He said, "I am going to look for Mrs. Walkley's Maud. She was struck by something as she came here, and some neighbours brought her along, and the other children; but Maud's missing."

"Then you mustn't stay for me. I shall be all right now. I wish you hadn't waited."

The Rector still stood for a moment. He was not a hero. He hated to be out in the rain, even with an overcoat and some good boots. And now he was insufficiently clad and wearing bedroom slippers. And besides, his cough. He had been tired when he went to bed last night, and now, after barely escaping with his life from the collapse of the Rectory.... And what a loss for a poor man such as he! His library was known to book-collectors throughout the country. It was only last month that a self-invited dealer had offered him two thousand pounds for it. An absurd price! He believed that it was worth four. And it was insured for only three hundred pounds....

Certainly he did not want to go into the storm again in this half-clad condition to look for Maudie Walkley....

If the height of heroism is to be measured by the depth of disinclination or cowardice from which it springs, rather than from a 'sea-level' of normality, there was no braver deed in that night of a million of hidden heroisms that the advancing waters would cover than that of the Rev. Peter Smithers, stumbling down the slippery side of the hill into the rain-swept darkness, in his useless search for a child that was already dead.

Lost and bewildered, knowing only that he was somewhere in the lower meadows, he turned sharply more than once at the thought that he must be heading for the unfenced danger of the river-bank, till he knew that all sense of direction had left him.

He tried to read the stars, but the sky was dark with cloud already tinged with a faint red glow, that would be deeper before the morning came. He tried to locate his position from the light of the burning Rectory, but that fire was fading now, and others shone or flickered around him…. The faint light did not prevent him stumbling over a horse that lay flatly on the ground. It sprang up in panic, neighing with a voice that started half a dozen around it. The Rector tried to avoid their rush as they came upon him. He started a stumbling run, not looking where he went…. At the last moment a great horse that was almost upon him tried to turn, either to avoid collision or from a greater peril which it perceived better than he. But the wet flank struck him as it swerved. He lost his balance, and was aware that his feet were slipping beneath him as he fell. He called out, "Oh, my God!" once only as he fell into the weed-grown water, and died, as so many died that night, not knowing the full extent of the catastrophe that overwhelmed the world.

In the fire-lit church, beneath the shadow of the chancel wall, Muriel had joined the huddled group of refugees, some of whom were in little better plight than herself, and most of whom were in a terror which she did not share.

A weak and frightened voice came from one of Mrs. Walkley's wounded but rescued children, "Oh, mummy, it does bleed," and she felt her way to adjust the clumsy bandages with more skilful fingers than had been previously available.

What more, she thought, could she do? The mental habit of many years made her less concerned at the physical ruin around her than for the spiritual attitude of those who met it. She knew the power of song in the darkest places of the earth, among the lowest of her kind. It must not be one of her private favourites. It must be a hymn they knew.

"Abide with me. Fast falls the even-tide.
The darkness deepens. Lord with me abide."

Her voice rose, weak and solitary against the elemental fury of the storm.

Then a man's voice joined her. A rough, loud voice, as of an outdoor worker; it could be imagined as of a carter, who used it mostly as a horses' call. Then others, tuneless enough some of them. Voices that halted and quavered beneath others that were of a stronger quality.

"Change and decay in all around I see,
Oh, Thou, Who changest not! Abide with me."

What matter that the weak sound was beaten down and swept along to perish in the fury of the louder wind?

It was the voice of two thousand years. The Christian miracle. The assertion of immortality. The voice which was first heard in the serene confidence of the Founder of a faith transcending all its foolish creeds, "If it were not so, I would have told you." In the triumphal boast of the greatest of His apostles, "O Grave, where is thy victory?" What matters, if all things change and fade, whether the process be slow or sudden, to those whose appeal is made to the unchanging God.

CHAPTER FIVE

DAWN came on a ruined world. A world that was strewn with wreckage. A world in which all the interdependent complexities by which its civilization was sustained had been rudely broken; on fence, and farmhouse, and forest, that the storm had flattened, on burning cities that rose up, a pillar of lurid smoke, as the wind fell, there came the light of the indifferent dawn. And as the north wind slackened the water came across the sinking land. Not violently, as it had poured, one huge and dreadful wave, into the sunken Mediterranean basin; a wave which millions must have seen—but who that saw it could have lived to tell? Gently, inexorably, as the dawn-light pierced the heavy pall of air, red as with volcanic dust, tainted with the smoke of a thousand fires, the water rose. It spread gently over the Essex marshes. It lapped against the Thames Embankment with something more than a tidal lifting. Lapped, and spilled over, and spread widely, and more widely, in among the burning streets; for in London, as in every city in Southern England, there had been more conflagrations in the falling buildings than there was any hope of quenching, and every hour the fires had got a surer hold, while beneath the feet of a populace that fled the flooded fire-fringed streets in an ever-greater congestion of panic there were a million rats that squealed and dodged as they made their way to the higher ground which, in its turn, would fail them.

Watchers in the early morning, on the hills above the Severn Valley, looking down the broadening stretch of the Bristol Channel, saw a succession of advancing ripples, long, gentle ripples, stretching from coast to coast, as though a giant stone had been thrown into the central waters; and as each ripple spread it lapped over a few miles farther of the level land. There was an upward rush of water in the river channel. Gloucester—Tewkesbury—Worcester one by one, as the morning passed, were underneath the floods. At midday the long waves heaved and broke against the barrier of the Malvern Hills. During the afternoon the inexorable advance spread out around this ten-mile barrier, and flooded the higher Hereford levels on the farther side. Then it seemed, in one appalling moment, that the whole land westward of the Severn cleft broke off, and Wales, with all its hills, slid downward, to be covered by a rush of water that had already drowned the lower Irish land. Eastward the water moved, drowning the Cotswold hills, meeting the flood that had risen in the Thames valley at an equal rate, lapping higher and higher around the northern Oxford wolds and against the ridge which is the watershed of England, leaving tide-swept shallows, and islands here and there, with casual salvage of beast or man that fled across it just as the circling waters closed, or that had not tried to fly. But farther north the land broke off, as it had done to westward— broke off, and sank away.

And all that day the northward roads were choked with crowds that fled the horror of the southern flood, to perish even more surely when the farther north should sink beneath the waters. Ceaseless lines of rapid, over-loaded motors, held up continually by the impedimenta of the storm-strewn roads, or by the accidents of their own impatience; offering wild rewards—anything but the priceless-seeming benefit of the lift in the overcrowded vehicle—to pedestrians who would help to drag aside the broken tree, to clear the rubble of the fallen wall; cursing the slowness of men who worked heroically to keep the roadways clear, or frightening the slower cars with threats or actual violence into the byways that soon became as congested as the wider roads.

So the day passed, and the next sun rose on an ocean that had spread from the Rocky Mountains to the northern coasts of Africa, and had obliterated the isolation of the Baltic Sea.

CHAPTER SIX

WITH the first dawn the wind had somewhat lessened the relentless pressure of the night, lessened also in the steadiness of its direction, till, with the broader day, it became variable both in force and direction, a matter of short and violent gales, and sudden calms, and fierce whirlwinds of contending air.

With the first light a straggling company from the church porch came out to survey the havoc of the storm.

For the most part they were a white-faced group, cowed and bewildered by the magnitude of the calamity which the morning showed them. They were in no physical condition to regard it bravely. They were shaking with cold, or stiff with rheumatism, after their vigil in rain-soaked garments on the unfriendly stones. They were hungry, and uncertain how to look for food. They saw a world in which the familiar buildings, that held the endless things that they had come to regard as the inevitable necessities of life, were burnt or fallen. They gazed at horizons, livid or dusky red, which told of more than local ruin. Vaguely they realized that there was no help but in themselves, and they were untrained in self-reliance, as they were unpractised in self-discipline.

All their customs, all the tendency of their laws for a generation, had discouraged their initiatives and reduced their freedoms. They had been taught the ethics of slavery. They had not been encouraged to think, nor allowed to act. They were not permitted to build even their own houses to their own designs, or to teach their own children as they would. Everything was under the direction of appointed specialists. Even the money that they earned had been withdrawn from their control in ever-larger proportions, so that it might be spent for them more wisely than they would be likely to do themselves.

It would be unjust not to recognize that there was often much of wisdom in the ways in which they were controlled and herded. We may say, as we please, either that they had been reduced or raised to

the level of domestic animals. On the average they were better
housed, better clothed, and better fed than their grandparents had
been. Perhaps the advantages of liberty may be overrated. If they
had sold their freedom to the bureaucrats for a mess of pottage it
was a savoury mess,, and their bowls were filled very punctually.

But now they were faced with a calamity which could not be
reported to the proper authorities, and their instinct to stand about
and wait for the appearance of uniformed men, and for the appropriate relief fund to be opened, was obstructed by a cold, bewildering
doubt as to whether there were any shepherds left for the sheep to
look for. Even the Rector had disappeared.

A babble of voices broke out, foolish, exclamatory, or lament-
ing.

Two of the Rectory maidservants made their way up to the still
smoking ruins. There was nothing left unburned except an old red-
brick barn on the western side of the house, and that had fallen in
ruin. It had contained nothing which would repay the toil of delving
among the brick-heap—or so they thought. Later there might be others who would think differently.

Beside the barns were the pigsties, which were still standing.
The Rector's sow rose on her hind legs as their voices reached her,
and put her snout over the top of the gate. In the later morning she
would do so again, grunting angrily that her expected meal had not
been brought with the usual punctuality. That evening she would
make repeated useless efforts to jump the gate, and fall back baffled.

A day later men would come searching with murderous purpose
for such as she, but would find the gate burst through, and the sty
left empty....

The little crowd spread out from the church porch, the more ro-
bust leading their different ways to the ruins of their cottage-homes,
and perhaps to find such food as the gardens offered—which was
not much on the first of June—or to search apathetically, with
stunned, bewildered minds, for those that the night had ended.

There was one man, Ben Millett, the local grocer, who found
his wife lying in the little yard behind his burnt-out shop. She lay
half dressed: a large, ungainly woman, who had stayed after he fled
in an effort to save some of the stock. She had not entirely failed, for
some cases of provisions had been piled against the farther wall of
the yard, but it seemed that the storm had overcome her, and she had
fallen with her head against the pump-trough.

Ben Millett did not attempt to raise, or even to touch her. He
stood fascinated, observing the tyrant of twenty years so fallen. He

noticed that her feet were charred, and the shoes partly burned away. Surely that would have roused her had there been any life remaining! He stood silent before a hope that he scarcely dared to rely on. But surely, surely she must be dead!

He only moved when young Rogers and his aunt and mother came into the yard together. They took no notice of the dead, but began to search among the boxes that she had salvaged at that fatal cost.

He heard the voice of the elder woman. "Sugar's no good to we. Here, Harry, smash this one. It's tins o' something."

He roused himself as from a dream, stepping over the burnt legs of the dead to protect his property.

"Look here," he said angrily, "you mustn't do that. They're not yours. That salmon's two-and-three-pence a tin."

Harry Rogers, engaged in smashing one of them with a coal-hammer, remarked that he'd have some breakfast if they were four-and-six.

His aunt interposed civilly that "Of course, we'll pay you, Mr. Millett."

Mr. Millett said, "When?"

The women's dresses had no pockets, and they had no money. It was not evident how or when such a debt could be settled. But Harry had some paper money in a trouser-pocket. At his aunt's urgency he passed a ten-shilling note to the protesting grocer.

Mr. Millett, a very honest man, wished to give change correctly. He remarked that he had no money "on him." He looked at his ruined store. A search for the cash-till did not seem a very hopeful project. He must go to the bank, where he had enough of savings to stock half a dozen of such shops, should he wish to do so. But the bank itself…. He looked down the wreckage of the once familiar street—the street in which he had lived since he was a child of three, when his father had come from Foxhill to take the position of ostler at the Ring o' Bells—and he realized that the bank itself…and, perhaps, all his savings…suppose that his real wealth were in that heap of boxes?"

Never mind the change now, Mr. Millett," the elder woman remarked. "We can take it in groceries. I hope you've saved something good besides the salmon."

"Oh, Harry, what are you doing?" his mother broke in plaintively. She had always hated waste, and he was smashing a second tin, and a third, recklessly open.

He had discovered a coal-hammer to be a form of tin-opener that causes spilling, and introduces dirt very freely. Never mind that. He would open one for each.

"There's plenty here," he said, pointing to the case, which still contained thirty-three tins of the same size.

Feeling an impulse of generosity at the sight of this plethora of a food which he rarely tasted, or enjoying the smashing of the tins, or from a mixture of these incentives—human motives are seldom easy to analyse—he burst another tin for their owner, and Mr. Millett, observing it, became conscious that he could also do with some breakfast.

He joined his customers very sociably, and as their appetites failed they had glances and words of pity for the dead woman three yards away. They almost forgot how she had been disliked when living. They became cheerful about the future with the consciousness of the food within them. Harry Rogers was a plasterer. There would be no lack of work for him. He could stay here, and make shift for himself. The women would go to their cousin's in Wolverhampton. It did not occur to any of them that the elements would have the audacity to interfere with important towns. What were Town Councils and Chief Constables for?

A motor-cyclist hailed them from the road, inquiring whether they knew where he could get some more juice, and was he right for Codsall?

He seemed glad to stop and talk for a moment. He told vague, wild tale of spreading floods in the south. He should go back to America. He thought the blooming country was done for. Meanwhile he was going north for the safety of the Yorkshire moors—if not farther. No risks for him. But he had a married sister at Codsall, and he meant to take her, if she would come. No, no kids. Only married at Easter. Yes, very bad getting along. Two spills in the last ten miles. A streak of blood on his cheek supported the narrative. Well, he must get on. Hoped it would last. Didn't look like getting any about here.

He gazed hungrily at the salmon-tins. Mr. Millett gave him his, which was nearly empty, his own appetite being satisfied, and was thanked for a welcome charity; but he had manœuvred, as the conversation proceeded, to conceal the reserves of food, and the skirts of Harry's aunt had been used as promptly and more effectually for the same purpose.

The cyclist went on, cheerfully enough, to his destined end. They did not know that he was the first of thousands....

At midday Mr. Millett was burying a remnant of his often-plundered stock in a little coppice, a field's-width from the road.

Five hours later he had heard with a sudden realization of his peril that Worcester was beneath the water. (He knew Worcester, where his brother had a corn factor's business, which made it seem suddenly real and near.) He joined the crowd that jostled and panted on the northern road.

CHAPTER SEVEN

MRS WALKLEY, setting out in a vain search for her missing child, whose death had cost the Rector's life, took the elder girl with her, but left the wounded Cora in Muriel's care.

Cora, a thin, anæmic child of seven or eight years, who had been knocked down by a blown branch, and whose right arm and side had been lacerated, was evidently unfit to walk, and Muriel, who had been nursing her in the darkness, offered to continue her charge when the daylight enabled the distracted mother to set out on her useless search.

She made a bed, of a kind, from some hassocks that had escaped the rain that drove through the church during the night. She went out to find some means of washing the wounds. She found an old enamelled bowl in a ditch at the foot of the Rectory garden. It had a hole in the bottom, but it was at one side, and it would still hold a good deal of water if it were tilted. So she was able to relieve the child's thirst, and then to do what was possible for wounds that were inflamed already.

By this time the church had emptied, except for one old man who had gone out with the rest and then returned. He was bent with rheumatism, and stood without speaking, leaning on a heavy stick, and looking down on Muriel's tattered and muddied form, and on the injured child.

At last he said, "It's milk 'er needs…. There's a cow in Datchett's paddock, as like as not."

Muriel looked up into a broad and weather-beaten face, wrinkled with age, with a spreading fringe of yellowish-grey hair. She thought of a sheep, but the eyes were smaller and less intelligent. The face did not alter its expression as she looked up. The life in the bent figure seemed remote and dull; but the words were good.

"Will you show me?" she said.

He seemed reluctant to move, or as though he had not heard; but in the end he came, moving painfully.

The paddock was fortunately near—just over the hill—and after an hour or more of alternate coaxing and dodging a cornered, frightened cow yielded some reluctant milk to Muriel's strange but not unskilful hands—not what it would have given in the garden shed to its own attendant, while it licked up the meal which was expected payment, but as much as Muriel herself cared to drink, and as much more as could be carried in the tilted bowl. For the old man would have none. He pulled out a chunk of bread and cheese from a capacious pocket. It was as though he silently implied that he was always adequately provided for such catastrophes.

At midday he disappeared. He did not return. Neither did Mrs. Walkley. Muriel never saw her again.

The child grew worse rather than better as the day advanced. She was weak and fretful, and at times somewhat delirious. Muriel would not leave her for long, but went out several times foraging for food, or to learn what she might of the conditions around her. She watched the crowds that struggled northward on the wreck-strewn roads. She heard the wild and fearful talk that urged the weaker forward.

The road beneath the hill was bad enough, but in the afternoon, when the child fell into a restless slumber, she made her way over the fields to the main road that crossed it at right angles, going north, and here she came to a hedge-gate, over which she saw a limousine on the farther side, with two wheels in the ditch, which half a dozen men were toiling to move forward, while an impatient block of vehicles fretted in the rear. It was a spot where a fallen tree had been dragged aside, but only just sufficiently for one car to pass at a time, and this one had been too broad, or too badly driven, to pass it safely.

There had been two ladies in the car, who had alighted, and stood on the uncrowded side of the tree, watching the workers. The men it carried had alighted also, but stood holding the doors, lest others should attempt to force a way in when the wheels were lifted.

Muriel crossed over to the ladies. She was not ashamed of begging—had done so many times—for others; not herself—in a hundred circumstances.

They stood, cool and clean and gaily clothed, looking with an aloof impatience at the slow lifting of the foundered wheels.

Muriel said, addressing both indifferently, "Have you any food you could give me? I have a wounded child in the church."

The nearer of the ladies looked doubtfully at her companion who answered quickly, "No, indeed. We haven't enough for ourselves."

"Nonsense, Ella," came a man's voice from beside the car, "we can spare some easily."

"Yes, of course," said another.

"If you once start giving to every beggar—" she began furiously, but the man did not heed her. He had entered the car, and had brought out a basket from its ample recesses.

"You'd better take the lot," he said, "you couldn't carry much without something to put it in."

Muriel took it doubtfully. She saw clearly enough that she was benefiting from some antagonism which did not concern her. She felt that the other members of the party looked disconcerted by the extent of the gift. She did not like to accept anything which was reluctantly offered.

"I don't think I shall need all this," she said, but the car began to move forward as she spoke. There was a rush to crowd in as it turned to the middle of the road, and the cars behind hooted their impatience to take the opening way. Muriel, basket in hand, was pushed aside and forgotten. She went back with a week's provision for the sick child and her frugal needs.

She walked back giddily, thinking at times that she was faint from the toils and exposures and lack of sleep she had experienced, at others that the earth itself was unstable beneath her. As she regained the church she knew that the weakness was not in herself alone. The ground rocked under her feet. She was glad to sit, and then lie flat, to reduce its effects. As the shocks continued she considered that the open skies were safer than any roof, however solid, and carried the child out of the church and laid her in the adjoining field.

She lay down beside her, and as the earth quietened for a time, exhaustion triumphed, and she slept heavily.

She still slept when the shocks came again, not with violent oscillations, but with a steady sinking beneath her. She might have slept on through the night in the open field, but, as the evening came, the child waked her, asking for water.

She rose to get it, stiff, and heavy of limb, and slow of thought, but with the changed outlook that sleep will bring.

She looked round, and saw no one. She heard no sound of human life. She felt suddenly lonely. Had all the world fled to some farther safety, and left her here to die? She looked doubtfully at the child as she returned with the needed water. Could she carry it? Not far. She reminded herself that God was everywhere. The earth was quiet now. The church still stood. The child must not lie out all night.

She carried her back to the cushions where she had lain before…. The sky was clear of cloud, and a waning moon looked down on a hundred leagues of troubled, tossing water where there had been rich cities and fertile English fields but a night before. Only here and there an island showed above the covering waves, and on the largest of these an old grey church still stood among the surrounding ruins, and within it slept an exhausted woman and a dying child.

CHAPTER EIGHT

THE short night ended. From the unshaken tableland of Asia, from the heights of the Himalayas, from the unchanged, enduring East, across the desolations of water that had been Europe, moved the regardless dawn.

It moved across a thousand leagues of new uncertain seas of no sure tides, where fierce and changing currents hurried the floating wreckage of a continent, now here, now there—hurried, and flung them back—the floating wreckage, and the floating dead.

It rose over some new-made islands in the western sea—islands with raw, unsanded, beachless coasts—islands on which some human life still endured among their storm-swept ruins—life that cowered terrified, or dazed, or maddened by the sudden calamity which it had experienced and perhaps survived.

It rose upon the old grey church where Muriel and the child still slept—where Muriel, exhausted by exertions far beyond her normal endurance, might have slept for many further hours, had she not been wakened by the weak reiteration of the cry for water from the dying child.

For she saw that the child must die unless some skill beyond her Own could be brought to aid her—would probably die in any case, as her experience told.

She hesitated as to what it might be best to do. She might find medical aid—if she sought it. She could not tell how far the settled order of civilization had left the world, or how few might be those who were still alive around her.

But when she tried to rise she found that the question was already answered. Exposure and exhaustion had left her too full of pain and weakness for any thought of walking farther than along the side of the field to the river below, from which she had been fetching the water that they required

Well, if it were God's will.... She tried to talk to the restless child when she had done what little was in her power for its physical comfort, but she could not reach its mind. It gazed at her with dull, unheeding eyes, or turned away its head in a sharp impatience.

Later in the day it was in a delirium of fever, from which it had little respite till its life was closing.

In the afternoon Muriel heard voices with a sudden hope. They were the voices of approaching men. They passed the door of the church, but did not enter.

She supposed rightly that they had gone on to the Rectory ruins. They would return, she supposed, by the same path. Here she was right again, but her purpose to call them changed as they passed beneath the broken windows of the church and she heard their voices in an interjected narrative which it seemed that two or more were giving to the other members of the party:

"If the...hadn't been standing underneath the crane...."

"Fetched him a wipe over the jaw, and he fell...."

"She'd got two ducks hidden under the seat...."

"Told him to...the skulking hound...."

It was too fragmentary for any meaning to emerge, but neither tones nor words gave expectation of any useful succour.

The next minute she knew that the party had turned in at the church door.

She heard rough voices and the stamp of heavy boots on the stones. She lay quiet, and saw them as they straggled up the aisle, though, as yet, she was unobserved. She recognized them as a group of miners—doubtless from the Larkshill collieries, which she knew to be no more than three or four miles away.

She saw the foremost man very clearly. Not tall. A blunt-featured face, not uncomely. He was looking right and left in the empty pews as he advanced. She thought of the basket of food which lay near to her hand, and wondered how much, if any, would be left when these unwelcome visitors had departed. But she was not greatly perturbed, having an invariable formula for such emergencies. It was a case for prayer. After that the control of the situation was in very capable hands.

The man looked straightly at the place where she lay beneath the wall with the child beside her. He looked her straight in the face, and then turned a rather broad back between her and his advancing companions.

"Nothing here, Jim," he said, to a tall, loose-jointed man, with a half-filled sack over his shoulders.

The man answered thickly, with an indication that he was something less than sober, but with a surprising fluency. The substance of his contention was that there was never any good to be got from a blasted church. He spat on the stones to emphasize his opinion concerning it.

A small man with a weak face and a goatish beard rebuked him with drunken solemnity. He appeared to suggest a possible connexion between the recent catastrophe and the infidelity of Jim Rattray. He also suggested that those who had escaped might reasonably be expected to show some gratitude for their Creator's favour.

Rattray's reply was again too picturesque for a literal reproduction. Its substance was that a Creator who preserved Monty Beeston, while disposing of so many millions of better men, must be weak in the head.

There was an uncertain murmur from the little crowd behind them. An uneasy murmur, from which emerged a desire that there should be less talk, and that they should 'get a move on' in some more profitable direction.

"Yes, we're best out of here," said the man whose back was offering a precarious shield to the woman and child who lay beneath the shadowed wall.

Jim Rattray turned with a sudden anger which may have been prompted rather by a personal antagonism than by the words of the speaker.

"I'm not taking orders from you, Tom Aldworth."

He took a step forward, steadily enough, with a threat of ultra-sanguinary intentions in regard to his antagonist's interior organs.

Tom Aldworth stood his ground, but declined the quarrel.

"I don't fight a man when he's in beer," he remarked, as one who mentions something too obvious for discussion.

Jim Rattray looked dangerous for a moment, and then pulled himself together with an apparent effort. He said something indistinctly that sounded like "All pals here," and turned to follow his retreating comrades.

Tom Aldworth went also, without looking round at those whom he had interposed to shelter.

CHAPTER NINE

MURIEL TEMPLE would certainly not have lain silent had she been possessed of her normal strength, nor was she restrained by any fear of the rough group that had approached so nearly.

She had walked unmoved through a kraal of hostile and rebellious Zulus to reason with a blood-drunken king, and been unconscious of heroism. If it were God's will that she was to be murdered (which she thought unlikely), there was no more to be said. If it were not His will, the heathen might rage and imagine a vain thing, but as to doing her any injury they had just no power at all. A (Christian) child could see that. She played a game in which she held continual trumps, and the fault was hers if she lacked the necessary faith to play them victoriously.

But she thought of the child, and of the faintness which had come to her when last she had risen, and she lay still, and left the situation for her Master to deal with.

The miners did not return, and three days later she found strength to dig a little churchyard grave for the body of Cora Walkley, who thus found a quieter resting-place than had come to most of those that sea and storm had ended.

With reviving strength, and being freed of the encumbrance of the dying child, Muriel rose on the next morning with a determination to learn more of the condition to which her world had fallen.

The leaden pall of damp and dirty air, which for a century had lain unlifting upon the English midlands, as it lay upon the valleys of the Tyne and of the lower Thames, and upon the industrial districts of Yorkshire and Lancashire, as though to hide their foulness from the indignant day, had disappeared, and the sky showed a blue depth such as the factory-worker had only seen when on excursions to the distant coast, and supposed with vague unreason to be a particular quality of the seaside air.

Muriel, whose life had been largely spent elsewhere, might have been less quick to notice its difference from the sickly struggle of frustrated light which had been locally known as a sunny day, but she was conscious of another quality, which she had no difficulty in defining. The air was salt. A fresh and pleasant wind came from the north, and it brought a strong scent of the sea.

"It can't be a mile away," she thought wonderingly. With all that she had heard and seen she had not realized until that moment how great might be the ruin that had overwhelmed the world.

Among the unconscious springs of conduct which she had not disciplined, because she had not understood their existence, or had not regarded them as antagonistic to the spiritual experiences or service which she supposed to be the only purpose of earthly existence, one of the strongest was the desire of exploration. She had little imagination. She was impatient of romance, or of the invented tale. But she liked new facts that came to her own experience. She liked to see and to know.

She determined now that her first enterprise should be to discover the meaning of the salt taste of the northern wind, and in doing this she must learn something of the conditions on which human life was continuing around her.

But first she made her way back to the ruins of the cottage where she had been living. She had seen, from the hillside, that it had escaped the destruction of fire, and she hoped to recover at least some of her personal possessions, and in particular the garments which she badly needed.

But her search was useless. Others had been there before her. The little well-tended garden had been trampled by many feet. There were the marks of wheels and of a horse's hooves in the soft soil. Beams had been dragged aside, and tiles and bricks were scattered.

The body of John Wilkes, which had been exposed by these delvings (he had been smothered in the bed from which he had declined to rise), had been lifted, with that of his wife, into the ditch which bounded the garden on its lower side. There had been a rough attempt at burial, a few barrow-loads of earth and stones having been tipped over upon them. Muriel might not have observed the grave of her late landlord but for a liver-coloured, smooth-coated dog which was gnawing at an exposed foot, and lifted a snarling head as she made her way round the spreading *débris* of the fallen cottage.

Everything had not been taken. She stepped among broken bedsteads and furniture, some tattered books, a washtub, and a dented bucket. But there was nothing left of personal clothing or bedding, of food, or tools, or utensils. She saw some of her private papers and letters blowing about the garden, but the box which had held them had disappeared.

Here was at least sign of human life, and there was hope in the thought, though she would have preferred to find her possessions where she had left them.

She reflected that there might be other houses down the village which remained unplundered, but before investigating further she was still resolved to explore the limit of the land, and the meaning of the salt wind that she had breathed that morning.

She made her way back to the church. For the first time she entered the vestry.

It contained little of value, a recent theft at a neighbouring church having made the Rector cautious about his own property; but there was an ancient chest containing surplices and other vestments, a few devotional books, and a wall-mirror with some brushes on a ledge beneath it. There was also an old brown jacket hanging behind the door, which the Rector had used when he busied himself with the church brasses, or on other matters of cleaning or decoration which he did not always delegate to others.

Muriel hesitated to touch anything. The Rector might return, though it was strange that he had not done so earlier. Mrs. Walkley had not returned. No one returned. Of the little crowd that had gathered in the church a week ago there was no one left but herself and a dead child.

Yet he might do so.

She looked in the mirror, and it confirmed the earlier verdict of her own judgment. She had a comb which she had picked up from the rubbish-heap at the foot of the Rectory garden. A really excellent comb, with not more than a dozen teeth missing: a comb that had been well washed by months of rain. It was a rubbish-heap of further possibilities. Many things might have been thrown out by the careless servants of a rather absent-minded bachelor which would be useful now.

She did what she could with this looted treasure. The Rector's hair-brush assisted. But she had found no means of mending her tattered garments, and now that she was going in search of civilization she became increasingly conscious of their condition.

She looked doubtfully at the old brown jacket. She felt that it would be a justifiable borrowing, but it did not attract her. She took it down, and was aware of a scent of stale tobacco which she disliked.

She tried it on, and found that it came almost to her knees. Her hands did not emerge from the sleeves.

There was a weight at one side. She discovered a pipe, a pouch of tobacco, a box of vestas about a third full, a stump of carpenter's pencil.

She emptied these out, except the matches, which were treasure not lightly to be cast aside.

The size of the coat was awkward, but the capacious pockets pleased her. They might be useful for many things. She was not only hunting her fellow-men. Her food was almost exhausted. And some covering she must have.

She looked at the fastenings of the vestry doors. She did not know who might come in her absence. She already felt a sense of personal possession and responsibility. There was one door which opened into the churchyard: a strong door, locked and bolted on the inside. Clearly the Rector came in through the church. The door into the chancel was also strongly made—a thick oak door, heavily hinged. There was a key in the lock on the inside.

She carried in a quantity of the hassocks and pew-coverings, which had been the only bedding she had known for the past week, and the food-basket, nearly empty now, locked the door, hid the key, and started out to seek her kind.

She was aware that she must make a queer figure in the ungainly coat, but she was not greatly troubled. She realized sufficiently that others must be facing primitive necessities, and overcoming them as best they could.

In fact, she need not have troubled at all, for she was not destined to meet either man or woman till she returned in the evening, except one doubtful distant sight of a laden figure which made haste to disappear as she sighted it, perhaps a quarter of a mile away. Had she made her way eastward to Larkshill, or to Cowley Thorn, she would have had a very different experience, and there was a scatter of human life to south and west; but she went up through the Rectory grounds, where she almost trod on a sitting hen as she tried a short cut through the shrubbery—a hen that dashed off her nest and flew squawking across the drive, leaving Muriel to the sight of a dozen eggs, and to consider their possibilities for her empty larder. But her hand convicted them of the warmth of incubation. She decided that the hen had been sitting, not laying, when she disturbed her. They were useless now, but she considered that a hen with tiny chickens may be caught very easily. She would remember the spot.

She went on by a field-path which went uphill in the direction she sought, and found an open gate into a larger field which had been ploughed but not planted. There was a cart-track by the hedge, and following this she came to another field in which oats were springing and a dozen sheep fed freely.

Beyond that she came to an open heath, which she supposed to be part of Cannock Chase, though she was not sure, knowing little of the geography of the district. Here the sheep were many, of all breeds and ages. They had broken through gapped hedges and fallen gates, and congregated according to their ancient practice on high and open ground.

Here Muriel turned and looked back. She could see for several miles, but there was no sign of ending land or of encroaching sea. South and east and west there must be a wide space of land which still endured above the water. She wondered whether there might yet be a further subsidence, but she was not greatly worried by the thought. After all that had happened the land yet seemed very solid, very firm. It is hard to distrust it.

But looking north again she saw nothing but level heath, and feeding sheep, and the sky-line beyond. In the air a black-headed gull circled slowly. She could not doubt that she was near the sea.

Yet it was farther than she had thought. She must have come two miles—perhaps more—and she was conscious of fatigue. She tired so easily now. Yet she realized, with a moment's wonder, that she had had little of the old pains during the last week; had thought little of the doom under which she lived. Perhaps it was not wonderful that she should forget herself with such happenings round her.

She would rest before she went farther. She lay on short, warm grass, and slept long in the sunlight.

She waked refreshed, and with a feeling of healthful vigour such as she had seldom felt in recent years.

She went on, singing:

> *"Heaven above is fairer blue,*
> *Earth around is lovelier green,*
> *Something shines in every hue*
> *Christless eye have never seen."*

It was a long time since she had thought of that hymn. She had heard it at a Convention for the Deepening of Spiritual Life which had been held in Birmingham over thirty years ago—before she had settled what her life would be—before Zululand had crossed her mind. But it was the clean, blue air and the pleasant sunlight which had brought it back.

39

She went on a little way, and stopped abruptly. The land broke off beneath her feet—broke off as straightly as though a knife had severed it. She looked down a cliff-wall of red marl; thirty feet below the ocean purred lazily in the sunlight, its full tide about to turn.

The sea was so quiet that a gull was sleeping on the gentle lift of the waves, its head beneath its wing.

There was no sign of northern land, no sign of boat or sail. Only when she looked north-eastward was she in doubt whether the land curved outward or a separate island followed.

Looking at the peaceful water, she might have forgotten the devastation that it had wrought, had she not seen a broken chair that floated almost beneath her feet. There was nothing else in sight to tell of all that the water covered.

She had loved the sea. But she saw it now as the implacable enemy of her kind. They might surmount its division; they might boast that they had subdued it; and then it would lift its waves and overwhelm a continent, and stretch itself in the sun to doze like a fed lion.

She saw the appalling cruelty of the waters. Her mind turned to the climax of the Apocalyptic vision—"and there shall be no more sea." Words which had meant little in the ears of countless millions who had heard them since they were written—which must have wakened feelings of resentful protest in the minds of many. She had herself been conscious of regretting that condition of beatitude. Was its feline beauty to disappear forever?

A man can learn to love the sea, as he loves a woman. He can love the wind also, but not quite in the same way. Air is not feminine, like water. The wind can be quiet and loving. It can be fierce and merciless as a wolf in its hunger. But not as a cat. It will not purr against your feet in the same way; it will not bite without barking.

The sea does not seek its prey like a dog; it does not hunt as the wind hunts. It may crouch very still the while it waits for its victims. It can be quiet and swift in its treacheries. It can caress with smooth and deadly paws.

It loves to lie in the sun's warmth, purring lazily, and half asleep, till it has lured its victims to its reach, as a fly will settle within range of a lizard's tongue.

You may do well to love, but it is always folly to trust it. Even though it respond to your wooing with the surrenders which its lovers know, it will not be loyal. It will turn with cold and cruel teeth, even on those to whom it has bared its beauty. It has the heart of a harlot.

CHAPTER TEN

MURIEL gazed at the ocean, which stretched northward to the horizon-limit, covering all the teeming life and wealth which had once been England to a depth which she could not estimate; and, though she pitied, it was without protest, as it was without fear.

She did not think of the elemental forces of nature as operating with impartial and implacable obedience to blind and universal law. She looked upon them as the servants of an omniscient and omnipotent God, of Whose household she was a servant also—a servant of higher rank and of more assured position. She would not have put it in that way. She did not readily think in metaphor, unless it were in the Hebrew imagery to which she had been used from childhood. But she was assured that the sea was powerless to touch her, unless it were permitted to do so.

She sat thinking for a long time, while the sun's arc declined to the north-west, trying to understand the conditions under which life would continue, and to decide how best she could aid it. She was puzzled that her immediate surroundings should be so desolate, though the explanation was very simple. But she knew, by the men she had seen, that there were those who still lived in the Larkshill district. If they were of uncongenial types, the greater was the call upon her to join them. The greater, also, was the need for her to consider how she could serve them in practical ways, her missionary experiences having taught her the power of service and the methods by which she might stoop to conquer.

She was not too ill to be of some use to God under these changed conditions. If it were not so, would He have preserved her when so many millions had perished?

Surely not too ill; though she was aware of a lassitude which made her unwilling to face the return walk, in spite of the growing thirst from which she suffered.... Her thoughts were broken by a scrambling and scuffling sound in the gorse-bushes behind her, and by the stampede of a dozen sheep that had been feeding near them.

She looked round, and caught a glimpse of a small white dog— a smooth-haired terrier—that was making excited rushes right and left at something that dodged it, but which she could not see.

41

Then there came the agonized half-human cry of a captured rabbit, and a moment later the dog came out of the bushes, its prey hanging limp and dying in its mouth.

Muriel could not know whether it had been previously aware of her presence, but now it came straight toward her, wagging a stump of tail in the excitement of its successful hunting, and laying the rabbit at her feet.

Muriel loved dogs. The stranger was well satisfied with the praise she gave him. He sat down at her side, his stump still wagging on the ground, his head lifted sideways toward her caressing hand.

The dog had a brass collar, with his name, and his owner's, inscribed upon it: "Gumbo. Please return to George Hinde, The Ridge, Lower Helford."

Muriel was not very clear as to the position of Lower Helford, but she supposed (rightly) that it was covered by the placid ocean beneath her. She wondered whether the dog's master would appear, or would she hear him whistle for the return of the wanderer. She resolved to introduce herself should the opportunity come. She felt that the owner of such a dog could not be an unwelcome acquaintance.

But no call came, and the dog showed no inclination to leave her.

Conscious of hunger, she began to think of the possibility of making a fire and roasting the unexpected meal. But there was little wood lying around, and she was unsure that the gorse-bushes would be dry enough to burn freely, even if she had had a knife to cut them.

She must not come out without a knife again—it must surely be possible to find one somewhere.

She decided to return at once; if the dog followed her she would conclude that he had lost his owner.

So she picked up the rabbit and returned, with Gumbo trotting very contentedly at her heel.

In spite of her physical weakness, it is probable that there were few survivors of flood and storm who were better fitted to face the altered conditions under which life must now be sustained. She had seen and shared so much of primitive living, had so often been reduced herself to crude expedient, that she was at once less perturbed by fear of privation, and better fitted to avoid its penalties.

Arriving home, she soon had a wood fire blazing on the open ground. A splinter of wood proved adequate to the skinning and preparation of the rabbit, and when she slept that night, in the added security of the locked vestry, with the dog at her feet, she thanked God in her prayers for the companionship He had sent her, and for the provision of the needed meal, with a gratitude which was not faltered by undue thought of the fate of George Hinde, or his family, that the waves had covered.

CHAPTER ELEVEN

AS Muriel had watched the ocean that afternoon, and tried to imagine the conditions under which human life could be continuing, she had resolved to lose no time, as her strength had returned sufficiently, in joining herself to those who remained alive, and that she would set out the next morning to Cowley Thorn or to Larkshill, where she felt it to be most probable that her search would be successful. It was characteristic that she did not give any thought to her own safety or to her own advantage. It was the duty of service which called her. However limited her strength might be, she did not doubt that she could do something, in their emergency, to aid her fellows.

But the next morning brought its own delays. She went farther among the ruins of Sterrington, and discovered, as she had expected, that there was much of probable or potential use which could still be salved from the ruins—much that weather and vermin were deteriorating, if not destroying.

There was, in particular, a detached bake house which had contained several sacks of flour, which had been only partially protected by the ruins under which they lay. The exposed portions had attracted the cow to which she had been previously introduced in Datchett's paddock, the Rector's wandering sow, and a young black pig with which we have not been previously acquainted; and when these marauders had made some tactical dispositions to rearward, in the face of Gumbo's vociferous protests, he had dashed into the rubble of flour and tiles and mortar and scattered a score of busy rats, of which he had got a grip of the rearmost, and returned to his new mistress shaking the life out of it triumphantly.

Muriel recognized that the flour ought to be salved, but she found it a laborious task. She emptied a sack which had been largely exposed and damaged, carried it up to the vestry, and then filled it, in the course of many journeys, by means of the basket which had been given her from the foundered motor; the dog keeping guard over the sacks in her absence. In the process of filling the sack she had emptied another, which was carried up and filled in turn, and this continued till she had salved nearly four sackfuls. After this the weather turned wet, and the remaining flour was largely spoiled, at least for any lengthened storage.

Meanwhile there was other needed food for which to forage, cooking to be done, and many things that hindered, and made the days pass quickly.

She had felt that Datchett's cow should be captured, and that its milk would be welcome, but she had difficulty in finding any enclosure that could be sufficiently secured without labour which she felt to be beyond her capacity.

In the end she got it into the Rector's orchard, where she tethered it while she strengthened hawthorn-hedges which had suffered little, because they were already so old and short, and thickly stemmed, and deep-rooted. The June grass was abundant among the uprooted orchard trees, and the cow settled down contentedly; but she gave little milk—little even for Muriel's modest needs. She was near her time for calving again, and the interval during which she had been left unmilked had nearly dried her.

Then there was no water in the orchard, and that meant a tub to be filled daily from a well in the rectory yard which still yielded freely.

Meanwhile Muriel had tried to secure the two pigs, and had succeeded, with Gumbo's energetic assistance, in persuading the Rector's sow into a sty adjoining that from which she had escaped previously, but the young black pig had evaded all her efforts, and had finally disappeared.

Having secured the sow, she became aware that she must release it again, or be content to remain sufficiently near the spot to feed it daily. And these things had not been done continuously, but between others, such as a determined search for sewing materials of any kind, on which she had been mainly occupied for three successive days before her efforts were substantially rewarded. And then there had been the work to do for which they were needed, the jacket sleeves, which impeded everything she did, to be shortened, and other tasks which it is needless to detail. And in that three days' search she had come on so many things which she did not need at the moment, but which she knew might be of irreplaceable value, and which she must also try to secure from beast and bird and weather.

And then the gardens. Already the weeds were rejoicing that the hoe had ceased to trouble them. They were beyond any possible effort from her; but on an impulse, one day, she had decided that she would at least save the patch of potatoes that Mr. Wilkes had been earthing-up on his last Saturday, and had spent the best part of the day in searching for a suitable tool before she could complete her labour.

One afternoon, while she was engaged in retrieving the contents of one of her most desirable discoveries—a stout leather trunk, which had only burst on its under side, and containing a wealth of silk and linen garments, undamaged, except that a mouse had found them to be an ideal nesting-place—two men approached the church who did not walk openly down the road, as honest men should surely do, but came furtively through the ruined woods, among fallen trunks and half-uprooted trees that yet showed a valour of green leaves upon their skyward branches.

They walked straight to the church, as men that had an assured object. The one who entered first was slim and rather short, young, and dressed with a surprising neatness, as though unaware of any change in the conditions of life around him. He carried a light sporting-rifle under his arm.

He glanced round the empty church and whistled to attract the notice of any possible occupant.

"Probably dead, or gone," he remarked to his rearward companion, a fresh-coloured youth, who was rarely talkative. "But we'd better look thoroughly now we're here. Tom was sure he saw them. And there's been a fire outside not many days since."

Bill Horton said, "Ah," and followed him up the church.

Muriel had grown careless about locking the vestry door during the day. She was becoming used to solitude.

Jack Tolley lifted the latch, and the two men gazed at a sight which left no doubt that they had found what they sought.

"Here's your chance, Bill, if you can't get Bella. There's one here that understands housekeeping. Ever seen so much flour in a church before? And here's half a hundredweight of Brazil nuts. It's like a harvest service."

Bill Horton said "Ah" again.

Jack Tolley closed the door, and retreated down the church. "We've got to find them," he said. "It's not likely they're far. But they might scare if they saw us."

He led the way to the Rector's orchard. "Keeps a cow too," he observed. "You're in luck today, Bill."

Bill Horton said no more than before, but his fresh complexion was a shade deeper than usual.

45

He knew well enough that he had no chance with Bella, and he had the desire for mating which is common to all healthy young animals.

He was here with Jack because he liked him better than Rattray, and he hated Bellamy, but he hadn't forgotten what they said...

They lay for half an hour in the orchard grass, watching the churchyard path, and were then roused to alertness by a sound of furious barking in the road below.

"That's dogs," said Bill, with more animation of voice than he had shown previously. He jumped the low hedge and ran down the field, followed by Jack Tolley at a more moderate pace. Jack did not approach anything, even a dog-fight, without circumspection—especially in such days as these.

CHAPTER TWELVE

MURIEL came up the road in excellent spirits, even more heavily loaded then usual, and with such articles as no woman, even an ex-Zulu missionary, can regard with indifference, especially one whose wardrobe was in the condition from which Muriel's suffered.

Even the dresses, of so little substance that they could have been concealed in a man's hands, gave her more satisfaction than she would have cared to analyse, or why had she measured them against herself before she had chosen them for the parcel which she was making?

She was walking as rapidly as she could—she tired less easily now than she had done three weeks ago—for there were heavy clouds coming from the direction of Cowley Thorn, and she was anxious to get 'home' before the storm should drench her plunder. Gumbo was trotting before her, equally impatient for his own reasons, thinking of the evening meal with the appetite of a young and healthy dog whose life had become an almost ceaseless rat hunt. He carried a salt cellar in his mouth, not because Muriel would have been unable to accommodate it in one of her ample pockets, but because it had become the custom for him to carry something, and there was nothing else on this occasion with which Muriel could content his urgency.

They were clear of the village, and in sight of the church which they were approaching from the lower road, when a dog jumped up from the wayside ditch, where it had been occupied on some business best known to itself, and stood in the centre of the road, with a lifted tail and an air of dubious hesitation.

Muriel recognized the dog. It was the liver-coloured mongrel that had growled at her from his interrupted meal in the cottage garden.

Gumbo dropped the salt-cellar. The two dogs advanced slowly. Their noses touched. It is impossible to say how much was communicated between them. It is a thought which might bring some humility even to the colossal conceit of men that a dog may understand the methods of human intercourse far better than a man can understand those of a dog.

But whatever passed it was a cause of instant antagonism. The dog that has taken to unmastered living will never tolerate those who are still content with a human servitude, and the ill-feeling is returned with even greater intensity.

The two dogs backed from each other, growling deeply.

There was the pause which often ends in one dog turning aside with an abstracted expression, as though occupied with other thoughts, or troubled by some uncertain recollection of a prior engagement: a movement which is commenced very slowly, but at a pace which increases as the distance widens.

But the liver-coloured mongrel had no thought of retreating from an enemy less than half his size, and Gumbo, aware that he stood between his mistress and the forces of anarchy, was equally resolute.

The rush of the bigger dog carried the terrier off his feet, and the two rolled together for some yards, a snarling, dust-hidden heap, from which they broke apart, with their positions reversed, Gumbo now facing his mistress, and the bigger dog between them.

The terrier was shaken and breathless, but he had managed to avoid the grip of the white fangs which had sought his throat in the scuffle; he had also taken an instant advantage of opportunity when he had snapped at a hind paw as the heavier dog passed over him, and had assured that his opponent would continue the conflict with a limping leg.

He had won the first round on points, but he badly lacked a referee who would call time and give him the minute's rest that he needed.

The big dog had no such intention. He came again with a rush that Gumbo dodged with difficulty, and the next moment the two were in a struggling heap again, with a flurry of snapping jaws, and a pandemonium of outcry, sinking to one rumbling growl as the big dog got the choking grip that it sought upon the throat of its enemy.

Muriel might be an exponent of the gospel of peace, but she was not of the kind to stand aside from a conflict of this character.

The stick she had picked up from the roadside was little help, as it broke the first time she applied it accurately; but it was unfortunate for the strange dog that, like Gumbo, he was still encumbered by his late owner's collar.

In Gumbo's case the broad metal band which prevented his opponent's teeth getting a firm hold beneath the throat may have saved his life in the extremity of the next three minutes, but the other collar offered an inviting grip for Muriel's hands, which became a choking one as her fingers worked in beneath it.

Bill Horton, watching the fight from the side of the road, with an expert's appreciation, was roused to unusual articulation at the lady's temerity.

"Don't do that, miss. You'll get bit for sure," he protested, as he advanced to her assistance, with no clear purpose in his mind.

Bill had no brains worth mentioning, but he knew a dog-fight as something very good to watch and very bad to join.

The choking pull of Muriel's hands in the mongrel's collar, and Gumbo's struggles beneath him, combined to free the latter animal from the grip that held him. The big dog, having his jaws free, became a greater menace to the woman whose hands were dragging at the tightened collar. For the moment he ignored the terrier, who had regained his feet, but was in poor condition to renew the conflict. He struggled savagely to twist free of Muriel's hands and use his teeth upon her.

"Don't loose now, miss," implored the anxious Bill, moving up to help, but uncertain how to begin. He saw that her peril would be increased at once should she loose her grip on the collar. She saw it too, and held on desperately.

Bill, having arrived at the idea, by whatever laborious mental process, that an extra hand might be useful to choke the struggling animal, made a grab at the collar. The dog, seeing his purpose, dodged, and tried to bolt, dragging Muriel along several paces. She stumbled over some impediment in the road, and came to her knees, her grip failing as she did so.

The dog turned on her quickly, the wet jaws striking her throat as a rifle sounded, and he collapsed on the road. He rolled over, howling dismally, the sound sinking to a whimper, which was quickly silent. He twitched, and lay still.

Muriel got up breathlessly from the dust. The two men were on their knees in the road, collecting an assortment of feminine garments which had scattered from the parcel which she had dropped when she went to the rescue of Gumbo, and over which she had fallen as the dog dragged her along. She looked ruefully at their condition, as she interposed to retrieve with more sympathetic and discerning hands than those which were operating upon them.

"I must thank you both," she said, as they rose and faced one another. Bill Horton grinned sheepishly.

Jack said, "That's nothing. But I'm glad we came. It was a nasty brute for you to tackle."

He looked with some respect at the woman before him. He thought vaguely that he had seen her somewhere. It was the voice of a cultured woman, quiet and musical. The figure was small and slight. He hesitated about her age. She was not young, but she had very clear grey eyes and a girl's complexion, her natural paleness being overcome by the exertions of the last five minutes. She might be forty—probably less. (Actually, she was five years older.) No, he could not recollect where he had seen her previously.

He said, "We came to tell you that it's not safe here, and to ask you to go back with us. We thought there were two of you. Are you alone?"

Muriel liked his directness. She answered frankly. "There were two. There was a child that died.... Why isn't it safe here?"

"I can't tell you in a word. Can we sit somewhere?"

Muriel hesitated. She did not care to introduce such strangers to her secret stores. Then the habit of a lifetime conquered.

"Yes; you'd better come with me to the church. That's where I've been living."

She turned her eyes to Gumbo, who sat licking his wounds, with as ecstatic a countenance as nature permits a smooth-haired terrier to exhibit. His tail thumped the ground in self-approbation as he saw that the attention of the party was directed upon him. He wasn't quite clear how the dog had died, but he was quite sure that he had done well. He would always remember the instant chance of the passing paw, and how his teeth had snapped it....

Bill Horton looked him over critically. "He won't hurt," he said, meaning something quite different.

Gumbo supported the verdict by jumping up, briskly enough, as they commenced to move toward the church.

Chapter Thirteen

MURIEL led her guests to the seats in the porch. She did not invite them farther.

She said, "It's pleasanter here than inside on a warm evening like this. If you'll sit down, I'll get you something to eat."

They sat down obediently, not saying that they had already explored her resources. She took the parcel from Jack, who had been carrying it since it had been reassembled from the dirt, and retreated into the church.

"It's a queer meal," she said, as she returned with a supply of pancakes, which she had cooked the night before, and had meant to last her for the next three days. She was sparing of fires, which meant matches. She brought some of the Brazil nuts also, of which they had already observed her store, and a tin of pineapple. "You're welcome to this if you can open it," she added. "I didn't make a very good job of the last."

Jack produced a large and complicated knife from a hip-pocket, which included a tin-opener among its numerous blades

They commenced with appetite, but Jack looked with some anxiety at the declining sun, which still shone fitfully through the clouds of a summer storm, though the rain was beating heavily on the stone path.

"We ought to start in half an hour," he said, opening the subject which he knew had to be faced, and with as little delay as possible.

"Do you live far from here?" Muriel inquired, speaking as casually as she might have done a month ago.

"About four miles—perhaps more," Jack answered. "But we came through the fields. It's a bit risky by the road as things are just now."

"How are they 'just now'?" Muriel queried. "Hadn't you better tell me from the beginning? You see, I know nothing."

She recognized that Bill Horton was unlikely to contribute substantially to the conversation, and addressed herself to Jack Tolley accordingly. She was a good judge of men, and she felt some confidence in his probable character, but she had not the slightest intention of going anywhere with them that night without a better reason than he was at all likely to offer. She was unaccustomed to be led by anything other than her own conceptions of duty or obligation.

Jack considered that she must know *something*. The events of the last month could hardly have escaped the notice of the least observant. He said, "It's hard to know where to begin. I'd better introduce myself first. My name's Tolley—Jack Tolley I'm always called. I was a clerk at the collieries."

"Yes, I remember you now. I thought I'd seen you before. I'm Muriel Temple. Don't you—?"

Yes, he remembered now. She had come to the colliery office, perhaps two months ago, with an introduction from one of the directors and a request that she might be shown over the mine. He had only walked across the yard with her, to introduce her to the foreman, but he did not easily forget faces. It was the difference in dress and circumstances. The unexpectedness.

"Well, Miss Temple," he went on, using a title which was already becoming obsolete in the chaos of the last few weeks, "it's this way. When the trouble came there were a lot of men down the mine. Some of them got out at once, and went off with the crowd. I suppose they're dead now. Some of them got caught down below. We got them out—at least, about eighty of them—by an old shaft which hadn't been used for years. It was an old working that ran— but I needn't go into that...

"And there were people still going north when the land sank.... I didn't see that. I was helping to get the cage to work at the old shaft.... But they say that the land just broke off and slipped away. They looked over the edges, and it was hundreds of feet below them, and they could see the people running about, and trying to get back, and it seemed hours before the water flowed over them. There must have been a great part of England that just settled down lower than it had been, and the water couldn't flow over all of it in a minute. But I didn't see that. I don't really know." He spoke with some irritation of mind. His mental operations were as precise and neat as his person. He had heard a dozen more or less hysterical accounts of that stupendous tragedy, and no two were alike.

"Well, there were hundreds on the main road who had kept in front of the floods that followed them from the south, and only got here when the land had broken and they couldn't go farther. They crowded the road beyond Cowley Thorn, and spread out along the cliff-side.... And there were those on the railway.... But I mustn't go into detail. There were a lot that died.... Some of them fell ill, and some seemed to go mad...and there was quarrelling from the first... and there was no law."

"There was God's law."

"Well, they didn't worry much about that. Not all of them, anyway. They just saw that they could do anything if they were strong enough…and then they found ways to get food, if they didn't trouble about tomorrow. We found a lot at Linkworth that wasn't burnt. That's why we haven't come much this way. And some of them got arms." Muriel glanced at the rifle, which lay across his knee as he talked, and he answered the unspoken comment. "Yes, we found some sporting-guns in a country house. I'm glad we did. It gave us a chance, or I mightn't be here now…. But the quarrels got worse. You see, it" mostly men that are left, and the women made trouble."

(Yes. It was an old tale. Women do make trouble. Muriel had observed that rather frequently.)

And then there was the drink. Butcher's got enough up at Helford Grange to keep them all drunk for a month, and he doesn't care who gets it if they pay what he wants. That's made the trouble worse."

(Yes. Drink does make trouble. Muriel knew that too. But she had not known how much trouble can be made either by women or drink when there are about four men to every woman, and there is no dread either of the annoying certainty of civilized law, or the deterrent severity of the administration of a savage chief.)

"So there's been a fair row," Jack concluded briefly. "And we've turned Jim Rattray out." (Muriel recollected the name, and then the man. She did not doubt that there had been good reason for his expulsion.) "And a lot of men have gone with him. They're somewhere down this way…. And Tom Aldworth said he'd seen two women here, and we'd better look you up."

Muriel said, "You say Jim Rattray's near here. Do you know where I could find him?"

Jack Tolley, who was not easy to startle, looked his surprise at the unexpected query, and an expression of vague bewilderment spread over the vacuity of Bill Horton's countenance.

"You'd be sorry if you did. There's some of the worst toughs you ever met in that lot. You wouldn't be safe with them if there were a squad of police in the next street."

Muriel looked unimpressed. Her experiences of the toughs of various races during the last twenty years, and of the best methods of dealing with them, had been rather numerous.

"It might do good, and it couldn't do any harm," she said thoughtfully. "But if you don't know where he is…?"

"I wouldn't say if I did."

"I'm sure you'd tell me if I really wanted to know." Muriel smiled "But I suppose there won't be any more trouble, unless Rattray makes it, if you've turned him out."

It occurred to her that she might carry out her intention without seeking the lawless one through the wilderness. She had an attractive vision of two hostile camps, and of herself as an envoy of peace between them.

Suddenly she decided that she would accept the invitation which she had received. It was what she would have been doing, in any case, in a few days. She had only put it off from day to day because there had always been something left over for the next morning's occupation.

"But I'm not coming tonight," she added. "I'll come tomorrow. And I shall want a cart. I know you've got one. Oh, yes, I've seen the wheel-marks. Are your people in need?"

"Yes, the flour'll be useful."

Muriel looked at him, and he felt the error of the "the." He realized that she knew at once that they had explored her stores in her absence. His respect for Miss Temple's capacity was increasing rapidly.

"If we bring a cart we shall have to bring enough men to guard it. We don't want them to collar everything you've collected here. But I wish you'd come with us tonight. It's not safe here alone."

"Oh, I shall be safe enough," she answered easily. "I've got Gumbo, and some good bolts."

Jack had the sense to see that it was waste of words to argue further. "Well," he said, "you'll see us again tomorrow."

He got up to go.

When they were out of sight of the church he stopped.

"Bill," he said, "I think I'll stay here tonight. It's the safest way. Tell Madge I shall be back tomorrow. And ask Tom Aldworth to bring Steve's cart, and about a dozen men, with the rifles. Tell him to come early; there's a fair lot to load up."

Jack went back to the orchard. When it was dark, and he judged that Muriel would be sleeping, he returned to the church porch, where he made himself as comfortable as circumstances permitted. He did not trouble to keep awake. He calculated that the dog would give sufficient notice of any approaching stranger, as he had rightly calculated that he would not disturb his mistress to announce the movements of one who had been recognized as a friend a few hours earlier.

BOOK TWO

CHAPTER FOURTEEN

ON the second day of the deluge, when the floods still rose, but the first violence of the storm had fallen, and the people of Southern England, knowing vaguely that the south of Europe was beneath the waters, and that the Thames valley was filling, had fled blindly northward, it was natural that many of them had crowded to the railway stations, seeking a means of transit which might be preferable to the dangers of the congested roads.

But the storm had left the lines in such condition that they would have been regarded as impossible under more ordinary circumstances. Viaducts had given way, and bridges had fallen in. Signal-boxes were wrecked, and signals had been swept away. Telegraph-poles and wires had fallen across the lines in many places. Gates and fences and blown wreckage of every kind had been scattered upon them.

Yet in such emergency some attempt had been made to overcome these difficulties. From one of the Midland towns a crowded train had gone cautiously forward, its occupants swarming out from time to time to clear the line of the more serious obstacles. It proceeded on its northward course for about fifteen miles, and then came round a bend in the line where it was confronted by a final obstacle; for here a bridge which carried a road over the line had collapsed completely. The driver, having come round the curve at a cautious pace, was able to apply his brakes in time to avoid an accident, the engine stopping within a few feet of the obstacle; but, unfortunately, they were followed by another train, which had taken advantage of their previous labours, and had been able to make a better speed in consequence.

Urged by the fear of the pursuing floods, it had run over a clear line at a steadily increasing speed, and with a correspondingly decreasing caution. It came round the bend at thirty miles an hour, and before its speed could be materially reduced it had crashed into the rear of the standing train which had preceded it.

Had the line been clear ahead, the accident might have been less serious. The hinder coaches of the standing train might have been telescoped or derailed, but it is doubtful whether the impact would have done more to the farther coaches than to hurl them roughly forward upon the line on which they stood. But they were so placed that any advance was impossible. The ruin of the fallen bridge was piled within three feet of the engine's buffers. The struck train rose like a caterpillar, while the other penetrated beneath it, the rearward coaches falling backward upon and around their assailant. Fire started among the wreckage.

Even had the work of rescue been prompt and efficient, the loss of life must have been heavy, but there was none here to give aid, except such occupants of either train as had escaped serious injury. Some of them did what they could; others, oblivious of all but the desire to reach the imagined safety of the north, continued their flight on foot, without regarding horrors which they had little power to alleviate. Here were heroism and cowardice side by side; selfishness and self-sacrifice. But the greatest courage could do little under such conditions. The wreckage burnt swiftly, and with it those that were dead already, and those that were confined beneath it, or too badly injured to crawl away.

The nest morning there had been about seventy people, injured and uninjured, still camping upon the scene of the disaster. The rear coaches of the second train had been uncoupled in time to escape the flames, and these supplied shelter. During the day they were joined by a number of the men that had escaped from the mine. Some of these gave what aid they could, which was little. The conditions were such that most of the injured died. As the days passed, others of the less fit succumbed to the combined effects of unaccustomed hardship and the shocks of personal loss and overwhelming catastrophe.

Some wandered away. Some continued to make their homes in the standing coaches. There were about fifty of these, men, women, and children, previously strangers, drawn from every class and circumstance of life. Some of the better men among the miners who had first come to aid the misery of the injured and helpless remained among them. Some wandering strangers joined them. In spite of the addition of about twenty of the miners, the proportion of women remained higher in this community than it was among the derelicts of the road, of whom those who survived the first weeks of exposure and hardship were camping among the ruins of Cowley Thorn, in the mining village of Larkshill, or in isolated ruins, or erected huts, scattered over the countryside.

North of where the land had fallen there had been the two parishes of Upper and Lower Helford. Of these, Lower Helford, a populous district devoted to the manufacture of locks and similar ironmongery, was under water. Part of the more agricultural parish of Upper Helford was still visible, but separated by a space of swampy ground which the tides swept over. But Helford Grange, an old country house occupied by a family which had owned the two parishes from Tudor times, lying two miles farther south, had suffered only from fire and storm, which had reduced it to a charred skeleton. Its cellars, which were extensive, remained undamaged, and in these a man named Butcher had established himself, of whom there will be more to say in his own place.

As the survivors adapted themselves to their changed conditions they found that there was little difficulty in sustaining life during the summer days. Many previously domesticated animals wandered over the country. Many wild creatures and birds could be snared or hunted. Fruit was abundant in the neglected gardens.

Being without ordered rule, security of property, or any settled leadership, they made little provision for the future, except in isolated instances, though they might talk of the necessity of so doing. They could acquire more for their immediate needs by random plundering, or by watching for the harvest that the tides would bring them, than by any productive industry. That for which there was no immediate need, or which was discovered in excessive quantity, was often flung aside or wasted. They found, as Muriel had done, that the days passed easily. If they found food for a few days, and were unmolested in its consumption, they would be likely to drowse in the sun, or take shelter from the rain, till the week was over.

Search for plunder was the principal occupation of the community, and even this was carried on without organization or forethought.

Some of the rougher elements, including a proportion of the miners, formed themselves into nomadic bands which wandered without any settled headquarters, destroying wantonly such findings as they did not value, or would overload their transit facilities.

As the weeks passed it was inevitable that some men should gain ascendancy over their fellows, either by character or mental energy, but it was unfortunate that there was no one man who became recognized as a natural leader.

There were doubtless those who were self-satisfied of their ability to take control to the general benefit, but they lacked the force of individuality to impress such a belief upon their fellows—at least, until the slow processes of the common experiences should have assessed them rightly.

There was, perhaps, only one man, Jerry Cooper, at Cowley Thorn, who had a clear purpose of taking control of the new community. He was confident of his ability, and was entirely selfish and unscrupulous in his intentions and methods. He was not generally liked, but had already established some local domination.

Jim Rattray, of whom we have heard and seen something already, was of a different kind. He was too lazy, and too rarely sober, to have any plans for the governing of his fellow-men. But he was popular among a certain order; he was quarrelsome and reckless, he had intelligence, and a considerable vanity.

In discussing the social order of the England which the floods had covered it had been customary to divide the population into "classes," as though they were of different castes and of permanent division. But the fact was that they were in a condition of continual flux.

The slum-bred child, the hardy survivor of a large family, of which half might have died in the hard school of elimination into which they were born, would find that money could be made by frugal thrift and energy, aided, it might be, by some caprice of circumstance. His children, born to softer conditions, would despise their father's origin, but would have sufficient shrewdness and enterprise to hold and perhaps increase the wealth that his industry had accumulated. Their children, probably fewer and weaker, and bred to the disadvantage of luxurious living, would most often succumb to the "misfortunes" by which their enterprises would be frustrated, and would gravitate toward the gutter from which their parents came—and from where a child or grandchild might emerge again to fight an upward battle, and to be scorned in turn by the children for whom he would recapture the ground that his parents had lost.

Jim Rattray's father, a prosperous Bristol brewer, had taken a common course when he had paid his son's dishonoured cheques for the third time, settled with the moneylenders who were feeding upon him, and seen him on to an Australian liner, with the promise of an annuity of four hundred pounds, payable monthly, which would cease as soon as he should set returning foot upon the soil of his native land.

Jim Rattray had outwitted his parent before he landed at Melbourne, by arranging with a boat acquaintance to impersonate him with his father's agents in that city, at the cost of a commission of twenty-five percent upon the monthly allowance, which was to be deducted before remitting it back to England, to which country Jim returned by the next boat, using the name of his new acquaintance for the purpose.

For three subsequent years he had experienced the difficulty of living his accustomed life without his presence becoming known to his family or to his previous associates. It imposed a new penalty upon such appearances in the magistrates' courts as had been part of the routine of his old life, and other disabilities which he found so irksome that he was considering the advantages of returning to the exile he had avoided, when the elements interposed to solve his problem, as they solved so many which had seemed to be of an impossible difficulty to those who faced them.

Among others of this fortuitous community who were destined to some prominence in the events of the coming months, it is sufficient now to mention two only, an ex-furnaceman named Bellamy and Tom Aldworth.

Bellamy was a man of enormous strength, and of a corresponding brutality.

He was of a black and scowling humour, dreaded by his companions, who had yet a greater fear of his geniality. For it was in the exercise of his ferocious strength that he found relief from his broodings. Having lived in civilized conditions under the shadow of the jail, and more than once in fear of the gallows, he had suddenly found a delightful freedom, beyond any possibility of his dreams, of which he had, so far, taken advantage (if we except some minor violences) on two occasions only.

Once was in the first week of panic, when he had been a scowling member of a little crowd at the cliff-side which listened in a wondering terror to a man who preached the Judgment of God, and an approaching hell, in a frenzy of religious emotion, which might have borne its natural fruits, under conditions so favourable, had he not pushed his way to the front of the crowd and addressed the self-appointed evangelist.

"Eh, mister, what's this about sending us all to hell?"

The man was inclined to be frightened by the huge form and sinister reputation of his interrogator, till he noticed the good-humoured grin that was obliterating his usual aspect of ferocity.

"'Except ye repent—'" he began.

"It isn't fire," interrupted the furnaceman, with a widening grin, "it isn't fire we're worried about just now. What's the best thing to put hell out? We've got too much round these parts."

The man, who was not unused to being heckled, and could usually retort to good purpose against a far more adroit opponent than Bellamy was likely to prove, began, rather neatly, to allude to the waters of baptism, but the furnaceman did not want to hear him. He lifted him easily with one hand on his coat collar, and dropped his suddenly squealing and squirming victim over the cliff-side before any of the spectators could have intervened, even had they had the courage to do so.

He turned to face them with a broad grin of satisfaction at the joke he had played.

"You won't hear of a better hell-quencher than that," he remarked genially, as he made his way through a crowd that opened very widely before him.

The other incident occurred about a fortnight later.

Among the flying population that had been stayed at the cliff-edge there was a young woman who had been a teacher at a girl's training college in London. It had been a condition of her employment that she should maintain an at least nominal celibacy. Amidst much chatter of so-called eugenic theories of race-production (mostly of a negative character, and as cowardly in conception as they were false in fact), there was an utter indifference of public opinion either as to the nature or number of the English children which were to form the succeeding generation They cared nothing that many thousands of the best of their younger women should be condemned to barrenness, or tempted to abortion, because it was considered an inconvenience that those who were engaged in the teaching of the children of others should be interrupted by the bearing of their own.

Contemning their religion and their race for a false expediency, where they might more reasonably have required that those should themselves have had a full experience of life who were guiding others across the threshold of maturity, they deprived the next generation of many thousands of those who would have been, both in mind and body, among the front rank of its most hopeful children.

It followed that her experiences of life had been as limited as was her fitness for the post she held. Like most of her fellow-teachers, she had lived cleanly, though they would talk among themselves with an ignorant viciousness. It had only been required of her that she should be an efficient transmitter of facts (most of which were not worth remembering) and an example of the negative virtues. Her disposition had been quiet, gentle, and inoffensive, and she had been popular both with her fellow's and with the girls she taught.

When the deluge came she had owed her life to the efforts of a chance acquaintance of the London streets, a grocer's assistant, who had persuaded her against the folly of crowding into one of the lifts of the underground railways a few minutes before they had ceased to work, and within half an hour of the time when the whole system had been flooded, with the loss of not less than half a million lives.

They had taken the northward road together, getting a lift from a kindly motorist for a sufficient part of the way to enable them to escape the pursuing flood, while not advancing to die beneath the devastation which was before them.

To the boy the flight had brought a romantic idyll, beside which a world's collapse had been an unimportant incident.

For ten days they had lived in a green arbour, where great trees had fallen across a natural hollow, making a dim green twilight above the sandy soil of the bank-side, and feeding on the stores of a gipsy caravan which had been wrecked and overturned and deserted.

At the end of that time they had ventured out together, and almost at once they had encountered Bellamy, with two congenial companions, roaming in search of any plunder that might be worth the taking.

Bellamy had looked at the girl, and at the puny size of her escort. He had told her with a good-humoured growl to leave that monkey and come along. The girl had hesitated. Actually she cared little for her companion. She had always liked big men.

What she would have done had the decision been hers cannot be certainly known, for Bellamy, seeing her hesitation, laid a compelling grip on her shoulder, at which the boy struck an absurdly futile blow, and was afterward conscious only of the huge hand that choked him.

The giant threw him aside contemptuously, with a broken neck.

"Come on, now," he commanded, with the affability which resulted from his successful violences, and the woman followed him, rather stunned in mind, but not altogether unwillingly.

A week later she came, a flying, dishevelled figure, to claim the shelter of the camp in the railway cutting, showing a hand of which three fingers were broken.

Half an hour later Bellamy had followed, a leisurely, good-humoured giant, come to recover and chastise his property.

He had been met by Tom Aldworth, the last of those whom it is necessary to consider before approaching the main stream of the succeeding incidents.

Tom was a young man whose love of adventure had led him into trouble in the earlier days, when he had been tried (and acquitted) on a charge of murder. He was, quite consistently with that incident (this is not the place for its explanation), of a solid reliability of character, which, as it became recognized, was giving him an increasing influence among his associates—an influence which was more quickly felt because he was already known to those who had escaped from the flooded mine, and who formed so considerable a part of the male population.

He was not brilliant of intellect, nor of more than ordinary education. He was without personal ambition. But he was free from private vices, and was doggedly anxious for the welfare of the new community, though he had neither the wish nor belief in his own capacity to guide it wisely.

But for Tom it is probable that Bellamy would have fetched the woman out of her hiding-place and carried her off to such punishment as his humour prompted; but Tom had promised her that she should not be taken, and knowing that there was none among them who would stand up to the giant at close quarters, he had used the half-hour interval in enlisting the support of those who had been most active in the expulsion of Rattray, so that he was prepared for the ordeal.

He met Bellamy on the bridge which spanned the dry bed which had once held the Rugeley Canal, and that he must cross to enter the camp from the western side, unless he should have preferred to clamber down the ditch, which was not reasonably probable, as he was not of the kind to avoid the direct approach, nor to have much respect for his adversaries.

Tom had a rifle under his arm, and he did not offer to move from the centre of the roadway as the giant approached him.

"What do you want here?" he asked curtly.

The attitude and words were sufficiently hostile, but Bellamy showed no sign of observing it.

"I wants a bitch o' mine that's run loose. A dark-eyed bitch with a red skirt. I know she's hiding near here. Reddy saw her crossin' the flat."

"There's a woman here with a broken hand," Tom answered frankly, "but you won't get her. You won't get anything here. You're warned off. The boys have told me to warn you. You'll be shot at sight if you come a step nearer than Larkshill Road after to-night."

Bellamy stood facing the now lifted rifle, as though he restrained himself with difficulty from rushing upon it. His face flushed with blood, and the veins swelled out on his forehead.

He tried to swear, and it seemed that his articulation was obstructed by his own rage. He turned away, muttering something about "choking him with his own guts." He may have known what he meant.

Tom watched him till he was out of sight, and went back to talk matters over with his companions. It was agreed that an armed watch should be kept in the future, both day and night, more especially at night, and that either Tom himself, or Jack Tolley, or a Welsh miner named Ellis Roberts, should always be one of the party.

CHAPTER FIFTEEN

THE next day Tom walked over to Cowley Thorn to see Jerry Cooper, and to learn whether they could gain any support from him in the stand they were taking. He went up Bycroft Lane, which now led nowhere but to the steep shore-cliffs, and crossed Hallowby Park, which was equally deserted. No one came there, for the mansion had been burned to the ground, the park was four square miles of bracken and storm-strewn oaks, and there was no hope of plunder in that direction.

Those who wandered abroad went inland, or eastward to where the new coast was shallow, with little bays, and depressions that trapped the largesse of the tides.

But the lodge was standing on the farther side of the park, and had its share of life, for the old woman who had kept it was still there, having been too lame for flight (and too incredulous also), and there were a woman and two children that the seas had thrown up a month ago in a foundered boat—a woman that Tom and his companions had rescued, and carried there, as the nearest shelter, and that had lain too weak and ill to be anything but a burden to anyone. Considering the isolation of the position, and the fact that their existence was known only to himself, he had considered that they might b' safer there than in any other shelter that he could offer, and in any case, the woman had been too ill to move.

So far, he had brought them food, and watched over their safety as far as he was able, and if he hoped for any ultimate reward from a woman who was regaining health and bad no other protector the time had not come to claim it.

So, after delivering the food he had brought, and lingering to give vague warnings to keep the children off the road, and to lock up at night (he kept the key of the lodge-gates in his own pocket, and he had made the park-palings secure, at least against any wandering animal), he crossed the road, and took his way over the neglected fields to Cowley Thorn. He saw no use in alarming those who could do nothing further for their own protection.

He found Jerry Cooper busily occupied in repairing the fencing of a paddock in which he had secured three horses.

He was in his shirt-sleeves, a heavily built man of about fifty years, hard of eye and jaw, who laid down his tools, and received him with a superficial geniality, which still seemed to require him to state his business, and begone when he had done so.

Jerry Cooper, a builder's merchant by trade, had made himself the richest man and the most powerful in the city of his birth. He had no doubt that a few years would see him in the same position again.

He was of no mind to be guided by Tom Aldworth's suggestions. He would play second fiddle to no man.

He listened to the tale to its conclusion without comment, and then asked bluntly, "What's it to do with me?"

Tom knew his defeat from the tone and manner of the question, and had no subtlety of mind to overcome the hostility which he recognized.

He answered with directness. "It seems to me we shall have trouble till we join together to stop that sort of thing happening."

"Well, shoot Bellamy if you want to. You needn't ask me. *I* shan't shoot you. Probably one of his pals will. But that's your lookout."

"I thought we might have joined together to get some order—and security," said Tom weakly.

"Look here, Aldworth," Cooper answered, in the tone which his employees had learned to dread in the old days, a tone domineering and merciless, "if you come here to me to talk, *talk sense*. What's this girl of Bellamy's to me? She hasn't come here. If she had I might have kept her, and put a bullet through the swine, instead of talking about it, and asking other men to help me to save my skin. You've got two women in Hallowby Lodge. How many more do you want?

"You come here with Rattray, and Butcher, and any other men who'll join in a fair deal, and I'll talk business tomorrow. Then you can make dogs' meat of Bellamy, for all I care.

"But you listen to this. There's not one woman to five men in this cursed place, and about half of those women are with your lot already, and now you ask me to help you when another bolts to the same hole.

"If you'll share level, we'll talk. If you won't, we may act in a way you won't like."

"It seems to me," said Tom, "if we go on those lines, the men may soon get fewer."

Cooper gave him an interrogatory stare before he answered:

"Perhaps you're right. But it needn't be if we talk reasonably."

"So I will," said Tom. "We don't make them come to us, and we shan't keep them if they want to go. That's reasonable enough."

"It's not reasonable enough for me. There's forty men in Cowley Thorn, and as many more between here and the coast, and more in Larkshill, and not twenty women that are worth sixpence among us.

"There's half a dozen here that keep to their own men, more or less, and two sluts, and Nance Weston. That's the lot in Cowley Thorn.

"Now you'd better think it over, and make a fair bid, or you'll have someone besides Bellamy to deal with."

"It's not our fault if there were more women in our camp than yours. They mostly came on the train. If others have come since I suppose it's because they think it's the safest place. I've told you that we don't force them to stay."

"I'll go further than that. I'll tell them just what you say. They can come here if they like. Even if they leave their own men, there's no law now to stop them. There never was much of that. But we shan't turn them out if they want to stay."

Cooper had made up his mind as the conversation proceeded. He had been considering the matter for some days. He was too good a business man to take any avoidable risk, but he knew that there are times when such a risk must be taken.

He thought he saw in this question of the women (about which, in itself, he did not care very greatly, one way or the other), a means of seizing the ascendancy at which he aimed. He knew that it was through the dissensions of others that the shrewd man triumphs.

A demand for a more nearly equal distribution of the female population could hardly fail to win him a general support and popularity.

He rapidly calculated the forces at his disposal. He added the followers of Rattray and Bellamy—he could dispose of them afterward, when they had served their purpose. Perhaps Butcher also? He was less sure of him, but he could probably be bought.

Anyway, he wouldn't be likely to help Tom Aldworth.

These thoughts passed rapidly through his mind while Tom was speaking. He was used to quick thought and quick decisions when business called for these qualities.

He said, "Tell them to make their minds up quickly, or they'll get it done for them. I'll give them three days."

He rose from the fallen trunk on which he was sitting. He turned his back on Tom without ceremony.

Tom stood looking at him for a moment. He recognized an opponent of a different quality from the brutal Bellamy. The man was clean, at a time when cleanliness was an almost obsolete virtue. He was suitably dressed for his occupation, at a time when clothing was apt to be neglected or fantastic.

Tom did not know the intended use of the horses, but he recognized that the man was working hard, and with purpose.

He walked back slowly, thinking rather sombrely of the future of those whom the floods had spared.

He went back by the main road, and almost ran into Bellamy, talking to a group of his fellows around a horse-drawn trolley, on which there was a barrel of beer that they had broached and were sharing freely.

Tom recognized the folly of having left his rifle behind that morning. He had been shy of going out as though fearful of danger. Now he had an impulse to run, which he restrained with difficulty. He walked on past the group with an outward coolness.

The giant only looked at him, as he passed, with the geniality which he reserved for his victims.

CHAPTER SIXTEEN

IT was still possible that serious conflict might have been avoided had not the following day brought another incident very similar to that in which Bellamy had been involved, and with a corresponding sequel.

Tom was anxious to avoid a conflict with Jerry Cooper. He saw that the direction in which they were heading might resolve the problem in the simplest terms by reducing the male population till the difficulty of numbers would no longer trouble them. He considered that, even for the women, this might be something less than an ideal solution, as it was unlikely that the survivors would always be those of their own selection.

He tried, also, to see the matter from Cooper's standpoint, and he may even have overdone this mental exercise, and credited him with a better case than would have been allowed by an impartial judgment.

He evolved a plan, at last, which was less perfect than he supposed it to be, but which supplied a possible solution of existing difficulties, and which was actually adopted at a later date.

He formed a sincere intention of inviting his opponents to a conference for its discussion.

But it happened on the following day that Jim Rattray, returning with some congenial companions from an expedition in the favourite Linkworth direction, and being in a half-sober condition, as they came along the southern limit of Spiller's Wood, where many of the trees were still standing, or showing a spread of green branches from shortened trunks (for the storm, which uprooted the northern trees of the larger woods, piled them against those that were farther inward till a solid barrier of resistance had been banked up against its power of further destruction, so that the southern edges might show little sign of damage after a month of leafage had covered their minor injuries), walking silently enough along the edge of a mossy bank, came upon a man and woman, who do not otherwise concern us, in some degree of affectionate intimacy, which aroused an amatory jealousy in the mind of the half-drunken observer.

It is an arithmetical fact that there were a somewhat large number of women of dissolute character in the England of pre-deluge days. It is happily true that it was possible to go through life without any first-hand acquaintance with this element of the population. But it is also true that, to such as Rattray, they were the only sort to be intimately known, and that it was possible to believe that all women were of a kindred quality.

Rattray, jumping down from the bank with the instant resolve to share her favours, was unrestrained by any element in his own character, and had the happy knowledge that there were no longer any laws to embarrass him. But it is fair to observe that he would not easily have understood the extremity of resentment which he occasioned.

The woman, being no worse than kissed, struck him fiercely. The man picked up a cudgel, and Rattray went down with a bruised head. Had he been alone that would have ended the incident. But his companions came tumbling down to his rescue. The man hit out boldly enough, but he was out-numbered, and belaboured with various weapons, till he fell unconscious, his skull fractured by a blow from an iron rod.

Seeing the man fall, they regarded him no longer, but as the woman had lacked the sense to run, and had endeavoured to obstruct his assailants, they now turned their attention to her, and, at Rattray's instigation—he having now recovered from the blow that felled him, and being in a somewhat more sober but very savage mood in consequence—they carried her off, a kicking, biting, protesting fury, to make such sport with her as their natures led them.

During the night she escaped, or they let her go, and she returned to the man she loved, to find him badly, if not mortally, injured, and, in this extremity, she made her way to the railroad camp, where she told the tale to a dozen indignant listeners.

She was a stranger to them, she and her husband being of those who had hidden from the earliest days, preferring solitude to the lawless risks of human association, but they could not refuse their aid for this reason. They brought in a dying man, and gave what comfort they could to a distracted woman.

Tom Aldworth's mind was of no exceptional ability either to construct or to penetrate, but he had a good share of that faculty of judgment which is known as common sense, and it assured him now that there was no probability of founding any settled order of living upon the condonation of such acts, or with the co-operation of those who had been guilty of them.

He did not alter his purpose of meeting Jerry Cooper, and any others he might bring, to discuss the position, but he took active steps to induce the better sort of the scattered population to come in to the protection of his camp and to assist its defence. He sent Jack Tolley in search of the women that he believed he had seen some weeks earlier in Sterrington Church, and placed an order with Butcher for a quantity of barbed wire, which was very promptly delivered, against his undertaking to supply four horses of a specified quality within one month of that date.

The horses which Tom had thus pledged himself to capture were required toward a larger order which Cooper had already placed, from which it will be seen that Butcher conducted his business with a large impartiality, and from which it may be deduced that he did not think that Tom's party would be wiped out very easily, or the credit given must have shown less than his usual caution.

CHAPTER SEVENTEEN

BILL HORTON delivered his message well enough, but was vague and self-contradictory in his estimates of the contents of Muriel's storehouse.

Tom Aldworth was annoyed. He wanted Jack's help for a dozen things. He doubted the wisdom of sending for the woman's belongings. Why hadn't he brought her back, and ended the incident?

They had three days to prepare for a conflict which seemed inevitable, and he had no wish to risk anything which might precipitate it earlier.

If he should send a cart along a road which ran through a part of the country where he had good reason to suppose that Rattray and his companions were camping, it would invite attack if it were weakly guarded. If he sent a strong force he would weaken his defences for many hours, and what might happen in consequence?

As to that, reflection encouraged him to conclude that the risk was not great. The movement would be unexpected. It was unlikely, if not impossible, that the scattered forces of his opponents would unite for a common purpose in time to take advantage of it.

Then, as to an attack upon the cart, he concluded that a possible combination of Rattray's and Bellamy's gangs was the worst that he need anticipate. He did not suppose that Cooper would be too scrupulous for such an adventure, but he recognized that it was not his way. He was a politician. He would instinctively manœuvre for popularity. To whatever purpose he worked, he would consider it essential to put a good face upon it. He knew the importance of window-dressing.

Then the flour, the quantity of which Bill had not underestimated, was badly needed. He decided to send, and he recognized that, if he were to do it at all, it could not be done too early.

He explained the matter to Ellis Roberts, a grizzled Welshman, who had once been a foreman in a Welsh slate-quarry, and had lost an eye in the blasting operations incidental to that occupation.

Ellis was not quick, but he was sure. He saw more with his remaining eye than did most men who were better equipped in that particular.

He agreed, after some thought, that it was worth doing, and that a daylight start would be best.

They discussed who should be asked to go, and how many.

Ellis thought four of the rifles would be enough. Tom grudged them. He had thought of two only. But he agreed. He knew that there were some firearms among the two gangs, though it was doubtful whether they had ammunition. He recognized that a show of such weapons might avert a conflict more surely than an increase in the mere numbers of the escort.

But he had only eleven rifles in all, and the position of his camp obliged him to defend a rather large area. He depended upon these rifles to check a possible rush from any side, and did not wish them to be too widely separated.

Still, he reminded himself again that there was no likelihood of any strong attack during Ellis's absence. It was probably the best way.

They decided not to send Steve Fortune's cart. Steve would want to make his own terms, which were not always moderate. The float would hold more, and with less packing. That was important.

The one thing which men had learnt thoroughly during the previous month was the art of transport.

"Probably be half the day loading up, even then," said Ellis. (I am aware that, being Welsh, he should have said "whatefer," but the fact is that he didn't. There are some Welshmen who don't.) "Can we get the float up to the door?"

Bill was uncertain about that, but not hopeful.

There was a pack-horse available, and Ellis decided to take that also. He collected half a dozen men eight with himself and Bill— and arranged to start with the dawn. There would be Jack Tolley also on their return, and he not only had a rifle but he could shoot straight, which was not a universal accomplishment.

They never knew whether all these precautions were needed, or whether they were observed at all, but they returned late in the afternoon without incident, having found the pack-horse a very necessary assistance.

Muriel was half astonished and half ashamed to realize the quantity and variety of her accumulations. They returned slowly, as she had insisted on the bringing of Datchett's cow; and a four-mile walk for such an animal, which is due to calve in a week's time, is a matter of less haste than dignity.

The Rector's sow did not come. Tom pointed out that the feeding of confined pigs was very unpopular in the community which Muriel was about to join. He shared this prejudice. It was far simpler to let them run loose, and shoot one when it was needed. Muriel, who had experienced the difficulty of satisfying its daily appetite, and was aware that it had become rather bony under her administration, had already some doubts as to whether she had not been a fool to recapture it, and agreed without difficulty.

Had it been fit for conversion into bacon, or immediate pork— but it was showing unmistakable signs of adding to the numerical ascendancy of its kind, and so the sty-door was opened, and a very happy pig went off down the field at a brisk trot, tail in air, and with no sentimental backward glance at the place of its confinement.

Muriel consoled herself with the capture of some week-old chickens and a protesting hen.

CHAPTER EIGHTEEN

MURIEL looked with an observant curiosity upon the road they traversed.

It rose clear of the Sterrington hollow, and ran for some distance upon the crest of a gentle ridge, where it had been bare of any height of trees along its edges, and the telegraph poles which had been planted on its southern side had fallen across the fields, so that the road itself was not encumbered by any serious impediments.

The fields might not have shown any great difference from their usual midsummer fertility, but that the fallen gates and gapped hedges had given free access to such animals as the storm had left uninjured. There was no sign of cattle, for these animals had congregated in the fallen woods and in the richer pastures of the lower lands, but there were a few sheep feeding upon a field of growing oats, one of which lay as it nibbled, and then rose awkwardly to trail a broken leg to another patch.

Apart from that there was an absence of the notes of the smaller birds, which had suffered most severely of all the creatures of the

70

fields, and a flock of gulls rose as they passed, and took flight to a farther feeding-ground.

But when they left the higher level, and had descended the hill to the colliery village of Larkshill, they came on different evidences.

The cottages that had lined the road, and spread out into 'courts,' and along side-alleys, had not been of a stability to survive the elemental discord. They had been flattened by the tempest, and had burst into fifty fires from the hot ashes of their broken hearths, to smoulder, a rain-drenched bonfire, through that night of horror and the day that followed. And as they burnt they lay.

There had been little effort to rebuild, or activity to search among such unlikely ruins.

Only the first cottage on the left, at the hill's foot, was already showing two rebuilt rooms, and Davy Barnes, helped by the two younger children, was working diligently at a further wall.

Martha, his mother, a meagre, work-worn woman, with wisps of greying hair hanging untidily about a burn-scarred face, came out to give a shrill greeting to Ellis Roberts, and a mute, shrewd stare at the unknown woman who was walking beside him.

"What yer doing with that beast?" she asked curiously, as Datchett's cow turned a slow head to observe the origin of the disturbance. "Shouldn't 'a' thought yer'd got feed for a rabbit from Larkshill Road to the sea."

"We're not as bad off as that," said Ellis—and then to Muriel's natural query, "you'll see when we get there."

Coming to where the south road entered the village, they encountered more obstructions upon the road, but they had been cleared sufficiently to enable them to make a tortuous progress. Shortly afterward they turned south by the ruins of the Plasterer's Arms, continuing for a short distance down Sowter's Lane, and then turning east again by twisting byways, because, as Ellis explained, the straighter road was blocked near Bycroft Lane by a tree which lay across it, and it had been found an easier course from day to day to follow the winding lanes than to remove the obstacle.

They came out again upon the Larkshill Road, almost opposite to the ruins of the ironworks, and crossed it to take a cart-track which had been used to deliver goods that came by road, and had run on past the works to the canal-siding.

A month ago waste ground, barren and blackened, rubbish-strewn and unfenced, had extended around the ironworks and the cottages that straggled toward the main road and along the nearer side of the canal.

Now the smoke-pall had cleared, the sky was a blue dome of healthful air, or white with cloud, and the coarser weeds and grasses were already struggling to cover the polluted ground and the fallen ruins of street and foundry. But this effort of cleanliness had had little support from those who were left to observe it. Their time had been mainly spent in gathering the largesse of the sea, or plundering the ruined country to southward. Precarious spoils, often useless in kind or excessive in quality, had been exchanged, quarrelled over, wasted, and flung aside. The main camp was out of sight, being in the hollow of the railway cutting, though it was at no great distance on the farther side of the canal, which had run parallel with the railway, but its filth and refuse, flung lazily aside, were clearly observable among the abandoned *débris*.

Perhaps such conditions were almost inevitable in such a community, without leadership or organization, which had lost two-thirds of its numbers in a few weeks from wounds and weakness; and had found the expulsion of some of those who remained alive to be a necessary condition of any tolerable existence. The fact that no infectious disease had broken out to complete their destruction may be attributed to the sea air and exposure to which they were compulsorily subjected—conditions which, commencing with the disadvantage of precarious and unsuitable food, had killed the old, the weak, the injured, and those who were unsound in any vital organ, but had hardened those who had survived their hardships.

CHAPTER NINETEEN

THERE had been much said, after the four years' conflict which had partially exhausted Europe, of the horrors and folly of war, and they are subjects on which overstatement is not easily to be achieved. But it is a confusing fact, which we may observe without basing any contention upon it, that there is no other impulse which unites our race, or arouses its energy, as does the shadow or the call of war.

The canal-bed ran north and south, continuing northward for about three miles, where it broke off abruptly above the ocean into which it had poured its waters. The railway line ran parallel with it for half a mile north of the camp, and then turned north-eastward, striking the sea at a somewhat shorter distance, for there was not more than a mile of land to eastward above the water.

The initial problem which must be faced in deciding the plan of defence of such a position against an equal or superior force is the extent of ground which it is necessary or possible to hold.

Tom Aldworth considered this problem without the benefit of any previous military experience, or knowledge of the art of war, and was confronted by a difficulty that has troubled many commanders of greater ability and experience—the line which appeared to offer the greatest natural advantages was more extensive than could be easily held by the small company that the camp contained.

The main population of the camp, including most of the women, and its most important stores, were located in the shallow railway cutting in which the accident had occurred. Here five coaches, each consisting of from six to eight compartments, and a goods-van, which had been uncoupled from the rear of the second train in time to escape the fire which had consumed the remaining portion, were occupied as living-rooms, and storehouses for the more valuable or perishable goods that had been collected.

Other goods were piled, and some huts were being erected, at the sides and farther back along the line.

The sides of the cutting were of a considerable height at the place of the fallen bridge, but declined from it until the line became level with the surrounding country about three hundred yards to the south.

Tom considered the fact that the camp was situated in such a hollow to be a military disadvantage, which was not as absolutely true as he supposed it to be—especially where the question of artillery did not arise—but there were other considerations which would have embarrassed the occupation of so limited a position. There was, for instance, no water-supply in the cutting; and other questions would have arisen, which must be avoided lest this narrative should be mistaken for military disquisition.

Not unnaturally, Tom thought of the canal-ditch as the strongest line of defence, and it was for this that he had bargained for the barbed wire which Butcher had delivered so promptly.

As Muriel's little party came along the outer bank toward the bridge which they must cross to gain the security of the camp, they could observe about three-quarters of the garrison, including most of the women, engaged in the laborious erection of an efficient fence, under the impulse mentioned at the commencement of the present chapter.

Tom saw them coming, and met them on the bridge, where he had previously encountered the discomfited Bellamy.

He lost no time in the formalities of introduction, for he was not a student of etiquette, and his mind was distracted by a score of contending questions which were brought to him for solution, or which he knew would be neglected unless he should assume the responsibility of decision. He was without any properly constituted authority. If he wished anything done he had to ask, not order. Argument followed more often than a prompt obedience. But there was a general disposition to come to him for advice or guidance, and there was no doubt that the popular opinion of the camp would hold him responsible for any disaster which might fall upon it.

He told Muriel briefly that Ted Wrench, who was standing near, would show her where she could sleep and could put any personal belongings which she wished to retain. He observed the sacks of flour with some satisfaction. If there should be anything in the nature of a siege.... He looked doubtfully at Datchett's cow—a tired and thirsty animal, hanging a disconsolate head.... He began to talk to Jack Tolley and Ellis Roberts about the impossibility of extending his defences to the lines which they had agreed upon on the previous day—an impossibility which was conclusively demonstrated by the rate of progress which the day had shown, quite apart from the question of how they could have been manned efficiently afterward.

"That little rat Reddy Teller's been here with a note from Cooper this morning," he went on; "he seems to be the general messenger. Cooper wants us to meet him tomorrow afternoon in Larkshill Road, outside the Plasterer's Arms. He asks that there shall not be more than four a side. (I suppose 'four' means he's got Butcher to join him.) We're to undertake that, if we don't come to terms, nothing's to happen on either side till the next morning. All the others can come, as we may have to consult them, but they're to stand back. That's how I understand it."

"I wouldn't trust Rattray's gang, or Bellamy's," said Jack.

"I wouldn't trust any of them. But I can't think of a better plan. You see, we've got to meet somewhere, or there's no chance of a settlement. We don't want a row, and we don't know how it would end. We can't make them come to us. If we go to them, just ourselves, they may try some tricks, whatever they promise. If we take a lot of the boys with us, we leave the women here unprotected, and we don't know what might be happening.

"This plan meets them halfway. I propose that we all go—every one in the camp that isn't too ill, even the children. They'll go armed, all except us, and stand back, and be there to know what's arranged. I've got a plan to propose, and we may get them to agree.

74

"If they try to fight us there—well, it's got to come some time. It'll be over all the sooner."

Jack said: "I don't like it. I don't think I'll come." He stood thoughtful and hesitant. "But I don't think they'll try any tricks. It wouldn't be Cooper's way. Not that he'd mind. But he believes in talk. He wouldn't risk a mistake. The others might.... But we could deal with them. We might tell half a dozen of the boys to have their rifles ready. They could cover the four of them, and they'd be done for before us, if they tried any mischief."

Tom Aldworth nodded, and then grinned as he said, "If Harry Swain's one of them, I hope he'll aim at me. I should feel safer than if he tried for the others."

Jack said: "What's the plan you've got?"

"It's this. You mayn't think it's much good, but we've got to look at the facts. It's true that there are half a dozen men left alive for every woman, and we were mostly strangers to one another a month ago. Getting the boys out of the mine made it worse, but it would have been bad enough without that. I suppose it would have made trouble anyway, but like we are with no law, and a few rotters among us, it was sure to make more than a bit.

"Well, we've had rows enough, and we look like having some more if we can't get something that every one will agree to. You know we've tried to get every one together before to get someone chosen to boss these things, and most of them wouldn't come, and those who did quarrelled as to who should vote, and what for, and we got no further. Most of us are too busy looking after ourselves, and some like things to go on as they are.

"But this plan of Cooper's will get most of the folk together, and if we agree to anything it may be some use.

"Now we've got to look at this. We *have* got most of the women here, and it isn't only Rattray's lot and the toughs with Bellamy that don't like it. The boys at Cowley Thorn must feel just about the same. That's what Cooper's building on. I think he means to make us all run when he whistles, and we mayn't always like the tune.

"But there's the fact. There's one thing that I don't like, and it shows how the feeling goes. I've sent to all the men who are scattered about Larkshill, and beyond, and asked them to help us. They know what's been happening, and there isn't one that's come. You know there's some decent ones among them. I don't say they'll help Cooper. I don't know. But there it is.

"Now I'm out of this. You all think I've got a woman at Hallowby Lodge, and, however that is, I'm not asking for two. I am going to say, why not let the women choose for themselves? Tell them they've got to chum up to someone, and give them a fair time, and if they don't, it's their look-out.

"They can make their own choice, and we'll stand by them, and settle with anyone who interferes...."

"You don't think Bellamy'll agree to that?" said Jack sceptically.

"No, I don't; nor Rattray; and we don't want either of them here at any price. It may be just as well if they don't. But it's fair for all, and it gives us something to fight for. We might get it agreed, and, if not, we shall know where we are."

There was a moment's silence from the two men he addressed. As all the rest would do in turn, they paused to consider the personal results that would be likely to follow.

Tom knew what was in their minds. Here were two of the best characters in the camp—if even they couldn't....

Ellis Roberts looked at his younger rival, "That goes with Madge?" he asked doubtfully.

"Yes," said Jack Tolley, and the two men joined hands on the bargain.

Tom saw that his plan would, at least, be assured of some support, and a hearing.

"I suppose it's us three," he went on, "but who's the fourth?"

That was a difficult question. The three of them were becoming informally recognized as a self-constituted committee of management. There were several others who might have claims, but the preference of any one would mean jealousy from the others.

"We'd better let them choose," said Jack.

"It's waste of time to call them off the work," Tom answered. He knew how much talk it would mean, and how probable that a row would end it.

"Why not have Miss Temple?" said Roberts.

Tom stared. It seemed absurd to suggest a woman, and one who had only joined them half an hour ago.

But Jack nodded. "Yes, that's a good idea," he said definitely.

"Well, you know her better than I do," Tom answered. "I suppose there ought to be a woman among us. It's their racket as much as ours. What sort is she?"

"She's been an African missionary," said Jack. "She knows her own mind, and how to make other people's up for them. She'll probably start with prayer."

Tom frowned. "We don't want any more of that now…. I suppose you know what you're doing."

"I don't agree there, Tom," said Ellis, "it's just what we do want. A lot more than we've got."

He had been a silent but liberal supporter of a little dissenting chapel in the Corris valley. It was possibly the ugliest edifice of its kind in Wales (a pre-eminence for which the competition was extremely keen), and its front elevation was ornamented with a scroll text. "It is the Lord's doing: it is marvellous in our eyes." There was no intention of levity.

Ellis Roberts considered that, if religion had been swept away by the flood, its disappearance had conferred no very evident benefit.

"Well," said Tom, "have it your own way." He reflected that she had got round the two of them very successfully—or why on earth had they brought the cow!

CHAPTER TWENTY

MURIEL followed her belongings till they came to the mouth of the cutting, where the line was level with the surrounding hills, and here, when her escort had tied the cow to a broken gate, they turned inward, and retraced a short distance along the line, the side ditch of which had been filled in and levelled to allow of such traffic, till they came to the rearmost of the coaches. The cutting, which was usually a scene of much coming and going, and disorderly activity, was now comparatively quiet, as the bulk of its population was working at the fortification of the canal-bank.

Ted showed her a compartment which he told her she would share with another occupant, whose belongings had already been moved to one side, to make room for her own possessions.

The lady was absent, and Muriel expressed a hope that she was prepared for, and would not mind, the intrusion.

"She don't count," said Ted easily. "She's crazed. That's why no one's been in with her before."

Muriel made no comment upon this information. She recognized that first-class compartments were not likely to have vacant accommodation without sufficient reason under the prevailing conditions. The craziness need not be of an aggressive character. She was used to facing difficulties as they came. She addressed her mind to the selection of such articles as she would require for her own use, and which could be accommodated under the seat or on the rack of the half-compartment which had been allocated to her. It appeared, by implication, that the remainder of her acquisitions would pass into communal storage, and that she would cease to have any special interest in them. She questioned Ted upon the organization of her new associates, and gained an impression of what may be described as an almost systematized confusion of communal and individual ownership, growing out of the accumulation of promiscuous stores which were often collectively acquired, and were otherwise in excess of any single requirement. A chaos out of which order might be resolved, but hardly without some intervening discords.

She found Ted Wrench to be a somewhat lazy youth—a condition which was the immediate cause of his present occupation, Tom having observed his shirking of the harder work at the barrier. He became sulky at the amount of unloading and rearranging that was incidental to the elimination of Muriel's retentions before the cart and packhorse could be taken to their further destination. He reminded her that the cow had still to be properly deposited. That meant half a mile's walk. Muriel placated him with Brazil nuts, of which she forthwith decided to retain as many as possible in her own possession. She recognized that needed goods were the only money of this community. Was it then reasonable to part with so much that she had laboriously accumulated? Well, they were offering her their protection, and they had carted her goods. Certainly, she would not be one to raise difficulty over such an issue. But she made a bargain with Ted (for some more nuts), that he should help her to enclose the space below the compartment for her hen and chickens—still in the basket of which we have heard before—when the cow should have been disposed of; and she got him to fetch some immediate water for that long-suffering quadruped.

Later she accompanied Ted to see where her cow was to be pastured, and, by doing this, she was able to understand why its coming had been received so coolly.

The land east of the railway fell away toward the new coast, and a stream, which flowed under the line about a quarter of a mile farther south, turned north-east, so that it crossed the narrow land between the line and the sea at a somewhat acute angle. The cattle which had been captured for the common use were confined within the area bounded by this stream, the sea, and the railway, but unfortunately, though its area was considerable, it was not fertile land. It contained the pit-heads of two abandoned collieries, and the slag-strewn ground was covered with a coarse and patchy growth, which, even in June, was unappetizing to cattle that could observe more verdant pastures on the other side of the stream.

It was also unfortunate that the stream was badly fenced, and was fordable in many places, so that it had become a continual occupation to watch these cattle, and to fetch back those which outwitted the irregular patrol, which was a general duty rather than particular to any individual.

The cattle were valued for the milk they gave, but they were already so numerous that they were grazing off the coarse grasses faster than their summer growth could adjust the balance, and several which had failed to maintain their milk-supply had been expelled during the previous week.

Under such circumstances, it was not surprising that an addition to the herd was regarded as a doubtful blessing, and the disfavour with which the cow of the departed Datchett surveyed the barren prospect around her made it quite evident that she was equally critical of the decision which had removed her from familiar fields.

CHAPTER TWENTY-ONE

THE summer evening was still light when Muriel went to rest, with a tired dog that had followed her all the day lying across her feet, on a more luxurious couch than she had known since the night when the roof of Wilkes's cottage had collapsed upon her.

It was true that three of the windows had been broken, either in the collision or by a subsequent violence, and that she did not feel free to close the door till her companion, whom she had not yet seen, should appear; for the coaches stood high above the line, and though rough steps had been contrived for most of them, to make ascent easier, the approach to this one, as to some of the others, was by no more than an upturned box, and it might not be easy for the "crazy" woman to open it from such a position.

But the evening was warm, the cushions soft and thick, and Muriel was conscious of that degree of physical exhaustion which makes a luxury of rest. She was not sleepy, and the thought came to her, with some wonder, of how much less fatigue she had felt than would have followed a day of such exertions only a month ago. Could it be possible…? If so, it must surely be that there was some work for her to do here, which must be better done than had been that of the previous years.

Her mind wandered to speculate on the real character of the woman with whom she was to live in such an intimacy. Her possessions, whatever they might be, must be contained in the two suitcases which had been pushed under the seat, and in the cardboard boxes on the rack. A little travelling-clock, pinned to the side-cushion, was ticking regularly. There was nothing of the squalid disorders of food and clothing and utensils, inside and out, which Muriel had observed of some of the neighbouring compartments. There was no evidence of insanity here.

Then she came. A dark-haired woman, good-looking in a quiet way, with gentle, rather wistful eyes. Her clothing, which had once been good, was weather-soiled and stained, but it was tidy and clean. She looked well. She did not look very unhappy. She greeted Muriel with a quiet cordiality. Gumbo, looking up inquisitively, thumped an appreciative tail on the cushions.

"I hope you don't mind the broken windows. There seems to be no means of mending them now…. I must introduce myself. I am Mary Graham…. Muriel Temple? What a pretty name. I shall be so glad to have you with me. I ought to have been here to welcome you when you came, but I couldn't leave Janet. I never do leave her till she goes to sleep. I expect they told you that. They think I'm crazy about her. But I can't break a promise like that, can I?"

"They didn't tell me anything," Muriel answered. "But I should be glad to hear."

Mrs. Graham sat down as she answered, "There's nothing really to tell. I just sit with her till she goes to sleep. I always used to do that… But I didn't think it would be so long."

And then the sympathy in Muriel's eyes reached some chord of suppressed sorrow, and her expression altered. She flung herself down upon the cushions in a passion of weeping. "*Oh, God, if she would only speak! I didn't think it would be so long.*"

Muriel was too wise to question her further. She crossed the narrow space that divided them, and soothed her with words which have comforted a million sorrows, till she went to sleep against the shoulder of her new companion.

In the morning she waked cheerfully, and went out almost at once, saying that she "must be there before she wakes," and shortly afterward Tom Aldworth appeared, having a natural curiosity to make the acquaintance of the colleague which his two companions had thrust upon him, and seeing the necessity of some previous understanding, if she were really to join the proposed conference.

Tom came to the point shortly enough, after outlining the position of which Muriel had gained some knowledge already.

"So we've agreed to meet them," he concluded, "to see whether we can save a worse row than we've had yet. They've asked four of us to go. There'll be Jack and Ellis, and they said you might make a fourth."

Muriel was pleased, and somewhat startled by the suggestion.

"If there's no one else who understands better," she said doubtfully. "You see, I don't know them. I don't even know the facts properly…. But if you really ask me, I won't refuse. I'll do what I can."

Tom felt that this new ally was something less than enthusiastic.

"I suppose you don't think we ought to give way, whatever they ask? You wouldn't tell us to hand over those women to Rattray and Bellamy?"

He felt that to be a test question. He didn't want any doctrine of non-resistance to be preached at the conference to such men as those.

Muriel answered him frankly. "No, I couldn't say that. Perhaps I ought to say that it's always wrong to fight, but there are some times when you can't really feel like that. I don't know that killing or being killed matters as much as we sometimes think"—she thought of the millions of lives that had been surrendered so easily to the indifferent floods—" but I think there's something wrong in ourselves, if we can't stop a thing like this."

Tom thought that was likely enough. He was quite aware of his own deficiencies. Muriel, who never worried an exhausted subject, changed the topic by asking, "What's the trouble with Mrs. Graham?"

Tom told it awkwardly. Even amid the deadening horrors of the last few weeks it was something of which he would not willingly speak, and he was shy of any verbal emotion.

She had been a passenger in one of the rear carriages of the first of the wrecked trains, with her daughter Janet, a child of eight or ten years. She had escaped uninjured, but the child had been crushed very badly in the lower part of its body. It had seemed unaware of its injury, but while she had nursed it on the bank-side it had kept repeating, *"Oh, mother, I'm so frightened. You won't leave till I'm asleep?"*

They were the words, he understood, that she had used on the previous night, while the storm had beaten upon their falling home, and her mother answered them with repeated promises, till she had died in her arms.

She had sat for three days on the bank-side, nursing the dead child, little noticed amidst the conditions that were then prevailing, and when at last it had been forcibly taken from her, and carried up to the field above the cutting, where a shallow trench had been dug for such bodies as had escaped unburnt, she had followed it, and had sat ever since, from dawn to dusk, on that common grave.

There had been attempts, at first, to reason with her, and to divert her mind from a grief so useless, but when it was found that she was beyond the reach of argument, that her mind was obsessed by the dying promise, and that she talked as though she sat beside a child who must not be left till sleep had come, she had been left to herself, though food had been provided for her.

"And you can see a thing like that, and still say there's a God," said Tom, with unusual bitterness. He had his own losses, darkening the recesses of his mind, as most of the other men had.

"It just proves it all the more."

"I don't see that," said Tom.

"Perhaps you don't try," said Muriel.

Tom, who was never eloquent, left her the last word.

He was, in fact, in some haste to be gone. He had a private expedition to make to Hallowby Lodge, which he realized that he might not be able to visit regularly during the next few days, and there were many things on his mind which were needing attention, and were unlikely to get it if he should leave them.

CHAPTER TWENTY-TWO

JERRY COOPER was destined to go to the conference with only two companions. He failed to secure Butcher's support, and was annoyed at the miscalculation.

He did not expect any assistance of military value from such a quarter, but Butcher was a gentleman (of a kind), and he was sensible that they would make a better show if he were present. He could not fail to realize that Rattray and Bellamy were not very savoury colleagues.

He even went himself to Helford Grange to solicit Butcher's support, and interviewed him in the cellar from which he conducted his commercial enterprises. On the way there he heard of the barbed wire that had been supplied to his opponents.

When he met Butcher, he went straight to the point.

"I didn't think you'd any use for Tom Aldworth."

"Who says I have?"

"Well, you've sold him some barbed wire, which won't help those on the other side."

"It won't do *him* any good. They couldn't put it all round that sprawling camp in a week. Besides, there isn't enough to go round—not to do any good.... You want horses, don't you?"

"What's that got to do with it?"

"He's to catch four of the kind you want, and hand them over to me within a month. You don't suppose I *gave* him the wire, do you?"

"He won't be catching horses a month from now. Not unless he changes his ways."

"Well, that's my risk, isn't it?"

"I don't really mind about the wire, but I want you to come in with us. You'd rather be on the winning side, wouldn't you?"

"I haven't heard of it yet," Butcher answered sourly. "I don't quarrel with anyone," he added. "Quarrels don't help business. That's my motto."

Cooper didn't give up easily. "You'd find we could work together," he said. "It isn't really the women. I mean to boss this show. You'd never get on with that lot. They'll clear you out as soon as look at you when they feel strong enough. You need protection."

"I don't need yours," Butcher answered, unresponsively. "They wouldn't quarrel with me, anyway. Nobody will. They'd lose too much if they did."

"*Lose?*" said Cooper sarcastically. "You've got more stuff stored here than the lot of us put together."

Butcher grinned.

"The best of it isn't here. It's well hidden. No, they won't quarrel with me."

He got up, and went down the dark passage, leaving Cooper in some uncertainty whether the interview was over. But he was not easily beaten. He sat on stubbornly, and, in a few minutes, he was rewarded by Butcher's return. He had a bundle of swords under his arm, a miscellaneous collection of small-sword, sabre, rapier, and cutlass.

"Rattray wants these," he said, as he laid them on the table before him.

"Well, why not?"

"He can't pay." Butcher's tone spoke his contempt for an impecunious customer.

"Do you want me to?"

"I don't care either way. I'll take seven pounds of tea, if it's clean. No dirt sweepings."

"Seven pounds is a lot. You know everyone's wanting tea."

"It may seem a lot, because we've found so little, so far. But it's a risk. Further on, the boys might find a warehouseful any morning. Anyway, that's my risk. Seven pounds is the price, and a fortnight to find it. You know it's to be got in small lots."

Cooper saw that he could do no more. "You shall have the tea," he said, as he got up, "if Rattray has the cutlery by the morning." He counted the swords before he left. He didn't trust Butcher, or any other man for that matter. But in that he was wrong. Butcher was quite straight in a bargain when it was made. He valued his reputation; though it was not one which every one would consider enviable.

Cooper was still anxious to secure support. He even tried Stacey Dobson, who had ceased to worry about anything if it were a fine day. He learnt, not for the first time, that the ways of wire-pullers are hard. He talked to many, and as he did so he adjusted his own position adroitly. He observed that the Rattray-Bellamy gangs were of a general unpopularity. He continued to represent himself as a restraining and (of course) dominating influence, where there was unreason on both sides, and where (he never omitted to emphasize this point) the scattered population of the north coastline and Cowley Thorn was getting badly left. If he gained little active support he created a general impression that he was working for the common good, and a vague suggestion of territorial unity, of which he well knew the value. It was Cowley Thorn against the railway camp, with Larkshill as a doubtful central constituency to be won by those who were the more expert at electioneering. Had he not cultivated the Bardsley ward of his native city for three years by such methods before he stood for the City Council, and was elected by a record majority?

He did not know what was going to happen, but he had some confidence that he would know how to turn events to his own advantage.

CHAPTER TWENTY-THREE

IT is rarely that the course of any event can be pre-imagined with accuracy, and this is especially true of one to which the attitudes and intentions of many minds must contribute.

Tom Aldworth had imagined a table in the middle of the road, with a row of four delegates seated on each side, and behind each row a listening crowd of their followers, the lawless Bellamy and Rattray's gangs restrained by the sight of the marshalled lines of his own adherents, and by the ready rifles which his followers could direct so quickly upon their leaders. The reality was somewhat different....

As to Muriel, if she imagined anything, it was of the nature of a public meeting which they would address in turn, and at which she could feel some confidence that she could do her part successfully.

She was one of those who can talk to a large assembly more effectively than to any single auditor. She spoke with a simple, clear directness, and an evident sincerity. She had a musical voice, which she controlled to the emotion which it conveyed, and she had the faculty of making every member of her audience feel that he was addressed directly....

The day opened very brightly, and her mood responded. She felt a renewed purpose in her life. God had still work for her to do. She felt as confident as when she had set out, after an older colleague had failed, to persuade a contemptuous Zulu chief to allow his wives to attend the Mission school. If only her voice...and God was quite equal to restoring that, if it should be needed. Song came as she thought.

> *Green pastures are before me*
> *Which yet I have not been.*
> *Blue skies will soon be o'er me*
> *Where the lark clouds have been.*
> *My joy may no man measure,*
> *My path in life is free....*

She made a prayerful effort for the humility which she was conscious that she too often lacked....

Even the disordered squalors of the camp gave her a subconscious satisfaction. It was all work for active hands and persuasive lips....

So she was quietly happy and confident when she set out with her new companions—a troubled Tom Aldworth, already aware that matters were not developing 'according to plan'; an observant but not forecasting Ellis Roberts, who took events as they came, and countered them with a slow and serious equanimity, as character and conscience led; and Jack Tolley, loyal to but somewhat aloof from the others, having a mind which was critical of all disordered and imperfect things, and who was most conscious of the reluctance with which he had surrendered his cherished rifle to Harry Swain's incompetent hands.

* * * * * * *

Of the scene which had been depicted in Tom Aldworth's imagination there was little that was objectively realized.

There was the ruin of the Plasterers' Arms, a comparatively static feature, and there was the expected table—Jerry Cooper, an efficient stage-manager, had seen to that. It stood in the middle road, opposite the turning of Sowter's Lane, and there were four chairs, of sorts, on one side, and three chairs, or rather two and an upturned tub, on the other. Cooper had no intention of having an empty chair on his side, to suggest the defection of an expected supporter.

But the crowds were not there—and the meeting terminated in a way which might have been foreseen as quite probable but which had not entered into Tom's somewhat worried calculations.

In fact, the event was a forcible illustration of the lack of leadership or cohesion which weakened the powers of any of the protagonists, either for good or evil.

Under the impulse of Tom's report of his conversation with Jerry Cooper, and of the three days' threat which he had received, and with the evidence of the two injured women that had fled to them for protection, the inhabitants of the railway camp had been roused to something approaching unity of action, which had expended itself upon the erection of the barbed-wire fence for which the material had arrived so promptly; but with the next day, and with the knowledge that their self-appointed leaders were meeting to negotiate a possible peace that afternoon, the impulse weakened, and the tendencies to wander out in little plundering companies, or to amuse themselves with their own occupations, or with the ubiquitous dice-box, reasserted themselves.

It was being said, and was not answered, that it was little use to fortify the canal-bank opposite the encampment, unless the same protection were carried north along the side of the line to where it disappeared beneath the waters, and south to the crossing stream, and then north-east till it came again to the seashore. That was not entirely true. If there must be a weak front, it is well to shorten it as much as may be, but it was sufficiently so to slacken the impulse of the previous day; and, anyway, there was no more wire.

The general feeling was that there was a day of respite, to be used by each for his own ends, and if there were to be trouble tomorrow, it would be time enough to think about it when tomorrow came.

If we analyse causes sufficiently, we shall find that the idea of the meeting would not have arisen at all but for Reddy Teller, a small, rat-faced man, a member of Bellamy's gang, who has been mentioned as the messenger who brought Cooper's invitation to Tom Aldworth.

Bellamy had no thought of any organized warfare, nor did he care a straw whether the remaining members of the community had no wives or twenty. He only knew that a woman whom he regarded as his property had found shelter in the railway camp, and that he had been threatened with a rifle when he went to fetch her.

For this insult he was considering the opportunity for a violent vengeance, and hesitating between the idea of a night raid, which might be the easier way of securing the woman, and a murderous ambush of those who had given her their protection, when Reddy Teller made the suggestion that they should enlist Rattray's support, and offered to seek him out with this object.

Bellamy was not enthusiastic. He liked doing such things in his own way, and without assistance. He had a brutal contempt for the men of the railway camp. He would have fought any three of them with his right arm pinioned. But he had a respect for their rifles. He gave a growling assent, and Reddy Teller, who hoped for trouble which would bring a more direct advantage to himself than the re-capture of Bellamy's woman (in which he could not be expected to take a lively interest), set out very promptly.

He found Jim Rattray without much difficulty. He was camping at a favourite spot about two miles to southward, where the river ran under the London road, and there was a gentle, shady slope from the road to the river level.

His camp was of a semi-permanent character, there being two small tents erected, and a spread of awning under the trees. There was much litter scattered about, but Jim was not without some instinct of tidiness, and most of their dirt was thrown Into the river from which they drank.

Teller found him seated with about a dozen companions, who were (for the moment) of a steadfast friendship, owing to the cementing influence of some bottles of whisky which they had secured.

They had also cooked a young pig, an old hen, and several rabbits of miscellaneous ages. Half a sheep could be seen hanging under the trees. Taking no thought for the morrow, they had good cause to be merry.

Jim Rattray was sentimental. He was singing a song which had survived the ruin of the world that had produced it:

> *"There ain't no sense*
> *Sitting on a fence*
> *All by yourself in the moonlight."*

He had a good voice. There was hilarious applause as the song ceased. He was quite willing to accept the encore:

> *"There ain't no thrill*
> *By the water-mill*
> *All by yourself in the moonlight."*

But he was interrupted by the arrival of Reddy Teller.

It must be observed that Jim was unaware of the anger which his actions had caused to Tom Aldworth and his companions.

A man had begun to quarrel with them, and he had been knocked out. What of that? He did not even know that he was dead, and, in any case, it was no one's business except their own.

They had made sport with a woman, and let her go. It might have been better to keep her, but it would have been troublesome, and tomorrow must take care of itself. What of that either? He did not even know where she had gone, and cared less.

But Reddy knew more than he did, and had a cunning tongue. He drew a picture of aggressive activity on the part of Tom Aldworth, to whom it was well known that Rattray had a particularly active antipathy. He represented the population of the coast, and of Cowley Thorn, as in preparation for armed hostilities against the railway camp, which was greedily absorbing all the remaining women. He made Rattray feel, in his own case, that they had nefariously pilfered his feminine property, and had refused to restore it, and, beyond that, he pointed out that if the camp should be successfully attacked, and Rattray did not participate, he would be shut out from any share in the resulting spoils; on the other hand, should the forces of Bellamy and Cooper be defeated owing to his absence, what fate could he expect from a victorious Aldworth? He continued to hint the importance of Jim's assistance, both of brain and hand; and the emotions of fear, and greed, and vanity having been in turn excited, he had easily secured the promise of his support.

Drunk or sober, Jim Rattray could always talk. It was by his tongue that he maintained ascendancy over his equally dissolute companions. He had no difficulty in arousing them to a like determination. He was eloquent upon the weakness of the doomed camp, and upon the richness of the spoils it held. He even thought that it might surrender without a fight when it realized the forces that were arrayed against it. He quoted Scripture, "to every man a damsel or two," being about the only text which he had retained from his childhood's teachings.

A suggestion from one of his companions that they were ill-equipped with weapons of offence for such an adventure was met by an assurance that they could be obtained from Butcher, against the promise of payment from the expected spoils.

He burst into song again:

> *"So it's up and it's over to Stornoway Bay,*
> *Where the liquor is good, and the lasses are gay...."*

Reddy Teller was inwardly sceptical about the credit to be obtained from Butcher's direction, but it was not his part to make difficulties, nor to loiter when his work was done.

He left with little ceremony, the chorus following him as he went:

> *"All for bully rover Jack,*
> *Waiting with his yard aback,*
> *Out upon the Lowland sea."*

He reported to Bellamy, and went on to see Jerry Cooper, who thereupon sent the letter to Tom of which we have heard already.

Jim Rattray had a few hours of discomfort, following an interview with Butcher, who assured him that he had no weapons for disposal of any kind, though he did not deny that he might exert himself to procure some if there were an immediate inducement to do so.

But the following morning there was a note from Butcher telling him of the swords with which he could now supply him, and with no awkwardness of condition to delay delivery. He took the good that came, without looking for explanation beyond his own very obvious merits.

His followers learnt of the proposed meeting with satisfaction. Supposing a more militant attitude on the part of Cooper's supporters than was the fact, the combination against the railway camp seemed sufficiently formidable to justify the supposition that Tom would offer terms of peace which would include the surrender of at least a large proportion of the women which the camp contained. They accepted Jim's assurance that he would agree to nothing which did not give them a fair share of the spoils. The bundle of weapons which he had distributed among them had increased their confidence both in their leader and themselves. They were content to wait his return, with the report either of the surrender of the camp or that war was to be commenced against it.

As for Bellamy, he sat down on his allotted tub (considered more fit to endure his weight than the chairs, which were of varying degrees of instability) with a simple object before him. He wanted his woman and his revenge. Anything which would give him these would have his support, and nothing else would interest him.

So the seven more or less self-elected delegates came together; but the expected crowds were not there.

There was, it is true, a solid body of men from the camp, and some show of rifles among them, but there was nothing but a miscellaneous and obviously non-militant crowd on the other side. Jerry Cooper, who might have made some objection to the show of force with which they were confronted, observed it with an inward satisfaction. He was too good a judge of men to fear that any treachery was intended, and he reflected that such a display would be likely to check any impulse of sudden violence which his colleagues might otherwise be disposed to gratify. Like Bismarck, he knew the importance of the imponderables, and he had no wish that public opinion should be outraged by the allies which circumstance had thrust upon him.

CHAPTER TWENTY-FOUR

THE table which had been provided by Jerry Cooper's administrative capacity was of exceptional size, and had been brought to the appointed place with some difficulty, and from a considerable distance. His was not the type of mind which overlooks the minor details of any undertaking to which it is committed, and it had occurred to him as of a possible importance that a sufficient distance should separate the rival parties to provide an obstacle to any sudden inclination to resort to physical arguments.

He had already seated himself, with Rattray on his right hand, and Bellamy on his left (a quick movement having been necessary to prevent Rattray from securing the central position), when Tom and his three companions approached, with the little group of their supporters a short distance behind them.

The three men looked at Muriel with some curiosity, both because she was personally unknown and was not of a kind to pass unnoticed in such society, and because they had not expected to see a woman among the deputation. None of them had been accustomed to regard women with any respect under the conditions which the flood had covered, though their attitudes had been widely different.

To Bellamy they were inferior animals, intended by nature merely for blows and breeding; Rattray was accustomed to meet them on an equality of degradation; Jerry Cooper regarded them as a necessary part of the race, but one which could have little place in the thoughts of a business man. He gave Muriel a hard, shrewd glance, which did not linger, but had appraised her keenly. She had discarded the unsightly jacket of the deceased Rector of Sterrington for the only alternative which she possessed—a selection from the plundered trunk which she had discovered on the last day of her solitude. In the result, she was dressed in a manner which it would have been difficult to match among the remaining women either of Larkshill or Cowley Thorn, and Jerry Cooper wondered, behind an expressionless face, if she could be an average example of the society of the railway camp. If so…. But he decided that it was more probable that she was of the nature of a traveller's sample, though he could not imagine why they should wish to display their goods, in view of the nature of the negotiations on which they were occupied. It only showed (which he already knew) that Tom Aldworth had no head for business.

But these reflections, though they may take some time to set down, were of momentary duration. Jerry Cooper did not intend that anyone but himself should take the chair at that conference.

He commenced at once.

"I suppose we all know why we're meeting here this afternoon. There's a few hundred of us who aren't drowned, and there's only a few score of women among us. That's bad enough; but it's worse when most of those women are in one camp, and they hold on to any others that come their way. There's been bloodshed already over this, and there'll be more if we don't talk sense here.

"I've got no grievance myself. I'm only here to get the whole thing settled. I'm here to see a fair deal. But you can't wonder if Bellamy and Rattray feel a bit sore—"

Tom broke in with "Let's have that out first. What's Bellamy's grievance?"

It was scarcely a wise interruption. Bellamy had a bad case. But its discussion was hardly likely to improve the prospects of peaceful understanding.

Cooper may have smiled inwardly as he answered. "It's just the usual thing. You've got his wife."

"His wife?" said Tom. "I thought—"

"You can call her what you like. It makes no difference. You know that. There haven't been many marriage-services in the past month. You've got his woman and he wants her back."

Jack Tolley spoke for the first time. "We're not keeping her. She can go back if she wants to."

He looked straight at Bellamy as he spoke. Something rumbled in the giant's throat, as though a reply were attempting exit, but he did not answer. He had little use for words. He looked at Jack almost amiably. He thought the time was very near....

Jerry Cooper took up the answer. "How do you know that? You wouldn't let him see her to find out. His woman bolts into your camp, and you say you don't keep her, not you! But when he comes to find out, you meet him with a rifle poked at his belly."

"Mr. Cooper"—Muriel's voice, quiet and restrained, broke into the discussion—"do you know that he killed the man she was with, and that he has broken three of her fingers?"

Cooper was not easily disconcerted. He answered with an attempt at an equal logic.

"No, Miss…? Miss Temple, we don't know anything. Your men won't let us. But I don't think there's much in that. I suppose the men fought for her, and the best man won. We can't help such things happening now. Who's to stop them? Anyway, I don't suppose she minded. She was with him a week. Then they quarrelled, and he was a bit too rough. But you don't ask why they quarrelled, or what she'd done to deserve it."

Muriel knew the weak point in the woman's case well enough, before Cooper mentioned it. She *had* stayed with him a week. She might have been too frightened to run before—or she might not. But no decent person would force her to return to his brutality. To look at him was sufficient to understand.

She answered frankly, "I don't know why she stayed with him at all. But if you see her yourself, and know that she has a free choice—?"

Cooper dismissed her civilly enough from the discussion.

"No, miss, it wouldn't. That's not the real point at all." He turned to Tom with a sudden change of manner. "The point is, what the hell is it to do with you? She wasn't your woman. We don't meet you with rifles at Cowley Thorn."

"It wasn't you, it was Bellamy," Tom answered. "We'll have no truck with him."

"Then you shouldn't keep his wife."

"We're not keeping anyone."

"Then send her back."

"Not unless she wishes to go."

"You mean she's to be another one for your lot?"

"We mean her to please herself."

Rattray broke in impatiently. "We're wasting time at this talk. They're to please themselves—are they? What about pleasing us? Fifty-fifty's the word. Tell them that, Cooper. That's a fair deal. Fifty-fifty, and our pick! We don't want the antiques. Tell them it's either that, or we'll take the lot, and the camp too."

Cooper turned on his impatient colleague, and his jaw set angrily. He wanted to manage the interview in his own way. He did not think that Tom Aldworth was capable of sustaining an argument against him successfully, and he was quite satisfied with the course of the preliminary exchanges. Rattray, on his side, objected to the secondary position to which he was relegated. Angry glances met, and words might have followed, but Cooper restrained himself with an effort. He saw Jack Tolley's smile as he watched them. He addressed Tom Aldworth again, in the manner of one who was trying to bring reasonable counsels to contending follies.

"You see what the feeling is. We can't let things go on as they are. The boys won't stand it. That's a fair offer enough. But we're here to deal, if you'll talk sense, as I told you before. If you don't accept, I suppose you've got something else to offer.

"Yes, I have," Tom answered. He was not naturally eloquent, but he spoke now with some fluency, his mind for some days having been full of the project which he was putting before them. "We're all agreed that things can't go on as they are. We all found ourselves here a few weeks ago, just as though we'd been wrecked. Most of the women didn't know the men, and the men didn't know one another, except those of us from the mine, and there weren't many women, and they're all sorts, and here we were with no homes, and no food, and all wanting help from one another, and no law but our own hands, and some just crazed with trouble, and some not caring what happened, and—so on," he concluded weakly, and then recommenced with a new fluency.

"I reckon we were bound to have some rows before we could settle down from that start, but we've had more than we need, and as we all get to know one another, they get worse. I don't understand why, but they do…. Now what I say is this: let the women choose. Tell them straight that they can each have the man they want, if he agrees, and we'll stand by them, whether we get left out or not. Give them a time to choose, and if they don't choose in the time, well, that's their look out. That's fair all round, and—"

"Is it?" Cooper interjected.

"Well, why not?"

Cooper leaned forward aggressively. The groups of spectators had increased, and had closed up as the argument warmed; and there was now an attentive audience, with no clean division between the supporters of either side. His electioneering instinct caused him to address himself to the minds of this larger concourse, rather than to his immediate opponents.

"I'll tell you why it's not fair, and why you know it's not fair. Do you think we forget that you've got most of the women in your own hands? 'Choose,' you say, and you know they've chosen already. We're to promise to back them up, and it's nice fools we should look.

"You ask us to play to your stakes, when you've looked at your own hand, and ours is face down on the table; and we say no to that. We say we'll have a fresh deal."

Tom was not quick to answer. The accusation was unjust to himself, and inaccurate in its implications, but it had sufficient substance to raise a murmur of assent from Cooper's supporters, and it was not easy to answer conclusively.

The fact was that, in the short period which had elapsed since the deluge came, the majority of the women in the railway camp had not formed alliances of any definite kind, though there were exceptions, and the camp had not been without its episodes of violence and jealousy, with more than one resulting fatality. The ultimate difficulty was before them there, as it was everywhere; but, on the whole, since the expulsion of Rattray's gang, the camp contained larger elements of self-respect and stability than were present in other sections of this chance-mingled population. For all that, if the women were confronted with such a necessity of selection, it might be true that they would incline toward the men they knew, and it was a fact that those of the railway camp would come off best under such circumstances.

As Tom paused, Muriel asked in her quiet, penetrating voice, "What do you propose, Mr. Cooper?"

The interposition was adroit enough, and disconcerting to Cooper, though he did not show it. His experience had taught him the tactical advantage of the indefinite programme. Heckle your opponents for details. Let your own promises be as vague as they are alluring. That was the way to win the maximum of support at the polling-booth, with the minimum of resulting worries. But such vagueness must not be allied with hesitation. Assertion must be prompt and confident, however worded. He answered readily.

"We propose nothing unfair, Miss Temple. We simply ask for a square deal all round. We don't think it's fair that all the women should be cornered in your camp, and we don't mean to stand it. When it came to threatening Bellamy here with a rifle when he followed his own wife, it brought matters to a head, and we're all come together now to see whether it's to be peace or war."

"Would you tell me what you propose, Mr. Cooper?" her voice was even pleasanter than before, and her eyes met his with a friendly frankness. It was as though she declined to regard him otherwise than as being as simple and sincere as herself in the endeavour to face the problem.

The happy individual

> *Whose armour was his honest thought,*
> *And simple truth his utmost skill,*

must have been a very skilful one.

Those who think that truth is easy to perceive or communicate can have had little practice in those occupations. Muriel's disconcerting directness was the result of many years of such mental exercises. She had sought truth very honestly, though she may not always have found it.

It will never be known how far Cooper would have risen to the occasion. He was in some difficulty, for while he felt that it was 'good business' to talk vaguely of the wrongs of his own locality, he was unsure how much active support he would gain if he should join with either Rattray or Bellamy in violent action to assert their claims. His constituents were uncontrolled, and there was no cohesion among them. Even those who would be glad to profit from any civil confusion might excuse themselves from the peril of getting knocked on the head, on a dozen pretexts.

But before Cooper could reply, Rattray broke in again.

"I'm damned sick of this talk." He turned angrily to Cooper. "Why don't you tell them what you mean? If there's only one woman to every five men in this curs'd place, well, there's fifteen men in my lot, and *we want three women*—and if we don't get them quietly, we'll take six. We want a plain 'yes' or 'no'—and we want it now."

Bellamy growled out for the first time, "Ay, that's the talk."

Tom Aldworth looked hard at the silent Cooper. "Is that what you say too?"

As he said it, a large drop of rain splashed on his hand.

Cooper hesitated in his reply. It was further than he had meant to go, and he resented the way in which he had been rushed by Rattray's interposition. But he neither wanted to break openly with his associates nor to resign the control of the situation at which he had aimed; and while he hesitated, the storm came.

It was a storm which those familiar with English weather might have foreseen as probable from the morning's brightness. It came in a sudden torrent of drenching rain, such as will disperse a riotous crowd which has stood the threat of machine-gun fire without flinching. There was little of near-by shelter to which to flee; little of ultimate comfort, or chance of change of rain-drenched garments, for most of those on whom the storm descended. In about two minutes the road was empty of all but a table, and five chairs, and an upturned tub.

CHAPTER TWENTY-FIVE

MONTY BEESTON was sober. That was not his fault. It was the misfortune of poverty. He sat on an upturned bucket, which, having a perforated bottom, had outlived its original utility, with a long-emptied beer-bottle beside him.

He had a quantity of second-hand safety-razor blades, from which he had cleaned a large part of the rust, and which he was sharpening upon a stone such as is commonly used for the whetting of scythes. It is not a method to be recommended either for the razor-blades or the fingers that hold them, but Monty, ignoring a still-bleeding cut, worked diligently. Had not Steve Fortune promised him four half-pint bottles of ink in exchange for eight of these blades, and would not Butcher give him at least three bottles of beer for the ink-bottles?

He had already learnt, somewhat painfully, that it was unwise to divert his eyes from his occupation, and Reddy Teller was within three yards before he perceived that it was not a resident member of the camp who was approaching.

"Goin' to shave that beard?" Reddy asked, meaning no offence, but seizing on the most obvious subject for opening conversation.

Monty looked up angrily. He did not like jokes about his beard, from which he had suffered in the old days. Now there was quite a considerable part of the male population who were cultivating (or neglecting) theirs. They might become things of beauty at a future date, but that was not yet. Reddy himself might have shaved during the past week, but it seemed unlikely.

Being annoyed, Monty Beeston became critical. He wondered what Reddy could be doing, and where he had come from. The speculation was not unreasonable. Monty had stationed himself in a position which enabled him to watch the cattle at intervals, while he laboured for his next drink. The field (if it could be flattered by such a name) sloped down before him; the camp was out of sight a hundred yards behind. It was not a thoroughfare. It was not a place where Reddy could have expected to meet him—or anyone. Reddy was not, strictly, a member of Rattray's gang, nor of Bellamy's, which had never been in the camp. He was tolerated, though not liked. But he appeared to have come from the direction of the river, which was strange, and he had last appeared (and only yesterday) as a messenger of Jerry Cooper, which was ominous.

Monty, who had sat there all the afternoon (except when the storm had driven him to shelter for half an hour), did not know what had been happening, but he thought that one spy might be one too many, and he said, with his usual mildness, "If I was you, I should clear. There's dogs—an' bullets."

Reddy did not seem as surprised at this remark as an innocent man might have been expected to be, but he stood his ground.

"Who says that?" he queried unpleasantly.

Monty did not answer directly. He only said, as mildly as before, "Well, I meant it friendly."

As he said this, he shifted his position, bringing into view a revolver of old pattern, and very large calibre, which he carried in his hip-pocket.

Every one knew of Monty's revolver. They also knew that he had a good supply of cartridges, but no one had seen him fire it.

It was, in fact, quite a good revolver, and the cartridges were also of satisfactory quality, but, unfortunately, they were not of the right size. This was a fact which Monty was careful to leave unmentioned.

Reddy Teller took the hint. He did not go back the way he came, but through the camp, and over the canal bridge without lingering. He made his way straight to Rattray's camp, having obtained the information which he had sought; for the hint had come too late.

A well-soaked Rattray, steaming in the sun as he walked, had returned to his camp by the river bridge, and had levied some reluctant garments from his companions, while his own were dried more completely.

The storm may have been partly responsible for the fact that nearly twenty men were gathered about the tents and beneath the awnings when Reddy joined them. Apart from that, the prestige of Rattray's gang had advanced in the mouths of men since it had become known that Butcher had supplied the swords. Not that anyone supposed that Butcher cared what became of them, or would risk a finger to save the necks of the lot. Rather, the effect arose from the contrary knowledge. It was not his feeling, but his judgment, which was supposed to be indicated. It was as though it should be known of a business firm that their bankers would back them up. Had Cooper realized this result, it may be doubted whether they would have got the swords.

Certainly they would not have got them could he have foreseen their leader's thoughts as he slouched home, steaming in the early evening sun.

The disasters of Rattray's life were results of deficiency of, or faults of, character rather than intellect. Even when drunk, you could not depend upon him to be entirely foolish. When sober, he could be of a very dangerous cunning, if there were sufficient incentive to overcome his natural indolence.

While the meeting was still assembled, he had seen the part that Cooper had aimed to play, and had determined to thwart him.

When the storm had dispersed them, he had made off at once in his own direction, without a word to either Cooper or Bellamy, and, as he walked, the vague impulse to be the first to move, and to move on his own, became a settled purpose, which he had resolved to put into action immediately.

He aimed, with the audacity which may deserve success in a good cause, and will often gain it in any, at nothing less than the capture of the camp, without the assistance of Cooper, and before he should have had time to develop his own plans, which Rattray rightly supposed would be of a more deliberate character.

The plan was not as wild as it may have sounded at a first hearing, though it was true that he was proposing to assault those who had ignominiously expelled him and his followers less than ten days ago.

But these followers were now more numerous, and better armed. The camp was threatened by other enemies, against whom it must guard itself at many points.

Finally, he depended upon the surprise of a night attack, and that this should be attempted at once, as he did not suppose that anyone would expect it to be made so promptly, in view of the inconclusive result of the conference, and the disunited character of their own association, which they had not entirely concealed.

He intended, if possible, to enlist the help of Bellamy, whom he felt that he could control or ignore when his use was over, and to face Cooper with an accomplished fact, and the ascendancy which would naturally follow.

The mind of Reddy Teller had worked along a different path to the same conclusion.

He would not have had the faintest interest in Tom Aldworth's proposal for the adjustment of the future relations of the community, for the sufficient reason that he would have known that no favours would be likely to come in his direction. He was of the kind that are always ready to join in any civil commotion, because it is only in times of violence or disorder that they can hope to gain the prizes which are the common objects of the desires of men.

To explain is not to exonerate; but if we attempt a rational understanding, we must perceive that it is much easier for those who are so equipped by nature that they may be the winners in an equal race to insist upon the merits of the rules that will keep all men to the beaten course than for those to appreciate or observe them who are aware that they have little expectation of anything beyond the dust that rises from the feet of the swifter runners.

Reddy Teller had been disliked at school: he had been disliked at the factory that followed. He had not the consolation that came to many who are disliked by their fellow-men that they are popular among women. Men might dislike Reddy; women usually detested him. Doubtless, the reason was in himself, but this did not make it more tolerable, nor prevent its reactions upon his own character. He was mean and furtive in his ways, and these qualities were emphasized in his aspect. He was of some mental acuteness, and of a restless energy, but these characteristics must be learnt by the experience of those who knew him, as his appearance did not suggest them.

He slipped in among the group, tolerated here, as elsewhere, but with no friendly greeting, till he came to Jim Rattray, to whom he spoke in a low voice.

Jim replied without cordiality, but invited him to walk apart.

"Been through the camp, have you?" he asked. "Well, I suppose you can. You're not one of us. You've got a good nerve, anyway. How'd they seem?"

"No-how," Reddy answered. "You'd have cleared it from end to end with them swords and a few pitchforks....

"But they was coming back as I left. It won't be quite as easy tonight.... But it isn't that I came to tell. It's the way I found, that they won't guess. You know the river's low, and there's fords we might try, but they might, be watched, and it's unchancy work in the dark, splashing through them. If they had a few rifles handy, there's some as wouldn't come back.... Then there's too much moon tonight for crossin' that flat ground by the works, and there's the ditch, and the wire as far as it goes.... But there's the bridge where the river goes under the line, that isn't watched or thought for, and the river's low there too, *an' there's room to pass under the bridge.* We'd be up the outside of the cutting bank in two minutes, and straight up the line. If they're sleeping, they'll have no chance; and if they're up and about, they'll be scattered away...."

Rattray listened carefully. The plan seemed good. He looked at Reddy Teller with some curiosity. How could he have foreseen that this information would be so opportune, and coincident with his plans of the last hour? Why did he act thus, as the jackal for other men? Perhaps, because it was the only way in which he could realize the plans he formed. He was not a man who would be followed by others.

So he thought; what he said was, "Could you find Bellamy?"

Teller answered at once: "I wouldn't tell him which way we're going. I wouldn't tell anyone. Let them find out when the time comes. It's talking spoils things like this. But he might have a go at the other end. It mayn't be much help. It's the right timing we couldn't do. It'ud be hard anyway, and he hasn't the sense. If he started too soon, it would just spoil it for us. They'd be watching all round for sure. I'll tell him half an hour after the moon shows, and we'll move at the first rise.... Yes, I'll find him easy."

He went off at once, without any comment from Rattray upon the programme he had suggested, or the reasons which he had advanced, but he left that individual somewhat disturbed in mind about the wisdom of the plan to which his subordinate was introducing him.

The method of attack from beneath the bridge appeared attractive enough, and it was desirable that it should be known to as few as possible in advance. A score of the greatest disasters of military history would have terminated differently had a similar caution controlled them. It might also be well for Bellamy to operate separately; he was not one to blend easily. But Rattray was too conscious of the numerical inferiority of the attacking forces not to wish that their movements should be simultaneous. The plan which Teller had announced was too much like committing suicide to save your life from an advancing peril. Because it was difficult to attack simultaneously, the timing was to be deliberately different.

Well, he could alter his own timing if he wished, so that the two should agree. Contented by this reflection, he strolled back to his companions, among whom the conversation had passed unnoticed, owing to a man named England having joined the company, bringing a somewhat rusty double-barrelled, muzzle-loading gun, which his industry had discovered in a poacher's cottage, together with a quantity of powder and small shot, which would have been more useful (or perhaps more dangerous) to him had he known how to load it.

He was now receiving advice from others of equal ignorance to his own, the use of the ramrod being very imperfectly understood, and the necessity of a wad of some kind being doubtfully asserted by some and confidently denied by others. Even if the necessity of a wad were admitted there remained an uncertainty as to the stage of the loading at which it would be required, and there was a majority of opinion that anyone who used the ramrod after the powder had been inserted would have his hand blown off as a natural consequence.

"Any caps?" said a man at the rear of the crowd, who had not spoken before.

It was a point which the owner of the gun had not considered. He looked blank. But a search among a small sack of other things which he had removed from the cottage discovered a matchbox containing a dozen or two of these necessary articles.

This point being cleared, the man came forward and examined the gun more closely, not concealing his contempt for its condition. "Might have been a good 'un once," he conceded. "'Bout the time o' the flood…. Meaning Noah," he added, aware that he had asserted an ambiguous antiquity. "Take a sword?" he inquired casually.

Yes, with some demur, the owner would take a sword. Having only just come into the camp, he had not shared in the original distribution of those articles. The exchange was made, with Rattray watching in the background, with some disposition to interfere, which was checked by a wiser discretion.

He had understood that the swords were his, and that he was responsible to Butcher for their value, though there had, as yet, been no question of payment.

Even if they were held in common, such exchanges might bring questions of a later difficulty. He was observing one of the inevitable confusions of a continued communism. But he had sense to see that the moment was inopportune for the discussion of such a question.

"Boys," he said, as he came forward, "we're not going to wait for Cooper. He wants to use us to take the camp, and then treat us how he likes. We're going through it tonight. Bellamy's going in at the other end, and we'll meet in the middle. You've only got to go straight ahead, and keep together, and not stop for the women till the job's over, and we'll have Aldworth's lot cleared out by tomorrow, as he cleared us last week….

"We've got a little surprise for them about the way we're calling; but that'll keep. You'd better get a good meal now, and some sleep, and we'll start fresh when the time…. You're not going to take that gun, Harding. It might give the alarm…. No, I don't mind the pistols. They're not likely to go off too soon."

CHAPTER TWENTY-SIX

MONTY BEESTON had made his headquarters under the goods van that stood at the rear of the railway coaches. He had stuffed it with sufficient hay to the height of the lines, and in places, against wedged boards, to the floor of the van that covered him. Here, amid the protections of wheels and axles, he lived like a nested rat, so that when he had squirmed inward, and was out of sight, no one would be likely to venture to penetrate after him with any hostile purpose, remembering the revolver he carried, and perhaps knowing also of a long-handled bill-hook which he kept somewhere in that dark interior.

Monty lay very happily in the mouth of his lair, for the night was warm, and he would have been stifled in its close recesses. He was not sleepy, for he did nothing during the day, and dozed or waked indifferently whether sun or moon were above him. He had drunk well, but not to excess, having manfully put aside till morning the last of the bottles of beer which had come to him as a result of his successful deal with the razor-blades.

It is probable that, among all that the floods had spared, there was no happier man than Monty. He had never accepted responsibility for the major problems of existence, nor doubted that the universe was conducted by those who were more competent than he professed or had any ambition to be.

He watched the catastrophe that had developed around him, as a dog might watch with a lively interest some operation of mankind, beyond the range of its understanding, but to which it was ready to lend its aid if its master's voice should require it.

He had constituted himself, much as a dog might do, the guardian of the general stores with which the van had been filled, and had been tacitly accepted in that capacity. He had no greater obligation to watch the cattle than had any other man or woman of this unleadered community, but he probably contributed more than half of the total time that was expended in this way.

The days went quietly and easily, and he was able to concentrate his mind upon the only problem that such an existence left him—that of procuring sufficient quantities of the beer he loved.

Peaceful by disposition, after forty years of romantic dreaming, he found a joy that any man might envy in wriggling back into the dark security of the den which he had constructed, and imagining the heroic deeds by which he would defend it from a world of foes.

The lack of female companionship did not disturb his serenity, for his solitary experience of the wiles of women had left him with a deep conviction of the depravity of all their kind. He had experienced a brief devotion for one who had fallen in love with a legacy surprisingly left to him by a great-uncle that he had never seen, and then, after a week of somewhat difficult happiness, woman and legacy had disappeared together. It was characteristic that he had made no attempt to punish the one, or to recover the other. He had gone back to his occupation as checker-in at the Larkshill works with an expression in his eyes as of a dog that had been inexplicably beaten by a friendly hand, and he had been careful to avoid any repetition of such experience.

The events that had now fallen upon the camp were such that he did not feel that they directly concerned him, but it was in the nature of life that women should be the cause of trouble.

It was in his own nature to prefer the present occupants of the camp rather than those who had been expelled with Rattray, or such wandering gangs as that of Bellamy, and to be loyal to those with whom he associated.

The long summer twilight had scarcely darkened, though it was past the midnight hour, and a low moon was showing through the south-eastern clouds, when a cry disturbed the silence of the night, which sounded in Monty's ears as though it came from the river, or perhaps from a farther distance.

Monty knew that a watch was being kept at various points, an that the whole circumference of the camp was to be patrolled at intervals, though it had been decided that there was no probability that they would be attacked so promptly.

Tomorrow all the women in the settlement were to be concentrated in the railway carriages, and an inner line of defence was to be constructed around them.

The precautions for the night were only such as cannot be omitted without disquiet, though there is no anticipation that they will be needed, as a man may go the round of his shuttered rooms before retiring, to test their bolts and catches, though he have no reason to suppose that any burglar will call to try them.

The cry did not alarm him, though it caused him to listen intently for a few moments. It was not in such a manner that a hostile force would declare its presence. There were no buildings in that direction, no scattered members of the colony who might have been surprised, and in peril.

Miss Temple's dog must have heard it also, for it barked sharply, but there was no further sound, and its voice soon quietened.

Monty dozed again.

CHAPTER TWENTY-SEVEN

THE storm which had brought the conference to its abrupt and abortive end had other consequences.

It was soon over, but it had been very heavy while it lasted. Such rain drains quickly off the surface of a heavy marl soil, and the river rose several inches. The difference only lasted for a few hours, but it was at its height when the attacking party came along the side of the river to the point at which it crossed beneath the railway. They had made a considerable circuit so that they might approach along the bed of the stream, which they did in single file, there being a narrow path along the riverside which was six or eight feet below the level of the surrounding country.

When Reddy had penetrated beneath the bridge, he had found a two-foot space of brick-paved, slightly sloping margin between the wall and the water, which he had passed without difficulty in the daylight. Now it was dark, and when he led the way, with his left hand on the wall, and his eyes upon the faint light of the farther end, he found it difficult to walk so that his right foot was clear of the water.

Still he went forward confidently, with the knowledge that he had done it once already, and Rattray followed him closely.

It was different with some of those who followed. The way was dark and strange; and they did not know but that a false step might plunge them at any moment into the river. They had been warned not to talk, so that they were without guidance from those that had gone ahead, and some of them were encumbered by miscellaneous weapons.

Yet they traversed it safely till the hindmost had entered, and Reddy was within a few feet of the exit, moving cautiously forward, with eyes and ears alert to the possibility of any watchful antagonist, when the foot of the man who was next behind Rattray slipped into deeper water. He recovered himself without difficulty, but in doing so he overbalanced the man behind him, who had been holding on to his coat, and who now fell into the water with a loud splash, and with the cry which had startled Monty as he lay with his head out of his burrow watching the stars.

The man was pulled out easily enough, and the file made its way clear of the tunnel without further misadventure, but the fear that the sound might have been heard, and have startled some dozing sentinel to a passing watchfulness, caused Rattray to delay his advance till he had been reassured by a sufficient period of continuing silence.

This pause had three consequences. First, it led to the capture of two of the patrolling sentries, who, their eyes being directed outward to the boundary of the camp, almost walked into the arms of the silent band, which had halted just below the top of the inner bank of the line, where it rose from the river-level. Surrounded by the swords and pitchforks of their captors, they bought their lives by meekly surrendering the two rifles they carried, and were warned by Rattray not to show their faces in the camp again. They disappeared into the darkness, and do not concern us further.

The second consequence was that as Rattray, his confidence increased by this episode, led his men up the line, with no further pretence of concealment, he heard a distant shot, and then several others, which told him that Bellamy had come into action before him.

He was well content that this was so, for if that attack should draw the majority of the defending forces to the north end of the camp, then he, being nearer to its headquarters, and having already captured its sentries, might possess himself of the citadel of his opponents before they should be aware of the double danger that threatened them.

If he could so establish himself, he would be indifferent, or even pleased, should they annihilate Bellamy in the meantime, with all his followers, providing only that he should have fought sufficiently to exhaust their strength and reduce their numbers.

The third consequence was that Monty, having heard the shots, was awake and watchful when the attacking force, now moving briskly enough, with weapons drawn and projecting at many angles from unaccustomed hands, came up the side of the line to the point at which the goods-van, at the rear of the coaches, concealed his presence beneath it. Although Monty had heard the shots, he did not immediately emerge from his lurking-place and rush northward into the battle. He had a good excuse for his delay in the fact that there had been an understanding as definite as was possible to their unorganized condition that those who were at the centre of the camp should not hastily leave it at the alarm of an outlying attack, unless it were clear that it was not in danger from other quarters.

There was another reason that was likely to cast the "sickly hue of hesitation" over the promptings of his natural valour. Like most of us, he had a secret anxiety—an anxiety to which we have been introduced already. How could he plunge into the conflict without revealing the emptiness of the weapon on which his prestige depended? And the prestige of Monty was not such that it could afford reductions.

As it happened (and as it so often does), the anxiety was entirely needless.

Monty heard the advancing feet. He heard Gumbo's furious barking, echoed, from farther distances, by the two other dogs that the camp contained.

He lay, looking out between the wheels of the van, the bill-hook ready to his hand. He saw Reddy Teller, and knew the purpose which had brought him to the camp a few hours ago. He saw the hated form of Jim Rattray. He was not quick enough to trouble either of these, nor the one that followed. The man who fell into the water should have come next, but, fortunately for himself, he had gone home. His substitute, stumbling over a bill-hook between the legs, supposed, not unnaturally, that he suffered from the sword of the man that followed, against the promiscuity of which he had already ejaculated some urgent protests.

Blows would have followed words had he not been too badly hurt for such arguments. He sat on the ground and swore.

Rattray looked round to add his own curses to the disorder, and to urge the speed on which their success might depend.

"Stop that damned dog, somebody," he said savagely, as Gumbo, his head through a broken window, expressed his excitement to the limit that his lungs allowed.

A man ran forward with a long pitchfork in his hand. He made a thrust at the dog, which was dodged successfully. As he thrust again, the dog was pulled back from the window, which was too high above him for the man to see what was happening inside, but he thrust the long fork in as far as he could, and reckoned he had finished the animal as he pulled it back. Certainly one of the prongs had penetrated something. As he recovered his weapon there came an unmistakably human scream from the dark interior.

Rattray, who had now come up, jumped on to the box which stood beneath the door and pulled it open.

The moonlight shone through the opening, and showed the form of Mary Graham lying on the floor, her head on Muriel's lap. Muriel had resumed the wearing of the Rector's jacket after the drenching of her lighter garments, and he thought that he had a man to deal with, till she lifted her head, and he recognized the cool and level voice that he had heard on the previous afternoon.

"It's no use coming in here. You can't undo what you've done."

A frightened Gumbo whimpered beneath the seat.

CHAPTER TWENTY-EIGHT

THE events of the next two hours might not be uninteresting, but to narrate them fully, with such analysis of the motives and characters of the two hundred people (more or less) who contributed to them (without which the events themselves would be frequently meaningless, and sometimes incredible), would be impossible within the space of a single volume—and there are other things before us which may be more worth telling.

The bare outlines of the progress of an ordered battle, between disciplined forces, which has taken place in open day-light, have often proved to be beyond the inquiry of the most careful historian. The accounts of eyewitnesses will have a baffling vagueness, or a bewildering inconsistency. But how much more must this be the case when confused and undisciplined fighting continues through two hours of darkness, over an indefinite area, and then breaks out again and again as the daylight nears, as groups of the defeated party are located, and attacked, and scattered.

The first clear fact which emerges from the confusion is the success of Bellamy's first attack. He had collected over thirty followers, about half being the regular members of his own gang, and the remainder constituting the most ruffianly elements of that fortuitous community. They had a variety of lethal weapons, though there were few firearms among them. He led them forward without subterfuge or obliquity He had a single purpose in mind—the recovery of the "red skirted wench" who had rebelled and escaped him. The others might go their own ways, but he would not be lightly turned from that purpose.

The frontal attack, which is so dangerously costly against an entrenched and disciplined force, may dishearten the less resolute by the confidence of its own assertion. Bellamy came straight on through the moonlight, and his followers could not hesitate behind their huge and resolute leader. There were some shots from both sides as the distance narrowed, but it is doubtful if any casualty resulted. A bullet may hit the mark at which it is aimed, but there are other possible directions, and they are more numerous Very much so.

He attacked from the north, where there was no canal-ditch to impede the advance, and the railway line was level with the surrounding country. Those who came to the aid of their companions after the first shots had warned them of the approaching danger must join themselves to men who were already retiring.

The fact was that there was no man there who would stand up to the giant, who advanced with no lordlier weapon than a stout, rather short cudgel. If he did not rap his opponents' heads with this implement as mechanically as a butcher might slaughter sheep, it was because they did not wait to receive his attentions. If shots were fired at him, they came from the safety of distance, or the hand shook as it pressed the trigger, and the uncertain light must be blamed that the giant was still advancing upon them.

He went straight ahead, for he was not searching blindly. If Reddy had told the truth—and woe to him if his information were inaccurate!—the woman was to be found in one of the isolated huts north of the cutting, on the inner side of the line.

There were several of these huts, and Bellamy laid a heavy hand on the door of the first, which had some pretence of bolting, and forced it inward. The door had originally been part of an outhouse, and had been pressed into this hut-building service. It was neither stout nor large. Bellamy, having forced it in, must stoop and crush his bulk to enter the black gap which it left him. He had no fear of the dark interior. He growled a threat to encourage anything living to reveal itself. He bent his head forward, peering with suspicious eyes. Then he stooped toward a bed in the corner. He grasped an ankle among the blankets, and drew out a woman, who began to scream and whimper.

He stepped backward from the hut, dragging the woman after him by the ankle which he still held.

He saw that she was a stranger, but he kept his grip, shaking her roughly. He demanded that she should direct him to the one he sought, if her unmentionable neck were to remain untwisted. There are those who would forgive her that she gave the information in this extremity, and there are those who would hesitate to do so. But, in fact, she told it gladly, having a reason.

It was the hut nearest the line. The one in which a fire was burning. This direction was unmistakable.

The hut was being built, or rebuilt, of brick, and had an open gap where a window had been, or was intended. The light of the fire, which was on an open brick hearth—a hot coal fire—glowed through the gap. Bellamy looked in through the window-space. The woman stood in the centre of the hut, the firelight showing her clearly. There was a rumble of satisfaction in the giant's chest as he eyed her. She looked sullen, but unafraid.

"The door's round the corner," she said surprisingly; "you can't come in that way."

That was obvious. The aperture was scarcely larger than the huge head that was gazing through it. He went round to the door.

The door was of the kind which is usual in cowsheds or stables. The upper half could be opened separately. It was open now. The lower half was closed.

As Bellamy appeared before it, putting a hand over to force the latch or bolt that still hindered him from his object, there came the voice of another woman from the shadow of the wall.

"Quick, Gladys, you'll be too late!"

So urged, the woman in the centre of the floor stepped to the fire, and lifting from it a bucket which was about half full of boiling water she flung a part of its contents at the figure that obscured the doorway.

It may be that the damaged and bandaged hand that steadied the bucket was unfit to control it: it may be that the woman's heart failed as her moment of vengeance came. The boiling water which he should have received full in the face partly splashed on the floor and partly struck his arm and shoulder as he stood somewhat sideways to open the door. But it was enough. He broke into an appalling howl as he turned and ran in a blind torment, not knowing where he went.

"Don't shoot, Jack! He's got his!" Tom said as the two came together, Tom from the river-fords which had been his watch, and Jack from the canal-bank, having both turned to what they supposed to be the point of the greatest danger. It was a foolish mercy, for

Bellamy was not killed, nor fatally injured, whatever might be the agony of the scalded arm and neck, or from the boiling water which had run so freely down inside his shirt-collar....

After the repulse of the giant, the tide of the northern fighting turned, and through all its fluctuant confusions we have clear evidence of repulse emerging, which proved itself when the daylight-came.

But the fighting with Rattray's gang is more difficult to follow, and had a different issue. The morning found the most part of them an undivided force that had retired upon a position adjoining one of the disused pit-shafts, where they were still far from defeated.

They had inflicted at least as much loss as they had suffered. They had one or two rifles and some ammunition. They had some pistols of various kinds, which had already taken a deadly toll of their opponents' lives, and they had the swords, which, however inexpertly used, had proved a source of sufficient danger and of a larger fear.

Reddy Teller was not with them. He was on his way to Jerry Cooper with a report of the result of the fighting as he had judged it to have gone at the first light of dawn.

Monty was telling anyone who would listen the tale of his successful prowess. He had some cause, as well as some disposition, for boasting. On the side-track beside the railway line two men of Rattray's party lay. They were both dead, and they had both suffered from the upthrust of a well-handled bill-hook as they passed the van in the darkness.

They were not pleasant to look on. The bill-hook had been whetted on the stone which had been less successfully used for the razor-blades, and it had exposed its victims' interiors somewhat freely. It cannot be said that it had operated more crudely than a motor-bus might have done any morning a couple of months earlier in a London street, but the swift descent of these derelicts of the flood from civilization to barbarism is shown in the fact that there was no hurry in the removal of the slaughtered bodies. Even a child might gaze at them unrebuked, and two did.

Monty Beeston, a very bloodthirsty character when roused sufficiently, as mild-mannered men often are, had picked his victims from the ambush in which he had lain. They were men he knew. Men that he was quite sure were better dead. We may accept his opinion without too curious inquiry into its origins. He had remembered something about his second victim as he made the thrust, and the hook had gone deeper in consequence. Now he lay harmless enough, though even more unsightly than he had been previously, and his face gave assurance that he had not enjoyed dying.

The race that the floods had covered had been utterly callous of human life if it crossed the path of its pleasures. Even when such casualties amounted to hundreds of thousands annually, so that they threatened to become a serious drain upon a population already diminishing its fertility at the call of the new worship, they only discussed means for the better warning of their victims. No one had the courage or the folly to suggest that they should abandon the most wasteful and insensate sport which a dying civilization had ever invented for the alleviation of the fever which was destroying it.

But, at whatever cost, they must avoid exposure of the unsightly. When they started moving the traffic in an unexpected direction, they did not fail to provide a waiting ambulance for the prompt removal of those that they would maim or slay.

At the urge of curiosity, they would subject many thousands of animals to deliberate torture. But while they cared nothing for the feelings of these creatures, they were insistent that nothing should disturb their own. The 'scientists' quickly realized the condition on which these abominations could be continued. They showed their contempt for the characters of their fellows by appealing to their basest instincts, assuring them that these practices might ultimately spare them from personal pain. They showed their contempt for their intellects by a swift reversal of their previous dogmas, and where they had been loud and confident in assertion that there was no radical difference between the bodies of men and animals, all being descended from a common stock, they now asserted, with an equal assurance, and without confession of inconsistency, that the gap between men and other animals was so wide that the latter really had no feelings that were worth considering, even if it were allowed that they could feel at all....

But Monty's victims lay on the railway-track, and he regarded them proudly. He had been too wise to fire a shot to warn his victims of the existence of that lurking peril! No one doubted his explanation. They didn't even listen very attentively. Most of them had their own occupations, some of them their own wounds, to consider.

The actual fatalities had not been numerous. In night-fighting of such a character between undisciplined forces it is likely that many blows will go astray, and nearly all the bullets. Most men, though they may be willing to take the lives of their enemies, will be at least as anxious to preserve their own.

Still, there were dead men, good and bad, and cuts and bruises enough: and less than half a mile away, in the very centre of their limited territory, their enemies were still an undefeated peril—a peril which might have been most easily dealt with had it been attacked at once, before it had any interval for rest or counsel.

But exhaustion was general. As the morning passed most of the men slept, and the day's tasks, and the duty of watchfulness, fell to women whose nights had been as wakeful and in some cases, as strenuous as their own.

It was after noon when a little group of men were gathered at the side of the cutting, arguing doubtfully about the best means of dealing with Rattray and his companions.

It was agreed that there could not be more than about fifteen men remaining with him. There were several errors in the details of this calculation. The two captured sentinels had the undeserved discredit of having joined him, which we know they had not, though their rifles had. It was not known that Teller had gone, nor that the man first wounded by Monty had crept away into the ditch of a farther field, under a quite groundless fear that he would be killed if he were discovered. It was known that two or three of Bellamy's lot, who had forced their way through the northern defences, had also joined them.

The actual number of Rattray's companions was nine, of whom two were wounded, though not to a disabling extent. They were comparatively well-armed, and consisted of some of the most desperate and lawless of the two gangs.

Like their opponents, they had spent the morning in sleep, setting a watch who had also slumbered; and had it been attempted they could have been surprised and captured without difficulty or loss during those early hours.

Later, they were awake and alert, though with no plans of aggression. They were now aware that the capture of the camp was beyond their strength, and they proposed only to wait till the return of darkness to retire from the conflict as best they might.

Tom Aldworth would have let them go. He felt that he had had enough of fighting, having done his share, and something more, during the night.

Jack was less sure. He feared a junction between them and Cooper, with further resulting troubles. It would be best to make the defeat as decisive as possible.

Ellis Roberts thought that Jack was right, but doubted whether there were sufficient courage and energy left in the camp to attack successfully. A failure would be worse than inaction. They could not order. They must depend on volunteers. How many would there be likely to be?

It was Steve Fortune who turned the scale. He had stood silent as usual, at the back of the group, listening to all that was said, a half-bred gipsy by his dark eyes and yellow skin, and by the coloured scarf round his neck. He spoke with a soft drawl, but with the accent of a northern county. He voted for a prompt attack, and he volunteered to join it. They had better end the lot, and get a sure peace for those who remained alive.

He said this because he was afraid. He was too afraid to wait. He had seen a man killed. A man that had shared his life for the past month. Who had been his pal, though they had exchanged few words, neither being of those who speak

But now he was dead. Dead, and lying in the rough grass, scarcely out of sight of where they were standing now.

Dead, as he had fallen when Rattray's sword had stabbed him. And Steve Fortune could not endure the thought that he might soon be lying in the same way. He must find out if this were so. He could not endure to wait. The image of Rattray was always before him. Let them make an end.

He did not say this, but the nervous desire to end the suspense communicated itself to those who heard him.

So, after some more talk, the little group scattered to collect volunteers for the attack, and after two more hours of argument, and hesitation, and weapon-borrowing, they assembled a force of seventeen, which was reduced by three before they started by the tears and protests of women, and increased by one under a contrary feminine influence....

The plan of attack was a cause of further discord, which almost led to the abandoning of the attempt.

They knew that there was rifle-fire to be faced, and no man wants to die by such means.

They had some reason to hope that no one among their opponents was expert in the use of such weapons.

Some of them thought that they should advance in single file, and that the individual risk would be thus reduced to a minimum. Most of them liked the idea well enough, providing that they were not at the head of the line. But it would be obviously disadvantageous when the attacking force reached its destination, and it was finally killed by a proposal that those who voted for it should lead the way.

Jack Tolley made the final suggestion. He said, "They won't get us if we don't bunch." He had the contempt which a good shot feels for those who cannot aim straight. "Suppose we spread out all round, and just go in as quickly as we can. We won't even fire till we get close. It's speed that matters. If they show themselves to shoot, I think I can promise to get one."

And so, as the afternoon waned, the attack was made.

Whatever may be said for the plan, or against it, it neither failed nor succeeded.

As it converged, Rattray's smaller force made an attempt to break through while their opponents were still fifteen or twenty yards apart from one another. It was a movement which appears to demonstrate the futility of such a method unless the attacking party has a great numerical superiority. But its results were capricious.

Jack Tolley was not directly in the path of the sallying force, but he was not far off on the left. Against the scatter of useless shots with which they advanced to break through the extended line, he fired twice with careful and deadly aim.

He could not get Rattray. There were others of the moving group who obscured him from Jack's position, but he killed a man of Rattray's gang who ran beside him, and wounded another with a shot that followed.

The man who was most directly in the path of the advance was Steve Fortune. He did not run, as he might have been excused for doing. He stood his ground, drawing a long cavalry sabre, which he had taken from beside the dead body of one of the gang (who did not appear to have found it very useful), and which he had been carrying sheathed under his arm as he ran forward.

Rattray was directly in his path, and would have avoided him if he could. There was nothing, from his point of view, to be gained by further fighting.

The long sabre-blade swept round, and he parried it with the sword he carried, a good weapon enough, but somewhat shorter and lighter than that with which he was threatened.

He would have dodged past if he could, but Steve did not understand his purpose. He knew nothing of sword-play, and thought that Rattray was attempting to pass so that he might stab him in back or side.

Steve was in a panic of fear, and grasping the hilt of his weapon in both hands he thrust straight at Rattray. The two swords met for a moment, blade slid on blade, and the two men came almost together.

Rattray's sword had passed under Steve's left arm, and some inches of the sabre showed brightly through the back of Rattray's coat.

It was the end of Jim Rattray.

Of the rest, four men escaped, and the others were killed, or wounded and captured, to stay or wander off to Bellamy's gang at a later date as their natures led them. Steve Fortune, somewhat dazed, but well content with the Homeric reputation which his fears had brought him, said less than ever. But the vision and the fear had left his mind.

CHAPTER TWENTY-NINE

REDDY TELLER made straight for Cowley Thorn, and found Jerry Cooper without difficulty. He was busy in the field in which Tom had seen him once before. But the field held six horses now.

Jerry guessed that he had news, and took him at once into the house he occupied.

Teller was introduced to an interior which showed none of the amenities of civilized life—it was more of a store-house than a home, and more of a workshop than either—but the lower rooms had been restored, and even glazed, and there were two men working on the roof, removing some tin sheeting which had provided temporary cover, as they progressed with the labour of reslating it.

He also noticed Stacey Dobson's man, Phillips, doing something to an opened drain.

Cooper's motives might be good or bad, but there was a hard efficiency about all his methods which must always be formidable to those who opposed him. If one must rule, he had surely a better right, and could do so to better purpose, than such men as Rattray or Bellamy.

Reddy Teller had little doubt that he was looking upon the future ruler of this land colony, and he meant to be as useful as possible to him, though it was scarcely a willing service. He suspected that, unless he could take his own advantage from the confusion, the end might bring him a very meagre payment.

He began at once. "There's been fighting all night at the railway camp. I expect you've heard something of it. I thought you might like to know more."

Jerry nodded to that. "I thought they would, and I hope they've got well licked," he said contemptuously.

Reddy noticed the tone, and was careful not to mention that he had instigated the movement.

"Yes, they're licked right enough," he answered, in a tone to suit the mood of his auditor. "Bellamy went in at the top end, and he's hurt or killed, so I heard say. I didn't see it. Anyhow, his lot's done. Rattray went through the river-bridge, under the line, and got right up the cutting. But his men didn't keep together. They were fighting in little group and being driven here and there, half through the night.

"Then, when the light came, they saw they were beat. Rattray's at one of the old pit-heads. He's got about a dozen with him. They ought to hold out there well enough."

Jerry was silent. The news was good, if only he could use the position as he hoped. If they must attack by themselves, he would much prefer that they should be beaten. A triumphant Rattray would be a dangerous enemy, or an intolerable friend. But if they were badly beaten, his own position was insecure enough. He wished he had not been so quick to challenge Tom Aldworth. He wasn't ready. He had allowed himself to be rushed by circumstance. But he was not one to waste time in useless regrets. He looked at Reddy Teller with a disfavour which he did not show. He was not one to reveal his thoughts, unless by intention. Physically and morally, he classified him as a dirty hound. If only he had his one-time foreman, Barty Brown, at his right hand, as he had had him for twenty years!—Barty, who never scrupled at anything which he was told to do, never opened his mouth at the wrong time, and was as loyal as a dog, for four pound five a week, and an extra fiver at Christmas. But Barty was doubtless dead, like a million of better men, and some worse ones. The thought had passed in a moment.

He said, "Is Aldworth hurt, or that Tolley fellow? He's the worse of the two. Have they lost much on their side?"

"I saw Perry lying dead, and I think that red-haired fellow— Wainwright, I think they call him—is about done for. Dodgy Perks did for him."

And Steve Fortune's pal, Conroy. Rattray struck him in the ribs. And there's two or three others of Aldworth's lot got knocked out, but I don't know who they were. And no end of them got hurt. But I think Aldworth's all right, and Jack Tolley."

Cooper grunted. The two gangs didn't seem to have done the railway campers much damage, if that were all.

"Reddy," he said, "you'd better—" and then, "What do you want for all this?"

117

Reddy's rat-like eyes glistened as he answered without hesitation.

"I want Doll Withlin."

"Um, I don't know her…. Well, we'll see."

Cooper was not one to promise freely.

Reddy, judging him shrewdly enough, was not dissatisfied.

"Well, find out what's doing, and what's said, and let me know."

Cooper turned away in the method of dismissal which was customary to him and Reddy took the hint, and went.

CHAPTER THIRTY

JERRY COOPER had decided upon his course of action even before he had dismissed the self-appointed spy with which fortune had provided him. His part must be that of one who interferes with authority, and in the name of order, between contending turbulences.

If he could get sufficient support, his programme would be easy enough. He judged quite correctly that the railway camp would have had about enough of fighting, for the time, and would be reluctant to encounter a fresh hostility, if he could only make his position sufficiently plausible.

Besides, there was little cohesion among any of these chance-mingled groups, and if it should appear that, one by one, every other section of the community was attacking the railway camp, would it not make even some of its own people think that there must be a reason for it?

So he thought, and was prompt to put his plans into action, while, with a characteristic caution, he schemed a retreat which would enable him to recover his position should he fail to gain the immediate ascendancy at which he was aiming.

He was made increasingly doubtful of his position, and roused to a greater energy, by the news which Reddy brought him next morning. The remainder of Bellamy's gang, with the giant himself, had been captured, disarmed, and expelled from the district in a public ignominy.

This would probably not have happened at all, had they not retreated by way of Bycroft Lane, and retired into the oak and bracken wilderness of Hallowby Park, and this coming, to Aldworth's knowledge, had alarmed him for the safety of the women and children that were living in the lodge on its farther side.

The fear proved a sufficient spur to translate a plan that crossed his mind into an active reality.

The inhabitants of the camp, after a day of rest, were in a very confident mood. They had collected the dead bodies of friend and foe, they had counted their wounds, and they had decided that their victory had been even more decisive than was actually the case, and that it had been very cheaply gained.

Tom was surprised by the number and spirits of those who volunteered for his new enterprise. He had not previously experienced the popularity that follows success, and that is so quickly ended by a later failure.

The whole thing proved too easy to merit any detailed narration. Bellamy and sixteen others of his own kind were surrounded while asleep in the twilight of the early dawn, and waked to find half a dozen rifles and as many pistols (including Monty's reputable though innocuous weapon) directed upon them, intermingled with a display of the miscellaneous cutlery which had been captured from Rattray's gang, and for the presence of which Butcher was ultimately responsible.

They surrendered tamely, submitted to being stripped of every offensive article which they possessed, and were publicly and ignominiously marched along the Larkshill Road, their hands tied behind them, their much-bandaged and dejected leader scowling sullenly in the rear, to be turned loose at last, at the confines of the village, with a warning that they would be shot at sight if they appeared again in the district. The hands of one only were cut loose, with an order not to release his companions while they should be in sight of the rifles that covered them.

So they had disappeared. No doubt, with the passage of time, to be a source of further trouble; but for the moment the spirit was gone out of them.

* * * * * * *

During the next two days Jerry Cooper enlisted the definite support of nearly thirty men, the best of whom may have been a young man named Rentoul, who was influenced about equally by love of adventure and of the horses that Cooper was collecting so diligently, and John Coe, an ex-farm-bailiff, who had been too ill to take any active part in the events of the previous days, and was still only able to walk with difficulty, but who was attracted by Cooper's obvious efficiency. Coe would have promised support to any man who would be likely to end the slack disorder, and rescue the ruined fields, by which they were surrounded.

For the rest, they were actuated mainly by the natural discontent arising from the belief that he had inculcated among them, that the men of the railway camp were monopolizing the female society that the floods had left them, and were endeavouring to force an agreement upon them which would perpetuate this condition. But those who followed his leadership would, if they were unable at the moment to assert their rights, at least retain their freedom to claim them when opportunity should become more favourable.

The men whom he thus enlisted were not all whom he could have persuaded to such a course. He had no use for wasters, or for such as would be likely to prove a source of future weakness or discord. He wanted men of his own stamp. Hard, unscrupulous, but not dissolute. Men who would submit to discipline, if they recognized the efficiency that enforced it. He was a good judge of such men, and he probably collected all that remained alive that were worth having.

But, having done this, he saw that they were not sufficient to justify him in an immediate trial of strength. The risk was too great.

Having decided this, he had a long talk with Rentoul, the one man alive who could ride a horse, and who had done so farther than the pedestrian wanderings of his fellows. The following morning Rentoul had disappeared, and Cooper's horses were no longer in the field which he had fenced to confine them.

A long interview with Butcher followed, and the next morning he walked over to the railway camp and sought out Tom Aldworth. He went very early in the day, because he was naturally an early riser, and he chose an hour at which he felt sure of finding Tom at the camp. He wished neither to make a formal appointment nor to risk an abortive call.

Some men might have hesitated about the reception they would meet, or even for their personal safety under such circumstances, but Cooper had no lack either of courage or self-assurance, and he felt no doubt of his ability to control any situation which might arise.

He walked easily in spite of his weight. He was still fleshy, but in better condition than he had been six weeks ago, and he had always been an active man.

He looked keenly right and left as he made his way through the fresh greenness of a country that had been washed by heavy rain in the night and was now responding to the warmth of the early July sun. He cared nothing for natural beauty. He knew little of agriculture.

But he saw everywhere disorder, waste, and confusion, which his soul loathed. If he did not understand agriculture, he understood building, and he looked with contempt at the slack incompetence of the efforts to repair or rebuild which he saw around him. *Law*. That was what was needed, *law*. Law to make the lazy dogs work twelve hours a day, till they got the place straight. Law, to make them do what they were told, and to tell them how and when to do it.

He had lived when there had been so many laws that no man living could even know them completely, and when they were being increased continually. Because a central parliament, however diligent, could not increase them with the required rapidity, they had had local assemblies in every town to supplement these exertions. He had himself assisted to make some hundreds of additional by-laws for the restrictions of the liberties of his fellow-citizens. He had never doubted the necessity of the work he was doing. It was true that a summons had once been delivered at his own door for an infringement of one of these regulations, but that was merely the blunder of an officer who did not know him, and two minutes on the telephone with the chief constable had settled that nonsense…

He had crossed the Larkshill Road, and passed the ruins of the ironworks, and crossed the canal-bridge, before he saw a human creature stirring, and then it was only an untidy slut (as he called her in his mind), who sat at the door of a half-fallen cottage, idly strumming on a banjo, to which she sang at intervals.

For some reason best known to herself she changed the tune as Jerry Cooper approached her and started a ribald music-hall ditty of the previous winter, on which a voice came from the interior of the cottage, "Chuck it, Doll; you know I hate that one."

Cooper remembered the name, and looked at her more curiously. So that was the young woman who was to reward the industry of Reddy Teller! She looked a worthless baggage. Probably didn't know how to boil an egg. What fools men were!

If he had hoped to find Tom Aldworth unready or unfit to receive him, he was disappointed. He met him talking to Ted Wrench at the top of the railway embankment. He was evidently giving some admonition to a youth who received it sulkily, but this ceased as Jerry approached, and he turned to receive him politely enough, though without cordiality.

Jerry did not want cordiality. He had come to ascertain if he had yet any chance of getting his own way, but he did not expect it, and without that he wished to quarrel—up to a point.

He commenced on a jeering note which he could make more offensive than the harsh and dominating tone which was his usual manner.

"Well, Tom, you're a great man now. You're so sure you can smash us all that you don't even need to keep a watch on who's coming over the bridge."

"There's a sentry at the old works. He'd give us warning of anything dangerous. But he'd let you pass," Tom answered easily. (Had Harry Swain really been awake or asleep, he wondered. Well, never mind now!)

Cooper scowled.

"I told you," he went on, "when you came to me for help, that we could work together if you'd talk sense, and you wouldn't then. I wonder if you will now. If we'd understood each other, they'd never have ventured here at all. Of course, you knocked them out, but there's some gone who might be alive now, if you'd listened, and it's just the same today. If we'd pulled together there isn't a dog'd bark without asking if it might, and we should get the damned place straight."

Tom said, "Well, I asked you to help us."

"You asked me to play your game."

"I asked you to help turn those brutes out, and now we've done it ourselves."

"Yes, you did that well enough. And now they're gone, can we deal?"

"I've no quarrel," said Tom. "But you're not liked here. That's plain talk, and plain talk's best. We'd best go our own ways."

Jerry glanced round contemptuously. There was nothing particularly in sight where they stood, but Tom knew what he meant before he spoke.

"It's the way of pigs," he said brutally. "You go your way, and I'll go mine, and we'll see who comes out top in the end."

Tom knew that there was some justice in the comment. There was little of order, method, or cleanliness in the camp during these desultory plundering days. He did not doubt that Jerry Cooper would handle matters differently if they should unite to support him. He knew that he himself lacked the force of personality that the position required, and he was unhappy because he could not settle his mind on a better man. But he did not like Jerry Cooper—nor trust him. No, they must go their own ways.

So he stood silent, and Jerry spoke again. "Well, you've had your chance. You can always remember that. I shan't stay in; this muck…. I don't say I shan't come back."

He turned his back on Tom as he said it, and walked away. The interview hadn't gone quite as he had meant it. He hadn't mentioned the question of the women—nor others. But he had not done badly. He was retiring because he had failed to rule, and he would be first in his own place, whatever it might be, but he had contrived to give it an aspect as of one who moves his seat in a public vehicle to avoid a verminous neighbour.

Tom wondered vaguely what he meant to do. He had no feeling of victory.

The next day Jerry had gone. What he could, he took; but he left most of his possessions, including, inevitably, the house he had been rebuilding. He could always face a small loss for a larger gain. He looked ahead.

BOOK THREE

CHAPTER THIRTY-ONE

COOPER disappeared into the deserted country to the south or west, and for the next two months very little was heard of him.

He may have known more than was known of him, for Reddy Teller appeared in Larkshill on several occasions, till it was made clear to him that such visits were unwelcome.

He certainly maintained communications with Butcher at Helford Grange; and it was known to those who rose sufficiently early that Rentoul would sometimes ride through the district in the early morning hours, which had once been sacred to cats, and milkmen, and market-gardeners. But his location remained unknown. The plundering expeditions, which still continued as the weather permitted, did not go far enough, or were not in the right direction to find him. But there had been fewer of these, because the weather broke a day or two after his departure, and there was heavy rain, which drove men into the shelters which they had erected during the previous weeks, and taught them the importance of rain-proof building. Even on the sunniest days, the ground was wet and unpleasant for camping. Fields of heavy, unmown grass hold the wet, and are unpleasant to struggle through, unless feet and legs are well protected.

Tom had only succeeded in capturing one of the horses for which he had rashly undertaken liability in exchange for barbed wire, which, like many larger military expenditures since the world began, had not proved to be of much ultimate importance.

The horses, of which there were now two or three herds feeding in the lower lands, were increasingly wild and wary, and neither Tom nor his friends had any previous experience in such enterprises.

Butcher relieved the difficulty by offering to take six boxes of matches instead of the three horses which were still owing.

The offer was less generous than it appeared, as he had received a message from Cooper that he was now getting all the horses he

124

wanted, and the order need not be executed, but the selection of matches in substitution, and the moderate quantity specified, was a shock to Tom, and to others to whom he told it.

They came of a race which must rank high, if not highest, among the most wasteful that the earth has known. It had declined to learn anything even from the forced economies of the years of war, and ten years afterward it had been as improvident as though such an experience had never entered its national life. Even when it announced to the not unintelligent or indifferent Eastern races that it could no longer afford the lives of its children, it still wasted sufficient food in its kitchens to have fed a county.

Every one wasted matches, and most would have shown an open contempt for anyone who objected to do so. It had happened that the goods which Mrs. Millett had saved from her husband's burning store had included a large case of these articles, and from this and other sources they had been freely scattered during the earlier weeks, and used without a thought of the time when they would become exhausted. But Butcher's ways were known. How large a proportion of Mrs. Millett's salvage had already found its way to his extensive cellars will never be told, but when he made open demand for any article, and put a high price upon it, it was a sure deduction that he had already cornered the available supplies as far as possible, and that he foresaw a shortage, against which he would be able to fix whatever price he pleased.

So men began to count their matches with care, and to give the unopened box less freely than they would have done yesterday. They remembered the lesson of a previous week when the price of tobacco, in all its forms, had been suddenly doubled, although every one knew that Butcher's men had looted an unburnt store, and it had been said that there weren't enough men left alive to smoke it in ten years' time. However that might be, other supplies had been getting short, and applications to Butcher had increased, and now it could only be dearly bought, and only for certain exchanges, such as tea, which had been in short supply from the first days, and was now at a fantastic height of comparative values....

The wet days gave more time for talk, and for attention to the interior amenities of the dwelling-places of the community. More time, also, for taking stock of what had been collected already, and hard work at times in providing additional protection for valued goods which had been allowed to stand out in the weather.

The tides, with a change of wind, threw up in a single day more of the buried wealth they covered than they had done in a month previously. Most of it was spoiled or worthless, at least for any immediate use, but there was still much which was worth the toil of transit, and the uncertainty of what the day would bring was, to many, an alluring gamble that surpassed any possible satisfaction that could follow a more regular occupation.

And amid such spasmodic activities the summer days passed quickly.

* * * * * * *

One day, Martha Barnes closed her cottage, haring sent her family into hiding (for reasons which will appear) among the Larkshill ruins, and made her way to the railway camp, seeking an interview with Tom, who was away at Hallowby Lodge. Not being one to be turned from her purpose lightly, she looked round, and observed Monty Beeston, seated on the bucket of which we know, and surveying the landscape with his usual diligence.

"Any bosses about?" she inquired, with a laconic directness which was her habitual economy.

Monty considered her without haste. She was a woman, and therefore of no importance. Probably a woman would know best how to deal with her.

"There's Miss Temple," he suggested.

"I don't want no truck with 'shes'. I've come serious."

Monty looked at her more indulgently. She was a woman of sense, though a woman still. But he had no better offer to make.

"Miss Temple's different," he explained vaguely. "She's the only boss here today."

"Then where's her?" said Martha, with no further waste of words in opposition to the inevitable.

Martha found Muriel on the off-side of the train, seated on one of the boxes by which she mounted to her own compartment. She was sewing a torn garment, and four of the five young children, which were all that the camp contained, were seated opposite to her on the down-line rail. Muriel had tried for three weeks to secure practical organization, and the reassertion of spiritual and moral values as she understood them and this was the extent of her victory. Four children, out of five, all of whom would have been useful to a surviving relative or some self-selected guardian, as cleaners, carriers, water-fetchers, or in a hundred other casual ways, had been released that Muriel might give them such instruction as she thought appropriate to their present circumstances, and the probabilities which were before them; and in two instances this concession had only been bought by services to be rendered to the children's needs, of which the garment on which she was then working was an illustration.

Martha surveyed the scene with some reduction of her usual grimness. She looked at Muriel, who had resumed the Rector's coat, as more suitable for her daily occupation than the war-path garments of the one-time owner of the trunk that she had plundered in Sterrington. Becoming aware that someone had paused on the other side of the line, she ceased the tale she was telling, and lifted her eyes from her work.

The two women looked at each other. for a moment in a critical silence. Within a year they were of the same age. The one was workworn, bony, and meagre; the other, though the capacious coat partly concealed it, still had the dim and graceful figure that she had kept from the youth that was so far behind her.

The one showed a lined and wrinkled face amid untidy wisps of greying hair, and her eyes, though bright enough, were small and sunken beneath their puckered lids; the other looked from eyes that were clear and wide open, beneath unwrinkled brows, and had a complexion that a child might envy. To a casual glance it might have seemed that a space of twenty years divided them, yet it might be that the body of Martha Barnes, reared in privations, and habituated to certain toil and to uncertain nourishment, had a more enduring vitality than that which outwardly appeared so much less battered.

Widely as their experience of life had differed, they were alike in regarding their bodies as subservient to their own wills, and alike, too, in a hundred ways which it would have surprised them about equally to discover.

"Can I speak to you, miss, for ten minutes?" Mrs. Barnes inquired.

Muriel had a trained memory for faces. She remembered Martha as the one who had exchanged words with Ellis Roberts on the subject of Datchett's cow—now the happy mother of a very promising calf—as they Lad approached the outskirts of Larkshill. She considered that the woman must have had some serious cause to come so far. She dismissed the children, and invited her visitor to enter the compartment in which she lived.

"We can talk here quietly," she said. "I had one of the children in here till last week. It was unwell, and there was a fear of infection, but it proved to be nothing but a result of bad feeding. I have been alone since then."

She may have felt that some explanation was needed for her degree of comfort in that crowded camp. She valued her solitude, but was doubtful whether she ought not to make a more definite offer to share it with others than she had yet done, since the child had gone back to its own place.

But Martha made no comment. She had something else on her mind.

"It's this way, miss," she began at once, when she was seated. "I've got three children left livin': there's two young ones, an' Davy, that's a grown lad; and there's a girl in the house that's not mine at all.

"When that mad rush came, there was a big motor ran off the road an' somersaulted down the field that's 'side the hill, above my cottage. I thought they'd be all dead; an' two was, but there was a girl with her head broke, an' a leg, an' I did what I could, with two children livin', an' one dead, an' not a wall left standin'. It was better when Davy came back from the mine on the next day—but it's waste talk of all that. We all went through it, an' here we are. But I did what I could for the girl, an' put her leg straight, an' in a day or so she comes round, an' her head healed itself, an' her leg mended in a month, or under, though not proper. It's a bit short of the pair, an' it's like it will. But she's all right now, bar that, an' a bit more useful than she'd 'a' been in her ma's house. She knowed naught when she got up, an' she don't know much now, but she's one to learn.

"'Well,' I says to Davy, 'there's no girls left in these parts, an' when you're more grown, come Christmas, you'd better have her than naught.' I reckon I saved her life, an' she's mine to give, if I wants; an' she says yes to that, though a bit slow-like, as some girls are."

"What does Davy say?" Muriel asked, as Martha paused, on approaching the point of her narrative. "Davy? He'll do as his mother says. He's a good lad enough."

"Then what's the trouble?"

"Trouble is I can't let her out of sight of the door, now her leg's healed, an' she's puttin' flesh on. There's Burke, an' Willetts, always round. An' there's a young lout Parkins, as follows her like a dog. Like a dog that snarls, when he meets my Davy, as I've told not to fight. 'You just keep clear,' I tells him, 'you keep clear of they, an' I'll see as you has her'."

"But if she likes one of these men better, Mrs. Barnes," Muriel answered, "I don't see what we can do to help you. We can't make her marry your Davy unless she likes."

"It's not that, miss. I'd manage that, an' not trouble anyone. Trouble is *I don't want my Davy killed.*"

"But surely, Mrs. Barnes, there's no danger of that, if he doesn't quarrel, as you say?"

"It isn't danger, miss—it's a sure thing, if things go on as they are. There's no law now, an' we're all made the way that we want most what we can't get…. I've known Burke since he was born. That's nigh on thirty years, an' he wouldn't have given two shifts o' work for the best girl that ever stepped. He was all for cards, an' the dogs, an' a bit o' drink at the weekend, an' Susie Clements 'ud cry her eyes out cus us laughed at her tryin's on, an' the way he wouldn't see what she showed him…. An' now it's said as there's no girls to be had, an' he's as bad as the rest, or a bit worse…. Trouble is, there's all talk, an' no doin'. There's been Cooper's talk, an' Tom Aldworth's talk, an' more talk that's worse, but there's no law to be feared of, an' what I say is Tom 'ud better start doin' something, or stop talkin' as though he meant as he would."

Martha, who seldom spoke at such length, now stopped definitely. She felt that the case had been fully put, and waited for Muriel's comments upon it.

Muriel was rarely slow to encounter a difficulty, or to speak her mind, however it might differ from those to whom she spoke it, but she hesitated now.

The fact was that she did not like Tom's plan, and felt that the difficulty (as far as she admitted its existence) should be fought on a higher plane. But she had had several discussions with him which had had the effect—an unusual one from such arguments—of bringing them to a better understanding and sympathy with their opponents' opinions. That was natural enough, because they were both anxious that the right course should be taken, rather than that it should be one of their inception, and to discover a satisfactory solution to such a problem is about as easy as to divide a square mile by a cubic foot.

But Muriel knew that it washer discouragement acting upon Tom's natural diffidence which had delayed any attempt to grapple with the difficult question of the marriage laws which should regulate the new community.

Muriel saw that Tom was being blamed for that for which she was largely responsible, and she answered accordingly.

"I'm afraid it's my fault, Mrs. Barnes, that nothing's been done since Cooper went. I think that marriage is one of God's laws that we can't alter. I didn't like Tom's plan, and I don't like it now. But I do see that there are things that we've got to face.

"I'll tell Tom what you say, and I'll promise that I'll let you know tomorrow what's going to be done about this. If Tom doesn't come over, I will…. I should like a talk with this man Burke, and the others."

"It isn't talk 'ull do much, miss," Martha answered doubtfully, "when there's three hungry men, and one platter o' food that's not for they. It's knowin' as it's hot to touch that'll do most…. An' there's times when a bad plan's good, if there's no better…. But I'll be gettin' back now. I left them hid in what's standin' o' Reynolds's outhouse an' Berry's sties over the wall…. Except Davy's gone to Butcher's for some lime we're needin', an' we can't go on that-like forever."

Saying this, she rose and went without formality. But the two women parted with a mutual confidence. Martha was shrewd enough to know that she had won a promise that would be kept, and Muriel recognized and appreciated the spirit of the woman who fought for her son's life, and would not make any offer of compromise with such a stake to consider.

CHAPTER THIRTY-TWO

MURIEL, being alone, faced the problem again, as she had done a dozen times before. A man should not be forced to marry any woman, nor a woman a man. There should be no marriage without love, and love cannot be forced. She felt also that there should be no unions of any kind without that which she considered to be a Christian marriage. How, with these beliefs, could she give any support to the proposals which Tom advocated? He had proposed that if any woman definitely elected her protector her choice should have the support and protection of all to whom it was communicated. As to the formality of 'marriage,' he was indifferent, one way or other. The old laws, the old social order, had passed away. What was the use of pretending otherwise? He supposed that other customs, and, in time, other laws, would replace them…. He would ask all men to support that, so that any who interfered should become a hunted outlaw…. But he would not go further…. If a woman would not marry at all, she must fare as best she could, he would not ask others to risk their lives in her defence. He did not say that this last condition was bad or good. He simply said it was no use to ask for something which you could not get.... Muriel, less used to be concerned for herself than for others, had realized very suddenly, with a pause of pulse and breath, that this question was one that concerned herself also. Was *she* to be told to choose one from this somewhat unshaved community? It was absurd....

There had been episodes in the past. There had been the youthful captain of the C. M. R.... He had been very hard to discourage.... And only she knew how many tears it had cost her.... But he had had no faith.... There had been so little in common.... She had never doubted that she had done wisely.... And there had been others before that.... But those things were long past now.... She was getting old, and her health...was it really so soon to fail her...? She did not tire so easily as she had done, or so she thought.... No, she would never do that...and surely others would feel the same....

She became aware that she was doing what Tom had lamented to her that every one did now—thinking only of themselves, with no thought for the common good. But, after all, what was best for each should be the common good also. And over all there was that which was right, as she saw it. The divine Law, which should be followed unswervingly, wherever it might seem to lead. "Heaven and earth shall pass away, but my word shall not pass away." That was the faith she held. Tangled with false traditions, with mistaken dogma, with the customs of the race that bred her, weakened by the infirmities of her body and the limitations of her mind, it still shone with the spirit of the Galilean carpenter: that dauntless, deathless faith, which, could it be shown that he were no more than human, would so proclaim, in triumphant paradox, that he were more divine. What could she do but trust God, and face the new, strange questions that arose with such wisdom as His Word supplied? She remembered the test which she had taken as her motto, when she had gone out to Africa, from the old Hebrew song of faith that had echoed down the millenniums: "I will fear no evil." How often since had it given her fresh courage and renewed her faith, in the lonely dangers and difficulties that her life had known. She put the whole matter resolutely aside, and turned to the tasks of the day.

For though she had dismissed the children, her work was far from over. She had, as was the case with all, the daily necessities of her own existence, where no shops were open, and no tradesmen called—tasks which might be light or easy from day to day, and which varied greatly with the standards of decency or comfort to which they clung—she had also the care of the sick, and of two or three who were still unhealed of wounds, and of the rather frequent accidents in the camp. She had long learnt that it was by this means that she could best establish an influence that could be used in other ways; and was consequently more competent than any other that the camp contained.

There would be Will Carless coming to her at midday. No one asked why he came so frequently, and stayed with her for ten minutes or more inside the compartment. He had a knife-wound in the side. Not a deep wound, nor one that need have been serious. But he had concealed it from every one. Would not now tell Muriel how it occurred, nor from whom he had received it. He had only come to her when its inflamed condition warned him that it would not heal without treatment. Of course she knew that it was Steve Fortune's knife that had done it, as she knew that Doll had the ultimate responsibility. Doll would flirt with her own shadow in the grass. Whatever her life might have been in the old factory days of hard work and unhealthy living, now, with abundant food, and idle life in the sea air and the sunshine, she was like a dangerous cat. She had the power to madden men with her sleek ways and her lazy laughter.

She had captured Will, a somewhat stunned, bewildered youth from somewhere in the south of England, in the first week after the flood. She may have liked his simplicity, and his inexperience. Anyway, he had waited on her like a dog, and she had lazed and lacked nothing. Muriel thought that she loved him, and was true to him—in her own way; but she would smile on any man for a gift, and do more than that to gain one that her whim might value.

Perhaps she might alter beneath the pressure of the elemental responsibilities, but it was her creed to take all and to give nothing. "No kids for me," she had told Muriel, yawning as she spoke, and looking at her with mocking eyes....

Does Doll know?" Muriel asked, as she adjusted the bandage.

Will looked unwilling to answer. Any reference to Doll seemed to make him uncomfortable. "She knows I cut myself, somehow." He was hurt that she had shown so little curiosity about the nature or extent of his injury, but he would not say that, even to Muriel.

"I think you ought to have told her. You don't give her a chance."

Will looked bewildered, and Muriel turned the subject quickly. She knew that it is so much easier to say too much than too little....

Later in the day she saw Tom. The day was fine and dry enough for them to sit on some of the rusting wreckage of the burnt train as they talked. Tom and Jack shared the foremost of the undamaged compartments. At least, it had not been entirely undamaged, but they had combined to repair it for occupation.

Tom said, "I daren't ask you to sit inside, even if it were raining. I never venture in when Jack isn't there. He always says something's been moved. There are more things in there than in any other three compartments, and they're all packed so that it looks almost empty. Where is he now? Oh, off somewhere after Madge, I suppose.... But what's the trouble with Martha Barnes?"

Muriel told him briefly. She added, "We can't hear that trouble's coming without our doing something to stop it. I'll go to see this man Burke in the morning, unless you'd rather."

"No, you'd do more than I could. I thought I'd found a way of stopping that kind of thing, but I suppose it wouldn't work, and most of them won't listen anyway. There's too many who want to go their own road."

"It isn't only that," she said. "You were disappointed because I thought you were wrong."

"Yes, that's true enough."

"Well, I want to tell you I'm not so sure as I was. I don't like your idea that the women have got to marry someone whether they like it or not, or be a kind of outlaw if they don't. But I don't suppose you think it's a good way either. But it may be as much as you could possibly get supported. And even those women who refuse mightn't be any worse off than they are now.

"I shouldn't consent for one. I don't know whether that will surprise you. But perhaps I'm too old to matter?"

She looked at him with the humour which she showed too seldom. It was of her nature that she took life too seriously. She could be kind, cheerful, joyous, sympathetic, but she seldom jested.

Tom did not know how to answer at once. Of course, she wasn't too old; but somehow it was true that he hadn't thought of her as being directly interested.

He said at last, "I know you'll do what you think right, law or no law; and if you marry anyone, he'll be a lucky man. But I don't think anyone here would worry you, or let the others outside."

"Then you'd break your own law as soon as it was made," she said, logically. But she was relieved at the assurance, with just a shadow of underlying bitterness (she understood that second's pause quite clearly), which she hardly recognized for what it was.

"I don't see," she went on, "why you shouldn't get the men together, and get the best agreement you can. I don't think you should ask the women. It isn't quite fair to them. But if you do it at all, it needs doing quickly. If you reckon, you'll find that about half the women in this camp are either married already, or most of us know who they'd choose without much guessing, and the more that's the case the harder it may be to get those who know they'll get left out to agree to anything like you propose."

Tom said, "It won't be easy. It ought to have been done sooner. I know that. And if we try to get the men together for anything there's many that don't come, and don't care. It's everyone for himself now, and the mess gets worse every week. I think it's partly because we had so much too much law before that every one's afraid now of beginning the same thing. We've got troubles enough, but no one calls for the rent, and if we can't do anything it's because we *can't*, it isn't because we're afraid we'd get a summons if we did. And no one starves with the shops full of food that they daren't touch. And no one's obliged to be at work at seven, or get sacked if he's late.... It's just the difference between being a wild animal and a tame one. There may be more comforts for the one, but the other's *free*. And if it doesn't get such good food in the winter—"

"Yes," Muriel interjected. "No one seems to think of the winter."

"I know that; and I've said it's a worse mess every week. But there it is. They'll all listen, and agree, and then they go off their own ways. They don't mean to be locked up again because their rates aren't paid."

"Isn't Butcher trying to get the old ways back?" Muriel asked.

"Butcher?" said Tom, jumping hastily, "that reminds me. I ought to have got Monty and Ted Wrench to go for the fish."

"What's Butcher got to do with the fish?"

"Well, he just has. He pays Burman, and he lets each lot of us have what we need. It saves trouble, and he just started doing it, and it goes on. Of course, we pay him with other things.... But I mustn't stay now."

Muriel did not try to delay him. She wanted some fish herself. There had been none for the last ten days, and they had not thought it worth while to send that afternoon. Now it would be two hours before the messenger would be back, and late for the cleaning and cooking that must follow.

The fish all came from Burman, the farmer on the island which had been Upper Helford. He kept to himself, and made it clear that it would be unhealthy for anyone to trespass on his domain; but having cornered the boats, he had taken to bringing a supply of fish twice a week when the sea was smooth enough for him to venture, which he exchanged with Butcher for such necessities as his island lacked.

The fish he brought were somewhat miscellaneous in kind and quality. There must have been strange feeding for them on the submerged lands. Lost wandering shoals must have fled starvation, or blundered upon some gluttonous, unfamiliar feeding-grounds.

So Tom went off to persuade the more habitual loungers to exert themselves to bring the fish, which they would otherwise have little claim to share. And Muriel sat puzzling herself somewhat over the complicated blend of individual and communal trading and ownership which was developing around her. She recognized that the subject was beyond her grasp, but she realized the position to the extent of seeing that the basis of the confusion lay in the unowned goods that could still be garnered from land and sea, and that when these sources failed, or were subjected to the assertion of individual claims, there must be some sharp adjustments, though their nature was beyond her guessing.

And when the winter came…? Perhaps if there should be privations there would be less quarrelling, or would it be as bad, or worse, but from a different impulse…? She remembered that in the savage lands she knew men were most prone to quarrel over the women when crops and game were abundant.

Jack Tolley came up as she rose to go. If he had gone to see Madge he was soon back…. She could judge nothing by his face, for he did not show his feelings lightly. She spoke a few moments on indifferent matters, and passed on. Could Madge really prefer Ellis Roberts, she wondered? Well, after all, why not?

CHAPTER THIRTY-THREE

MURIEL went to seek Len Burke the next morning, as she had promised, and found her task much easier than she had expected. Len might be formidable to men, but he was only like a big child when she talked to him.

He admitted that there were four of them (if he included Davy Barnes, whom he plainly held in contempt) who wanted Sybil Debenham, and that there had been rows about it, and might be worse ones. But it was all the fault of Martha Barnes, who wouldn't let the girl out of her sight. If they all had a fair chance...?

Muriel seized the opportunity to tell him of Tom's plan, and, to her surprise, she found an immediate supporter. Len had always prided himself on being a good sport. He would not only support Tom, he would get the others to come. When was it to be?

Tom wanted to get a meeting on Wednesday evening. But that meant nothing to him. Wednesday? Which day was that?

It was the day after tomorrow, she said. Today was Monday. He had not known or cared.

Tom had warned her of that. It made it impossible to call a meeting more than two days ahead.

There were many who still kept count of time. Butcher did, and watched for the punctual settlement of the credits that he gave so judiciously. So did others. But there were many who had lost count of days, and were glad to do so....

The meeting was held at the cross-roads as before, beside the ruins of the Plasterers' Arms, but this time the roads were crowded from side to side. There were few men absent, and not many women, though they had not been asked to come.

Tom had not sufficiently calculated that all the men who had already contracted any female alliance would be there, and would support his proposal. They had nothing to lose, and might have much to gain by its adoption. And there were many others who were assured, often on slender grounds enough, that a woman's favour was theirs, or confident from a general vanity that they would not be left unmated under such conditions.

They passed a resolution with cheers, and without any open dissension, that they would support any woman in the choice she made, and would expel or execute any individual who interfered or quarrelled to overset this freedom, and this having been done, the allocation of the unattached and of some previously doubtful women became the conscious preoccupation of the whole community, to which those who were already mated contributed their advice, and made or thwarted opportunity.

The railway camp, having the largest female element, became increasingly populous, especially in the evening hours, and more than one inhabitant of Cowley Thorn or of Larkshill retired from it in triumph, leading his living booty before the eyes of scowling but silent rivals—exits which would have been more dignified, if not more romantic in character, had not the man usually been bowed down with the weight of goods which his acquisition (or perhaps 'selector' would be the better word) was taking with her.

In other cases the favoured ones would join the wives that had chosen them at their own residences, so that the total population of the camp was not greatly altered, though its women lessened, and those of Cowley Thorn, where there had been scarcely any since Cooper had disappeared, taking five with him (such as were little loss), was considerably increased.

In this atmosphere the unions of those who had remained un-mated proceeded rapidly; not without some incongruities, for it would not be reasonable to suppose that selection could be made with the compatibility which had been instinctively required amid the freer choice of larger populations; not without some bitterness, and some open quarrels, of which one resulted in the expulsion of a man named Bryan, who wandered off to find Jerry Cooper and in-crease his following—the first instance of the public enforcement of enacted law, and, as such, an event of some historic interest in the development of this fortuitous island colony.

* * * * * * *

Muriel did not go through this period without adding to her ex-periences. She was approached in different ways by several men of diverse ages and character, all of whom she repulsed with the same impersonal friendliness. Among these, the diffident homage of the man Burke, whom she had interviewed on behalf of Sybil Deben-ham, was the most incongruous. This sporting character, having abandoned his pursuit of the frightened Sybil (losing nothing thereby, for when she understood that she could gain a respite from more urgent masculine solicitations by promising herself to the shy and youthful Davy she had taken that course as easily as his mother had prophesied) followed Muriel, like a frightened dog, at a timid distance, till she shortened the physical separation to explain the wider gulfs which divided them. There were others also; but when she had made it clear that she had no purpose of marriage, she had little reason to doubt that she could walk secure and unmolested, somewhat as a nurse may do in slums which other women could only traverse at continual peril.

She had the confidence of many, and gave some hesitant advice, though it was usually of an abstract character, for she had outlived the folly of supposing that she had the gift of altering the lives of others to their own advantage.

Tom was among those who made her a confidante of his troubles. He lacked the art of graphic words, such as will make the dull-minded see vividly that which is in the thought of the speaker. But he could state the vital facts so that they became real to one who had sufficient sympathy and imagination to see them.

Now he told fully what she had previously known only by hint or inference, or by the talk of those who themselves had little certain knowledge.

It began with the experiences of those who had struggled up to daylight after more than twenty-four hours' imprisonment with little hope of rescue, in a mine where walls caved in, and props gave way, and floods were rising—struggled up to the safety of the surface-world, to find that safety marvellously gone, and to a view of long-familiar scenes that had been wrecked around them.

To no others to whom storm came, and fire, and drowning floods, could the catastrophe have appeared so sudden, so inexplicable, so bewildering, as to these men who stepped out to an accomplished ruin.

A little band of them, of which Tom was one, had wandered round Hallowby Park, and found along its farther side that the whole country they knew was beneath the waters, and while they gazed at the tossing, sunlit sea in which so many things were afloat which were not good to look at, and debated with inward fears whether the water might not be rising upon them, a little boat—an empty boat, as they had first thought it—drifting before the wind, had grounded on a shallow place a hundred yards from the land.

And while they watched, a child's cry had sounded across the water, and Tom had swum out, and brought the boat to the land.

It held two living children, and a woman who had seemed dead. They had carried her to the little lodge on the west side of the park, that being the nearest building the storm had spared, and an old woman there, Mary Wittals, had taken charge of her and of the children, and, after a long illness, she was now living there in recovered health.

Tom had promised the old woman that he would provide for those who had been landed upon her, and he had kept his word, taking daily food and other necessities. He had endeavoured not to alarm these unprotected people during the time of their enforced isolation by explaining more than was necessary, or than must have been apparent from their own experiences; and while the woman had lain ill, if not dying, she had excited little interest or cupidity.

But she was now regaining her youthful vigour; she was a young and (Tom evidently thought) a very beautiful woman; circumstance had isolated her from the rough and primitive conditions of the past months; and she had, as yet, no conception of what she would have to face if she and her children should be brought to the railway camp.

The lodge lay out of the way of any likely wandering, for the road which ran north from the Larkshill district along the west side of the park and past the lodge went on only to break off at the new coast, and at a spot where the cliff was high and straight, and no one would go there in search of the harvests that the sea would yield on shallower shores. (Generally, the shore was flat along the east and high along the northern coast. It was at the north-east that the boat had grounded, and across the park, south-westward, that the rescued party had been taken.)

Those who knew had little interest in a woman who was regarded as Tom's property, who had been seen apparently dead from exposure or other causes, and who was reported still to be a bedridden invalid.

Now Tom's problem was to decide whether the time had not come when the isolation must end, and she and her children be brought into the camp.

"Isn't there more room at the lodge?" asked Muriel "Hadn't you better settle down there?"

"No, there's not much room at the lodge. There's only one room, and one bed, and there's Mrs. Webster and the two children sleeping in it, and Mary Wittals—to whom it all belongs, in a way—sleeping on chairs to make room for her visitors. I had thought that if Jack had gone with Madge I could have offered them this compartment, but that isn't the whole difficulty…. You see, she only looks on me as a friend, or a servant—and I know who she is."

"Who is she? And why shouldn't you know?"

"There's no reason I shouldn't, but it makes it awkwarder than it would be. You see, she's Martin Webster's wife—Martin Webster, the barrister—no? I thought every one knew him by name—he saved my life once, in a way. I'll tell you about it some time, but not now.

"Well, she thinks he's alive, and now she's stronger she wants to set out to look for him. Of course, she can't.

"They lived about twenty miles to the south, about where the land ends. From what she tells me, I should think it's quite certain he's drowned."

"Is she young?"

"Yes," said Tom, "Quite. Not very. She's got two children." (Helen Webster was actually twenty-eight—five years older than Tom.) "I suppose I shall have to go to look for him before I can propose anything else."

"What else do you propose?" Muriel asked.

Tom hesitated. It wasn't easy to explain. Of course, as things were, it had been taken for granted, among those who knew, that he had a first claim on those whom he had rescued, and for whom he had provided when they must have fared hardly—could, indeed, not have lived at all in the first days, had they been left unaided. But Helen Webster, however grateful she might be, did not realize the position. She was always friendly: was obviously glad to see him on his almost daily visits. But her friendliness was that of an older woman, of different education and social status—a distant friendliness, which may be a more effective barrier than dislike or discord.

And yet, while he had realized this, he had set his mind on her as being naturally, almost inevitably, his sooner or later, under the new conditions of life. He did not think it likely that her husband was living. He did not see how she and her children could easily exist without his support and protection. He did not see that she could expect it to continue permanently on its existing basis. Her own self-respect would reject it when she understood. He did not think that there were many in the very limited choice that now remained that she would be likely to prefer to himself. He knew that he would be fiercely resentful if anyone should interfere between them—that he would share the difficulty of peaceful adjustment of such differences which he had, so far, only attempted to solve for others.

"Well," he said at last, "I know she's free to make her own choice, but I reckon I've got the first claim."

Muriel saw clearly enough that he spoke without assurance, and that their relations could not have advanced to any confident intimacy. She remembered that Mrs. Webster was married, but such ties were being ignored or forgotten—perhaps rightly—on every side. So many had husbands, wives, lovers, that had disappeared, and whom it must be assumed that the floods had covered. But she believed that her husband might be alive. Thinking that, she would not be likely to consider Tom Aldworth in such a possible relationship till that doubt were removed. Muriel considered (reasonably enough, though quite wrongly) that her anxiety to be quite sure of her husband's fate might arise from a willingness to clear the way for another union. She wondered whether Tom would welcome any help from her, and whether she could give it. She could do nothing till she had some idea of what kind of woman Mrs. Webster was.

A barrister's wife, who had saved her two children somehow, in a drifting boat—that was all she knew.

"Is she pretty?" she asked.

Tom was not eloquent. He felt vaguely that "pretty" was not the right word. "Beautiful" would have been better. But the right word failed him. Possibly he did not know it.

He answered awkwardly, "Yes—at least…. It's more than that. She's *different*." He tried to think of another of the remaining women to whom he might compare her, and failed. "You see, she hasn't been through it, like we have."

"I see," said Muriel. It occurred to her, among other things, that Helen Webster might be quite capable of looking after herself. Anyway, she would defer the offer of going to see her which she had been about to make. Sooner or later it would happen. She had long since learnt to control her youthful inclination to butt in where she wasn't needed.

As Tom said no more she added, "If you've got to look for Mr. Webster, hadn't you better get it done quickly? You can't leave her there forever, now she's got well; and I suppose you don't want her here till you both know where you are."

"Yes," said Tom. "He was square to me. I reckon I've got to go. But I shan't find him. It oughtn't to take long to look. Hatterley's been wandering round down south, and he says there's hardly anyone there at all. It's just going wild."

He thought of himself as setting off alone—or perhaps Jack would come with him, if this trouble with Madge were over one way or other. Jack was a good, though not always a very sanguine, companion, and his quickness with the rifle gave a feeling of security to anyone who walked beside him. Also, he knew the countryside, and not only the now obstructed roads, from the experience of many nights of unsuspected poaching in the old days.

So he planned; but when he went, he went differently.

CHAPTER THIRTY-FOUR

JAMES HATTERLEY had no cause to complain that he had been born into an uncongenial century.

He had preached the advantages of a life of bare feet, nut-butter, and parsnips (raw), and had been living in the summer woods with a wife to whom he had been too "advanced" to unite himself with the formality of a legal marriage, while he lamented the decadent civilization around him; a civilization which had regarded him with an even more confident contempt, being assured by its own majority, and had disposed of him to its own satisfaction by describing him as a crank—a word which it had appeared to mistake for an argument.

Now James Hatterley and his wife remained, and the civilization of which he complained had disappeared around him.

There is much to be said for James Hatterley, and I am sorry that the first historical fact which must be put on record concerning him after the storm rose is that he was badly frightened. His bare feet and his habits of simple living gave him an enormous advantage over his fellow-survivors, and the increased difficulty which had arisen in obtaining regular supplies of nut-butter must be accounted a triviality in that comparison.

He should have emerged from his hollow oak on the second day, or the third at latest, and taken control of the survivors of an effete generation.

Instead of that, he lay close, and watched, and did not like what he saw, and lay closer than ever.

He had to fight once to save his wife from a stranger's familiarity, which he did sufficiently well, but he realized more vividly than ever that he was now in a world in which a summons for assault could not be 'issued.' It may be that a prolonged diet of parsnips and nut-butter improves the health so much that the joy of living becomes too great to be lightly risked. Anyway, he lay closer than ever, keeping his wife beside him.

None the less, though he lay close, he looked out, and his eyes were good.

He saw Bellamy's gang going south, at as good a pace as the two-horsed cart that carried all their permanent baggage could be persuaded to move. He was under cover, on an elevation nearly a quarter of a mile away, but he could tell most of the men, including the huge form of Bellamy himself. He saw the two old hags who had been their only feminine associates since they had been marched with roped hands through Larkshill village. He saw another woman among them. One who did not go willingly. He could not tell who she might be.

His wife, lying beside him, had better eyes, or could use them to better purpose.

"That's Marian Hulse," she said. "I wonder how they got *her*."

"Such things ought to be stopped," he said firmly. He rose up as he did so.

"You're going to interfere?" said his astonished wife.

"No, I can't do that. But I'm going to let them know."

He set off at once. He did not understand his own motive for this activity. Probably it was composite in character. Most motives are.

He came to the patched cottage on the southern limit of Lark-shill, where Marian Hulse had been living with John Pettifer (a man of sufficient placidity to endure her tempers), but he found it empty. The door hung inward by a single hinge. The window was broken in. Brick-ends lay on the floor, and there was blood on one of them. There was more blood on the hearth.

James Hatterley went on across the fields to the railway camp. Tom Aldworth was away, but he saw Jack Tolley and Ellis Roberts, who had kept their word and held their friendship since Madge had exhibited the caprice of women by choosing the one who was twice the age of the other, and of the more battered appearance.

He saw John Pettifer also, who had been left for dead on his own hearth, and who now sat on the bankside, with a bloody bandage round his head, and a face of unnatural pallor, telling once again, to an ever-increasing group of listeners, the tale of the early morning hours.

It had been scarcely light when they had surrounded the cottage. (The days were shortening now, though the warm weather continued.) They had thrown brick-ends through the window when he would not open, and he had returned them by the same way.

Finally, Bellamy himself had forced the door. John had attempted to defend himself and his wife with a carving-knife, but Bellamy had seized his arm, and a broken wrist showed how the struggle for the knife had ended. Then Bellamy had thrown him down, so that his head struck the stone floor, and there he had lain unconscious till the chance call of a neighbour had found him.

Tom came up as he talked. He said, "We've got to stop this. Who'll come with me to get her back?" The men looked at each other. There was indignation enough, but less resolution, in their expressions. Where were they to go? Who knew where Bellamy's gang might be now? Would it not be too late to do anything? Who knew, even, whether Marian had been taken willingly? She was not popular. There was a feeling that anyone who had taken her might soon wish he hadn't.

James Hatterley, listening at the rear of the group, spoke in his rather high-pitched voice, and every one turned round to look. He was not generally known, and any stranger was an excitement in a community which was getting to know every one else.

"They've gone off down the London Road. They've got Marian Hulse, and they're making all the pace they can."

"Any horses?" said Jack.

"There's a rather big cart, and two horses to draw it."

"That won't help the pace. How many are there?"

"Over twenty."

"Teller there?" asked Tom.

"Yes."

"It's that damned rat's doing, more like than not," said Jack.

Ellis Roberts, to whom he spoke, only nodded in reply.

Jack went on, "It's no use wasting time to get a party together. I'm fresh enough. I've done nothing all day." (Which was scarcely accurate.) "If there's anyone who'll come with me we'll find where they are before morning, and then if you fellows don't settle the lot you'll deserve whatever happens afterwards."

Tom said, "Of course I'll come, Jack."

"Better not, Tom. If I get a chance, I shall put a bullet through Bellamy; but if we're going to attack the whole gang we'll want more help than we shall get here tonight. If you get the boys together, and you're the one who can, I'll be back before morning."

"I do, Tom?" said Ellis Roberts laconically.

"No thanks, Ellis. I'd set a pace that wouldn't suit you after the first few miles. You come, Bill?"

Bill Horton said, "Ah."

Ten minutes after the two men set out together. They passed Monty Beeston sitting outside his lair. He was whetting his bill-hook with great diligence.

CHAPTER THIRTY-FIVE

JACK TOLLEY was not back as quickly as he had expected. Under Reddy Teller's cunning direction the cart had turned off the road, pursued a byway for some distance, returned by a field-track, and then left the road on the other side.

They did not expect any prompt or vigorous pursuit, nor that their direction would have been observed, but Reddy was one who liked precautions.

Jack observed with some annoyance that the fleeing party had either failed to scatter the clues which the etiquette of the case demanded, or he was too dense to observe or too foolish to understand them.

Even when Bill Horton discovered an empty meat-tin in a field-side ditch, Jack had difficulty in deciding how long it had been thrown away, and was utterly unable to deduce in which direction the individual(s) who had thrown it aside had been moving at the time.

Probably this should have been apparent from the angle at which it lay, but Bill had lifted it up without proper observation of such detail, and could only contribute his usual mono-syllable to the investigation.

Indeed, this absence of any evidences by which the movements of the gang could be trailed neutralized much of the effect of Reddy Teller's ingenuities.

Jack's pursuit was speedy, and his search thorough and systematic. At midday he located the gang, which had camped in a wooded space, unloaded the cart, and turned the horses to graze.

Most of them were resting after the exertions of yesterday. Jack, profiting by the poaching experiences of earlier days, which he had practised for several years without drawing suspicion upon himself from any direction, was able to get close enough to ascertain that Marian was not there.

He returned to Bill Horton, whom he had prudently left some distance away, in doubt about the course to follow. She might have escaped, or been released, and there might be little gain from a further search. He could not challenge Bellamy for information while only Bill was with him.

It would be best, he decided, to return at once, and come in force to settle, once for all, the issue that had arisen. Whatever might have subsequently happened to the girl, the outrage remained, and others would surely follow, should it pass without reprisal.

But as they returned, in a narrow lane, not half a mile from the place where the gang was camping, they came on the body of Marian Hulse. Her clothing was torn and disordered; her right arm lay awkwardly, being dislocated at the elbow; her face had an expression of savage anger, that even death could not entirely obliterate.

"Bellamy's work," said Jack. Probably it was not the work of Bellamy only, but there was his signature in the broken arm. Had he not seen a woman's fingers and a man's wrist broken by the same hands?

Bill Horton said "Ah," as usual, muttering something else which was not fully articulated. His fresh colour showed an unusual pallor.

"The sooner the boys know this, the better," Jack said, but hesitated to leave her unburied, even though he might cover her from the flies. There were too many roaming dogs and other wilderness creatures now, which might increase in ferocity and contempt for mankind on such a diet.

Yet what could he do? He had no tools suitable for digging. He could only decide that the sooner they were back the better. Perhaps it might be well for the others to see also....

There were over fifteen miles of cumbered roads and rough cross-country to be traversed, but they were back at the railway camp while the sun was still in the sky.

He told the tale to Tom Aldworth, and the others who clustered round to listen. Indignation stirred as they heard it, and the thought that no woman could be securely left, nor any small party wander far afield, as they were beginning to do again with a return of fairer weather, while such men were living around them.

"If we start early in the morning—" Jack began.

But for once Tom was the cooler, and the more reasonable.

"There's no real hurry now, Jack. We'd better get all the men together, and do it thorough, and once for all. We've got to settle that lot, and we don't want any to escape to Cooper, or anywhere else. There'll be trouble enough with him too before we've finished.

"If we get things arranged tomorrow and start the nest day, it's as much as we shall do now."

Jack saw that he was right. He had become restless and impatient for action lately. It was not usual for Tom to give him wiser counsel than his own. He knew quite well that he could judge more accurately and see farther than Tom could often do. But he was content to let him lead, and give him a very loyal support. He himself would nearer be a leader of others—he knew that as clearly as he knew other things. He was too detached: he saw all sides at once. Never a leader, nor one to be led very easily. One to see but not to succeed, he thought rather bitterly. Even Madge....

CHAPTER THIRTY-SIX

TOM'S counsel was good in itself, but it had another reason which he had not mentioned. To exterminate Bellamy's gang would mean leading an expedition into the very district in which Mrs. Webster believed that her husband might still be living. Forty men can search more thoroughly than one or two, and it would be in the general interest to discover what that district might hold of human life or of material things. He determined that this should be done, and that he would go over to Hallowby Lodge the next morning, and come to a clear understanding of what his position would be should the search be unsuccessful, as he anticipated.

He had not been there that day, waiting for Jack's return, and hardening the resolution in his own mind not to be put off with any further indefiniteness. It was so much easier to make such resolutions than to keep them when Helen Webster stood before him...

Muriel told the news to John Pettifer. She had set his wrist as well as she could, and dressed his other injuries, and tried to get him to lie down in her own compartment, but he sat on her wooden-box step, staring blindly before him. She supposed he had loved the ill-tempered woman.... Now she had to tell him she was dead, and how she died....

He heard it without any change of expression, except that tears began to fall slowly down his cheeks.

Then he made an attempt to rise. "God blast—" he began. He made an involuntary gesture with his bandaged arm, that pulled it from the sling, and the sudden pain stopped the curse midway.

He sat down again while she examined the wrist and rearranged the sling.

He looked at Muriel, and said in a quiet, natural voice, "She was a brave woman, Miss Temple. I knew they'd get nowt from her."

Muriel said what she could, but what comfort was there to give?

Outside the goods ran just below, Monty sat getting the last of the evening sun, which would disappear over the edge of the cutting in a few minutes, though there would still be two hours of daylight. He had resumed the sharpening of the bill-hook, and looked up at Muriel as she passed him to fetch the water which she would need for her evening meal. "Bellamy's guts," he remarked in cheerful explanation, as he plied the stone.

Muriel only smiled in answer. She preached a gospel of peace, and she would hold that evil can be overcome by good rather than by its own devices, against any appearances of circumstance, but she had learnt that there are times when speech may be worse than useless; she knew Monty Beeston, and did not waste her words.

CHAPTER THIRTY-SEVEN

THE next day was busy with preparations, and with canvassing of the scattered population to secure volunteers for the expedition.

Sympathy with its object was general, but personal excuses were many. State of health, or of boots, lack of weapons, sometimes a frank unwillingness to leave an only partly trusted woman for so uncertain a period, were among the reasons put forward.

Some, who were unwilling or unable to go themselves, offered the loan of weapons, or to help to guard the camp while so many would be absent. It was a general objection that there must be enough remaining to protect the women.

No doubt it required some quality of courage, or willingness to take the chances of life, to volunteer for such a conflict, leaving a woman (and perhaps a child) to the mercy of circumstance, under the conditions that were then prevailing.

But over forty promised to assemble on the following morning—and over twenty came. The remainder included those who had promised without sincerity, or had spoken under an impulse of indignation, which the night had weakened, or were withheld by the reproaches or the tears of women.

But Tom, looking at the assembled force, was well content. It included most of those on whom he had cause to rely, and he had already learnt that numbers (of the wrong kind) may be a source of weakness rather than strength, especially where there is no effectual discipline to control them.

They were twenty-three in all when they started, with three led horses to carry such stores as they required, for they would not impede their mobility with vehicles which could not be moved freely aside from the cumbered roads.

Of the men of the railway camp, Jack Tolley was there, of course, and Ellis Roberts. Monty also, and Bill Horton, and Harry Swain (with a borrowed rifle, which made his society a somewhat perilous enterprise); and, rather surprisingly, Ted Wrench was there; and—even more so to most—Steve Fortune wasn't.

Tom was in good spirits, being one who was always roused by adventure and movement, and having a special cause in the fact that he had, at last, brought himself to the point of having a straight talk with Helen Webster, and that a clear bargain had followed.

He was to search for the missing barrister in the southern country from which her boat had drifted. If he should fail to find him within a month, she was to resign herself to his ownership and protection.

That was the best he could make of the bargain, even in his own mind. She had not professed that she was willing to consent to such an alliance—had, indeed, told him plainly that she had no feeling for him beyond a compulsory gratitude—but she had given way at last before the implacable logic of circumstance.

He had made it clear that she would have no safety for herself, nor provision for her children, apart from a continuance of the service and protection which he had given for some months already. Had she been alone, she might have found courage to take the risk of setting forth to search for one who she tried to persuade herself might still be living, though there could have been few women less fit by temperament or past experiences to face the dangers of such an enterprise, but the children made it impossible…

He had no expectation of finding Martin Webster alive. It was not a reasonable probability. But he would search fairly and well. He did not expect that it would take a month, and he did not suppose that any of his companions would be willing to be absent for such a period. But they had agreed among themselves that there should be no return till Bellamy's gang should be wiped out. He could not tell what time, or how wide a search, that might involve. But that must be the first task to which he must direct his mind, and it appeared that it would take him into the country where Martin should be found, if he were still living. Beyond that, he must be guided by opportunity.

But he had little doubt that he would come back with a good right to claim the reward on which, rather by convergence of circumstance than by the impulse of his own nature, his heart was fixed.

CHAPTER THIRTY-EIGHT

ON the evening before the expedition set out Tom had confided to Muriel the nature of his understanding with Helen Webster. This was a natural continuation of the confidence which he had already given, and was also impulsed by the necessity for making arrangements for her support during the uncertain period of his absence.

If Mrs. Webster were to remain in the isolation of Hallowby Lodge, it was necessary that there should be regular supplies delivered of many things which she had not acquired a habit of seeking for herself—which would have been impossible during her illness, and which Tom had continued to supply since she had recovered her health. Milk, in particular, he had rarely failed to furnish daily, and for the continuance of this and other supplies for which she had become accustomed to rely upon him he had arranged with Will Carless, whose ready offer to join the expedition he had refused on the ground that he must ask this service from him, and also (in his own mind) because he thought that Will's absence would almost certainly lead to trouble with Doll Withlin, who was not a young woman to be safely left to her own devices. Next morning he was additionally glad that he had not accepted Will's offer, when he observed that Steve Fortune was not among those who assembled for the expedition. He did not wish to avenge one tragedy to find another awaiting his return....

He could trust Will, also, to do what he undertook; and he was free from any jealous suspicion that his confidence would be abused in his absence. Indeed, the idea of any familiarity between Will Carless and Mrs. Webster was an incongruity to the imagination. The idea brought vividly to his mind how different she was from most of the women that the chances of flight and flood had left living around him, and from that realization he saw, with an unwelcome clarity, how deep, in her eyes, might be the gulf which separated himself and her.

Muriel listened to the tale he told, trying to visualize the woman to whom his attentions were so plainly unwelcome. She had witnessed some strange matings during the last few weeks. Doubtless such things were inevitable now. Some of them were turning out well enough. She hoped this one might also. She liked Tom Aldworth. But she wondered about this barrister's wife whom she had not met. Would she be content to remain isolated with her children at Hallowby Lodge, now that she had recovered her strength? There seemed no sufficient reason, now that she and Tom had arrived at a definite understanding. Also, she might be safer at the camp under such conditions. She put this idea to Tom, and ended by asking, "Would you like me to see her?"

Yes, Tom would be glad of that.

So next morning, when the expedition had started, she set out for Hallowby Park.

Under the directions which Tom had given her, she did not go by the main road, for he had left the lodge gates locked, and neither they nor the park-palings could be easily surmounted, but she went up Bycroft Lane, from which she could enter the park on its eastern side.

She went alone and fearless, though most of the women were becoming reluctant to do so. There was not only the danger of human violence. Cattle and dogs roamed loosely over field and road, and with an increasing ferocity, though it was also true that they showed an increasing desire to avoid the neighbourhood of mankind, and were of no active danger to those who did not seek them, unless they should come together by a mutual blundering.

But none of these dangers, either from man or beast, was very great in the district through which she walked. Hallowby Park lay in the north-eastern corner of the island, with the railway camp and the districts of Larkshill and Cowley Thorn curving round it, south to west, so that it was bounded on two sides by the not distant sea, and on the others by the most populated part of the island. The animals within this area had mostly been captured or killed, or had deserted it for the emptier inland spaces.

Yet the way Muriel went showed signs enough that the iron hand of civilization had been lifted from it.

Bycroft Lane was very old, and deep, and narrow. It had never led anywhere within memory or tradition except to Bycroft Farm, and who knew but that some old-standing habitation of man might have been there, with a deep-worn lane approaching it through the oak woods, when Caesar came to Britain?

It had never been more than a narrow, deep-rutted hollow between high banks, with the park-palings at the bank-top on the left hand going north; but now it was choked with weeds from bank to bank—weeds of such height that Muriel found the nettles sting her face as she slipped or stumbled in the cart-tracks which she could not see. And the thick tangle was wet about its roots, although the weather had been finer during recent days, and her ankles and worn-out shoes were quickly soaked. But the steep bank and the high park-palings were not an attractive alternative, and she held on (half wishing that she had kept to her older garments, and the Rector's coat, rather than drawn upon the reserves of the plundered trunk) till she came to the place of which Tom had told her, where some high ladder-steps at the bank-top supplied a way for pedestrian traffic into the park; but climbing this, and seeing a better way ahead, where the rabbits kept short pasture between the bracken, and finding that she had suffered little damage, beyond the clinging of many seeds that must be brushed or picked off with some patience, she was glad to think that she was dressed with some appearance of respectability, for she had a feeling as though she were calling upon someone who still belonged to the world that the floods had covered.

It was sunny between the oaks, some of which still stood up stubbornly, though their shattered forms, and great limbs flung loose and dying, showed how much they had suffered.

She kept as straight as she could, choosing the broader paths, and came out to what had once been a wide expanse of lawn before the front of the Hall. But the Hall was now a charred ruin, with nothing more than some roofless stone walls partly standing, and on the lawns the grass had grown thick and long, and lay over as wind and rain had beaten it. There were tall weeds also, growing on what had been a gravel drive, though these were not as dense or heavy as was the lawn, so that Muriel could trace her way without difficulty. She noticed that the drive showed signs of a pathway vaguely trodden through its weedy growth, and that this turned off across the lawn as though to approach the ruins, and wondered whether any human life could have found shelter in that desolation.

But she went on with no inclination to investigate this possibility, and soon saw the broad, locked gates that closed the drive from the public road, and on her left, as she approached, a small, stone-built lodge, built against a sloping bank that rose at that point above the height of the gates, and which, with its squat shape and solid stone construction, had enabled it to endure the elemental fury which had cast down so many more imposing structures.

Muriel knocked at the closed door, and it was opened by a rather stout and elderly woman, who walked with an habitual lameness.

She did not look at surprised to see Muriel as might reasonably have been expected after some months of isolation, but answered with a respectful civility. No, Mrs. Webster was not in. She had gone out with the children.

"Could I find her?" said Muriel.

Mary Wittals looked at her visitor, and scarcely hesitated in her reply.

"Well, miss, she's likely gone up to the Hall gardens. We gets no vegetables now, since the fire, and the gardeners leaving, unless they're fetched. She's most likely there, with the children.... No, she never goes out of the park, and there's not many that pass these days. Things be quiet to what they was...! We're all getting on, as you might say."

Muriel wondered whether the old woman attributed the recent changes to the advancing age of the planet or of its inhabitants, but she did not follow the subject.

She said she would try to find Mrs. Webster, and the door was closed politely, after giving her a glimpse of a small but very comfortable interior, with a grandfather clock ticking sedately against the farther wall....

The Hall grounds lay behind the house, and the kitchen-garden was on the western side, so that Muriel, following the dim track in the grass which she had previously noticed, came to it first, when she had passed the stables—burnt out, like the main structure—and made her way along deeply weeded paths, between a luxuriance of neglected vegetables and competing weeds, seeing no one, but guided, as she paused in some uncertainty at the lower end, by a sound of children's laughter in the orchard that lay beyond.

Climbing over what appeared to be the tree-crushed ruin of a rustic summer-house, she descended into a tangled wilderness of green boughs, through which any progress must be indirect and difficult. The orchard was not large, but it had contained some old pear-trees of great size, which the storm had broken short, or uprooted, and these fallen giants had either crushed or, in some cases, actually held upright in their places the smaller standard trees between their outstretched branches.

She came on the children and their mother together, and if Helen Webster was surprised to see such a visitor, she did not show it.

She was seated on a fallen log, watching the two children—brown-limbed babies of four and two—who had been gorging themselves with raspberries (overripe, and falling at a touch of reaching fingers), and had now stopped to observe the spasmodic jumps of a frog in the undergrowth, stimulated by a cautious approach of

Mary's deliberate juice-stained finger, while her elder sister, more excited than she, alternately rebuked her for teasing, and encouraged her to incite it to a fresh activity.

"I am Muriel Temple. Tom Aldworth may have mentioned me," said Muriel, as she reached the group.

"No," Helen answered. "I don't think so. But I always had a bad memory for names."

In fact, Tom had mentioned none, and had always been vague and reticent about the affairs of the outer world.

"But," she went on, smiling, "no one's asked for a card. Visitors aren't so frequent that they're unwelcome. And I suppose we're both trespassing, really—if anyone trespasses anywhere now. There's room here."

She moved along the log as she spoke, making space for Muriel beside her. She looked at Muriel's dress, at her general appearance. Her boots, she admitted, were bad enough, but she did not look *quite* what she would have expected to emerge from Tom's lurid hintings. Had he misled her to get that hateful promise? And how and why had Muriel found her here? She felt sure that it was not an unexpected meeting.

Muriel took the unspoken point with her next words. "Tom told me about you being alone here. He cannot come himself now, because they're gone after Bellamy's gang—but I expect you've heard about that. Will Carless is to bring the milk and other things till Tom comes back…. But why don't you have a cow here of your own? There are plenty about. You might just as well have had mine. It wasn't welcomed very warmly where it is. Tom ought to have thought of it…. You'll like Will Carless…. So I said to Tom I'd come and see whether there was anything that you might need that Will wouldn't think of."

Muriel stopped with a feeling that she was explaining too much. It was as though she were being required to excuse her presence. It was too impalpable for resentment.

Helen did not answer directly, for her first purpose was to probe the conditions of life from which Muriel had emerged so suddenly.

She asked, "Is he married?"

"Married? Oh, you mean Will Carless. Ye-e-s." The doubtful drawl of the word was involuntary, and she went on to explain it. He's living with Doll Withlin. The women aren't changing their names now. At least, Doll hasn't." She added, "Of course, things are so different." She didn't wish to give a bad impression of Doll. "People can't marry just as they did. There's no one to marry them."

154

Helen said, "Yes, I've understood that…. It was good of you to come. I've got so much to ask you, I don't know where to begin…. Joan, you mustn't tease Mary. She won't hurt it."

The two children looked up as their mother spoke. They saw Muriel for the first time. Joan stood irresolute, but her younger sister advanced with a slow solemnity. She stood before Muriel, gazing at her in silence with wide-open eyes.

"Nu," she said, indicating an overall of a somewhat startling blue that she was wearing.

"And mine," came a quick word from Joan, and her sister ran to her side.

Mary still gazed at Muriel with an unwinking intentness. "Kiss," she directed solemnly, and was in Muriel's arms in a moment.

The frog hopped away forgotten.

Joan looked jealously at the captured lap for a moment. She would never like to be left out, or to come second.

"I'll have muvver's," she announced. "Muvver's best."

Helen took up the child's first word in a tone of apology. "They do look rather startling. But Tom brought the material, and I had nothing else…. I expect anything's difficult to get now. It was very good of him to trouble." She did not wish to show a critical ingratitude, but what better could you expect of Tom?

"I expect they'll fade in the sun," Muriel answered, with professional hopefulness. "But how beautifully you've made them."

"You don't really think so," Helen smiled. "I never tried before. But they had to have something. While I was ill they ran about in the clothes they had, till they were both half naked."

"Then I think you've done wonderfully."

A child's overall is not a very difficult article to cut out or make, but no garment can be easy to unpractised hands. Muriel thought that Helen need be, economically at least, dependent on no one. She had learnt enough herself of the unpopularity of the needle in the railway camp, and of the demands which would be quickly made upon anyone who had skill and willingness to use it.

She looked down at the child that lay so quietly with eyes that never left her face, and then at the restless Joan, already showing signs of a wish to leave the lap she had chosen.

"How like you she is," she said, alluding to the elder.

She would have said, "How beautiful they are," but that she was not of those who will speak of a present child as though it were incapable of comprehension, or as though it learnt to speak a language first and to understand it afterward.

"Do you think so?" said Helen. "I suppose Mary is more like her father. So people say—used to say...." She stopped as the words brought back a past of which she feared to think, and a future which she feared to face.

Her hesitation brought to Muriel the same realization of the gulf between past and present, though her reactions were different.

All the difficult adjustments, all the lawless violences of the past months, all the tests of body and character which had fallen upon the remnant of her race that the seas had spared, had passed Helen Webster by, in her illness and isolation, and now she looked and spoke as though she were still of the forgotten days, which were already receding into a mist of unreality.

Muriel had the faculty of judging the qualities of her associates which is acquired most often by those who live widely and variously, and have mental contacts with numerous and divergent types.

She saw a woman who had beauty, and more than beauty—charm, distinction, and a self-possession that would not easily be shaken.

She saw one in the dawn of youth, looking, indeed, after the months of convalescence, too virginal for motherhood.

But she saw more than that. She saw the character of one who was reticent of emotion, and reserved from action, to whom life had been something to be discussed, observed, criticized, rather than to be felt and lived. One who would give trust, and show sympathy, even friendship, freely enough, but would not give her own confidence lightly.

And what a wife—how absurd a wife!—for Tom Aldworth.

But, as she had seen already, there must be incongruities in the matings of so small a society. And who was there better than Tom? There was Stacey Dobson, at Cowley Thorn, who, in education, manners, and outlook, might be more of her kind, but he had not shown any desire to marry anyone. He only appeared to wish to be left alone with his books, and with servants who gave him a loyalty difficult to understand under the new conditions....

Her mind wandered into speculations on what kind of man Helen's husband had been—a successful barrister, doubtless much older than she. It was not a profession for which Muriel had any respect. Men who spoke to their briefs. Without honest conviction. It was unlikely that such a man would be of much use under present conditions. He would find his level, and it might not be a very high one.

But his wife was loyal—more than merely loyal, anxious that he should be sought when search seemed foolish, and, Helen being what she was, that said something for him. And the children.... Muriel knew enough of life to understand that such as these were do not derive from one parent only. They were beautiful children. What would the new conditions bring to them as they grew older? How much could be retained of the lost civilization, even by such as they? How much was worth retaining?

Clearly enough, she saw them as the one supreme importance to which all else should yield. If the children of this new community could be reared graciously in body and mind and character, what else mattered? Otherwise, what remained?

As she thought thus she was already answering Helen's questions as to the conditions of life in the railway camp, and in the country beyond it. They were quietly searching questions that, in all their variety, led to one line of inquiry—how far had Tom Aldworth been accurate in the description of existing conditions by which he had gained that hateful promise, and what hope was there that her husband might be found, and the nightmare ended? The fact was that the appearance of Muriel had made the position to which she was committed at once more real and more obnoxious. Having no love for Tom, and regarding him as of another social order, of a different range of sympathies from her own, she felt such a union to be a degradation. But if she had really been left alive in a world of savages even this must be endured for the sake of the children that she could protect in no other way. But suppose it were not a world of savages at all? Suppose it were one in which there were many others such as herself? Then it would be twice intolerable that there should be such to behold her shame.... And Muriel, not by what she said; but by what she was, had made her doubt.

Muriel, remembering what Tom had told her already, easily understood the drift of the questions, and her answers showed it.

Helen, who had no intention of exposing her feelings, or of confiding the position in which she stood to this acquaintance of an hour, realized what she was doing, and took the fence as it came.

"I see you know that Tom has promised to look for my husband, Miss Temple? Do you think there is much chance that they may find him?"

Muriel understood that she was not supposed to know more than that, and that anything which implied that Tom had confided further, or would suggest any intimacy of understanding between Helen and him, would be unwelcome, if not resented.

As it was, Helen looked at her in a speculation that she had only partly hidden. Was it possible that the woman whom Tom had sent, who knew so much, might be an alternative—perhaps a way of release? But Helen, not being given to let her inclinations deflect her judgment, put the thought aside. Muriel was not the sort to be attracted by Tom, and Tom seemed a boy to her; Muriel was ten—fifteen—possibly twenty years older, and she had no children to reduce her freedom.

Muriel was saying, "I don't know, Mrs. Webster. I don't know how you were parted. But I was alone a good while, and no one came my way. Every one seems to think that most of the people who are left alive are at this end. They came on till the water stopped them. You can take that either way. It does mean that, if he did stay in those parts, he might not have been heard of here."

Helen said, "It was when he had gone to get some things we needed that the water came. It seemed to be everywhere all at once. I found a boat on a park pool. There were no sculls, so we just drifted. I was hurt before that, and I suppose I got soaked during the night. That was how I was ill for so long. But I've learnt since then that the water couldn't have covered much farther than where we were. But I couldn't do anything while I was so ill—and having the children, too."

She had a secret feeling that Muriel might have done more, that Muriel would have found somewhere to leave the children, some way to search....

It may have caused her to add, "I pray all night that he will be found. I feel sure somehow that he isn't dead. I suppose you believe in prayer?"

Yes, Muriel believed in prayer, but she could not say that Martin Webster must be living because his wife prayed for that to be. How many prayers had the floods silenced forever?

She said gently, "I think there is a good chance that he is alive, and we will pray that they find him for you.... I suppose that I ought to be getting back...." She looked at the sun, which she had learned for many years to use as the most natural reference, and which others were beginning to use in the same way. Watches might get damaged in rough work, or would break down, one by one, and there was none to mend them. And the sun was an enduring alternative. Also, they saw more of it than in the old days.

158

Helen became awake at once to the fact that it was afternoon, and to the duties of hospitality.

"Won't you come back with me?" she asked, with an evident sincerity. "It's not more than ten minutes' walk, and there will be a meal ready. Not that the children will need much after the fruit they've eaten. I was afraid to let them have so much when we first found our way here, but they run about all day, and it doesn't seem to hurt them."

Muriel said she must return, but would be glad to come again, if she might; and they walked back through the weed-choked garden together. When the flood came at the end of May it must have been fully planted and in good order. Now, with four months' growth of unchecked weeds in fertile soil, the crops were not always easy to find, but they were there, and most of them had held their own, more or less successfully, against the unusual competition.

Vegetables were plentiful, for many more than the little family at the lodge, and some were already wasting in consequence. They discussed what could be saved by storage, and the labour it would require. Should Helen mention it to Will Carless? Muriel thought not, even to him. She did not wish to start wandering parties coming here from the camp, or elsewhere, especially while the best of the men were absent. But she would be glad to come again herself, and to bring any news there might be of the expedition.

So they planned, and parted; their prudence reasonable enough, but to be rendered futile by the events of the coming day, as so much careful human planning must always be.

CHAPTER THIRTY-NINE

ALTHOUGH the shortening of the summer days cast the shadow of autumn over those who were sufficiently sensitive to perceive it, the weather continued fine and very warm, with the occasional heavy storms which had been frequent during this first island summer.

On the day following Muriel's visit to Helen Webster there was little activity in a camp from which the more virile members had departed, most of its remaining population finding sufficient occupation in the routines of their daily life, which were already establishing the obligations and interdependencies without which men cannot easily congregate, however primitive may be the form of life which contents them.

And the condition of these people was not one of a primitive simplicity. It was complicated by tradition, habits, and some continuing practices of the highly organized civilization from which they came; while at the same time they had fallen, from ignorance and lack of any common directing purpose, to disorders and degradations which would have astonished the most primitive savages of any established tradition.

They ate, borrowed, quarrelled, cleaned, gossiped, and gamed, as the morning passed, or occupied themselves in sorting or exchanging the miscellaneous uselessness of their accumulations, or in some fresh salvage or constructive work.

In the later morning, some of them were mildly curious when a sound of rifle-shots was heard from the direction of Larkshill or Cowley Thorn, but this feeling was excited rather by a wonder as to the firearms that could be in use than by any fear of hostile attack.

Shots might be fired at any time at bird or rabbit, or to pick off the finest of a litter of running pigs, but it was doubtful now whether there were half a dozen effective firearms of any kind left in the district, and fewer that were in the hands of any who were likely to use them.

Curiosity quickened when the sound came more loudly—a dozen shots or more that followed one another in an irregular volley, and that were nearer than before. But these were succeeded by a long silence, giving time to discuss the nature of the noise they had heard, and the possibility of it having a quite different origin from that of their first presumption.

Only Steve Fortune, with an uneasy doubt of whether he might not have made a mistake in thinking that he would be safer here than with the militant body that he had declined to join, made his way over the canal bridge, and looked across the desolation that surrounded the derelict ironworks, to see the solitary figure of Will Carless approaching without any sign of panic, but at something more than an ordinary rate of progression.

Steve decided that he had news that it would be worth while to hear, and sat down on a heap of bricks that marked the path of the fallen stack, to await his coming.

Will paused as he came up to him, and spoke with some evident excitement:

"Cooper's in Larkshill!"

Steve did not look perturbed, and his apparent coolness had its effect on the younger man. Steve did not consider the news to be very serious. It was imagination, not facts, that overcame him. And the rivalry of the two men had its effect on both in such a contact.

"Was it him shooting?" said Steve. "I shouldn't 'a' thought there's one left in Larkshill now that 'ud fight a sparrow, unless it's Pellow or Harris."

"They're not fighting," said Will. "They were all firing at Davy Barnes. He's got off on Todd's bike down Sowter's Lane, to fetch the boys back if he can. They say he got through safe, but I don't think anyone really knows. They say Cooper's lot rode off Cowley way. Anyway, they hadn't come through Larkshill beyond Bycroft Lane."

"Rode?" asked Steve.

"Yes, so they say. They say he had about sixty men, all on horseback, and armed with rifles. Martha Barnes gave the alarm, and they were bolting for cover before he got to Larkshill. We'd better see the women do the same here."

"Where?" drawled Steve, and Will Carless looked blank.

He hated the way that Steve always made him feel young, especially when Doll was about. But the question was not easily answered. There was plenty of cover beyond Larkshill, and about Cowley Thorn there were thick copses and shattered woods, where those who would might lie more closely, and be more hardly followed, than would have been the case before they had felt the force of the tempest. But what cover was there in the cindered flats that lay on both sides of the empty ditch of the canal, and the bare, grazed fields between the line and the sea?

"Well, they'd better know," said Steve, as Will made no answer; and the two men went back together.

It was fortunate for the inhabitants of the camp that Cooper did not appear with sixty men or with six, for there would have been no practical difference. Having nowhere to hide, its inhabitants made no attempt to do so. No one can blame them for that.

They swarmed together as the news spread, and made their way to the canal bridge, where they could see as far as the farther side of the Larkshill Road—which was on a slightly higher level—and would have warning of any hostile approach, though it is not clear that they would have found any advantage from that circumstance. There was some show of weapons among the men, and some show of courage in the presence of the women that they should protect, but the best, both of men and weapons, were away somewhere in the south, and any force of armed and mounted men that had been halted by sight of the front of resistance that they were likely to offer would have shown its ignorance of those with whom it dealt.

The only word of useful counsel came from Muriel Temple, who proposed that they should go forward to the Larkshill Road, and follow it to Bycroft Lane, and so, turning off there, might gain the shelter of the high bracken in the park, where a hundred might lie close and take some finding.

It was an audacious proposal to advance more than half-way along the road which those from whom they fled would take, but it had the logical strength of being the sole hope, however slender it might seem. But the timid crowd stood listening and hesitating, when every moment must augment their danger. They heard a distant shot, and then another still fainter. They decided that Cooper's objective was his old locality, and with the opportunity to gain their security the inclination died. It is no defence to recognize that they were right in fact, for the reasons were beyond their knowing.

They stood there for an hour of waiting silence, and then began to scatter, one by one, to their previous occupations. But Steve still stood among those who watched and listened. At last there came the sound of two shots, almost as one, and then of others in quick succession. They were nearer than the earlier ones had been, and more to the right.

"Bycroft Lane, or thereabouts, I reckon," said a man at Steve's elbow.

"Someone ought to see what's happening," he answered, in his soft drawl. "I think I'll go and find out." He felt that he could endure the suspense no longer.

The group of those that remained watched him cross the barren land, and disappear to the right along the Larkshill Road. He was a hero once again in the open mouths of many women, and the thoughts of men. But he knew that he had gone only because he was in too great a fear of the danger that he could not see.

CHAPTER FORTY

STEVE FORTUNE made his way as far as the turning of Bycroft Lane without meeting anything larger or more formidable than a rabbit, though he saw a woman, whom he failed to recognize, with a child in her arms, farther along the Larkshill Road as he turned up the lane.

He went on up the narrow, weed-grown hollow, and he came on a brown horse, saddled but riderless, which lifted a startled head and moved off as he approached.

Steve was both alarmed and puzzled. It confirmed the rumour which Will had brought that Cooper had come with a mounted force. Steve remembered the great elm which lay across the Larkshill Road, and wondered how a troop of horse-men would surmount the obstacle, or by what other way they might have come. He supposed the horse to be a sign of the nearness of human enemies, and he looked round carefully. For some minutes he stood and listened in silence, while the horse resumed its grazing.

He remembered the gaudy scarf he wore, and, with a new instinct of caution, he pulled it off, and pushed it into a pocket as he stood.

He heard nothing, and began to look at the horse with a new idea. Here was something to be acquired: something on which he might possibly escape the surrounding dangers.

His father had been a horse-coper. He had ridden bare-backed as a boy, though seldom since.

The animal was well equipped, though the saddle and bridle were evidently adapted from different sets of harness. A good horse enough, though he had seen better.

He moved slowly toward the horse, but it was shy and suspicious, and turned away up the lane as he advanced.

Then it stopped, as though there were something which it feared to pass. It moved nervously from side to side of the road, and then turned back, and made a rush past him, and down the lane.

Steve made no useless effort to follow. He went on more slowly and cautiously than before. He came upon the body of a dead man. The man was Bryan, who had been expelled from the camp after Cooper left. He had been shot more than once through the body, and in the arm.

This explained the shots they had heard, but who could have fired them?

There was a carbine lying near the dead man's hand. Steve picked it up, and saw that it had been recently discharged from one barrel. The other was still loaded. But the man had not shot himself, and whoever had done so had left his horse and his weapon.

Steve took the carbine. He took some cartridges from the dead man also.

He went on with no less caution, but with some added confidence, and in more bewilderment than before.

He came to the spot where the stile at the bank-top gave access to the park. That was the way he had meant to go, and he saw no reason to change his purpose. Horsemen could not go that way. Bracken can give excellent cover. If he went on up the lane he would be unlikely to find anything but the sheer cliff-fall to the sea, which now broke it off. Every reason led him to choose the park.

He went straight on, not seeking the paths or the open spaces. The rabbits scattered before him. There was no other sign of life. He lay down in a deeply sheltered spot, feeling a pleasant security. It was warm, and he was glad to rest. He puzzled over what he had seen, and could find no solution. It was not his nature to be content under such circumstances. He must seek, and know. He got up again, and went on through the park.

He kept on through oak and bracken, well south of the drive, but seeing the ruins of the Hall in the distance. He approached the lodge, keeping well under cover. He had not been here before, but he knew that it must be here that Tom Aldworth kept the woman and her children.

He considered that he could gain nothing by approaching it more nearly. If the woman were lying close, she would know little or nothing. If she had been taken, his approach would be equally futile, and a useless risk. He did not want to risk anything. He had no purpose of interposition, whatever might be happening. He had no instinct of communal responsibility. But he wanted to *know*. Till he knew he would have no rest from the fears that vexed him.

He followed the park-palings—high, close, wooden palings, not over-easy to scale, nor wise to attempt without knowing what might be on the other side. He came to a place where a rotten cross-piece had failed and several of the uprights had been forced aside. He stepped through into a grassy ditch that ran along the side of the road. The weeds were scanty here, and there was a narrow path across the ditch, as though there had been a passage-way through the fence for some time, though he thought that the forcing of the boards was recent. The ground in the ditch was still soft from the storm of yesterday. It showed hoof-marks. Steve looked at them with attention. Two horses—if not three. And all entering. He could not see that any had left. And there was the fresh mark of a bike-tyre. He supposed that that must mean that Davy was back. But what was he doing here? If Davy were back, perhaps Tom had returned also? He went slowly down the road toward Larkshill, with an eye on the cover that grew abundantly on the high bank at the farther side, ready to retreat to its shelter at the first sign of life upon the road before him.

But it was not life to which he came. It was death again. Rentoul lay on the road, shot through the back—Rentoul who had ridden away with those first six horses that Cooper had got together. But there was no horse here, and still no sign of any human life.

The silence and mystery, to which some men would have been insensitive—might, indeed, have seen little of mystery that any of a dozen explanations would fail to satisfy—terrified Steve Fortune.

There was something to him inexplicable in these dead men of Cooper's gang that he stumbled over on the lonely roads He had feared that Cooper would have made a fierce and fatal attack upon a population unorganized and almost unarmed for resistance. He would not have been so surprised—indeed, scarcely so terrified— had he come upon the dead bodies of men shot down in defence of their wives and homes. But this was something beyond explanation, and he could not rest nor return till he had resolved its mystery.

Yet he hesitated, as such men will, to take the bolder course of returning through Larkshill, where there must surely be evidence enough, probably voices enough, to tell him what had occurred.

He resolved to make inquiry at the silent lodge....

He went back through the fence, and made his way through the bracken the more cautiously that he thought he heard the sound of horses' hoofs approaching up the road he had left. But though he went cautiously, and on foot, he took the shortest way, keeping the high palings within his view, and knowing that he must come upon the lodge by that direction.

It followed that he was already ambushed in the thick ivy that overgrew the bank-top above the lodge when the horses which he had heard came out from a wider circuit through the bracken, and the sound of their approach caused him to lie close, just as he had decided that he could descend in safety.

He saw two horses, one of which was ridden by a woman, and the other riderless at her side. There was nothing in such a sight to alarm a man who lay in the ivy above her, with a double-barrelled carbine against his hand.

Yet Steve lay very still, for the mystery deepened. The woman was a stranger whom he had never seen before, and she carried a child before her. He had never forgotten a face, even in the old days, and now he could have sworn to every woman that he had seen through the summer months. But that was not all. It was not men only that he remembered well. He did not forget horses either. The led horse he had not seen before, but the chestnut mare on which she rode was one of the six with which Cooper had departed from Cowley Thorn. It was the one that Rentoul had ridden, and Rentoul lay dead on the road.

The woman rode astride, and with the easy carriage of one who was well used to the saddle. She wore a belt with a heavy pistol at one side, and a long sheath-knife at the other.

He thought for a moment that she had killed Rentoul and taken his horse. But that did not follow—was indeed, unlikely, if, as he supposed she should be one of Cooper's gang. She might have come up after he had been killed by others, caught his horse, and changed from her own, which was certainly the inferior animal, if it were the one which was now beside her.

His guesses were partly right, but, as is usual with such constructions, when he guessed correctly he misled himself further in consequence.

Of one thing he was sure. This was not the woman that Tom had kept at the lodge. He had never seen her, but he had heard her described. Besides, this one was not of a kind that would have remained so long in solitude.

Whoever she was, she reined up at the door as at an expected termination, and Steve heard it opened, as she slipped from the saddle, he could not see by whom, but he saw the rider's face, as she turned after setting the child to the ground, more clearly than he had done before. It was the face of a woman dark of brow and of heavy, shortened hair, young, comely, and resolute. He took little account of her dress. It was little indication in these days (as, indeed, it had been little for many earlier ones, though from different causes), but he heard her voice, the surest means of classifying women either then or now:

"I must find them if they're not back, but I think they'll be quite safe. Here's one of them, anyway."

He heard the voice that answered, which he knew must be that of the old lodge-keeper, though he could not catch her words. He saw the rider tie the led horse to a tree at the side of the drive, and leave the other loose beside it, with a word of praise and petting.

He observed that she moved without any indication of nervous haste, but with a purposeful energy.

She went off at a brisk pace across the park, taking the way that led past the Hall, and onward to Bycroft Lane, walking as one who took a familiar way, and hitching her belt round, so that the pistol came easily to her hand.

Steve was sure that this was not a woman who could have lived among them either unknown or inactive. Yet she appeared to be known where Tom was keeping his invalid and her children, and to be occupied in their interests.

He did not feel the mystery to be less, but he felt that its solution would be here if he waited.

He had not lain for half an hour longer when he heard the feet of another horse approaching up the road. It stopped outside the gates, and a man, who was also a stranger to Steve, dismounted quickly. The horse had a second rider, in whom Steve had a fresh surprise when he recognized Davy Barnes.

He heard the man's voice, not unkindly, but with a commanding curtness. "You can go now, Davy." Steve knew the voice for that of one who was used to the direction of others, and who gave such an order without diverting his mind from more important considerations.

Davy walked off down the road.

The man pulled out some keys, and unlocked the gates, though not as one who was accustomed to do so. He led his horse through, and fastened it beside the brown gelding already tethered. He stood for a moment, as though irresolute, before a door that remained closed and silent. Steve, always sensitive to the moods of others, thought that he was divided between hope and fear as he did so. But he was not of a kind to hesitate in facing the event that met him. After that moment's pause, he stepped resolutely to the door, and knocked upon it.

The old woman opened at once. Once again, Steve could not hear what was said very clearly, and that which he did hear confused him. But he saw the woman come out into the drive, and point across the park. The stranger walked off rapidly in the direction that the rider had taken.

Steve was feeling both thirst and hunger, but he still waited. Everything which he observed increased his curiosity and his conviction that he was at the centre of the mystery, though he could not read it. His somewhat nomadic ancestors had been accustomed to such observations, and had learnt that knowledge may be power also. To know the date on which a woman did her week's washing might avert the danger of having to hang about, and excite suspicion, before the moment when you would strip the line.

He had not to wait much longer before he saw a group returning across the park in an evident amity. The man carried a child. There was a second woman. Steve showed his quickness of eye when he decided that it was the one of whom he had caught so short a glimpse upon the Larkshill Road. And she had carried a child, which was probably the same that the man was carrying now.

As they disappeared into the lodge, Steve began to piece matters together more successfully than he had done before. He remembered a vague tale he had heard, just as Tom's party were setting out, that some of them had promised to help him search for the missing husband of the woman that he had been keeping here. It had sounded a silly tale, and as such he had put it out of his mind. But now it returned. Here plainly enough was the missing husband, the father who had regained his children. The other woman was with him in some capacity less easy to understand.

He decided that Tom had returned with new allies, to whom these people belonged, and that Cooper had been defeated in consequence.

He had learnt sufficient, and could go home in peace. Yet he delayed. It would soon be twilight. He did not suppose, even under existing conditions, that three adults and two children would stay all night in that tiny lodge. If he should wait and follow, he might still remain at the centre of knowledge. But the course of another hour, during which nothing happened, except that afternoon had passed into evening, had disposed him to wait no longer, when Tom came across the road, and entered by the gates, which had been left unlocked. He went straight into the lodge. He had come, Steve observed, by the field-path which led directly from Stacey Dobson's place on the road to Cowley Thorn.

Steve waited a few minutes longer, but no one came out, and though he still did not suppose that they would all remain there for the night, he did what a wiser man would have done much earlier—he went home.

He had learnt a good deal by the medium of his eyes, but he realized that his ears could now continue the inquiry to better purpose. He concluded that Tom and his party had returned, and that his previous surmises had not been far from the truth. But such conjectures, however accurate, left much to be explained, many details to be discovered. He went back to the railway camp, where he expected to learn them.

Chapter Forty-One

MONTY BEESTON sat on his accustomed bucket, but with more than usual regard for the ease of his body. He had pulled out much hay from his lair beneath the goods van. It covered the bucket, and was stuffed behind it, and before the wheel of the van against which he was leaning. For Monty, though very happy, was very tired. Every bone ached, and he could imagine the size of the blisters upon his feet without the ordeal of inspection. He had experienced the toils of war, and he claimed a full share of its glories.

His bill-hook lay beside him, and his revolver butt stuck out prominently from his hip-pocket. Was it necessary to say that it had not been fired for reasons which it would be indiscreet to mention? Was it necessary to say that the bill-hook had been occupied upon no greater object than the division of a dead pig? Had it not been carried boldly enough into the tunnel darkness? Could it do execution where there had been no one left to slaughter on its arrival?

Had it not been thrust out manfully at the horsemen who had ridden down the Sterrington hill, and would it not have been effectual to bring at least one of them to the ground, but for the fact that it was less than twelve feet long? Was that Monty's fault? (It was quite heavy enough as it was for a hot day.) Monty had done his part, and his feet confessed it.

There had been—alas!—no beer to rejoice his return, for that which had been found in Bellamy's cart had been consumed last night; but a large jug of milk stood on the sleeper beside him, a tribute from those whose curiosity he had gratified.

He thought that he was tired of talking, but when Steve strolled up, having been previously repulsed by Will Carless with a turned shoulder and a muttered oath (the cause of which he had guessed very easily), and began to question him in his quiet drawl, he found that it was still a pleasure to answer. He even offered the remainder of the milk (having already drunk to the limit of his own capacity) to so satisfactory a listener.

"Settled Bellamy?" Steve inquired.

"No," said Monty, "the new captain done that. Him and his gal. Fine gal her be." He spoke as one who encounters an improbability, but is constrained by truth to admit it.

"The new captain?" said Steve.

"Yes, we've got a real boss now. Captain Webster. Captain Martin Webster."

"You mean he'd killed Bellamy before you got there? How many has he got?"

Steve imagined a numerically superior body that Tom had encountered after it had executed its own vengeance upon Bellamy's gang, and to whom he had been forced to yield, upon such terms as he could obtain.

"There's none but him and the gal," said Monty. "They was in the long tunnel, down the line. They killed Bellamy when he went in to fetch them out. And Smith. And Donavan. And Reddy Teller. And a lot more. Then we come up, and finish it off. Bill Horton's dead. Navvy Barnes killed *him*. And Roberts. Roberts shot Navvy."

"Ellis Roberts dead?" asked Steve, to whom the rapid list of fatalities was somewhat bewildering.

"Yes," said Monty, "Navvy knocked his ribs in with a spade, after he'd shot him. So Ellis said…. Harry Swain's hurt, and Andrews, and Ted Wrench, and Tedman—Bob Stiles knifed him over the stuff. That's about all." His voice had a note which was almost regretful, as though he feared that the list of fatalities might seem inadequate. "Bellamy's lot's done in, all except Hodder and Timms, and an old woman, that's brought back."

"What about Cooper's?" asked Steve.

"Ran like rabbits," said Monty. "Just ran. Some's pris'ners. Some's dead. Some's gone…. Cooper got off," he concluded, with a regretful homage to a truth which could not be permanently avoided.

"I know some's dead," said Steve. "I've seen Rentoul and Bryan."

This was news to Monty. He inquired eagerly for details, which Steve gave very willingly, though with his usual slowness.

But it was difficult to get any clear impression from Monty's narrative. He was not false to the facts as he knew them. He did not even exaggerate. But he was picturesque. He saw the high lights only. He had a journalistic mind. We may learn more if we listen to Tom Aldworth, who is back at the camp at last, and is telling Muriel of the crowded incidents of the last two days, and of the perplexity which now confronts him.

CHAPTER FORTY-TWO

"YES," said Muriel, "I should like to know what's happened, if you've time to tell me."

"I want to tell you," Tom answered, "and I want your advice, though I don't see how anyone's can be any use. It's just waiting to see what happens."

"Is it true," Muriel interposed, "that Ellis Roberts is dead?"

This brought Tom to a definite explanation, and reminded him of something outside his own preoccupations.

"Yes, that's true, and I'm very sorry it is. He was too good to lose.... I suppose Madge will go to Jack now."

"Jack's been very good about Madge. What happened?"

"Well, we came straight on Bellamy's lot. There was no difficulty about that. They hadn't moved much from where Jack and Bill found them. But there was fighting going on, and we thought they had fallen out among themselves, which was likely enough. We never got out of that idea till the very end, and it nearly made more mess than there is now.

"I don't suppose you know, but there's a long tunnel on the line near there, and we found some of Bellamy's gang at one end, and some at the other, firing into it. It was plain enough that they were fighting with some inside, but we couldn't tell who, nor what it was about.

"I asked Ellis to take as many of the boys as he liked, and set about the men at the farther end of the tunnel. There were only five or six, and I thought if we caught one we could find out what was happening. It was there that we got most of the damage. There was that brute Navvy Barnes, Martha Barnes's brother-in-law. He killed Bill Horton with a spade before Ellis shot him, and got Ellis himself in the ribs with his last blow. Ellis didn't seem to be so much hurt, and he came back to us with Hodder, that he'd caught as I'd asked him, and left the boys there to hold that end of the tunnel, but he was dead before morning.

"I tried to get the truth out of Hodder, as to what the fighting was all about, but he didn't tell the tale straight, or I wasn't quick to take it the right way, and we still thought they were quarrelling among themselves, and I got Jack to take Ellis's place in charge of the farther end that we'd captured, and Reddy Teller'd gone in at mine, and I took the boys in after him to end it.

"We found a mix-up fight going on, and we took them in the rear, and they ran, what was left of them, past a trolley that stood on the line—a flat trolley, one of those the repairing gangs used to use for themselves and their tools—and there was a man and woman lying down on it, and firing right and left. I called out to settle the man, but not to hurt the woman, and the man spoke to me, just quiet

171

and clear as I said it, 'I didn't think you'd shoot *me*, Tom,' and I knew who it was in a second, though I couldn't have guessed in the bad light, and him so altered, and I knocked up Jack's rifle just in time."

"I suppose that was Martin Webster?"

"Yes, it was him sure enough. And the words brought it all back, when I was tried for shooting a man, and thought I should hang for sure, and he got me off. That's how he is. Quiet, and quick, and always the right word, and yet not hurrying...."

Tom stopped, as though he felt some difficulty in continuing his narrative, or his mind were on the past scene that was brought back to him so vividly, and Muriel said, "How does Cooper come into it?"

"I don't know that," said Tom. "I mean, I don't know how he heard we'd gone off, unless Butcher ratted, and I can't see why he should; but Davy Barnes met us as we were hurrying back, and he took us across the country to cut Cooper off at Sterrington...."

"Who's *he*? Davy?"

"No, of course. Mr. Webster. I didn't tell you we'd asked him to take command. He's a better man than we've got here, and he showed it then. He saw the only chance there was, and he didn't lose any time talking. We almost failed, as it was. Cooper got through, and most of his men, but we knocked out two or three, and captured one, and some horses. We got Betsy Parkin back, and Tilley— Goodwin's Tilley, I mean. They only got off with Nance Weston, and she's no loss."

Muriel did not argue that. She said, "Had they done much harm in Cowley Thorn? They didn't come through Larkshill, nor here."

"No. We think they must have guessed we were nearly back, and got scared. Though we can't tell how they heard. They shot Stacey Dobson. He wouldn't bolt with Phillips and Betty. I don't know why they did that. The Captain's got his house now. It's the best there is, and it's only right he should have it."

"The Captain?"

"Yes. I mean Mr. Webster. It's what we're all calling him now.... We asked him to take it on, and he said no, unless we gave him a free hand to do just what he liked with everything, and we'd sign to that, and we talked it over, and all signed. It seems to give things a chance, anyway. And we've promised to stand by him, and make the others do the same, or turn them out if they won't."

He fell silent again, and Muriel saw that there was still something left unsaid. She remembered that he had made no further mention of the woman who had been with Martin in the tunnel.

She said, "Was he really alone? I thought you must have had a good deal of support from somewhere to make Cooper run, as they say he did. They say he had sixty men."

"Sixty? Well, he didn't. Nor twenty, when we saw him. That's just talk. I don't think he could have brought all the men that went off with him. It was just meant for a quick raid, to do what damage he could. He seems to have got horses for the lot, and taught them how to ride, and I suppose he thought that made it easy.... And so it did, near enough."

"But you said there was a woman with Mr. Webster. Did she come back with you?"

"Yes—at least, not all the way. When we turned off to cut across Cooper's way home she came straight on to the lodge. I suppose the Captain was anxious about his wife, and...."

"Not alone?"

"Yes—no—at least, she came on Davy's bike. I don't know how far. Then she got one of Cooper's horses. She's not like any of the women here. She can ride, and shoot straight. I think it was she who killed Bellamy. They'd killed half a dozen, more or less, when we came up...."

"What were they fighting about?"

"Oh, just the usual thing. Bellamy'd caught her, and she'd escaped, and he tried to get her again, and kill Mr. Webster, and she reckoned she was his wife."

"Martin Webster's wife?"

"Yes. Of course, he didn't know that his wife was alive. He's gone back to her now."

That seemed natural enough. But there were points in the tale that puzzled Muriel, and she felt that there were things on Tom's mind that were still unspoken.

She said, "If Mr. Webster's gone back to his wife, where is she now—the other woman? You don't give her a name."

"Oh, her name's Claire something. I don't know any more. She signed with the rest when we all signed, but she put Claire Webster. She said that was her name now."

"But she didn't know then that his wife was living?"

"Yes, she did. That's just it. They both knew. And I asked the Captain what he meant to do, and he wouldn't say. They both knew, and I suppose they talked it over, and they're no worse friends; but when I asked the Captain what he intended to do, he wouldn't say anything, except that the women must decide, and that that was my own law.

"So I thought he meant to stick to Claire, and might leave Helen to me. He can't want both.

"And then there came this news about Cooper, and Claire says at once, 'Shall I go to see that your wife's safe?' or something like that, and he looks glad, and off she goes—and it's lucky she did.

"It seems Cooper had sent two men to the lodge, and they'd made off with Mrs. Webster and the children—I suppose he thought they were mine, and meant to do me a bad turn—and Claire rode after them, and got them back, I don't just know how, but I know she shot Bryan dead in the lane."

"You haven't told me where she is now."

"That's the queerest part of it all. When I'd arranged about Dobson's house, I went straight to the lodge, and there they all were together, as friendly as could be. I suppose they haven't told Mrs. Webster anything, though I can't even tell that for certain. And then the question came up, who should go, and who should stay, and was it safe to take the children so late, and Claire said she'd stay with them, and the Captain said yes, that was the best way, and we went off, he and Mrs. Webster, and me to show them the road, and she stayed there with the children."

"Well, that seems plain enough."

"Yes, it may, but it isn't. Or why don't they say so, plain out? I asked the Captain if he meant to give Claire up, now he'd got his wife back, and he wouldn't say. And she doesn't act like he's giving her up either, and yet—well, I can't make it out either way."

Muriel said, "I can't quite see what's worrying you about that. I know you hoped for something different, if the Captain, as you call him, hadn't been living. But he is, and he's gone back to his wife, and surely that's final.

"I'm sorry about the other one, but it's a matter between themselves, and they seem to have decided it in the right way."

"It isn't only between themselves," Tom answered. "If he's gone back to his wife, it leaves Claire free for someone, and every one understood that Claire was his wife, and now they find he's got another, they want to know where they are. They've mostly seen her now, and she's one that most would be glad to get. There was a lot of talk as I came back through Larkshill. Even Butcher's on to her. He saw her ride through Larkshill, and he said it was about time he had a pick. He thinks he can buy anything that he wants."

"Well," said Muriel, "I suppose your new law will settle that. She can make her own choice."

"Yes, if she means to," he answered, doubtfully. He had seen something of Claire Arlington (or Webster), and he could not easily think of her as allying herself with any of the men who were still unmated round them. "Yes, if that's what she means—and if it's the law tomorrow. But the Captain's to make his own now.... And I've promised to get the others to agree to that, and I'll do what I said. But he can't want to have both. If he doesn't want to give Claire up—" He left the sentence unfinished, and went off without apology, leaving Muriel to climb into her own apartment by such light as the moon supplied, and to the sound of Monty snoring in the mouth of his lair, about ten yards away.

Muriel lay down, but the problem which Tom had presented did not leave her mind. She was sorry for Tom. She saw that he still had a doubtful hope that Martin might prefer the new love to the old if a choice were forced upon him, as it seemed that it must be. In that case, Tom's claim to Helen would be a strong one. But in the alternative, he appeared to have no more claim upon Claire, even should he have any wish to urge it, than anyone else in the camp.

She sympathized with the discontent in his mind, and recognized that he was acting well enough in still giving his loyal service to Martin as, she thought, even if a harder test were before him, he would continue to do. But though she was sorry for him, she was more sorry for others. She saw the difficulty of Martin's position. She realized that much must depend upon the character of a woman that she had not met. But if they had believed Helen to be dead—as was natural, indeed inevitable, that they should—and had then fought, at their lives' risk, to maintain the integrity of the bond which they had formed between them, it was no light thing that he should not only repudiate her for the sake of his recovered wife, but should do it under such conditions as should oblige her to accept an alternative, and probably unwelcome, lover. Would she submit to such a condition of life? What complication might her refusal make? What dangers for herself or others?

Muriel could not clearly visualize this woman whom she had not seen, this woman with blood on her hands, who had won the admiration of the woman-hating Monty, who appeared to Tom to be of such a kind that Martin Webster might be willing to give up Helen to hold her, if such a choice should be made inevitable. She could not visualize her, but she felt that, so far, she must have acted well—with a rare courage, and with a rare generosity. She appeared to have risked her life for the recovery of his wife and children. She had volunteered to guard those children while he returned to her rival's arms. Muriel recognized that there might be something different here from the simple problems of human jealousy, or lust, or greed, with which her experience had been too often familiar. She saw, though the thought was scarcely definite in her mind, that the constants of human experience arise from the constants of human character and environment. Here environment, though no less powerful than of old, was of an unshaped fluidity, and the variations of character were therefore asserting themselves round her with a greater emphasis.

Then she thought of Helen. Suppose that, forced to decide between them, Martin should find it beyond his resolution to discard her rival? Knowing little of Martin, she could not readily assess this probability. But if it were so, she saw not only how great might be her grief—for she had read correctly the strength of affection which her reserve had covered—but of her humiliation also. Not merely left, as so many had been left before her, for a younger or a more attractive rival, but left under such conditions that she would be forced, almost inevitably, into a union which she did not desire, and which she would regard as a degradation. So Muriel judged her. She could refuse, of course. But what would follow under these lawless conditions, which had scattered the countryside with death during the last two days?

And then, what would be the position of her children under such circumstances? Martin dead, they would have become Tom's care, and his mother would have bought his protection of them at the price he asked. But Martin living could hardly consent to such an allocation. She saw that the fact that Helen was not only his wife, but his children's mother, would make it almost impossible for him to discard her, even should he wish to do so.

Always honest with herself, though the clear logic of her mind might be often warped by beliefs which she regarded as beyond inquiry or criticism, she was surprised to recognize the position to which her thoughts were leading. Marriage to her was a sacrament. Monogamy was fundamental institution of Christianity, divinely blessed and enjoined. She had never examined the bases of this belief. It was too fundamental, too obvious. But with an intellectual candour, which was the more admirable because of the hostilities of belief which confronted it, she admitted that the position was not an easy one to determine.

Her sympathy for Helen weakened with the reasoned conviction that it was not likely to be greatly needed. She reminded herself again that Martin had gone back to her with the knowledge of Claire—even, it seemed, at her own suggestion. And, besides, there were the children. If the scale should be disposed to tremble, they must surely turn it in her favour. That was natural. Under the surrounding circumstances, it was almost inevitable.

But what would tomorrow bring for the one who had rescued her rival's children, and now slept with them at her side?

BOOK FOUR

CHAPTER FORTY-THREE

IT would be illogical to conclude that Phillips had no Christian name because he was never known to produce it.

As a manservant, which had been his first occupation, and his father's before him, he had no occasion for this distinction.

But even when his employer died, about two years before the period with which we are concerned, and he was persuaded by circumstance to take over the plumbing business of a deceased cousin in Cowley Thorn, he was never known to use it. He retained the business name of J. T. Couthlin and Co., and signed his letters and endorsed his cheques in a name which obviously was not his.

He was engaged to marry Betty Cotwin, Stacey Dobson's housemaid, in the coming October, when it may be presumed that it would have been disclosed upon his marriage certificate, but even that occasion did not occur, for the flood came, and when the routine of the plumbing business departed he realized the necessity of extending his immediate protection to that young lady, and took up his residence with her on the following day, with Mr. Dobson's decided approval.

Stacey Dobson had never been responsive to the pressure of outer circumstance. He had lived his own life in his own way and when the storm struck, and the news of flood and ruin assailed him from every side, he met the proposal of his frightened servants that he should join the discomforts of the northward flight with an indifferent but final negative.

His house was large, substantially built, isolated, and protected by the rising ground beyond Cowley Wood from the full force of the storm. It lost much of its roof: its upper rooms were damaged by falling timber. But beyond these injuries, and some internal displacements, it survived the fury of the first night, and it was from the window of an almost uninjured library (some plaster had fallen on

178

his shoulder from a cracked ceiling, but it was nothing more than a clothes-brush would rectify) that he told the servants, who had spent a miserable night on the lawn, that they could please themselves, but that he would be obliged if they would not interrupt him further.

The fact was that he was composing a sonnet on Mutability, and the sonnet form is sufficiently exacting to make such interruptions almost intolerable.

Only Betty remained. She had already acquired a broken head, and some other damages, in attempting to rescue some of her master's property from a roofless bedroom, and excused herself from joining the exodus of her fellow-servants by explaining that her head ached, and she did not feel fit to go.

Stacey Dobson did not fail to understand the loyalty of her decision. He even made a moderate protest against it. But it was somewhat perfunctory. He really doubted the wisdom of the wild migration which was proceeding around him. He was repelled by thoughts of the miserable conditions of food and shelter which this flying population must endure, if the floods should spare them. He could not understand anyone being willing to get hot and dirty today, to reduce the possibility of being drowned tomorrow.

He said, "What about lunch?" and Betty understood that the subject had left his mind. When the whole world is going mad around you, and the very earth seems shaky, it is very comforting to have such a master.

As Betty would not go, Phillips remained. He joined her under Stacey Dobson's damaged roof nest day, and two young people were entirely happy.

The result showed how far it might still be possible to maintain the amenities of a drowned civilization under sufficiently favourable conditions.

Stacey was more than willing for these unpaid attendants to share the benefits of what remained of his roof, providing that his personal wants were satisfied as far as possible, as entirely reasonable—indeed, it was assumed on all sides, without the necessity for discussion arising.

Under Phillips's efficient hands, and with the assistance of the knowledge which he had acquired in the course of his experiences as a master-plumber, the house soon became rainproof once again, though its upper story remained in a condition of partial wreckage. The drawing-room, which had suffered little, and which adjoined the uninsured library, was transformed into Mr. Dobson's bedroom. Renovations of the dining-room were completed later, and when the events occurred with which we have been dealing it had been actually repapered and decorated and was ready to be used again, if there should be anyone who would require to occupy it.

Betty's determination that her master should not be annoyed by any difference in the service which he received, whatever might be the extent of the surrounding confusion, would have been of little avail in itself without the assistance of Phillips, capable and experienced, anxious to please her own desires, and sharing her pride in the manner in which the house was still maintained.

Stacey Dobson was a reasonable man, and (in his own way) a good master. His debts, by the mercy of heaven, had disappeared in a night. He had no care in the world. He remained quietly among his books. His meals were still good and regular. If the menu showed an occasional monotony or omission, he was kind enough to pass it in silence. His bath was always ready when he required it, and he declined to notice that it was not filled in the old way.

So long as these conditions continued, he was not so foolish as to vex his mind by inquiring how soon they might collapse, or what might be the extent of the cellar-stores that Phillips' foresight was industriously accumulating.

When the alarm of the approach of Cooper's horsemen had reached them, he had insisted that Phillips should take his wife to a place of safe hiding without delay, even at the risk that the lunch should suffer.

When he had lazily refused to point out where they had gone to the impatient raiders, they had shot him in the garden-hammock in which he lay.

Tom heard of his murder while he was trying to persuade the inhabitants of a much inferior dwelling-place to vacate it, so that their new leader might be accommodated with an appropriate dignity, and being refused with some ingenuity of excuses, he lost no time in pursuing so desirable an alternative.

He found both Phillips and Betty were willing to accept a new service of such a character, and to acquire the reflected dignity of waiting upon the family of this newly elected ruler, and they were probably happier in so doing than had they asserted a right which could not easily have been disputed, and claimed the house and its contents, as its only remaining occupants.

CHAPTER FORTY-FOUR

IT was characteristic of Helen Webster that she had neither any disposition to avoid the subject of the woman who had shared the intimacy of her husband's life, nor did she allow it to disturb her mind, during the first hours of their reunion. It was not merely that her joy was too great for the intrusion of any minor discords. It was rather, though not solely, because she had a confidence in Martin's love too deep and well founded for any jealousy to disturb it. She had also acquired a habit of leaving the practical difficulties of life for him to deal with, which reassumed its influence now that they were again united. She had no doubt of his intention, nor of his capacity, to do whatever might be right, and as far as she spoke of Claire at all, it was to express the gratitude which she felt for her own and her children's rescue, a realization of the hardship of the position, and of the generosity with which Claire had acted toward her. It was well, she felt, that she had been consolation and help to Martin when he had believed that she herself was dead. But as to any possibility of her own displacement, or of an enduring rivalry, the faintest, briefest doubt had found no entrance to disturb her mind.

If Martin saw farther, if he saw that a question might be approaching which it would be her part to answer, the fact that he was silent need not imply that her confidence in him was without foundation...

It was still early on the following morning, and she was occupied, with a natural delight, in taking stock, under Betty's guidance, of the resources of her new home, when the sound of horse's hooves on the road disturbed them with recollection of the alarms of yesterday.

Phillips went out quickly, to return with the news that it was only Claire who was approaching, with one of the children before her.

They met her at the gate, and with a laughing word she gave the child to her mother. She had one of the horses for Martin also. "A king can't walk," she said mockingly.

Phillips, who knew less of horses than of most things, held the offered bridle with a show of confidence which he scarcely felt. Martin took it from him with a query as to the suitability of the or-

181

chard, from various standpoints, for its temporary confinement. They went off together. Claire would not get down. She had promised to return quickly for Mary, and had been delayed already.

Helen, with a recollection of the Claire of her rescue of yesterday, and of eyes that had been hard and merciless as she had fired her automatic into the body of the falling Bryan, found her less formidable than she could have expected in this laughing mood.

As she went back into the house, with Mary in her arms, to be handed over to the admiration of the waiting Betty, it seemed a very quiet and happy world, in which summer was still supreme; and if there were a chill in the morning air to remind them of an approaching autumn it passed unnoticed.

The condition of the house of which she had become the mistress so easily, and the atmosphere in which it was still conducted, assisted to persuade her, even after the experience of yesterday, that the pictures of surrounding degradation which had been given to her had been too luridly painted, and of the stability of an established order in which competent ant deferential housemaids were still available.

Had Fate designed to mislead her, in a spirit of impish humour, it could scarcely have contrived a better method with its remaining material.

Betty, though with a wider knowledge, was conscious of a somewhat similar feeling. After the nightmare of the past few months, a mistress had appeared such as she had supposed to be no longer existing, one who seemed to have been kept aloof from the violences and vulgarities which had degraded the world around her—as, in fact, she had.

Phillips, using a file on the walk below for the discipline of a rebellious lawn-mower, was of a similar complacency. He regretted Stacey Dobson's death—though less acutely than Betty, whose tears had only been restrained by the hurried requirements and excitements of this new service—but death had become a very frequent neighbour, and he admitted the kindness of a fortune which had brought him so promptly another master whom it would be an honour to serve.

Only Martin, clothed in a fortunately fitting suit of Stacey's in place of the filthed and tattered apparel of yesterday, and seated at Stacey's desk, which he had swept clear of its contents so that he might commence to use it for his own purposes, was already experiencing the unescapable penalty of any form of pre-eminence, in the anxiety of doubtful thought which might need, at any moment, to be translated into swift and confident action.

He was still seated at the desk, working with the brain-tiring speed and concentration with which he had once been accustomed to get up a complicated case, when time had seemed impossibly limited, and was making a series of rapid notes of the almost endless things which he would require to know, or on which action might be needed for the organization of a chaotic community which hesitated between an old civilization and a new savagery, when Tom came to make his report.

He was able to announce that a number of those who had not gone on the expedition, and had not promised Martin their support, had now been persuaded to do so by himself and others.

After many questions had been answered he took Martin's instructions to canvass the remaining men, and to send any to him who might give service of particular kinds, as well as any who seemed to show an active hostility, if they could be so persuaded.

Martin told him that he proposed to work quietly there for the next three days, after which he would probably require a meeting of his supporters—if possible, of the whole community.

It was evident that Tom had done well, and that he was prepared to continue the service that he had offered. But when these matters were concluded, he did not go. He had still one subject which must be raised, but on which he did not feel it easy to speak.

Seeing Martin engaged as he was, and clothed from the resources of Stacey's ample wardrobe, he was too strongly reminded of the lawyer who had put his briefs aside to defend him without hope of fee, for no better reason than that his mother had once been in the service of the family; and had saved his life, when such a result had seemed to be beyond reasonable anticipation.

This memory, and an honest belief that Martin was the one man who could rescue them from the disorders into which they were sinking, confused his resentment at that which he felt to be an injustice, but the nature of which, even in his own mind, he was unable to formulate.

"You'd better tell me," said Martin, who could guess well enough what was coming.

It was Claire, of course. There had been reports at first that she was Martin's wife, and as such she would have been secure from molestation. But then Helen had been seen as they had walked from the lodge last night.

DAWN, BY S. FOWLER WRIGHT

Now they wanted to know which was his wife, and which wasn't. Told that his real wife was Helen, they had concluded that Claire was unattached, and to be had by the promptest wooer. Butcher had been in Larkshill last night, which seldom happened. He said that he had come to see James Pellow about some smith's work that he wanted. Probably he had really come to learn the truth about Cooper's raid. Anyway, there he was. He had certainly made the trouble worse.

The fact was that the law which had been adopted at Tom's suggestion was now working to its natural consequence. The available women having been definitely mated, those men who were left had a feeling of being permanently shut out, and it is a position which always improves the flavour of the forbidden fruit. They had been restrained from any violent reaction, in some cases by their own characters, and in others by the strength of opposition which would now be arrayed against them. It was a fact of few exceptions that the men who had secured the available women were those who were best adapted, in brain or muscle, for the conditions of the life around them.

The instinct to gain security for home and children, which is fundamental to women, had operated as it was bound to do, and they had chosen for the qualities which would give the greatest assurance of such protection.

The destruction of Bellamy's gang, the repulse of Cooper, and the memory of Rattray's end would give little encouragement to any thought of active rebellion against the law which had left so many with no hope of home or household, but this very condition must make them the more alert to any chance of altering the restriction under which they lived.

The appearance of Claire, and the news that she was apparently unattached, had caused an unprecedented excitement. Butcher himself was said to be a candidate, and one who, whatever his physical disadvantages might be, would not readily admit defeat. It was at his instigation that a meeting was to be held that afternoon, at which it had been proposed that Claire should be present, and should be pressed to make her choice from among them.

Martin listened to this tale, and said little. He saw that Tom might have influenced the matter differently, in view of his supposed relations with Helen—might, at least, have averted an immediate difficulty. But it was useless to say that now.

He only said that he would have no meeting called in the future, except by himself. As to Claire, Tom could tell them all that the law still held, and she should choose as she would. He would say no more, but he must have Tom's promise to support that, wherever it might lead.

Somewhat reluctantly, being still mystified as to Martin's ultimate purpose, as he had been from the first, Tom gave the required promise.

Having this, and judging that it would be kept, Martin dismissed him with few further words. If there were trouble about a meeting that afternoon, for whatever purpose, Tom was to get together those he could trust, and they were to disperse it, by force if necessary, referring to him only if the position should be sufficiently serious to require it.

Martin judged that it would be inexpedient to appear to take the possibility too seriously, or as something which he could not rely upon Tom to deal with, but he saw clearly enough that if his authority should be challenged, from whatever quarter, or on whatever issue, he must assert it promptly and absolutely, or his rule would be over before it had well begun.

As to this matter of Claire—well, he saw that much must depend upon her own intentions, which he could only guess, but he thought that he was acting rightly in a position which had no precedent.

His thought was interrupted by the sound of voices coming through the open window. He could see nothing, for they came from the front of the house, and the library window was on its southern side, but he heard the voice of Claire raised in an indignant anger, "Well, you can call it off," and Tom's reply in a tone of apologetic protest, the words of which did not reach him. She must have stopped Tom at the gate. The voices went on for some time, but softened somewhat, so that he could hear no more of what was said. He considered that Helen would be there. Claire was bringing Joan, and Helen would be certain to go out to receive her. He judged that the crisis had come, as he had supposed it would, but more quickly.

Then the voices died away, the library door opened, and the two women came in together.

Helen spoke with her usual quietness, but there was too full a sympathy between them for him to fail to recognize the controlled emotion which her words concealed.

"Claire is—is staying here. She wanted to go—but we owe—I owe her too much for that," and then, with a quick instinct of error, "it isn't what we owe, but what we need. Martin, I want her to stay with us."

She lied easily, as did most women of her social rank in the England that the seas had covered, but she may never have lied meanly, and she lied nobly now. And as she lied she realized that the lie might become truth. In such times as were before them she might yet be glad of such a comrade. And then—wondering if they understood all that she meant to give—she added, "I told Tom that you want us both…that we are equal in all things…. I think it's the right way. It's the only way now."

Claire found no words in response. Offered all that she had instinctively felt her right, offered it so generously, against the whole weight of the traditions and customs of the race from which they came, and against the natural jealousy of her kind, she had a reluctance to take it, and in the pause Martin answered,

"Yes, it's the only way…the only right one…. I think you both know that I couldn't have foreseen this…but the old laws are gone…. I don't mean that they were bad in that way…but we've got to think them out afresh…. I suppose, according to tradition, I ought to have chosen one of you and deserted the other—and the one might be happy afterwards, but I don't think the two could—they would always have a consciousness of having acted basely to the one that was left. At its best, it could be no more than a cowardly way of avoiding a difficulty…unless either of you had wished to go…. I think you had the right to decide that."

Then Claire spoke. "But I'm not sure that it is right to stay. It will bring trouble…. No, I'm not sure that it is…. You'll have enough without this."

Martin answered frankly, "Yes, it will bring trouble at first. I don't know how much, but I think it will bring it quickly. After that we shall be stronger, if we survive. It will be best in the end.

"I've undertaken to rule this crowd, and I don't mean to turn back now. And to do that I've got to fight them over something. It doesn't much matter what. But I need a fight. I don't mean violence. But I've got to show them who's in control, and when they've learnt that they can have all the freedom they're fit for.

"It's not going to be easy. There's so much to be scrapped, or rebuilt. But you can both help me immensely. I don't think there'd have been much chance if you'd decided differently. It's the only chance to face new conditions boldly, and we should have failed at the first fence…. But we should be able to do a great deal together, we three."

Helen spoke again. She had adjusted the defensive armour which had seemed to slip for a moment, and had regained the self-control which had rarely failed her, in whatever emergency.

"It mayn't always be easy, but I think it rests with ourselves. I think it's hardest on Claire, in a way. We've got back what we thought we'd lost, and she's got less than she thought she had."

She was aware, as she spoke, that she thought of Claire as something that came in from outside. They might take it in, but it would be alien still. She and Martin were one. Martin knew that. Perhaps Claire knew it too. She recognized in Claire a large-natured generosity which would simplify the adjustments that they must face together. But primarily it would depend upon herself to make such a household happy, or even tolerable. With the mental aloofness which was of her nature, she tried to regard it as an experiment of unusual interest, at which she should be ashamed to fail. Surely her love for Martin should be sufficient to protect her from any risk of failure. She said, "It's the eternal triangle in a new shape," and was uncertain whether the metaphor were absurd or witty.

She looked at Stacey's clock, still ticking over the fireplace. It was past midday. They had spoken slowly, with pauses pregnant of thought, and more had passed than the words would have held at a smaller time. She was relieved that they had understood each other so well without emotional expression, from which she always shrank. She said, "It must be time to see about lunch. I wonder what Betty's doing," and went out as she said it.

Left alone with Martin, Claire spoke with her usual directness. "I don't know now that I'm right to stay. I don't think I would, if I didn't think of the child that I may have. But I don't know even that. I could find somewhere to go to. I'm not bound to stay with this crowd. I found my way about a good bit before we met.... I'm sorry for Helen.... You love her better than you do me. It's right you should." Martin answered with the frankness which had become habitual between them. "Perhaps I do; and perhaps it's natural I should. But I don't know, and I don't want to think. I know that what has been in the past cannot be altered, and ought not to be ignored—and I know that I need you both."

"It may come right," she answered, "if we all play fair, and I think we shall. We're that sort, rather. Martin, you haven't kissed me since—"

Helen, coming back, found them together, with Martin's arm round her. They did not move as she entered, but Claire looked up, and said, "You know, Helen, he'll never care for me as he does for you. I suppose it's because you were first.... And because you're different from me. But I'd rather have it so than have anyone else in the world—or what's left of it."

They were finishing a belated lunch, that drawled neglected as the talk swayed between narrations of their separate experiences and speculations of the future, when a noise of altercation arose in the hall, and three men, pushing past the protesting Phillips, entered the room together.

CHAPTER FORTY-FIVE

THE first of the three was a tall, thin, elderly man, very narrowly made, which gave his height a grotesque effect. He walked with a permanent stoop, as though to discount this effect of deformity, but this manner rather emphasized than concealed it, and gave him, as he moved, the appearance which Claire had recognized when she told him with more truth than courtesy, that she would remember him, should she wish to marry an eel. For this was Butcher, of whom we have heard more than once or twice already. Henry Butcher, once junior and acting partner in the firm of Butcher, Trent, and Butcher, stockbrokers, of Colmore Row, Birmingham.

He was accompanied by his son William, a young man of twenty-four, of too little individuality to merit a detailed observation, and James Pellow, a man of about the same age, or somewhat older, of a rather melancholy aspect, having a smear of coal on one side of his face, and wearing a soiled apron of basil skin, which suggested, truly enough, that he had been engaged in the work of a smithy before being called upon to join the deputation (if such it were) in which he now figured.

It had been a fiction of the old days that all men are equal. The belief (so far as any believed it) was pernicious in its fruits, as falsehood must be. It had not even resulted in giving men an equality of opportunity, to which equity would entitle them: it had not even given them equality of legal right, the scales of justice refusing to move except for those who could weight them with surrendered gold.

There were seven present here, including Phillips, who stood, passive but alert, at the open door, but none among them doubted that the issue of this invasion rested between Henry Butcher and Martin, who had risen to meet him.

188

Earlier experiences had taught them both to estimate position coolly and rapidly. Martin saw that the intruders were unarmed, and though he was aware of hostility, he felt no apprehension of an appeal to the argument of immediate force. Before Butcher could speak he had taken control of the situation.

"You needn't wait," he said to Phillips; and then, turning to Helen, "I don't suppose you or Claire will want to, either. I suppose these gentlemen wish to talk to me. But there's no reason that Betty shouldn't clear the table."

His tone was quiet and decisive, but Butcher broke in brusquely, though with a voice which was little louder than his own, "The women had better stay."

Martin met his glance with one of courteous wonder. "The ladies will please themselves," he said, as one who states the obvious. "Won't you sit down?"

To be just, we must observe that the dead Stacey had his part in setting the tone of this interview. The room had an air of leisured dignity, such as was already fading from the memories even of those who had been accustomed to such surroundings. It was improbable that such another room existed in the houses which were now occupied, or which remained derelict and unplundered.

The men sat, though doubtfully. Helen and Claire went out.

Martin said, "Perhaps you'll tell me why you've called so—abruptly." His tone was light, but conveyed subtly that they had placed themselves in the wrong by their mode of entrance, as though they had advanced a plea of inferiority.

Butcher answered, unabashed, "We've come to find out who you are, and to take charge of the woman. We have come in the names of about ninety men by whom we have been nominated to see you. We don't want any trouble, but the woman must come with us."

The words were suave enough, but the tone was rasping. Martin did not reply instantly. He looked at his questioner. The scrawny throat worked curiously. The left hand appeared to be shrivelled, as by neuritis. The man's clothing was soiled and slovenly, but Martin was too used to appraising his fellow-men not to know that he had been of some social status in the old days.

Physically, he judged him to be a wreck, as he was—and with additional infirmity arising from the exposures of the first days. Yet, like many others, he was finding a returned vitality. Hardship and exposure had killed many. In many they had developed latent diseases. But those who had not died were, in many instances, finding a degree of health beyond their previous imaginations.

Butcher, on his part, was aware of the atmosphere of the room, and of the quality of his opponent. He had not guessed that Stacey had a house like this. Even his old residence in Westfield Road had not contained a room of such quiet luxury—and now his headquarters were a range of cellars! Good cellars, no doubt. Light and dry. But cellars all the same. Martin, armed by old practice for a battle which must be of wits, not weapons, countered his attack with a curter query.

"Who are you?"

Butcher said, "I am Henry Butcher. This is my son. This is James Pellow, one of Tom Aldworth's set."

Martin recognized the hit. How much did Butcher know of the support that Tom had promised? Of the plan that had been based on so insecure a foundation? What was the significance of one of Tom's party, if such he were, being a member of this intrusion?

Showing no sign of his thought, he answered in turn, "I am Martin Webster. I have been living farther south, where the land is deserted. I came here yesterday. Tom arrived very opportunely, when I was attacked by some lawless rogues that you had turned out of this part of the country. After that I took control of his party, at their own request. You seem to need someone to do that, judging by what was going on when I arrived."

Butcher refused this gambit. He held to the object which had brought them.

"It's the women we want," he answered. "How many are there?"

"There are three women in this house," Martin replied, with precision. "I understand that one has been here from the first. She is Phillips's wife. I don't suppose you want her. Of the two others, one came with me. The other has been my wife for many years."

"Yes," said Butcher, "I heard that. Well, you can take your pick. You can't have both."

"I hadn't heard of that law," Martin answered, smiling slightly. "I was told that the women chose. Now you say that I can pick which I will! Have you made a new law today?" He turned to the melancholy blacksmith, who had not spoken, and who now shook his head, without breaking his silence.

"No?" said Martin, smiling again. "Don't you think you should know your own laws before you come to explain them to me?"

Butcher answered, with a higher note in his voice, for he was angered by the tone of banter that met him, "I haven't come to argue here. You can do that tonight. You've got to bring her to Cowley Common—one or both—by two hours before sunset. If you're not there, you'll get fetched."

"I shall not come tonight," Martin answered coolly. "I am calling a meeting for Thursday. We shall all come to that. I shall have something to say then."

James Pellow spoke for the first time. "Thursday?" he said vaguely. Like so many others, he had ceased the counting of either dates or days. After disputes, and confusions, and discordant reckonings, the attempt had been very generally abandoned. What need was there of such reckonings when no one recollected beyond yesterday, nor planned beyond tomorrow? And, apart from this, there was a feeling among many that they had been a part of the old servitudes. They had the taint of the compelling sound of the factory siren.

But Stacey's calendar still hung on the wall, and it had been one of Betty's duties to correct it daily. Otherwise Martin might have known no better than the men who faced him. But there was no need to mention that!

"Yes," he said, "Thursday. It's Monday now."

He would have said more, but Butcher broke in.

"I don't know who you think you are, but—"

Martin interrupted quickly. There was something in the working of that scrawny neck which had brought another scene to his mind.

"Oh, yes, you do. I was *Courtfield Against Marlow*. I cross-examined you about the date on which the transfers were executed."

Butcher did not often show his thoughts, but he had been ruffled throughout by the tone which the interview had taken, as Martin may have meant that he should be, and he was now obviously startled by the unexpectedness of the retort. In the second of silence that followed Martin turned from him, and addressed himself to James Pellow directly.

"If you're a friend of Tom's, he'll tell you that we're not coming to any meeting tonight, because I'm not ready, and I've got other things to do. Thursday is three days from now—it's Monday now—and on Thursday we shall come, and I hope every one else will be there. After that we shan't waste much time in meetings, unless some of us want to starve when the cold comes.

"Tell Tom I depend on him to see that there's no trouble to-night. As to that, he knows what he's to do. But if anyone comes here to make it they'll get plenty."

He turned to Butcher as he continued, I don't want to quarrel. It will be better for all of us if we can work together. It's only Cooper who'll profit if we fall out. Can't you wait three days? I shall be ready then to discuss everything."

Thus addressed, Pellow did not reply, but he looked round at Butcher, as though expecting him to do so. Butcher hesitated. He disliked Martin for several reasons. He thought him dangerous. He had never troubled about Tom. He considered that he was more astute, and that he had become more powerful, in his own way, than Tom was ever likely to be. It suited his plans quite well that Tom should busy himself in defence of the community. In fact, with his own defence, among others. And he was entirely pleased that Cooper should have his following also. There would always be such as these to keep the peace, or to quarrel between themselves, so that wiser men might prosper. But the real power was his. His more securely with every day that passed. The power of wealth.

He did not hesitate because Martin's words were conciliatory, or his voice persuasive. He did not intend that Martin should control this community, unless he could control Martin, which he thought unlikely. Nor did his mind deviate from the object which had brought him there. Like his son, and Pellow, he had no wife. He bitterly resented, in his secret mind, that no woman had shown him favour, even with the solid advantages which he could offer. But he was not one to seek his ends by obvious or violent means. He had tried threats, which had failed. And he recognized that to threaten further would be of no avail, whatever might be the sequel. He thought that Martin would be beaten, and the wish went with the thought. But suppose he were not? There would be no advantage in having committed himself to an open enmity.

He rose slowly, signalling by a jerk of his hand for his son and Pellow to do the same.

"You'll come today," he said, "if you're wise. If you don't, it's your risk, not mine. I'll tell the men what you say, but it isn't likely they'll wait. We've warned you fairly."

With these words they had reached the door, and with no further leave-taking they went out.

Martin followed to the outer door, and watched them go up the road together. He saw that Pellow had found a voice, and that Butcher gave him what appeared to be a facetious answer.

He went back into the house, and found the women together. Under Betty's guidance, they were busily occupied in reviewing the resources of the establishment.

"Well?" said Helen, as he approached. She was interested, rather than concerned. She had an acquired confidence in Martin's ability to deal successfully with any difficulty which might confront him—a confidence which he might not find it easy to sustain, under the conditions of life which were now before them.

"Only talk, so far. But we mustn't take it too lightly. I want Phillips." He went on to find him.

CHAPTER FORTY-SIX

"PHILLIPS," he said. "What's Butcher?"

It appeared that Butcher was medicine and commerce. He was more than that. He was wealth and power. He had made his habitation in the ruins of Helford Grange. Fire had levelled it with the ground, but the cellars were dry and extensive, and in these he lived, with about a dozen followers, including his son, who had been a medical student in his third year.

The younger Butcher, and a woman who had gained some experience as a dispenser, and who was also of their party, were the only two known to be remaining alive who had any knowledge of medicine or surgery as it was practised in England in pre-deluge days. This fact alone gave him an assured status, and assisted to enable him to accumulate stores with impunity, which another might have found it difficult either to acquire or hold.

From the first, Butcher had set his mind to the cornering of various articles, mostly of the less bulky order, which he foresaw would be in demand after their supplies became restricted. He had traded these articles fairly enough, and had continued to accumulate with diligence. He had enlisted the help of several men, especially such as had particular knowledge which could be usefully employed, and who were of that order of mentality which can give good results under the influence of a stronger will, but is not separately formidable.

He claimed that there was nothing which could not be obtained from Helford Grange, if the price which he asked were paid—a price in other articles of his own naming.

He did not usually supply his customers' requirements immediately, but would state a day on which they would be in readiness. This may have been unavoidable in some cases, and he may have gone to much trouble and search to maintain the reputation which he desired, but it is probable that it was more often the result of a policy of concealing the extent and variety of his accumulations.

His followers were quiet and industrious. They did not menace the interests of their fellows in any open manner. They carried no arms. They took no sides. They had declined, under his instructions, to take part in the conflicts which had resulted in the expulsions of Bellamy and Cooper. If there were any provision for the defence of the Grange itself, it was not outwardly visible, nor apparent to those who called there for advice or barter.

Neither he nor his followers produced anything. They lived by barter and acquisition. Under the conditions which had prevailed, they cannot be considered entirely predatory or parasitic. Their activities must have resulted in the conservation of many useful things which might otherwise have been destroyed or wasted.

Martin observed that an ascendancy was being established which was not based on physical force, and with which he might have to reckon seriously and promptly if another authority were not to be developed beside his own, which might ultimately prove the stronger, and of a very doubtful benevolence.

He reflected that the problems of government are always the same. The civil power and the power of finance are at perpetual issue. Here was the old power in a new form, and he must conciliate or uproot it.

He was aware that the repeated lesson of history is that autocracy cannot continue unless it be allied with those who govern in finance and commerce.

King John had drawn the teeth of financiers, but in the end they had accomplished his ruin.

The Tudors had allied themselves with finance, and had established an absolute monarchy. Was it not the power of finance alone which had delayed the Armada for twelve vital months, while the Spanish Philip had learnt in bewildered wrath that his orders for Baltic stores were refused, on a hint from the London merchants, until he should have paid in cash against a *pro forma* invoice?

When the Stuarts preferred the agricultural interest, had not finance turned and destroyed them?

It was a truth which could be illustrated from every chapter of the history of civilization.

If he would establish an autocracy of any kind, he must control or conciliate commerce, in whatever form he should meet it. But did he wish to do so? Should not his aim be rather to establish a freer democracy than the older world had known? But even so, was it not under such conditions that finance became the more intolerable menace the more dominant power?

Suppose that the better aim should be to establish a simpler form of living than had been the ideal of the earlier days? An agricultural community, in which the manufacturing and trading interests should be controlled, if not eliminated? Even then, would not the financier triumph?

Was not the Mosaic Law an example of the difficulty of formulating a code which could resist such dominance? There would, at least, be one of its provisions—the prohibition of usury—which he would do well to remember.

There were few of the drowned world from which he came who would not have mocked the thought. Its industrial and commercial systems had been built on that foundation, so that it might have become impossible that they should survive its withdrawal. Yet he saw it for what it had been, with all its splendour—a palace built on sand—or, rather, upon a swamp of more sinister potentialities.

So his mind wandered, and he must recall himself to the insistent needs of the moment. And yet the rapidity of thought is such that it had been but a passing minute, while Phillips stood, silent and deferential, awaiting his further questions.

But he only said, "Thanks, Phillips. That will do," for the thought which was now in his mind was one which was best left unspoken. What was the significance of Pellow's presence with Butcher? Pellow, who was said to be of Tom Aldworth's party. Pellow, who could not be drawn into speech.

It might mean much or little, but he would ask nothing which might be construed into a doubt of Tom's loyalty, or of his ability to influence his own party successfully. He was already realizing something of the isolation of those who rule: gaining something of their habit of reticence.

He was puzzled also as to the significance of Butcher having appeared as the leader of the deputation. He had kept himself aloof from all previous controversy, as the trader will, till he considers that his purse is jeopardized too seriously for further quietude.

Possibly his attitude might be still undecided. Possibly he had come to form his own opinion of the proposed ruler. Possibly he might have spoken differently if Pellow had not been present.

Martin considered that it was unlikely that he had been actuated by a simple desire that Claire should be surrendered. From her own account of her interview with him, it appeared improbable that he could hope that any personal advantage would follow. He might conceivably have been actuated by a desire to revenge the insult which he had received, but Martin judged that his feelings would not easily deflect his judgment on such a question.

But all this was speculation, and might be absurdly far from reality, though it might well be that by the success of such guessing he would stand or fall.

His mind faced an urgent issue, which might be vital. Was there cause to fear an immediate hostility from those whom he had refused to meet till his own time, and should he make defensive preparations of any kind against that contingency?

He had given instructions to Tom to deal with such a position, and he did not think he would fail him. But he might be finding an unexpected difficulty in keeping his party together.

Martin recognized that, by his own dispositions, he was alone, and almost defenceless, against a combined attack Alone with Phillips and three women and two children. Protected only by the prestige which he had established, and the improbability that such hostile elements as might be arraying themselves against him would act without the knowledge of those on whose support he must rely, and with such concerted promptitude.

He recognized that his attitude in regard to Claire had placed a ready weapon in the hands of all who might desire to oppose him.

More than that, it gave a motive for hostility to many who might otherwise have been well disposed to his cause. And even those who had given him their adherence had done so before this question had arisen to test them.

Yet he did not think it likely that there would be any attack to be feared that day, or that it would be made without warning. He trusted Tom. Besides, there was Jack Tolley, whom he had not seen since his coming to Stacey's house. He did not think that Jack was very enthusiastic in his support, but he was one who would very certainly be loyal to the side he had taken, and he was one who could be trusted to watch, and to judge the position well, and to give warning, if it should be needed.

Finally, he decided that the probability of any danger threatening the women without sufficient warning was too slight for it to be expedient that he should be observed making preparation against it. Above all, he must show confidence.... It might have been better to go at once to this meeting that they had offered, and to have faced them at once, with Claire beside him, trusting to the ascendancy which he had already gained, and to his ability to control an audience.

But having decided differently, having challenged them at the outset by saying that they must meet him at his own time, it was essential that he should show no fear of the security of his own position.

Thinking thus, he let the hours pass. His mind was busy with many plans and speculations that jostled one another, so that he had an unaccustomed difficulty in keeping his thoughts on any single issue.

On two sides of Stacey's library bookshelves rose from floor to ceiling. He began to examine these volumes. They had acquired an altered importance.

He could not tell how widely, or how utterly, his civilization had fallen. But it was at least probable that a thousand years of human effort had disappeared beneath Atlantic waves.

It might rest with him to decide how much or little should be done to conserve the wrecks of the old literatures, of the old sciences, of the old philosophies and religions...

Stacey's library was as cultured and varied as had been the contents of his own mind. Fiction and *belles-lettres* predominated. In the bulk, these books appeared to Martin to have become of a doubtful value. Certainly the more modern fiction, with its morbid introspection, its lack of humour, and of any sane estimate of relative values, its assumption of the normality of vicious living, its lack of fortitude or of ideality, would have little to offer that men would longer care to read, or which could be worth their reading. At the best, they were unimportant. They could await the verdict of leisure.

There was some biography.... That could wait also.

There was a good deal of history. His eye fell on Motley's *Dutch Republic*, on Prescott's *Conquest of Mexico*. He passed along the shelf in a thoughtful silence.

Then he came on a little group of scientific text-books. They may have been the best of their kind, but they could contain little beside the total of knowledge—physical, chemical, biological—that the ages had accumulated and the seas had covered. Still there could be no other end. It had been inevitable—always. It was only the date which had been unknown, which must always be uncertain. Did not every civilization that the earth had known begin with a tale of flood, and of the few that survived it?

It seemed pitiful, if this were all that remained from so large a harvest. But there must be other books elsewhere.... And yet, if all were gone, was it so entirely regrettable? They had held such power for good—and for evil also. It was hard to say.

And beyond these he came on a little group of the disciples of the hoary cult of the Witch of Endor. He read "Oliver Lodge," "Arthur Conan Doyle," on the covers. He did not doubt that they were well-meaning men, not intending harm to any. Men so much to the liking of their own time that they had both been knighted. Humble men, who accepted without protest the verdict that a knighthood is the fitting reward of their calling from politicians who would not have dared so to insult a successful brewer or barrister.

Martin was something other than a typical lawyer, but he could not avoid a flicker of contempt for the ineffectual. To refuse a title is one thing. To accept a fifth-rate article from a man who would have despised it for himself....

He became aware that he was wasting time on trivialities that the floods had ended.

As for the books, it seemed incredible that they should influence any but the feeble-minded; yet he knew in the past.... Well, Betty should burn them tomorrow.

But how, he wondered, could the best of the old knowledge, or at least some of it, be conserved, and its falsehoods ended? Who could be competent to discriminate? Could he claim such competence? Were he of the generation that would follow, would he not resent such action having been taken?

This last thought brought another. What could be the system of education on which the next generation would be reared? He saw that this would bear directly upon the earlier question. The peculiarity of recent years had not been the extent so much as the wide distribution of knowledge among those who had little inclination or capacity to digest or co-ordinate it. Many thousands who never exercised their minds at all.... The increased leisure that had been almost universal.... Not that they had lived quietly. Far from it. But the hours given to routine labour had been abnormally short—had been shortening continually, even as the labour itself had been specialized further into more intolerable monotonies.

Previously there had been a small section of the community who were expert in arts and sciences of which others were ignorant. The farther back we inquire, the more primitive the conditions we encounter, the more marked is this division, till we find, at the foundation of every civilization, a priestly order reserving to itself a body of inherited knowledge, which the general community is permitted to approach, if at all, only by the medium of allegorical tales, the true meaning of which is quickly lost, even if explanation be given.

Which was the better way? Martin saw that the question was not a simple one. A privacy of knowledge places a great power in hands that may abuse it. Against this was the fact that knowledge given out to a whole people becomes uncontrollable, either for good or evil. And how much knowledge there is, curious to acquire, which can be used for evil only! Even should a new poison be discovered, its nature and use would be made known to all men, even though the civil power, acting at a somewhat higher level of sanity, might make regulations to hamper its distribution.

Perhaps there was no absolute answer. The great error of the latest developments of Western civilization had been its tendency to treat all men as alike and equal. An equality of opportunity might be good—might be ideal—but it had gone beyond that. There were some volumes of *The Golden Bough* upon the shelves beside him. They brought recollection of a stray sentence of their author—he could not recall exactly where it occurred—"No abstract doctrine is more false and mischievous than that of the natural equality of men." That, at least, was an error which he could avoid without difficulty. It is not one which finds nourishment in the soil of primitive circumstance.

He saw that knowledge had been made a fetish, so that those who pursued it were regarded as though they could do no wrong. Knowledge, under its new name of science, was a sacred thing, however foul or foolish, or by whatever cruelty it might have been obtained. Even the chemists who had increased the horrors of human conflict had not been reasonably exterminated when that conflict ceased....

But these speculations were most probably no better than an idle folly. The force of circumstance, and the conditions of the life before them, would be stronger than he. The problems which would arise with a daily urgency would be different from those of the old days, and experience might be of little use to decide them.

Martin stood at the window as his thoughts wandered. He observed that Phillips had resumed his work on the lawn. He noticed that most of the garden was in a wild disorder. There had been no attempt to tame it. But there was a small portion round the house that he had kept under control, and there the order was absolute. There was no weed on the well-rolled gravel beneath the window. The edges of the smooth-cut lawn may never have been better trimmed.... To try too much, and to fail entirely.... He wondered if there might be any wisdom to be gained from this man who worked with so clear a purpose. He threw up the window.

Phillips looked up as he did so.

"Would you like Betty to get some tea, sir?" he inquired, in his usual deferential manner.

"No, I wasn't thinking about tea. I was wondering whether this life is better or worse than it used to be. I wondered what you'd say if I asked you. Was it better than it is now?"

Phillips showed no surprise at the question. He thought silently for a moment, doing his best to satisfy his master's requirement as naturally as though he had been asked to find him a corkscrew. But his reply was unexpected.

"No, sir. I shouldn't say that. There's some things that's better, and many worse. But I've noticed one thing. There haven't been any suicides."

Martin looked at him in a momentary doubt whether the answer were to be taken literally. But Phillips was a man of a literal mind. Not at all one who would be likely to offer his master an untimely jest. Martin realized that he was merely stating a fact. It might not be one of any significance. The population was not large. Even in the older world it might have been possible to discover a district of some hundreds of inhabitants where there had been a period of several months without such an occurrence.

But finding that his master was silent Phillips continued to develop the subject.

"You see, sir, there was one last year in Cowley Thorn, and four in Larkshill. There was the girls that tied themselves together to drown in the round pool; and Dr. Raikes that shot himself from overwork, or so they said, and the grocer in Church Street that was hanging when they came together for the creditors' meeting, and the bank cashier at the Midland and Southern; and the year before there was a young couple that gassed themselves at Larkshill, when it came out that they'd got no money left and weren't married at all, and—well, there'd been others, more or less, all the time, and I just thought that there might have been more now that things are so much worse, as we all say; and so far there's been none at all."

He paused, as though in some doubt whether he had said too much, in reply to a question which he should have answered more shortly.

"Yes, Phillips, go on."

"Well, sir, I don't rightly know why it is. Things *are* worse than they were, and there's been wrong things done that couldn't have gone on before, and them that do them just laugh, and do worse to-morrow. We're not as safe as we were. But we're not held down as we was.

"I think that's what makes it more worth while to keep alive. It's not so easy to do, but, somehow, it's more worth doing. We used to be held down till we couldn't move. I don't say we weren't held down comfortable, but there it was. We was held down hard, and if we ached to move—well, there was only one way, and there was some that took it."

"But it was a free country, Phillips. The laws were made by the people themselves, for their own security and comfort."

"Yes, sir, they did all that. I don't say they didn't. But I shouldn't call it *free*. Not when you couldn't help having a summons sooner or later, try how you would.... I had one myself the week before the flood, and when I think of it, it makes me half glad it came, and I didn't have to go, and my mother died without knowing. But you don't want to hear all that."

"Yes, go on. What was the summons for? I shouldn't have thought you'd have made a mistake of that kind in a century."

"It was the business I took over. It had been called J. T. Couthlin and Co. for fifty years, since my mother's uncle started it; it's he was J. T., and I kept it on, and used the same name, as Bill did before me, and thought no wrong—and what wrong was there? And then I was summoned because I wasn't carrying it on in my own name."

"Oh, you mean the Business Names Act. You should have registered."

"Well, sir, I didn't know, and I'd done no wrong, and I went and told them at the station, and they said, 'Then you ought to have known. You'll be fined five pounds, most likely.' And my mother was too old to have understood. She'd have said I'd disgraced the family, and must have done something bad to be fined like that. She'd almost sooner have been seen in a pawnshop than had the police knock at her door.... No, sir, I shouldn't call it a free country. It wasn't bad in its way, and it was very safe if you kept quiet and went the way you were told—but I sometimes think it may have gone on about long enough."

CHAPTER FORTY-SEVEN

MARTIN, turning from the window, observed that Betty had entered to lay the evening meal with the formality which Stacey had always exacted, even though there might be unavoidable variations in the nature of the fare provided.

Claire and Helen came in together.

Martin noticed with satisfaction that they appeared to be on terms of a very cordial intimacy, though his knowledge of the ways of women was sufficient to tell him that it was a fact of no certain significance.

From a score of animated questions of contrivance and management which they were discussing as the meal proceeded, Claire turned to him to explain the nature of the defences which Phillips had provided against the emergency of attack, and which he had shown her with an evident deference, which had caused her some inward amusement.

"I think he was almost nervous, till he found that I really admired his ingenuities. He appeared to regard me as an expert on such questions, till I told him that we only specialize in tunnels.

"But they seem to have had a bad time here during the first weeks—and, in a different way, later. He has got the kitchen separated from the rest of the house, and the windows barred and the doors. His arrangements for spraying unwelcome callers with boiling water, and keeping on the supply, are really remarkable. And there are relays of red-hot pokers for hand-to-hand fighting.

"I wondered they didn't retreat into the kitchen yesterday, and defend themselves there, but I suppose they didn't know how many men Cooper was bringing, or how long they might stay…. Isn't Phillips talking to someone?"

Phillips was. The voices went on in the hall for some minutes. His own, quiet and deferential, broken occasionally by another, somewhat louder, and of a more open-air quality.

Then he appeared at the door.

"Mr. Burman, of Upper Helford, is waiting to see you, sir. I told him you were engaged, but he won't go, and he says he doesn't want to be long, because of the tide."

"Do you know him?" Martin asked.

"Not well, sir. He supplies the fish."

"Then the fishmonger must wait."

"They're good fish," Helen remarked, with appreciation. "Don't make him wait too long."

The fish which earned this commendation were a kind of sprat or pilchard, of which a liberal supply had been distributed on the evening before Cooper's appearance had disturbed the routines of the district.

Besides these fish, there were eggs on the table, milk, some unleavened cakes, butter of Betty's making, some apples, and a weak solution of the precious tea. Certainly, Stacey had not starved, if this were an example of the fare that had been provided for him.

"He isn't exactly a fishmonger," Phillips began, with some hesitation.

"What is he?" Martin asked

"Well, sir, he was a farmer in Upper Helford, and his sons cleared out with the rest, but he wouldn't leave. He's got two or three men there. You can see them from the cliff. And he just goes on farming. He doesn't let anyone go over, and when we've had a boat, once or twice, it's disappeared in the night."

"Do you mean he's on a separate island?"

"It's scarcely that, sir. Anyone might cross at low tide, if they could get through the mud, where Helford brook used to run, but there's barbed wire now along the other side, and a stiff climb it would be."

"Isn't Helford where Butcher is?"

"No, sir. That's Helford Grange, where old Mr. Carson lived, that owned Upper Helford; and Lower Helford too, for that matter. But the Grange is a mile or more to the south, the other side of Cowley."

"Don't people go over at all?"

"Well, sir, Jim Arter tried, and he was lying this side again the next morning with a charge of shot in his back. Mr. Burman had warned us what it would be, and he just went to find out."

This was the man who was now standing in the hall demanding an audience with Martin, with a shot-gun under his arm.

Phillips mentioned the gun.

"All the same," Martin decided, "I think we'll see him, even though the gun may be the one which was discharged into Mr. Arter's anatomy. I don't suppose he's calling with a programme of promiscuous homicide. Apart from that, he sounds interesting."

It was the haystack which was mainly responsible for this decision. In the course of fuller explanations than there is space to chronicle, Phillips had mentioned that the top of one of these erections could be observed from the opposite shore, as an evidence of his farming activities. Martin felt that this placed him definitely on the side of those who would seek to conserve rather than to ruin. The fate of the investigating Arter was of a less certain significance. They knew from their own experience that he might have deserved his end.

"All the same," Claire remarked, "I shouldn't care to sit with my back to him. Habits grow so easily now."

"Well, no one need," Helen said, only half seriously. "There are four sides to the table." She was less used than were the others to the proximity of potential violence, but she would have felt secure against more than one intruder in her present company. Yet she added, "Shall we go?" with a doubt whether Martin would prefer their absence, which would not have occurred to Claire.

"No. Why should you?" And, while he answered, the question settled itself.

"I'm afraid the tide won't wait," said the voice they had heard in the hall, and the door opened to admit a man rather largely made, wearing a wide-brimmed hat, and garments that were consistent enough with the character of farmer-fisherman which had been attributed to him, terminating in a pair of brown leggings and substantial boots.

He glanced round the well-appointed room and at the well-laid table with self-possession enough, but with an evident adjustment of mental perspective, which resulted in an apologetic, "Pardon, ladies," and his hat came down in his hand.

He showed a mass of shaggy, grizzled hair, merging into a beard that was full and brown. He may have been nearer sixty than fifty, but he looked ten years younger. His face was weather-beaten, but not showing any other signs of loss of vigour. His eyes were deep-set, beneath bushy brows, grey and keen, but not unkindly.

He leaned his gun, an ancient muzzle-loader, but looking in as good condition as its owner, against the wall, as Martin asked him politely, "Won't you sit down?" and indicated the farther side of the table.

Phillips placed a chair and withdrew.

"You will like something to eat after your voyage," Helen said pleasantly. She was too practised a hostess not to deal with the situation easily, though she had some hesitation in placing this informal visitor socially, and her voice had that note of aloofness—remote rather than condescending—which came into it so easily.

204

The man hesitated, from whatever motive, and glanced keenly and thoughtfully round the little group before he answered. Then he said, "Thanks, ma'am. I've got half an hour," and took the waiting chair.

Claire thought, as she passed the apples, "She'll always do the queen stunt better than I should." If Martin were to be the king of an island state, she had no doubt of who would be better adapted for the part of official wife. But for John Burman's presence she would, no doubt, have said it, with her usual frankness.

Burman ate, and surveyed the fare. He was quite at his ease. "I see you're careful with the tea," he remarked, looking at Martin.... "I reckon that thief Butcher's got plenty."

"Why do you call him a thief?"

"You're new here," Burman answered. "Tom tells me you've settled Bellamy's lot, and set Cooper on the run. I suppose Butcher'll come next."

Martin declined to be drawn. He said, "It was really Tom who settled Bellamy's lot, and saved our lives in doing it. We had been obliged to kill Bellamy before that.... I'm afraid there'll be more trouble with Cooper.... Yes, they've asked me to take control. Are you with us?"

Burman did not answer quickly. At length he said, "I'm not with you. I may be for you. That depends on what you mean to do. I'm not against you so far. I came to learn.... We shan't quarrel if you leave Helford alone."

Martin considered. Here was another unforeseeable factor. A declaration of independence at his very door. Of independence, but not of active hostility. So he understood it. He might make himself lord of Cowley Thorn, if he would, and of the deserted mining village beyond it. He might take possession of all the wilderness miles to southward—and westward too if the same conditions prevailed. But he was to understand that Upper Helford was foreign ground.

He did not know what other complications might follow should he accept this position. But he liked the man. And he needed friends. He answered diplomatically.

"I don't want to disturb you. From what I've heard, Upper Helford has been able to look after itself. But I think I can ask your help, because it seems to me that we shall be fighting your battles.... You've got a haystack."

Burman was not slow, but he did not follow this. He said, "It's not for sale. We shall need it for our own stock in the winter."

"That's what I meant," said Martin. "What other stacks are there?"

"There's not one that I know of," Burman answered.

"Well, how long would they leave yours when they learn what winter means? There are cattle everywhere, running wild. You can judge what will happen to them when the frost comes. You're a farmer. You can tell better than I can. I suppose it depends mainly on whether the season be severe or mild.

"But it won't be only the wild ones. There are cows fenced up, more or less, all over the place. Everyone seems to be living largely on the milk. I don't know how it is that there has been so little fore-thought, except that there's been so much to plunder, and so much quarrelling, and most of the men would have said that a cow just stood in a field and grazed all the year round if they'd been asked six months ago.

"If we can do something to organize things now—if it's not too late—I think you should be willing to help us."

"Maybe, yes," was the cautious answer, "if that's what you mean. But I can't do much this side. I won't risk—" He broke off abruptly. "I'm helping now with the fish. And a pinch of Butcher's tea or a pound of tobacco is all I get back. But they mayn't last. They come and go. There's times when we catch none, and times when we bring up strange sorts that we daren't eat. But there's mostly a few congers. There must have been a fair upset down be-low. And we can't fish when the weather's bad. I won't have any risks. The boat's not fit.... But I think, maybe, you've come about the right time."

He sat silent for a minute or two, as though he were weighing Martin's problem in his own way, and then spoke again.

"I'll tell you all I can. You see I've watched it from the start, and held them off.

"There was a crowd along the edge soon after the land broke. They came up for hours. They were all sorts, but most of them were crazy with fear. Some of them went mad. Most of them had no shel-ter. They fought over the food they found. They lay in the rain and died. There must be three or four hundred left alive, all told—maybe more. They're well enough. I reckon the weak ones have died off. But some of the best died too—or got killed. They quarrelled over the women, when they'd found how to get food and to keep alive. There were things done that are best not told. But no one worked, except to make some shelter for themselves, and those that had the women wouldn't leave them out of their sight. And if they weren't fighting each other they'd be plundering in the ruined houses, or getting things from the old gardens, or catching rabbits, or watching the sea for what it leaves when the tide falls.... And the time soon goes, and when you plunder you have to take what you find, not what you want. And I reckon that most of them knew little of country ways.

"If they'd made the hay, I don't know that there's one among them that would have known how to build a rick, let alone thatch it.... Butcher looks ahead, in his own way. He won't starve. But he only plans for himself. He isn't a shepherd. He's what his name says.... Yes, I reckon it's about the right time. There's some decent ones among them, but they want leading. There's that missionary woman ought to help, and there's Ellis Roberts—you could trust him."

Martin said: "Ellis is dead. I didn't see him alive." He told briefly what he knew of the matter.

"That's bad luck," said Burman. "There's worse left." He rose, saying that he would miss the tide.

Martin felt that this man could help him in many ways, and that his goodwill would be worth getting. He wondered how he could win a similar confidence.

"We mustn't ask you to stay now," he said. "We know the tide won't. But, if I may, I'll come and call on you tomorrow. I should like another talk when we've more leisure."

It had entered his mind that to offer to go alone into Burman's territory, after what had happened to the adventurous Arter, would be a sign of confidence which might attain his end, but he quickly learnt his mistake.

Burman was half-way to the door when he spoke, and he swung round instantly.

"No," he said, with a note of anger in his voice, for which there seemed little provocation. "I allow no one my side." Then he paused abruptly, as though a new thought had entered his mind. He looked at Helen, who had risen courteously at his abrupt signal of departure.

When he spoke again the anger had left his voice, which had a note of hesitation, even of awkwardness, of which he had shown no sign previously. "If you like," he said, "I'll take the girl."

"I think not," Martin answered quietly. The proposal was as puzzling as it was audacious. It might be a jest, or a foolish insolence. But Martin did not judge the man as likely to err in such directions. In the present social disorder, it might even be taken as a serious offer of marriage. He might not understand the existing relationships.

Helen stood silent and self-possessed. A smile at the absurdity of the suggestion parted her lips. She was no more sure than Martin that she understood, but she felt no resentment. In fact, she liked being called a girl. She was proud of the youthful slimness which had survived the ordeal of motherhood.

Burman was quickly conscious of the ambiguity of his proposal. He added, "If you trust me, I'll trust you. She shall come back tomorrow, if the calm lasts."

"I think not," Martin repeated. "I trust you well enough, but the suggestion is unreasonable. There is no occasion for hostages. It would mean possible discomfort to no good purpose. If you wish to work with us we shall be glad; but, if not, I think you will be the loser."

"You offered to come yourself. I only want to be left alone." He appeared to realize that the proposal was hopeless, and attempted no further argument, but he was plainly disappointed at the refusal.

"I don't mind going," said Claire.

She spoke impulsively. The love of experience, of adventure, may have impelled her, but she was aware also that the impulse sprang from that clear and sudden realization that Helen would always be the "official wife." If she were to do her part to make a success of the strange *ménage* into which fate had thrown them, it was outside the house, rather than in it, that she must prove her value. It was fundamental that she thought less of what might be gained than given.

She had formed her own opinion of Burman, and did not fear him. Beyond that, she felt that there must be some reason for such a proposal, and she was of some curiosity to probe it.

Her words drew the glances of those around her in a surprise which was general.

Helen made an exclamation of protest. It sprang not only from a generous objection to an ambiguous and perhaps dangerous enterprise, but from a sudden realization that she wished to keep Claire beside her, that she was already relying, in an atmosphere of dimly apprehended dangers, upon the more buoyant and vigorous personality of this strange protagonist.

Claire looked to Martin as she spoke, and saw the assent which quickly followed his first surprise and reluctance. He would much rather have gone himself. He would have rejected the thought of Helen going alone, even had she been willing—which it would be difficult to imagine—with an abrupt finality. But Claire was different. He did not think that any treachery was intended, though there was an impression of mystery, which might prove to be of much account or of little.

The thought was in his mind that they had taken hands at a game which could not be played without risks, and that these risks would be greater should they hesitate to meet them boldly.

Burman looked directly at Claire for the first time. Previously, his attention had been directed to Martin: his admiration to Helen. His offer had been deliberate, with a motive which they could not know. It had been to take Helen. Not any woman who might offer.

Claire was conscious of a glance that was shrewd and penetrating. She felt that she was being comprehensively appraised, as might have been a heifer at Helford market six months ago. But it was too impersonal for resentment.

"I can't wait more'n a minute," he said, and Claire, rightly taking this for assent, answered, "I shan't be half," and went out of the room.

Helen followed her at once. They heard her voice, "You'll need—" as the door closed.

"She'll be quite safe?" Martin asked.

"Yes—if the calm lasts."

Martin said no more on that point. He had not been thinking of the danger of water.

A minute passed, and Burman glanced restlessly at the door. He was clearly uneasy at the delay.

"Sister?" he said abruptly.

In a few words Martin told him the true position, including the claim upon Claire which was being made by the rest of the community. He felt he could judge the man by how he accepted the confidence.

Burman gave no indication of his thoughts. "You won't loose her?" he queried.

"No. What I have, I hold. It is how they wish it to be.... I shall meet them with their own law 'The women choose.' We did not intend the position, but, it having arisen, it seems the only right thing to do."

Burman offered no opinion on the ethical aspects of the problem.

He said, "I'd back you'd come to in a scrap."

It was not all that was in his mind. He would have congratulated Martin on the fortune which had given him not merely a plurality of wives when his neighbours lacked them (which might not be universally regarded as an unmixed advantage), but upon the more evident fact that they both appeared to be of more than average quality.

But he was not a man of fluent speech, except upon farming topics. Had he attempted it, he would probably have remarked that they were both cup-winners, or commented favourably upon their potentialities of procreation. Which is not to say that he was a fool, which he certainly was not; nor that he was not a gentleman, on which it may be best to reserve opinion, but he had not, like Martin, made an occupation of the use of words.

He was an expert farmer—which is one of the most difficult and exacting of human occupations—and his vocabulary, like his seed-corn, was chosen for utility only....

Claire, being a woman, was more than the half-minute she promised. Had it been otherwise it would have been useless to write it, being incredible.

But, though she was more than half a minute, she was less than ten, which may be accounted for righteousness.

She had, in fact, little preparation to make, having improved her garments earlier in the day, to the extent that either Helen's or Betty's resources, and the extremity of her own needs, had rendered possible, and had had a moment's annoyance that Martin had not noticed the change.

During her present retirement she appeared to have done no more than to resume the belt of yesterday, with the knife and pistol which she had used to such good purpose in the tunnel fight of two days ago.

If she had made other provisions for the night's absence, they were not outwardly visible It must have been some months since her head had known anything but its natural covering against either rain or sun.

Burman looked at her belted ironmongery with more interest than satisfaction.

"If you don't come friendly—" he began.

"It's not for you, it's before," Claire answered, with sufficient clarity.

Burman nodded. "We'd best be moving," he said restlessly.

Claire followed him through the door, waving a hand of casual parting. "Back tomorrow.... Take care of the chestnut," her voice came back cheerfully through the closing door.

CHAPTER FORTY-EIGHT

"WILL she be safe?" Helen said doubtfully, as the sound of their steps receded. She was not quite easy in mind, feeling obscurely that Claire had taken a risk to which she had been invited, and which she should therefore have accepted if anyone were to do so.

This was unfair to herself, for there was no necessity for anyone to have done it, and it had been Claire's own proposal that she should go; but feelings are not logical. She was aware also, that Claire was better able to protect herself than she would have been in any possible complications.

Martin answered, "I think she'll be safe enough. It's queer that he should refuse my offer, and yet be willing to take a woman. There's something we don't understand yet.... I don't suppose she gave it a thought, but it's a fact that it removes her from the scene for the time, if Butcher or the others should try to make any trouble."

Helen recognized the cool quickness of mind which seemed to give Martin time for analysis and decision under any urgency of circumstance. She did not think of this, it was a familiar knowledge. It gave serenity to her own mind, though the "two hours before sunset" were already passing, and Butcher's threat was upon them.

Then Jack Tolley came, bringing a pheasant which he had shot, and this being delivered into Betty's capable hands, he came into the library.

"There'll be no trouble today," he reported. "There's been a heap of talk, and some quarrelling, but our lot knew their own minds, and the rest didn't. Briscoe talked big about what he'd do, and Pellow keeps quiet, and Butcher's trying to make all the trouble he can, without coming into the front row, but I think they mostly mean to wait to hear what you've got to say.... I think you'll get them all to the meeting.... It's what happens then that's going to settle it.... Pellow may need watching. He's quiet, and stubborn. His sister's married to one of Butcher's men.... He helped us turn Bellamy out. He's a good fighter.... But he wouldn't come with us this last time. I don't know why. He's hard to drive, but if he trusts you he'll come willing.... Tom's been after Burman. He thinks he might help."

He began to explain about Burman. Martin stopped him to tell him of what had happened, and of Claire's going.

Jack made no comment, being unsure whether he had been told all the truth, or what else might underlie her departure.

Martin asked if he could stay for a time. He had a project of compiling a complete register of the population of his new dominion, with details of each individual. In particular, what occupations they had previously followed, so that he could have a comprehensive knowledge of the human material at his disposal.

This was work to Jack's liking. He was used to the pen. He liked method. He would willingly stay for an hour, though he must then return to his own concerns.

They were on this work together, when Phillips announced that Butcher was again requesting an interview.

It was sunset without, and the shadowing of the room was already warning them that the work could not be continued much longer. The resources of the house did not include any provision for artificial lighting under the new conditions of life. It was a problem which was only beginning to become serious as the days were shortening.

"Yes, I'll see him," Martin answered. "I expect we've done for tonight," he added to Jack. "No. Don't go. You'd better hear what he's got to say this time.... Yes, of course you'll stay."

The last words were to Helen, who was reknitting a damaged garment for one of the children.

Butcher entered without formality. He pulled a chair up to the table, and sat down so that Martin was opposite him. He ignored the others.

"May I see you alone?"

The tone was something less than rude, but it lacked courtesy. It was not a command, but it assumed that assent would follow.

"I don't see any need for that."

"I think it would be better. There are one or two personal matters which I should like to talk over."

"I am willing to hear them."

"I would prefer to see you privately."

"I never see anyone alone now."

It was a decision made as it was spoken. Martin guessed that the man had come to propose some form of alliance, whether in good faith or treachery, and he had no mind that such a bond should be suspected between them. It was best that Jack should hear.

He thought that Butcher was annoyed and disconcerted, though he was too practised in control of voice and expression to disclose his feeling.

"Just as you like," he said easily. "I only thought you might prefer it, as it's a business talk. It doesn't matter on my side. I ought to tell you first that I succeeded in getting you the extra time you wanted. Though it wasn't easy."

He turned his eyes to Jack, who had made a half-articulate exclamation at this version of the events of two hours ago, but Jack's face was expressionless as he bent over his work, and he said nothing.

"I've got you the time you want," he repeated, with added emphasis. "But what happens when we meet can best be settled beforehand. If you want the girl, I don't say that it couldn't be managed. Or if you want to settle Cooper, and control things here in your own way, I don't say that mightn't be managed either. It needs someone. But if you want both, you'll ask too much, and you'll get nothing. If Tom's lot stand for it, there's too many others that won't."

He paused, as though for Martin to answer, seeking to gauge the effect he had produced. But Martin only said, "Well?" as though discussing a matter in which his interest was perfunctory.

Butcher went on, "You've got one chance. If it were known that Tom and I would both support you, you wouldn't have much trouble. Not at first, anyway. If you'll say what you really mean, I may find I can make a deal. I've come in a friendly way to talk it over."

"And if I won't deal you think you can head the opposition successfully?" Martin suggested.

Butcher shook his head.

"No, I don't quarrel," he said, "I've too much to do. But you'll fail without me. You can try if you like. You'll learn when it's too late."

"I shall not fail," Martin assured him confidently. "Don't let that idea mislead you. It might be a dear mistake.... What do you want?"

"I want to know what you mean to do," Butcher answered, with some reason behind him.

"I will tell you on Thursday."

"It won't do then. We must know before that."

"Tell me what you want."

Butcher did not find this easy to do. He really wanted an alliance with Martin which would have secured his commercial activities—an alliance preferably to be made in secret. But he was not yet willing to propose it plainly.

"If we were assured of peace and security—" he began.

"For what?" Martin interrupted curtly.

The interruption confused Butcher for an evident second. Then his practised suavity in negotiation resumed, and he answered readily.

"For our lives and property, and—"

"I couldn't promise you that. As for your lives, there may be men among you who may be needed, should I decide to deal with Cooper, or should he attack us again. There will be no security till he's finished, one way or other. And there'll certainly be no promise of security for those who don't help. Besides, there may be risks of other kinds to be undertaken."

"Then you would destroy all individual freedom? Do you think you can make military service compulsory? Even service for other purposes?" Butcher shook his head sagely. "Believe an older, and perhaps a wiser, man when he tells you that it couldn't be done. Even as things are, it couldn't last for a week."

Martin smiled slightly "You assume too much. I don't intend to make anything compulsory. You can join Cooper tomorrow if you prefer. The roads are open. But I'm not going to have my best men risk their lives, and perhaps lose them, for the benefit of those who do nothing. They'll do their part, or clear.

"Then as to property. How do I know what you have, or how you have gained it, or for what purpose it may be needed by others? Take an extreme possibility. Suppose the spring should come, and I should find that all the available seed for some necessary crop should be in your hands. What do you suppose I should do?"

"But if that were so, I should be prepared to sell it. It would not be reasonable to suppose that I should be holding it for any other purpose. Surely you would not support any man who would take it from me without payment? That would be anarchy. If you allow such things as that, no man will save anything. There will be no incentive to labour. You would reduce every man in the end to a common poverty. I suppose that you would support me in selling it at a fair price to those who would require it."

"At a price of your fixing?" Martin answered "Not for a moment." He leant forward, and spoke slowly and decisively: "Mr. Butcher, I would sooner hang you. If we are to work together at all, we must understand each other clearly. There will be no lack of incentive to work if I have my way. Every man shall have the fruit of his labour, and shall sell it at the highest price he can get. I have watched the other incentive—the incentive of starvation. I will have no man working on such terms that he has a scanty margin for himself after he has handed the bulk to others.

"You may sell your corn at your own price *if you have grown it with your own labour*. You may sell fish at your own price *if you have caught it with your own nets*. But not otherwise.

"That, at least, is how it seems to me that it will be best to have it…. But I may see reason to change my view. I cannot tell. You may barter for your own need, and I will protect you to hold what you gain, even though it may be coveted by others. But if you gain by barter that which you do not need, so that you may take a later advantage of the necessity of others, I may interfere to protect them… And there is one change about which there is no doubt at all.

"There will be no charging of usury. Not even though you label it 'interest,' and profess that its moderation renders it harmless. A spade today has the same value as a spade three years hence. To think otherwise is to support the subtlest and most devilish slavery that the world has known."

Butcher did not appear to resent this plain speaking, nor to regard its personal aspect. Rather, he appeared interested. He was adept at concealing his thoughts.

He said: "I have heard that kind of talk before, and it sounds well, but it won't work. You'll find you can't go far without capital in some form, and you can't use capital without some risk of loss, and you can't have risk of loss without some prospect of gaining. You'll find that's the real point, and I don't know how you'll get over it. But perhaps you do. I shan't interfere."

He spoke as one who listens to a youthful folly, such as can only be taught by experience. He did not oppose. He only advised— and smiled.

Martin did not answer directly. "There is a form which all who joined us agreed to sign." He saw that Jack had it in readiness. He passed it over.

Butcher's face was expressionless as he read it—twice, and very carefully.

At last he said, "If I sign this, does it mean that I adopt your views, or believe in the possibility of their success?"

"No. Naturally it cannot. I cannot control your beliefs, nor could you do so yourself. But you can control your conduct—as I might do; were it necessary. It means obedience. Neither more—nor less."

"And if I decline?"

"I shall do nothing till Thursday. After that, those who do not sign will go—how far I will tell you then. I may put them afloat."

"You can't do that; there are no boats."

Martin, who, for once in his life at least, had said more than he meant, thought it best to pass the retort in silence.

Butcher made no further comment. He wrote with practised ease a somewhat illegible signature, beneath the neat regularity of Jack's handwriting.

He rose immediately. He said, "You can have my name now. I won't wait till Thursday. You can tell the others I'm with you. You'll find my support's worth having. I'll say good-day now."

With no further ceremony, and giving no time for reply, he turned, and went.

Helen looked at Martin with troubled eyes. "Do you trust him?" she said doubtfully.

Jack was silent. His thoughts were on the implications of what Martin had said. Was it practical? He was more concerned with immediate troubles and necessities. Much of what Butcher had said sounded reasonable enough. What they wanted was order, forethought, and industry. Martin's ideas seemed too remote. He was not disloyal, but his mind remained open. He became aware that Martin was speaking.

"I don't trust him at all, beyond the point at which his interest may move with ours. I suppose he came here to insure his risk. That's a good sign. I don't think he'll be dangerously treacherous—not unless he were quite sure of our weakness. He may hope to use us in the end. I should say that he has patience to wait his chance.... Probably when I'm murdered and half-forgotten he'll still be trading.... But it's a good sign that he came. I suppose Cooper helps he prefers the whips to the scorpions. And he probably thinks he can outwit anyone who talks as foolishly as I do.... Even Jack thought I had more sense." He turned a sudden smiling glance to Jack Tolley with the last words. But though Jack may have been surprised to learn that his mind was read so clearly, he was not disconcerted.

He answered: "No, sir. Not quite. I'm not sure that I understood. But I expect you're right. I only thought that there are a lot of things that want doing before such questions will matter, if they ever do.... But I think you're right about Butcher. He thinks we shall have our own way, for a time, at least, and he didn't mean to be the last to come on to the winning side."

"What was my mistake about the boats?"

"Well, there aren't any. There was the one that Mrs. Webster came in, but it disappeared. And there were two others—none of them was fit for the sea. They all disappeared the same night. Then there was a sailing-boat washed ashore, badly damaged. Dick Pugh patched it up, and it went also. Every one thinks that Burman steals them, but there's proof."

"He seems enterprising," Martin commented. He would know more about him when Claire returned.

But the next day came, and though the sea was calm, Burman's boat did not appear at the expected hour, and Claire did not return.

CHAPTER FORTY-NINE

AS he went out of the gate Burman turned to the right. It was the opposite way from that which Claire had ridden in the morning, and she looked round with an alert inquiry as the walk proceeded.

The district had been well wooded, oak and ash lining the hedges, and copses of young timber and hazel-thickets filling the hollows.

Cottages had been scattered here and there, usually well back from the road, with occasional larger houses.

Now the trees were fallen or scattered, some of them still showing a valiant effort of green on their uprising branches, though their trunks were prone, and their roots were largely extruded.

They met a man of Butcher's with a skip of fish on his back. He passed a word of civil greeting to Burman, and gave a look of silent curiosity to his companion.

Claire judged that her departure would soon be known to others. She wondered whether any effort might be made to prevent it.

"How far is it," she asked, "to the boat?"

"Maybe a mile—maybe more," he answered.

"It's a pity we didn't use the horses," she said. "I suppose someone could have taken them back." She assumed that he could ride.

"You might have said so earlier. I didn't know you'd got any," her companion answered.

His pace was fast, even for Claire, and he seemed disinclined to talk.

He turned off from the road to the right at a broken stile. They went by a well-trodden hedge-side path, on which a young bull confronted them. It showed a red wound where it had been gored in the shoulder.

Driven from the herd by a parent twice its weight, and having been chastised for its presumption, it was in a mood to make trouble.

Its front hoofs pawed as they approached, and its head moved threateningly. Claire saw a red and sullen eye, and would gladly have turned aside, but Burman did not change his pace or direction. He had sent too many of its kind to the butcher.

Before it had made up a sulky mind whether to contest the path or to yield, it was aware of a rough push from a gun-barrel in its ribs, and a voice that made no doubt of who was master here. It turned away with a new confusion in its mind having had reason to suppose that the human race was of a somewhat softer kind. It concluded that it was a bad day for young bulls, which would have been confirmed had it understood the farmer's thought and the words that followed.

Claire was aware of some muttered contempt for the town-bred people who had made such an exhibition possible. Then he spoke aloud. "Understand cattle?"

"Not much," said Claire. "They seem to understand you."

"There's two hundred," he said, "to be found without going very far from here. Round them up. Keep the best through the winter. Kill and salt the others. Don't keep more than you'll feed when the snow comes."

He walked on in silence.

On their right was a field of oats, wind-beaten, cattle-trampled, lifting bare stems from which the grain had already fallen.

From it there came the piteous squealing of a snared rabbit.

"I can't stand that," said Claire. She forgot the haste of their progress, and made her way toward it.

Burman looked at her curiously, and followed.

Birds rose as they advanced, rooks, gulls, and other sea-birds, and a pair of magpies. Burman cursed audibly, seeing the dropped grain on which the birds had been feeding.

The rabbit had been snared in a run which crossed the field. Its cries ceased as they approached. They came on a woman kneeling. She pulled it out of the snare, and broke its neck with a practised hand.

"Why don't you catch them decently?" Claire asked.

She looked up startled. She had not heard them approach. "They're no odds," she said sullenly.

They looked down on a brown-skinned woman, with dark, furtive eyes. She wore a red silk skirt, very soiled and tattered. It was her only garment, unless a necklace of rubies could be said to increase the total. Her left hand had been injured, and three fingers were bent like a bird's claws.

Still kneeling to replace the snare, she looked up at Claire. She had heard of her already, though she had not seen her. She guessed who she was at once. Strange women were not numerous.

"Did you really kill him?" she asked.

"Kill who?" said Claire.

"They say you killed Bellamy."

"Yes, he's dead. Did you know him?" She did not suppose that anyone would have had an affection for Bellamy.

After Bellamy had been driven out the woman had chosen a placid, fair-haired giant, a miner named Vincent. She had chosen him because she liked big men. She had taken longer but not much) to learn that she disliked placidity.

The man came up as they were talking, two dead rabbits dangling from his hand, and a cudgel under his arm.

"Treat 'er cruel, 'e did," he said, pointing a thumb at the kneeling woman.

Stooping over the snare, she made Claire no answer. It was true that he had treated her cruelly. Her broken hand was his signature. Never would she forget the brutal strength which had subdued her, nor the sight of her weaker lover lying before them with a twisted neck, and the blood trickling from his mouth. The brutal strength that had held her...and she had his child in her body now.... How she hated the woman that had killed him!

Claire was sensitive of the unspoken antagonism. Conscious also of the falling twilight, and of Burman's urgency, she turned back to the path.

They came to a place where the land sloped down to the water. Here there had been a plantation of young firs, which had met the full force of the gale. A path had been cleared through fallen trunks and broken branches; otherwise they must have waded among them, for the storm had literally flattened them against the hillside.

Looking over dead, upstanding boughs, and green, upthrusting saplings, and weeds that often grew beyond her height in this incredible chance of unobstructed sun, Claire had short glimpses of familiar sea, until they turned right-hand, to descend a narrow eastward hollow, in which some of the smaller trees were still standing, and, as it widened, they came to the water.

The tide had turned an hour ago, and the boat, moored to a tree that grew at the water's edge, was straining on the rope that held it.

Two men rose as they approached, and began to haul her in. One of them was a stranger to Claire. The other was Monty Beeston.

They looked at Burman's companion with a natural wonder. Every one knew that visitors were not welcomed at Upper Helford. Perhaps she had deserted Martin for a more exclusive companionship. So they speculated silently.

There was a husky whisper from Monty as Burman dropped into the boat before her.

"Going willing?" he asked anxiously.

"Quite," she said. "Back tomorrow." She judged that the woman-hater would have been pleased to attempt her rescue had she denied it.

She jumped into a boat that swayed two feet below her.

The boat was small for the open sea, but heavy for a single rower. Burman had strength, but little skill. In fact, he had never seen a stretch of water larger than the local reservoir till the ocean paid him this unexpected visit.

They were in an alley of water less than twenty yards across, with wooded banks on both sides, from which they ran out quickly, as the tide drew them.

Burman was none too quick in getting the boat's head straight, and the sides of the narrow channel were perilous with up-jutting trees, which Claire could dimly see as she bent over the boat's side in the deepening dusk.

That was their first trouble. The water was full of obstacles. Burman had learnt a way of safety at full tide, but the last hour made a difference.

He told this briefly as they came clear of a little headland and the open sea was before them.

"Oh, I expect we shall manage," she replied, with unruffled cheerfulness.

"Can you swim?" he inquired.

"Yes—a little." The dusk hid the smile with which she answered.

"I can't," he said. He pulled harder. He watched the receding shore, using his left only.

Claire shipped the rudder, which had lain in the well of the boat.

"Tell me where to steer for, and we shall get on better," she suggested.

"Can you?" he answered, with relief in his voice, for which she could see no sufficient occasion.

She looked round. Behind them, the land they had left showed abrupt cliffs, amid which the little channel from which they had issued was no longer visible.

To north and east the falling night showed nothing but open sea.

On her left hand, as she sat at the tiller, was the peninsula, or island, of Upper Helford. At this state of the tide it was completely isolated.

Lower Helford was beneath their keel. At low tide it would be barely covered. Ruined buildings, not yet completely demolished, the broken spire of a chapel, and the head of a mine-shaft would show above the water.

The eastern shore of Upper Helford was steep, though its height was not great. The raw, new coasts that were being formed by sea and wind were very different from those that had endured for millenniums. There was no sand, no smoothness. Soft soils were still being subjected to swift corrosion. Their surfaces were fanged with numerous projections of wood and stone and metal from the remains of human activities, and with the stumps of broken trees.

He rested on his oars for a moment to give her the directions for which she asked.

It appeared that there was no place for landing on this side. They must go round the head of the peninsula, and land on its western coast.

Looking landward as he spoke, Claire noticed a herring-gull on the water, scarcely two oars' length distant. It was not troubled by their presence. It was not troubled by the waves. One by one they seemed to slide beneath it, and pass on, and leave it serene and indifferent. The east coast of Upper Helford was about a mile in length. Already they were almost level with its northern limit. Beyond it the summer sunset had faded, and a planet brightened. Every second that Burman rested the position of this planet altered, drawing closer to the dim lift of the land's edge.

"We are drifting fast—" she began.

"Yes," he said. "We left it too late." He started rowing again. "If you go for that star you'll be about right now. We'll have to keep close inshore as we go round, and risk it."

The seagull had not greatly changed its position. Claire wondered whether her imagination had deceived her, and they were not really drifting so rapidly—but perhaps the current took the bird also, though the waves appeared to pass beneath it.

The water was rougher here, and they had taken a little over the side as they had lain broadside to the waves, but they rode better as the oars moved again, and the boat's head came round to the rudder's urging. The gull passed into the darkness behind them.

To steer toward the light of a setting star may be a sound enough method, for a time, on a still water, but with the side drift which was pulling them out to sea the proposition was different. Still, the directions were clear, and they needed no star to guide them. She must round the land as closely as she dared (or as she could), and when they were on the western side it would be time enough to ask for more definite directions as to their landing-place.

The sea was not really rough. As they came round the headland they met a breeze from the south-west, but it was not enough to disturb it greatly. But now and then they would pass through a space of more turbulent water, and once Claire thought she heard the noise of breaking waves on her right. It was too dark now to see more than a short space around them, the shadow of the coast they were passing, and a few stars that were brilliant overhead.

"Is there any land to the north?"

"You'll see tomorrow," was the only answer.

Burman pulled hard. He was not inclined to talk. He was, in fact, very frightened. To every man his own perils. He would rather have faced the fiercest bull that ever breathed, with a cudgel for his defence, than been here, on this night of waters, of which he had learned just sufficient to dread them.

Nor was his fear entirely unreasonable. He knew that when the tide was high there was little current, and he could keep a track of a proved depth, and make an easy landing. He had found that every minute of delay made the current stronger, and increased the hidden dangers beneath him. He knew little of the power of the helm, or of the assistance that Claire could render.

Had he been alone he might have failed in a very difficult struggle. As it was, they made their landing well enough, at a spot where a row of pollard willows showed dim heads above the water; and passing these, and crossing a submerged field, where the oars touched bottom more than once, they turned into the deep pool of a little land-locked bay, and were hailed, as they grounded on a gravel bank, by a boyish voice from the darkness.

CHAPTER FIFTY

IT is easier to pull down than to rebuild, easier to criticize the building of others than to erect a superior edifice. Martin Webster, considering his plans for the improvement of the community on the second morning of the short interval which he had claimed for thought and decision, became aware of these differences.

It was easy to see the defects of the civilization that the seas had covered.

Its laws, with which he had been exceptionally familiar, and of the administration of which he had had experience at close quarters, were too numerous, too complex, and too costly. Some of them were inequitable, and some were stupid. Their general nature was such as to enable the privileged class which administered them to grow wealthy at the expense of the state upon which it preyed—a greed which had become so arrogant that the very head of the English Government had been content or obliged to accept a lower rate of remuneration than that which was required by the law officers whom he employed.

At least, he resolved, there should be no lawyers in his new state, if he were really destined to found it. A man should bring direct complaint; and a law should be so published and so worded that all should know and should be able to understand it.

Every one conversant with litigation, as Martin had been, knows that the rights of any dispute are rarely all on one side, and that it is often of minor importance on which side the verdict falls. It is only important that the dispute shall be settled promptly, and without oppression of the losing side.

English justice had been fair enough (with some important qualifications), but it had been dilatory, operated with a routine publicity which was often regardless either of the feelings or the interests of those concerned, and always ruinously oppressive to the side against which the verdict fell.

But these were defects of procedure or administration rather than of the law itself. They were defects of age rather than youth. They were such as, having seen their evils, he could avoid very easily.

The question of the new laws which he must formulate was larger and more difficult.

There was the question of the social and political position of women, which had agitated the newspapers and tea-tables of the past civilization. Some of the political aspects of that controversy would not recur, for he had no intention of passing over the decision of any question of moment to the chance majority of a general vote.... He had not supposed when he supported their claims to increase of freedom and opportunity, from generous instinct rather than a considered judgment, that he would one day be in a position to legislate upon them.

Might there not be evidence of difference, if not of inferiority, in the fact that he was in a position to do it?

The men had chosen a leader. The women had made no effort to do so.... Possibly the whole question would resolve itself without difficulty. Yet he was unsure. He had been taught to suppose that women live subordinate or even servile lives under primitive conditions, and that this is at once a result of barbarism, and a cause from which it continues.

Yet even this did not stand out as a clear fact when he examined it closely.

The advance of civilization (if advance had been) did not show a progressive advance in the position of women which ran parallel with it.

He remembered that basic allegory of human fate in the opening chapters of Genesis, in which women were warned that the pursuit of wisdom, the advance of 'civilization,' would rob them of the physical equality of a savage mating, and of the intellectual precedence which is usual among all the mammalia who have the care of the young to stimulate their mental processes.

Probably the radical cause of all resulting difference was in the loss of physical equality. The women made the men work, and the men gained by losing, which is the constant equity of creation. There was no fundamental reason why the female should be physically inferior. It was not generally true of monogamous animals or birds—usually the reverse.

Then should he tell the women to dig their way to equality? He smiled at the whimsical fancy, and sighed for the futility of all efforts of government. He could think much, but he knew that he would be able to do little

Even thinking was of doubtful value.

The ideas which seemed so simple, the faiths which seemed so sure—they would recede as the mind approached to examine them—recede faster than it advanced, until they were in an atmosphere of doubt and shadow.

He knew that if he had asked a hundred people of the drowned world behind him they would have assured him that the women of their time, whether for good or evil, had advanced into a wider freedom, a greater responsibility, than had been known before to the civilization of Western Europe.

Yet when he examined this assumption it became less obvious than he had supposed.

It might be just possible to imagine a Joan of Arc in the twentieth century. It would be more difficult to imagine an Ethelfleda of Mercia. It was not a question of capacity, but of opportunity. As warrior or as administrator, the woman of a thousand years ago seemed to have had opportunities which had not been kept or recovered.

So he vexed his mind with these and a score of similar questions, and a score of times he reminded himself that they could not be of an immediate urgency, and that there were things that were. And then, when he had doubted whether the fact that he could consume the vital hours in such speculations did not demonstrate his unfitness for the position he had assumed, he became doubtful of his own doubt, reflecting that though the first steps may not go far in any direction, yet it may be everything, in the end, that they should have started in the right one.

As his thoughts wandered thus, he went on with his examination of the books around him....

He opened a book on physical jerks, which was eloquent upon the advantage of lying on the bedroom floor and waggling the legs in the air before dressing every morning. Probably it had done good in its time. But it could go to Betty now. He hoped to provide his new subjects with some more useful activities.

He came to a shelf of poetry, which included most of the acknowledged masters of English song. He had never taken poetry very seriously. He was surprised, as he opened volume after volume, to realize how little difference the floods had made to the value of these, and that there could be no thought of destruction here. His glance fell on one of Robert Browning's lyrics, "Is she not pure gold, my mistress?" There was nothing obsolete here. "Many waters cannot quench love, neither can the floods drown it." Yes, the poetry must remain, because it dealt with the unchangeable things.

Here was a business directory of the Midland Counties. Surely that was a book which had ended its utility. He paused in the act of consigning it to the condemned heap. Might not its tabulated list of civilized activities prove a guide by which he might avoid the over-sight of any occupation which would conduce to the welfare of the new community?

He took the book to his desk, and settled to the task of analysing its contents.... It was startling to observe how few men had been engaged, even in the business circles with which it dealt, in actual production either of the necessities or comforts of life.

For this analysis, he divided them under general descriptive headings, such as Growers, Makers, Mongers, Feeders, Body-patchers, Housers, Furnishers, Heaters, Clothers, Movers, Teachers, Restrainers, Coercionists, Newsvendors, Assessors, Insurers, Stock-brokers, Bankers, Gamblers, Amusers, Lawyers, Credulity-profiteers. These main heading required much subdivision, as, for instance, the Body-patchers included Surgeons, Physicians, Chem-ists, Herbalists, Dentists, Chiropodists, Manicurists, Nurses, Ocu-lists, Hairdressers, Makers of Pills and Rouges and Powders, and many others.

He had finished this, and was compiling a second and much shorter list of the occupations which were of a really useful charac-ter, when Phillips announced that Mr. and Mrs. James Hatterley had called, and that the gentleman appeared very anxious to see him.

"Show them in, Phillips," he said, and the next moment found himself shaking hands with a small, wild-haired man, scantily and picturesquely attired, and wearing sandals of flexible leather, which he had made for his own use, with some demonstration of dexterity.

He introduced himself as a "Christian Socialist," and by other names which indicated the birth-dates rather than the nature of his enthusiasms, and discovered a mind of somewhat confusingly con-tradictory beliefs and theories, and of a very angular surface.

He indicated that he had come to accept Martin's authority, if he were satisfied of his spiritual soundness on various points of im-portance, but not otherwise.

Martin judged that he would himself have been quite willing to guide his neighbours to an earthly paradise, but had found them in-disposed to take him seriously.

His wife was a vague-eyed woman, with untidy hair. They were one of the rare cases of a man and woman having survived the first catastrophe together, and both outliving the succeeding days of pri-vation and violence. In this they must have shown some adaptability to circumstance, even though fortune may have done its share.

Martin let the man talk while he studied him, giving a sympathetic hearing, and, at times, acquiescence. Hatterley had a mind containing many ideas, with which it was littered untidily. He had intelligence without judgment.

Martin saw that he might be a very useful tool, if he could handle him successfully, but the handling might not be easy.

The man was of a perversely combative nature.

He had been a pacifist in the old days, ready to fight furiously for the right to deny the moral justification of fighting under any circumstances. He had abandoned this theory, under sufficient provocation; and one of Cooper's inefficients, whose neck was permanently awry, and who trailed a damaged leg, had been a source of discouragement to any whose complexes might otherwise have prompted them to attempt the acquisition of Hatterley's wife. That is how he would himself have stated the position. He had been the apostle of many crazes, and had believed that a study of complexes, and the interpretation of dreams with a fantastic grossness, could do something better than add a new jargon to European languages.

Martin found himself catechized as though he had been an election candidate—as, in fact, he was, though it was a candidature without a declared opponent, and one which it had been declared in advance would be asserted by force, if it should be necessary.

But force is clumsy and dangerous. To be obliged to appeal to it would be in itself a confession of failure. Martin preferred the mental weapons in which he had a trained efficiency. If he could make captures in single combats, such as this (for the lady was silent), he might hope to establish the new authority without serious opposition.

He learnt that his visitors slept in a hollow tree, and that they found it healthful. Mr. Hatterley was sure that a 'return to nature' would be equally beneficial for the rest of the community, who were showing a contrary tendency to re-erect their fallen dwellings, retarded only by indolence and incapacity.

Listening to the Hatterley gospel, Martin thought several things which he did not say. His mental processes were not eased by the happy faculty possessed by his visitor of confining his attention to one side of any subject with which he was occupied.

He knew that nature, having ruthlessly destroyed the more diseased or unadaptable of those that the floods had spared, was already giving a higher measure of health than they had previously known to those who had survived the ordeal. He could not tell that the same path might not be followed farther with advantage to the race, and perhaps to the individual also. But he was also aware that a king's palace is no more 'unnatural' than is a bird's nest or a fox's earth. They are all departures from 'nature.' They are all artificial adaptations of environment. And an ant-hill may represent a more complex, as it certainly represents a more lasting, civilization than any which has resulted from human congregations.

It also occurred to him, though he did not say it, that the supply of hollow trees suitable for family life might be insufficient to accommodate the population for which he was assuming responsibility.

But he pleased his visitor by agreeing that wood is a better and cleaner fuel than coal, that hand-craft is better than machine-craft, both in the quality of its products and its reactions on the producers, and that many things had been wrong in the past which men of exceptional intelligence should now combine to alter.

He learnt that James had been an ardent believer in the advantages of a diet of bananas and nut-butter, of which the supplies had failed, but he was still an aggressive vegetarian. He suggested that the possibility of producing butter from hazel-nuts should be promptly investigated. He admitted that in the urgency of the interval he had become a drinker of milk, and had eaten eggs. Even fish at times.... But he appeared to look to Martin to save him from the necessity for any future depravities.

Martin replied that it was a subject to which Mr. Hatterley had probably given more thought than he had himself (James looked pleased), and he would always be glad to take it over with him as opportunity might allow. But he thought it would be inexpedient— indeed, impossible at the moment—to attach any penal consequence either to the consumption of milk, or the catching of rabbits. He pointed out that, while cows should remain, calves would continue to be a very natural consequence. About half of them would always have a radical incapacity for the production of milk, and they would almost certainly be destroyed at birth, were there no prospect that they would be eaten at a later stage of their existence, and—from their point of view—the advantage would be less than obvious.

As to the separate question of the suitability of flesh as an article of human diet, he pointed out that he was again confronted by the fact that it existed, for the moment, abundantly, whereas many alternative articles of diet were restricted or entirely lacking.

He concluded, "But I shall want your help in matters which are more urgent, and may be very difficult."

If Mr. Hatterley were not entirely satisfied, he had the sense to see that he had got as much as he could expect, and a more open-minded reception than he could hope to meet from any other possible authority. Also, he did not like some aspects of the life of the last few months. He had felt rather hunted. He was about to say that Martin could enroll his support; when the lady spoke for the first time.

"We're a lot better for the milk," she said definitely.

Hearing the tone, and observing that the man accepted the dictum without protest, Martin modified his first impression. There might be more character here than was suggested by the surface indications of her colourless and rather loose-boned structure. He reflected also that few women are vegetarian at heart, whether because they are more sensible than men, less sensitive, more selfish, or more naturally carnivorous.

Perhaps it may only be that they are dominated more absolutely by the herd instinct. They are never quick to believe that a majority can be wrong. They are rarely willing to face singularity for a theory. Beyond that, they are less moved by generalities. To excite their sympathies you must not talk to them of cattle, but of a particular cow, and, if possible, it should be one which they have seen quite recently.

This difference may show that women have less imagination than men, or, at least, that some women, of one race, at one time, may have had less.

Whether this difference had been fundamental, or the result of lives of more limited opportunity, was a question on which civilization had been experimenting when the flood had offered its own solution to all its problems. Perhaps now.... Martin became aware that his thoughts had wandered.

His visitor was talking about cows.

"Not so much as you might suppose," he was saying. "Some people have got cows that are milking well, but more of them are going dry because they haven't been properly milked or fed. If they're shut up in a byre they're a lot of trouble to feed, and if they're left in the fields they break out sooner or later and join the wild ones.... Most of the wild ones have got calves now, but it's not safe to go near them.... Gerda can." He looked at his wife with approval.

"They don't mind me," she said, with the same definiteness as before.

Martin felt that the subject of milk was exhausted.

He had a thought that he might find a use for these people, which would remove one from the list of the immediate things that he had resolved to put in hand.

He left his desk, and went over to the table, inviting his visitors to come forward also. He spread out a large-scale map of the county, with which the library had supplied him. He pointed to Helford and Cowley Thorn, indicating the coast as they knew it.

He went on, "We suppose, from many evidences, that we are on an island of very limited area, but even that we hardly know as a fact. Of this supposed island we are familiar with the north-east corner. Some of us have been down the east coast, the length of which is about sixteen miles in a straight line. From the south-eastern corner I know myself that the land is flooded as far as sight extends. There are some who have penetrated inland for ten miles or more, and have found little but deserted country, and the ashes that once were towns, but they have not reached a farther coast.

"The man we captured from Cooper's gang says that they have gone farther in search of horses with the same experience.

"Now what I want is someone who will follow the coast completely round, and who will have sufficient intelligence to make a reliable report upon it.

"Would you do this?

"It may be difficult, or even dangerous.

"It seems unlikely that we are the only people living, particularly along the northern coast, of the extent of which we know nothing. But you will notice this. Beyond Helford there was the high common of Cranleigh Chase, extending for about seven miles, and for that distance there was no north-ward road. Beyond that, the principal main road runs east, north-east, and would not be generally chosen for a northward flight. But if the northern coast extends to, or beyond, that point, there may be as many people there, or more, than we have here.

"Anyway, it is best to know."

James Hatterley looked at his wife. Evidently, he had no thought of going alone. But he looked eager. A new project excited him.

His wife said, "Yes, we'd do that." She looked pleased also.

Martin was well content. They would do it more intelligently than most, and they might be a nuisance at close quarters during the next few weeks.

James Hatterley had a somewhat similar thought. He considered that Martin's supporters might have some strenuous experiences before them, which he had no passion to share. But he understood wilderness living, and keeping to cover when safety required it

Let him have a tracing of the map, and he would mark the coast-line upon it. If it were no more extensive than they supposed, he should be back in a fortnight—perhaps sooner.

They went off in a very satisfied temper, leaving Martin to wish that he could find congenial work for all his new subjects with an equal ease.

CHAPTER FIFTY-ONE

AS the boat grounded Claire saw a boy's form appear vaguely out of the darkness, with an exclamation of reproach for the lateness of the return, which was checked abruptly—no doubt, she thought, as her presence was recognized.

"It's all right, Chris. Tie her up now, and come on. We'll talk at the house," said Burman, as he lifted a small sack from the bottom of the boat and led the way into the darkness, with Claire behind him.

"Careful here," he warned her, a moment later, as he began to mount some steps in a confronting wall of blackness. "There's no rail, but you'll be right if you follow close."

She could scarcely see the steps, but she realized the advantage of 'following close' under such circumstances, and did her best to keep pace with one who climbed an accustomed way. It seemed that the steps, which were of wood, ran up the side of a cliff that rose like a wall, so that she could steady herself with a hand that pressed against it as she climbed.

It was lighter as they gained the top, and followed a narrow path between bushes of prickly gorse—a path that began to descend, after a stile had been crossed, and came to a field where cows bulked dimly, to some farm-buildings, and beyond these to the farmhouse itself.

It was not more than five minutes' walk, and they were entering the kitchen as Chris joined them after securing the boat.

An oil-lamp was just alight on the table, and Burman turned it up, showing a low, oak-beamed room, with a large and ancient hearth.

"I thought you'd need it tonight, Dad," said the voice behind them.

"We haven't had a light yet. We go to bed when it gets dark," Burman explained. "We save here."

Claire was conscious that she was being inspected with some curiosity, and that introductions were lacking.

"I expect your son—" she began.

"Daughter," Burman corrected.

"Your daughter is rather surprised that you've brought a visitor."

"She's very glad to see one," said Chris. "I expect you're hungry. Dad's usually starved when he comes back."

Claire explained that they had had a meal not very long before, but Burman dismissed the idea. Chris would fry them some ham and eggs. He sat down heavily in a fireside chair, after inviting Claire to one that was opposite. He had rowed hard, and was feeling exhausted by the physical effort, and by the strain of his fear that they would have been driven out to sea.

"We'll leave talk till tomorrow," he said, but whether he spoke to her or to his daughter Claire could not tell. She was content to be silent herself, and to observe the ways of her new acquaintances.

She watched Chris, adroitly active with the frying-pan, and decided that she would still have taken her for a boy, had she not been informed differently.

The girl may have guessed the observation which she was receiving, for she looked round at Claire, and saw her clearly for the first time in the light of the leaping fire. For the lamp only illuminated the table, and made the shadows visible round it.

Meeting Claire's eyes, she broke into a moment of laughter.

"They're Sam's," she said. "Some he left. I looked awful in them at first, but I've filled out since then."

She still looked slim enough.

"I was just his height, so they don't do so badly now.... I suppose you're staying with us tonight, but I don't know where we shall put you up. I don't expect Dad thought of that."

The words might have seemed inhospitable if spoken differently. But they held a light-hearted friendliness which robbed them of ungracious meaning.

Her father, who had been considering the problem for the last few minutes—it was true that he had not thought of it earlier—was relieved to hear it mentioned.

"There's good straw over the hen-loft," he ventured with some timidity.

"She can't sleep there, Dad."

232

"She's slept on worse than straw," said Claire. "It sounds heavenly." She yawned as she spoke, for it had been a long day of some incident, and she was conscious of a healthy tiredness.

"We can't do better for tonight, Chris. Now can we?" her father asked.

Claire thought of a time, not many months ago, when she had slept on a bare patch of land that the seas submerged daily—slept till she was washed by the returning waves, and had to leave her haven for that last swim that had so nearly ended…. She made it clear that the straw would not be unwelcome.

* * * * * * *

She had promised not to leave the loft before Chris should call her, lest the men should be surprised at her presence, but the undertaking was needless, for she was still sleeping when the noise of the pushing-up of the trap-door disturbed senses which had become alert, even in sleep, to the danger of surrounding movement.

She half rose from the depths of the clean straw in which she had buried herself as Chris advanced toward her.

"No, don't get up. I want to talk to you here. I've got ten minutes. I've told Ned that I shan't take him out today unless he does the pig-feeding. I shall have breakfast ready in half an hour. You won't take that long to get ready. That's the best of sleeping like that."

She sat down on the floor, chin in hands, elbows on knees, and regarded Claire attentively. She gave a little sigh of relief.

"I'm not going to ask you anything now. I know Dad wants the first innings. But I want you to promise that you'll tell the real truth, whatever Dad asks you to say."

Claire said, "I don't know what you mean, but that sounds easy to promise."

"Then you do promise?"

"Yes, I'll promise that."

"Then that's all right. Can you fish?"

"Not particularly. Why?"

"Because I'll take you out later on, and we can talk then. You'll have to see Grandmother first…. I mustn't stay now. Breakfast's in the kitchen. I've told the men you won't shoot them."

"How many men are there?"

"Two. Three, if you count Ned."

"Is that all there are of you?"

"Yes—except Grandmother. The boys wouldn't stay. That's why I've got Sam's clothes. They're better for some things—and they save mine. I don't know when I shall get any more. We don't get much for the fish besides tea and tobacco. Dad doesn't mind— he says it's safer.... But I mustn't talk about that yet.... I really must go now."

She jumped up lightly, and disappeared down the ladder. Then her head appeared again, as she called out, "Come inside in two minutes, and I'll have some hot water ready. That's what I came to say. We're not really savages."

Claire followed a few minutes later.

CHAPTER FIFTY-TWO

AFTER breakfast, before the talk with John Burman which was to explain the purpose for which he had invited her, Claire had sat for more than an hour with his mother, a bedridden woman, obviously of great age, but with her faculties still clear, and had guessed something of the trouble from the anxious questioning which she had encountered, and the allusions to the granddaughter which had recurred continually.

Anyway, she was not kept in doubt when he began. He came to the point immediately.

"Well, ma'am, you've seen how we live, and how few we are. You can guess how we'd have fared if we'd not kept to ourselves. But it's the girl that's the trouble. No one knows that there's one here, and I don't mean that they shall. Not till times change, anyway. She's quite safe here, though she's a bit too free with that young lout she takes out to the fishing."

"But she's only a child," said Claire.

"She's not as young as she looks. She was at college last spring. Came home for Whitsunday, or she wouldn't be here now. Her brothers cleared, but she chose to stay.... Well, she doesn't like being cooped here.... The fishing kept her quiet for a time. That was her idea.... She used to go fishing in Cornwall.... So when I found a sailing-boat that we could patch up—I don't let them keep any boats on the other side she started fishing with a net we used for the beasts.... But she's done better than that now.... Well, she promised me she wouldn't go over to the other side, nor be seen on this—not that that would matter so much in those clothes she's wearing now, and she'll keep her promise right enough while it lasts, but she's saying every day now that it won't last much longer.

"She knows there's hundreds on the other side, and things happening, and she feels out of it all. When I tell her how things are, she thinks I just talk to scare her. I thought if she heard the same tale from you she might learn that older folk know best.

"She's just a child, as you say, and I wouldn't have her see what's going on on that side, not if she were as safe as a church.... But you'll know what to tell her better than I, and maybe she'll hear reason from you."

"You want me to tell her just how things have been, neither better nor worse?" asked Claire. "Well, I'll do that. But I hope they'll be better soon. You won't want to keep her here alone if we get them straight? She can't be here all her life, can she?"

John Burman did not look very pleased at this suggestion. The fact was that, real though his anxiety for his daughter might be, he valued his isolation on other grounds. He might value his daughter most, and he had no doubt of the sincerity of the motive which he expressed, but he also valued the farm which his ancestors had held for four hundred years. True, there had always been the obligation of the annual rent to be paid to the owner at Helford Grange, but it was centuries since there had been any difficulty about discharging that, or any thought of the possibility of being dispossessed from the property that they had held so long.

He answered, doubtfully, "We must talk of that when it's done. We'd best take things as they are now. I'll be glad enough to see them changed, but it's not done yet."

"I think there's going to be a change, and I think it's coming soon," said Claire confidently. "But there may be trouble first, and I'm sure Chris is best out of it. I'm quite willing to tell her that. You'd better keep Ned ashore. I shan't want him listening. We'll have a good talk in the boat."

"You think you'll manage?" he said, rather doubtfully. "Ned's a handy lad, and she's taught him a good bit."

He was not quite sure what the nature of this conversation, which required no auditor, was going to be.

"Yes, I can promise that. I'm quite used to boats," she answered easily. She remembered the worry of the night before, which she had thought so needless.

He looked at her speculatively.

"Did you kill Bellamy, as the talk goes?" he surprised her by asking.

"More or less, I suppose. There wasn't much choice," she answered. Would everyone always look upon her, she wondered, as having blood on her hands? If they could only understand how easy—how inevitable—it had all been.

"I shouldn't like her to get those kind of ideas," he said vaguely, but Claire knew what he meant.

CHAPTER FIFTY-THREE

"YOU'D better let me steer, if you can manage the sail," Chris said, "the wind's right, but it's only at one spot that we can get her over Low Meadow, even with a good tide."

Seen by daylight, the little harbour, in which were moored the fleet of boats which Burman had collected, was a gravel-quarry, into which the seas had poured on its lower side, so that the water which it contained was much deeper than that of the flooded fields over which the waves had advanced to fill it—fields which Chris still called by the names which they had borne for a dozen generations in the mouths of her ancestors.

Claire saw the wooden steps which she had climbed in the darkness, an old disused flight to the level of the higher road, which had become the only means of reaching the part of the quarry-floor which remained unflooded.

The fishing-boat was small, but stoutly built, lugger-rigged, such as were common on the Welsh coasts, being hired to visitors for summer sails, and used for fishing at other seasons. It was not difficult to handle, but it drew more water than the one on which Burman was accustomed to visit the mainland, and there was reason for Chris's sigh of relief as they left the willows behind them, and felt the stronger breeze of the open sea.

The wind blew from the south-west, scarcely enough to roughen the water, which lay to westward, with an unbroken surface sunlit and placid, but northward it showed ridges and knolls of land, too low and small and sea-swept for any human use.

The boat went smoothly onward, keeping to the edge of the shallower water, Chris talking all the time of the flooded land beneath them. "That's the hundred-acre that we've just left. Dad'll never forgive the sea for taking his two best meadows. You wouldn't believe the amount of hay we used to get off them every summer. I don't, anyway. It gets more every time Dad talks about it.

"There used to be three poplars," she went on, "where it ended. They were in Barton's field, not ours. I suppose they're flat now. Sam climbed one, and carved his name on the top, one holiday. He said I daren't, and I went half-way up, and came down again. I thought I should get blown off when the tree swayed. When he'd gone back to school, I tried again on a quieter day, and got up to where he had. The top looked farther off than it had done from the ground, but it was a good height. I meant to put my name over his, but it seemed mean when he'd gone back, and couldn't try again, so I put it just level. They're dirty trees to climb.... Yes, it's quite safe. There's quite a channel. It was all low along Bishop's Lane.... I've promised Dad I'll never go out where they could see us from Cowley Common.... Besides, it's here I get the best fishing, where the level keeps changing.... I don't know why, but I know where they come up.... Oh, it's safe enough. I've been aground once or twice, but I've got off. Dad doesn't worry. He thinks a boat's safer with a sail.... But I wish I'd learnt to swim.... Could you really? I should love to learn.... We're not going to fish today. We'll just anchor, and talk.... Have you really had such ripping times? You looked as jolly as a pirate when you came in last night."

"Some things are jollier to talk about than to live through," Claire answered. "It's been a hateful time, and it looks as though there's more trouble ahead. You'll never know how lucky you've been to be out of it. Fighting isn't jolly, except in books. It isn't jolly to get killed. It isn't jolly to hurt others, and watch them die. And it isn't jolly to know that your friends may be getting hurt or killed to protect you."

"I don't care," said the girl; "it isn't jolly to know things are going wrong, and not to be able to do anything to help, or to know what's happening. You might better be dead than that. You're just as dead as though you'd got killed, and you feel meaner."

"I know how you feel, but I think your father was right, all the same. You couldn't have done any good, and it's he who might have been in danger, if they'd known you are here. I hope things are going to be better, but if you understood how they have been—"

"How can I, when Dad won't say a word he can help, except 'promise not to be seen'? They can't be killing each other all the time; they'd be dead before now instead of eating a boat-load of fish every time I catch it."

"I'll tell you all I've seen, and all I've heard. You ought to know for yourself."

"I thought you looked the right sort.... Luff a bit. We can anchor in that pool.... That's about it.... There's no hurry about getting back.... There's some food under the seat."

So they sat and talked—or rather Claire did—a narrative broken by a battery of eager questions, till she became uneasy at the sight of the waning day, and remarked that it must be time for them to return.

Chris assented easily, but her comment on the information she had received did not suggest that the desired impression had been very deeply made.

"Golly, what a lark it all is!" she said gaily, "But you don't know everything. Nor Dad. I've got something to show you when we get back, if you'll promise not to tell."

"I'm afraid I shall have to go home when we get back. It's getting late now."

"You can't get back tonight. It's too late already."

"I'm afraid I must. I promised definitely."

"Well, you couldn't. Not till tomorrow. It wouldn't be possible for Dad to get the boat back. You don't want him drowned, do you? Besides, I really have something to show you. Something you'd never guess."

CHAPTER FIFTY-FOUR

THE following morning Burman came with the morning tide, which was not his custom, bringing a note from Claire.

DEAR MARTIN,

If I'm not needed, I may stay a day or two longer, but let me know if I am, and I'll be back this afternoon. I've got something on here rather interesting, and it might possibly be important, but I'll explain it when I get back. I am quite safe and well. Love to Helen, and, of course, to yourself. Kiss the babies for me.

CLAIRE

Martin sent a brief answer that there was no need for her to return till she wished. Perhaps, he thought, if she stayed away over Thursday it might not be a bad thing. The note was cheerful. He knew that she could take care of herself.... And he was finding already that he had little time to think of anything which was not forced upon him, little for his recovered children, little even for Helen....

Jack had come again, with a surprising amount of neatly tabulated information. He had prepared a census of the known population, with names and descriptions, and had found it to be somewhat larger than had been previously estimated, and even more disproportioned.

Excluding Cooper's gang, who were regarded as outlaws, and those at Upper Helford, whose numbers were not certainly known, it summarized:

MEN*WOMEN*CHILDREN

In and round the Railway Camp—54/33/5
Larkshill and beyond—40/23/7
Cowley Thorn and the North Coast—98/39/8
At Helford Grange—9/4/0
Scattered—107/56/11

Totals—308/155/31

Martin left him congenially occupied in tabulating these records, with notes upon the past actions, characters, and capacities of each individual, and analyses of the support or hostility which they were likely to offer, while he rode over to the railway camp, the condition of which, and of the surrounding country, he was anxious to see.

He went alone, having told no one of his intention, not even those of his own household, till the moment of starting. He realized that he must now move abroad at some personal risk, not knowing what secret enmities he might have excited, or what plots might be contrived against him. A shot from the hedge-side, finishing his activities, might be a welcome solution to others beside Butcher, of whom he did not judge that such a form of argument would be probable, unless at a more vital emergency. But such risks must be taken, and they would be lessened if he should make it a rule not to let his movements be known beforehand.

The brown gelding on which he rode was Claire's gift to him. He thought with satisfaction of her captures. Apart from Cooper's gang, he had observed no use of horses for riding. It would give prestige, as well as mobility, for his own household to use them. He decided to secure one for Helen. Perhaps one of those captured in yesterday's skirmish would be available.

He kept to the main road through the ruins of Larkshill, meeting no one, and came to the fallen elm, where his horse took the jump well enough, though unwillingly. He passed the narrow, weed-choked entrance to Bycroft Lane.

Beyond that point, where the Larkshill Road bent to southward, Jack had warned him that it was blocked by the fall of a factory, and other obstacles, and that he would make the better progress by a field-path which he would find on the west side of the road, and which he must cross again at a lower point.

He found this path easily. It was narrow, but worn hard. There were no impediments of gate or stile. They had not been removed, but avoided by the more slovenly expedient of diverting the pathway through the broken hedges.

Even to Martin, who had a trained faculty of observation, though he had not the eye of a farmer, the state of the fields was appalling.

Had it been merely told, it might have sounded incredible. Four months ago they had been tamed and planted. The pastures had been grazed green and smooth, or enclosed for cutting. In the arable fields the roots were sown or the corn was springing. It did not seem possible that four months' neglect could have made so great a difference. But they had been the four months of the year into which the most part of its growth is crowded. And hedge and fence, having been gapped and broken by the storm, and breached by the cattle, had ceased to give the old protection.

Then it must be recognized that the land, for the most part, had' been negligently farmed, and was far from having been 'clean of weeds in the spring-time.

The farmers of those last days had been dispirited, and many' of them were too near the edge of insolvency to provide the minimum of labour which was still recognized as necessary. The standard of good farming had been reduced with the substitution of machinery for the men and horses of cleaner days. The fields were persuaded to a bare fertility by the use of chemical dressings. The crowded urban populations lived mainly on imported foods, and were governed by those who sought their votes rather than their security or their welfare, and were content for these conditions to continue.

Faced by such a position, it could not be said that the farming community had done its best to overcome it. They remembered bitterly the brief years of war-time prosperity which they had been allowed to experience. By successive manipulations of a paper currency, the Government of that day (whether intelligently or under the blind control of those interests that would ultimately enrich themselves) had given a temporary prosperity to the farming and trading communities, which had been cynically withdrawn as soon as they had served their purpose. Many farmers had been induced by these conditions to purchase their farms with an inflated currency, and had mortgaged them to their bankers for a fraction of the cost, but which was really their entire value, to enable them to complete such purchases. They had mortgaged them at the price of a hundred head of cattle, not guessing that three years later it would require the sale of two hundred to repay the debt. They did not understand how they had been cheated. They looked upon it as on the operation of some obscure natural law beyond human control. And the banks thrived.

It is to be said also that they did not work as their fathers had done. They talked more, while the land lay neglected. They crowded to the great shows, parking their motors in hundreds while they discussed their grievances and lamented their poverty—and the silent evidence of the motors condemned them. Vehicles for which few sections of the community had less real need, and which represented all the forces which were inimical to their prosperity, as well as a national waste of energy which had reached the verge of insanity....

It was not a summer that had lacked fertility. In the fields where Burman had toiled in Upper Helford, though he had been short-handed through the loss of his sons, and diverted by many urgencies, hay and corn had been heavy in yield beyond precedent—perhaps, in part, because the haze of dirt which had hung in the air of the English Midlands since his boyhood had at last been lifted, and the white clouds parted to skies of deeper blue than could have been seen before in ten years' watching.

Elsewhere they were fertile also, but they were weed-choked, trampled, and infested with vermin; and flocks of sea-birds, forsaking their accustomed diet, fed freely on the ungarnered grain....

Martin got no sight of his goal till he came to the limit of a field which a tall hedge bounded. Even mounted as he was he could see little beyond it, except at one point, where it was broken at the top of a steep bank down which a man might clamber, but a horse could not easily be ridden. At the foot of the bank he saw that he was back again upon the edge of the Larkshill Road, with what had been a line of straggling cottages upon its farther side, on which the ground did not rise from the road-level.

Of these cottages nothing now remained but scattered mounds of bricks, where the searchers for any likely plunder had turned them over. Beyond them the country was flat, and he could see over it for some distance. At one point he thought that there was a glint of sea.

Four months ago the scene on which he looked had been one of the saddest products of the folly and greed of man that have ever repulsed the light on which our lives depend. Ruined ironworks showed ahead: a pit-head or two to the northward. Ground spread with the unseemly entrails of earth responded slowly, even now, to the wooing of sun and rain, and only patches of the coarser weeds had attempted its conquest. The bricks of fallen buildings, even though they had escaped the flames, were so blackened by the dirt to which they had become native that they showed as though charred by fire. Between the ruins of the ironworks and the nearest pit-head—perhaps half a mile away—he thought he recognized signs of the encampment to which Jack had directed him. A trodden path which showed in that direction, straight ahead, and almost at right angles to the road beneath him, confirmed this supposition.

He turned his horse to the right, seeking a place at which he could descend to the road in safety.

The hedge was high in places, but lower at others, so that there were times when he could see the road, as he kept closely beside it.

Looking down thus, he saw a man standing. He could not see his face. He was well grown, but he gave an impression of youth. He was standing in an obvious uncertainty He went a few paces along the road, and then returned. His foot kicked the ground on which he gazed. He twisted in his hands a stick of some pliable wood, which bent without breaking.

Farther down the road there came the lilting sound of a banjo.

Martin continued his way. He stopped again when he came to the spot from which the music proceeded. Here there was a green recess in the bank, and the hedge was gapped, as though some creatures, man or animals, had found that the side was not too steep to clamber.

In the hollow, half sitting, half lying, was a young woman, with a banjo on her lap.

She did not see Martin, who looked down on her at leisure.

The sight was pleasant enough. She was of attractive aspect, and she was evidently well content both with herself and the world.

She wore no hat, and showed a head of black and glossy curls, lightly restrained by a green ribbon.

Her dress, though not innocent of crease and stain, was very brightly coloured. Slim, extended legs were silk-stockinged, and her shoes however acquired) were neat and new.

She strummed the banjo idly, humming snatches of song between which she bit into an apple which lay half eaten beside her. Footsteps sounded on the road, and she looked up doubtfully As she recognized them a frown darkened her face, and her lips set sullenly.

"So you're here," said the youth that Martin had seen already, pausing at the gap

The needless information obtained an answer of equal brevity. "And here I'll stay." She touched the banjo to a defiant note.

Martin saw his face. A mere boy. He was five years younger than she—perhaps more. He had a face which was naturally good-tempered, but was now distorted by a combination of anger and misery.

He stood irresolutely, and she added, "You'd better clear. You won't get much if you stay." Then, as he stood silent, he added, "You get me what I told you, and then we'll talk."

"You know I've—" he began.

"Ada's got two," she answered.

"I don't know why you chose me, and treat me like—" he began again. "

Those that choose can change," she interrupted quickly.

"I'd see you dead first."

"You're the kid!" she mocked.

His glance fell on her left arm. She drew it back quickly. It had three bracelets on it, of which the lowest flashed with a setting of diamonds. He stepped forward and seized the retreating arm, drawing it roughly upward.

"Stop it, Will! You're hurting!" she said angrily.

He took no notice. His fingers went under the bracelet, breaking it off her arm in two pieces, and the next moment the fragments of the gaudy toy were flung over the road into the farther ditch.

"You can tell Steve he'll go the same—" he began, but did not finish, for she had swung round her other arm and struck him on the face.

"And now you'll get it," he said.

He had got a good grip of her before she guessed his purpose, but, when she did, there was a moment of furious struggling, with screams of protest. "Will, you brute! I'll tell Tom Aldworth!"

The invocation was unfortunate.

"Tom told me to do it. He said, 'Do it well, if you don't want it to end in murder'." His voice, though somewhat breathless, was almost apologetic, but he had got her well over his knees, and the stick was descending.

Martin did not move. He was not at all sure that there would be wisdom in interference. In the end he might be thanked by neither.

The woman was now screaming abuse and protest, mingled with shrill cries as the strokes caught her.

But he only held her down the harder and pulled her farther over, to operate on the back of the stockinged legs.

"Tom said, 'Do it well'," he repeated, with the same note of apology to her protests. But when her tone changed to a note of pleading, and "I didn't mean it, Will. I didn't mean anything.... I won't do it again. I won't really," and the blows paused, Martin judged it time to leave the scene unnoticed.

If they might not have thanked his intervention, still less would they have been likely to welcome the knowledge that there had been a spectator of this domestic difference.

CHAPTER FIFTY-FIVE

MARTIN rode on thoughtfully. Here was another aspect of the dearth of women and its results. "Those that choose can change." He; wondered whether Tom's legislative wisdom had provided for that contingency. The young man known as Will was a stranger to him, though he judged that he was one of Tom's party. He had not joined the expedition against Bellamy. Probably he had been among those who had feared to leave their women unguarded—not, it seemed, without reason.

He was glad that he had observed the incident and retired unnoticed. Knowledge is power. To those who rule it gives the power to act with wisdom. Accurate knowledge is the greatest need of those who would guide others wisely or rule with justice. And the more absolute the power the more difficult it is to obtain information which is accurate and unbiased.

The power of knowledge is greatest when it is unsuspected. The realization of this was the second lesson in the isolation which he had chosen.

He came to a place where field and road drew to a common level, and a fallen gate was little obstacle to his passage, though his horse must step with caution among its broken bars.

He decided to ride back to the point at which he had first struck the road, and take the path which had shown on the farther side. It would be the quicker way in the end. He considered his horse's feet.

The pair whose vocal and physical arguments he had observed must have heard his approach before he could have seen them. He passed at a quick trot, not looking toward their retreat. But he was aware that they were close together, and he thought that the man's arms were round the woman, whose face was hidden.

He found the path easily, and walked his horse forward, for it was not wide or clear enough for any speed to be ventured.

A short distance ahead he saw three men. They were not coming toward him. They were stooping round something at the side of the path.

They rose as he approached, and he pulled up to speak to them. Two he knew already. They were out for a day's shooting, or trapping, and had rifles under their arms. Martin wondered (as Jack had foretold) what reserves of ammunition were available, and if there had been any thought to conserve it. Suppose that the only remaining quantities should be in the hands of Cooper or Butcher? That, like a thousand other things, must be the subject of a prompt inquiry.

The third man was a stranger. Hearing him called Steve, and supposing him to be the giver of the bracelet, Martin looked at him with speculation. He was a sallow-skinned man. Young enough, but a growing baldness had caused him to protect his head from sun and flies with a coloured handkerchief, knotted at the corners. With greater conventionality, but less evident reason, a similar handkerchief was round his neck. Below that he wore a fancy waistcoat and a pair of moleskin trousers. He did not indulge in a shirt—a garment which appeared to be falling into a very general disfavour. A fancy waistcoat may be left unwashed for a few months with a less evident protest.

Steve had laid down an empty sack, and was occupied with a white smooth-haired terrier, of which he was the apparent master, whose eagerness for a rat, which had found precarious safety under some sheets of corrugated iron, had caused the halt.

The sheets had been the roof of a shed which had been crushed beneath the weight of the falling stack of the iron-works. The stack had been large and very high. Its ruin lay stretched across a wide extent of waste land, hard trodden by many feet, and scattered with broken crocks and perforated buckets.

The men had found that they could raise the sheets a little, but could not remove them without displacing a greater weight of bricks and mortar than they were inclined to attempt for such a purpose.

The dog sniffed and barked round the edge, its stump of tail quivering with excitement.

Martin considered the dog from a new, or rather from the old familiar, aspect, as the friend and comrade of man. He had become used to regarding them as a hostile menace. He did not like the man's look. He thought his eyes to be cunning and shifty, but he wanted to know him, and he took the shortest route to his confidence when he asked, looking at the dog, "Are there any more like him?"

"No," said the man. "T'old bitch bolted. This one baint mine. It's Miss Temple's." He spoke with some traces of the dialect of a northern county, but in a very soft and drawling voice, alien from its spirit, and giving an effect which it would be tedious, and probably vain, to attempt to interpret. His voice gave him an unexpected individuality. Martin understood how he might attract a dog—or a woman.

Talking of dogs, he learnt that more than one of those that had, at first, attached themselves to human owners had heard the call of the wilderness and disappeared. The one that had belonged to Steve had become restless when a dog howled in the darkness, and had slipped away, and not returned.

So they went; but for those that still preferred the abodes of men their wilder relatives were developing an implacable enmity. They fought at sight, and the wild dogs would unite to chase and kill their domestic cousins should they wander among them.

Talking of this and of the possibility of preserving the purity of some of the old breeds led to the question of how much might be the extent of the remaining land, or of the men still living upon it.

"I want two or three volunteers," Martin added, "who will find out what Cooper's doing, and how many are with him. I want them to go beyond him till they come to the water again, and let me know if there are any left alive who might be friendly, or needing help themselves."

He did not expect any immediate response, but Steve Fortune answered, "I'd do that," in his soft drawl.

246

Here was a man that would take some knowing. Martin wondered whether his voice would rise or quicken if he were told the fate of his gift, or the punishment that had followed.

But he must not stay talking here. He had a further object. He asked if he were taking the right path, and the men looked at each other doubtfully. He was on the straight way right enough, but he couldn't keep on it. At least, the horse couldn't. There was the canal.

He admitted that he didn't want to swim the canal. He supposed there would be some other method of crossing. But they told him that it was no question of swimming. The canal was empty. But it was not easy for a horse to cross it, and the bridge was half a mile away.

Steve said, "I'll go. You won't need the dog." He passed the sack to one of the others. Martin understood that a guide had been provided.

As the man walked beside his horse, Martin questioned and listened, learning new things from the leisurely answers he received, as he always did when he approached a fresh mind, and the altered conditions were presented from another angle.

He learnt, among other things, that Steve Fortune was satisfied. It was true that there had been bad times, with deaths and cruelties and disorders, but those were past. Those who remained alive were in very good health, and some of them—Steve, anyway—found it a much pleasanter life than he had spent under the industrial servitude from which it had rescued him. His first desire was that nothing should disturb or end it. Winter? Yes, but they would find food enough. Look at the cattle! Anyway, if they had to go short it wouldn't be with shops of food all round them, and cops and jails for those who wouldn't starve without protest.

Steve was a conservative. He had found it possible to live very comfortably, and he feared change.

He admitted that it would be an advantage if women were more numerous, but even on this point he gave no indication of any personal grievance.

Martin listening to this, and much else, was left in doubt of whether this man were a coward or a *poseur*, or of a selfishness too simple and absolute for any diffidence to disturb it.

As they followed the western bank of the canal-bed, Martin noticed that the opposite side had been fenced with barbed wire, but that this protection had been pulled aside in many places, where foot-tracks crossed the ditch.

He had not come to the bridge before he had seen many indications of the rough and sordid existence to which even these people, who had been represented to him as the best element of the population, had descended.

He passed four men and a woman, who sat on a patch of grassy ground, playing cards. The men played, the woman watched, looking over the shoulder of one of them.

She said something in the man's ear, as Martin rode up. The man shot him a sudden glance from beneath a mass of shaggy hair that overhung his forehead. The glance was not friendly. He took no further notice, bending down to the game. Martin did not know any of them. He had a trained memory for faces. They gave him no greeting.

He saw that they were staking a few sticks of tobacco, and a heap of shining jewellery, among which some large diamonds glittered from ring and pendant. Probably the tobacco was the more highly valued now.

Gaining the camp, and inquiring first for Tom Aldworth, he learnt that he was away, and that there were few left in the camp that morning.

A large ship's mast had been washed ashore, and Tom had got a party together to salve a quantity of wire rope and ladder which were attached to it. He had tried to get every one to join, but there had been many refusals, Steve and his friends among them. There were those to whom such a suggestion only meant that they must think of some more congenial activity, as an excuse for refusal, rather than spend the day with the laziness which they had intended.

The uses of wire rope are many, but there was no immediate individual urgency to prompt them to share in the rough and heavy labour which would be necessary to secure it.

A suggestion that the wire might be used for the more effectual blocking of the fords by which the cattle so often escaped across the river was met by the argument that the land on which they were confined was poor and exhausted, and that the real requirement was to move them out of, not to confine them in, the present area. So, as usual, there had been ready talk, and reluctant action.

Hearing this, Martin did not stay at the camp. He rode over the flat and barren waste that lay between it and the sea

It was true enough that the cattle needed removal. Such grass as grew in this area had been grazed bare, and it was too late in the season for further fertility. It would have looked even barer but for the fact that cattle cannot graze as closely as sheep or horses. But the urgent removal would require much repairing of fence and hedge, and the milking herd would be farther from the camp if they were put upon the richer pasture south of the river, and so nothing had been done, beyond the periodic expulsion of the less useful animals.

Martin rode along a beaten path, formed by the dragging of many heavy objects from shore to camp, and easily found the band of workers round the broken mast, which lay half covered by a falling tide.

He found Tom, and about a dozen helpers, who had already detached a quantity of wire rope and hempen cordage, and were now grouped round the cart which had been intended to assist its transport, but which was exhibiting a weakness in the felloes of one wheel, which foretold a breakdown in the first fifty yards to anyone who was not of an exceptionally sanguine temperament.

Neither horse nor cart appeared to have suffered from underwork on the rough tracks they followed, and the former, turning a patient head toward the arguing group of its masters, appeared to regard the difficulty with a quiet contentment.

There was a confused murmur of greeting as Martin rode up, not deficient either in respect or cordiality, and the group parted for Tom to advance to his horse's shoulder.

"What's wrong?" Martin asked.

"More than we can put right here. We might patch the felloes, but the hub's cracked, and that's loosening the spokes, and that's what's making the trouble. The axle's about done for too. Butcher's got a spare wheel he wants to sell us.... But we can't do anything here without Pellow.... And it's a question whether he'd come. We miss Ellis Roberts with things like this."

"Well, I want to talk to you. Why not walk back with me, and see Pellow yourself? They can go on stripping the mast as the tide falls, and getting ready to load."

Tom agreed readily, and they walked back together.

"I suppose you're fairly sure things will be right for tomorrow, or you wouldn't have been busy on that?" Martin asked. "It didn't look very urgent."

"I'm not as sure as I'd like to be," Tom answered. "There's too much talk, and the more they talk, the less they're sure about anything. I tried to get them on to that job to keep their mouths shut, and give them something to do. But they wouldn't come, except those I'm sure of."

"There's no fresh trouble?"

"Not exactly. Only they're wondering what you mean to do, and whether they're not promising too much. They're afraid of having to obey a lot of laws they won't like. Miss Temple says the same."

"Says the same? Says what?"

"She says it's no use making a lot of laws."

"I want to see Miss Temple. My—Mrs. Webster told me about her." (Should he say "my wife" or "one of my wives" in the future?)

"I think you'd better."

"Has she much influence?"

"She might about turn the scale. I don't mean merely a majority. We shall have that, with Butcher's lot coming in. Jack says that's certain. But we want more than that, now you've said you'll turn out those who won't join. We couldn't turn out nearly half.... And we couldn't turn out the women."

"But Miss Temple wouldn't want to leave us? I thought she was about the best helper you'd got."

"I don't know. She's the sort you can't turn. I think she means to help us, in her own way. But she could get about half the women in this camp, or hold them off, and it's not much use having the men alone."

Martin saw that. The idea of the men having sufficient loyalty to him to turn their wives into the wilderness because they declined his authority was absurd.

In a rash moment he had said that the women, equally with the men, must pledge their support, and whatever difficulty followed must be overcome, if he were not to fall at the first fence.

"I don't think there'll be any trouble about that," he said easily. "I expect they'll vote together—the women and their men—when the time comes. Is it only with the women that Miss Temple's influence counts?"

"No. There's about ten men—perhaps twenty—here and round Larkshill, that will do anything for her. Men like Burke, some of them, that won't for me.... And she can talk—especially when people get together. Straight, simple talk, that persuades. If she comes tomorrow, and says your way's wrong, she'll get every one who's doubtful against you, and shake the rest."

"Well, I don't know that. I can talk a little myself," Martin answered. "But it's best done first, and alone. I'll see her now, if I can. She seems to have some ideas. Is she the sort that won't change?"

"No, I wouldn't say that. She won't mind changing if you show her she's wrong. But if she thinks you're wrong, she'll say what she thinks…. It's all religion with her…. And getting people to clean the camp."

CHAPTER FIFTY-SIX

MARTIN found Muriel busy with some domestic work at her own location. She offered him a small, work-hardened hand, and asked him to enter the compartment which was bed- and living-room combined, and was, even so, a more luxurious dwelling than was the portion of most of those round her.

She called Monty, who was somewhere near, and he took charge of the horse.

The sky had clouded, and a fine rain was commencing, so that he was glad to accept the offered shelter.

After a few words of initial courtesy, he said directly, "Tom Aldworth tells me that you don't think these people need laws or is it only that you think they don't want them?"

"I think they don't need laws, they need leading."

"Meaning?"

"Meaning just that. They don't need laws. They need decisions."

They were both silent for a moment: Martin because she had expressed an idea which had been inarticulately present, but discouraged, in his own mind; and she because she waited for his response.

Seeing him silent, she went on.

"Mr. Webster, I'm not a lawyer, and I haven't got your capacity. I know we need someone to take control, and I know I couldn't. I've thought of every one here, and there's no one really fit, or not that every one would obey. I want to help you if I can, but that's what I think, and if you make a lot of laws and penalties—and I suppose laws must mean penalties—straight away, I think we shall have more trouble, and I don't think even you—I don't think anyone—could prevent it.

"It seems to me," she went on, "that laws should come gradually. If you should make laws I for one shouldn't promise that I should obey them. I should want to know what they would be, and then I should want to think.

"We've had one law already about the women. I told Tom that I shouldn't take any notice of it, and fortunately no one's made any trouble about that." (Was there a tone of bitterness in her voice, that denied the smiling of lips and eyes? It was so slight, if so, that Martin could not detect it with certainty.) "The idea was good enough, but the law was silly. There were so many things that might happen that we couldn't foresee. We're not ready for laws yet. They'll break themselves, or get broken. I don't know whether you'll understand, but I can't put it plainer than that. We don't want laws, we want leading."

"I see what you mean quite clearly," Martin answered. "You mean you want orders dealing with immediate needs, rather than permanent laws dealing with general principle of conduct or policy.

"It isn't such a simple alternative as you might think. It will lead to something like what we used to call case law—that is, one thing at a time will be decided on its merits, and the next time there's a similar difference, or anything like it, there will be an appeal to what was decided then; but it may be best to start in that way."

"May I ask you this? If I begin in that way, will you come and speak in my support on Thursday?

"I'm going to ask a good deal, if you do. I don't look upon it as a country that's to be governed, but rather as a ship that's to be steered to port—and a ship that's among the rocks, if it isn't on them.

"It's not a case for arguing, or thinking that we can steer two ways at once. I'll concede all you ask. You shall have leading, not law. Shall I have following, not argument?"

"I don't like promising too much," Muriel answered. "I shouldn't do what I thought wrong, and I won't promise blindly. But I think you're right. I think it's the only way we'll succeed, and that I ought to agree.

"I'll promise this now. As long as I'm here, I'll give you all the help I can. If I can't follow, I'll come and tell you, and if you ask me to clear out—well, I'll go."

"I think that's all I could ask, and more than I could expect," Martin answered, "and I think it means that, with your help we shall succeed. I'm very glad I have seen you."

"I don't think," Muriel answered, "that you'll find that my help makes so much difference. But I don't think that it matters so much whether we succeed or not. I know we can't always feel like that, and we shouldn't do much if we did. But I was sitting up most of last night—it was fine, and not very cold, and I was—not well enough to sleep. And I was watching the stars, and thinking how short our lives are, and how we are small and lost in the great space that we can see, but could never reach, and I thought of those terrible words of Paul: 'without God in the world.' I had never felt alone, as I did then.... And then I thought of all that the seas had covered, not the men and women only, but all that they had built and made— all the buildings, and the pictures and books that they thought so wonderful—and they just passed in a day, and the stars continued.... It was all so trivial that had gone.... And then faith came again, and I thought of the promises of God.... And it seemed that nothing that comes to us—nothing that we gain or lose—can matter, except how we face it.... And then I thought of the lines of an old hymn that you've probably never heard, or might think silly:

> *He hath His young men at the war,*
> *His little ones at home,*

and I thought that, if there's nothing hard to face, it may be that God doesn't think we're worth trying. As though He knows we'll break at any test, and He just leaves us in contempt...."

She stopped abruptly, and then added, in a different voice, "But you've got other things to think of. You must forgive me going on about my own thoughts. I suppose we all get these moods at times. And I've had no one to talk to lately.... But you won't want to go through this rain. It won't last much longer. It's clearing now to the south.... You can depend on any help I can give. I believe you've been sent to help us.... There's only one thing that could make me feel differently, and I feel sure I've no cause to doubt you there. But I hope you won't mind telling me. I think we ought to know—and we're bound to know, one way or other."

She paused a moment, as though hesitating how to frame the question, and Martin said, "I'm sure you wouldn't ask anything without reason." His thought was, "Am I going to lose her support after all?" He did not doubt what was coming.

"It's about Helen. You know I saw her before we knew that you were found—and then we heard that there was another. Of course, every one's talking about it. Some say that you mean to keep one, and some the other, and some say that you want to give Helen up, but can't because of the children, and some say you mean to go on as though you'd married them both—and I was thinking about this last night, and I saw how difficult it must be, and I thought, if you had the strength to do right in a position like that, you'd be the one to get things straight here. Would you tell me what you do mean to do?"

"Miss Temple," he answered, "I can't expect you to look at a matter of this kind quite as I do; and I can only say that if I lose your support I shall be sorry—I should be sorry even if it meant less than it does. I hoped that we should be friends, and it is a friendship that I should value. I hoped that you would be friends with—with Helen and Claire. But there can be no disguise about the decision that we have made. It didn't rest with me only. I consider that I am bound to both, and to that we stand. It is Helen's view, as well as mine. It was her independent decision, as I felt sure it would be. There is no law to guide us now, as you have said, and we had to think what was right in circumstances which could not have been foreseen."

"I didn't say there was no law. There is God's law always to me."

"Well we don't think we are going against that."

"And you thought I should?" Muriel frowned slightly, as though the implication were not too pleasing. "Well, perhaps it was natural. But I thought about this last night, and I couldn't be sure. I thought you were bound to Helen. 'Whom God hath joined'.... the words wouldn't leave my mind. They're not easy to understand. They were used to baffle a trap, and I suppose they're not meant to be easy.... And then I saw suddenly that 'God' didn't mean a priest. It meant something greater than that.... And I thought that, if you'd all meant to be loyal to one another, well, this was the test, and if you all came through the right way, it meant that there's still something better left in the world than the hateful things that we've seen here."

CHAPTER FIFTY-SEVEN

THERE were over four hundred people gathered on Cowley Common, sitting on grass or heather, or standing between the gorse-bushes in the background.

The sun shone warmly, though October was opening, and, except for a passing gull, there was no sign on that open heath of any change having come to the world since Cowley fair had been held on the same spot a year before.

Curiosity had proved more powerful than Tom's earlier efforts for the common good, and there were not ten people absent who could, by any possibility, have been expected to come.

254

Martin spoke first, from a raised knoll of land which had often been a showman's vantage-point for declaring the wonders which a penny would disclose to such as penetrated the entrance of his curtained booth.

He saw Tom's supporters grouped together, and the gleams of a dozen rifle-barrels among them showed that he was leaving little to chance.

He saw Butcher, with his household servants, marshalling themselves as near as possible to the place from which he would speak, as though to allow no oversight of the importance of the support they gave.

He saw Muriel Temple moving quietly from one to another doubtless making it clear that she would support him.

He felt a certainty of victory such as he had sometimes done as a difficult case approached its verdict, and which he had never known to mislead him.

He was glad that Helen was beside him, though he had discouraged her presence. But she did not lack courage, and she had felt that, in Claire's absence, it might fall upon her to defend both herself and him, and to avow her own approval of the decision which had been made.

His only anxiety was that Claire had not returned. He felt that this might be misread, and, having ceased to doubt her safety, he would have preferred that there should be no possibility of the construction that he had not wished her to come.

But it was too late to alter that now.

Muriel came up to him. "I understand that Tom's going to speak, and then Butcher. If there's no one else, I should like to say a few words after. I don't think Butcher ought to have the last word today. But I shall have to ask you to lend me your knoll. I'm too short to talk to people from the level."

Martin did not speak very long. He felt as he commenced that the attitude of many of those who heard was anxious, critical, and non-committal, though there were few who were really hostile.

He reminded them that he stood there at no suggestion, as it was at no desire, of his own.

He had been asked to take control, and he had agreed to do so on one condition—that he should be obeyed without question.

He spoke of the prevailing state of disorder, and of the lack of forethought, or of any planning for the common good, and the murmurs of assent were frequent, but he felt that the tension of those who heard him was undiminished.

He went on to say that he did not intend to impose new laws which would reduce their freedom, but, for the time at least, till they had reached a more stable social condition, he asked only for obedience to the orders which he would issue—he asked only that they should all work heartily, as he should allocate their parts, so that they might take full advantage of such remains of the past wealth as were still available, and might provide for warmth and shelter, for food and clothing and comfort, during the winter which must now be near them.

If disputes should arise, they must be brought to him, and he would try to settle them fairly, and they must pledge themselves that in such cases they would accept his decision.

But it was no time for doubts and divisions. If any man would not work with them in this way, now was the time to speak, and he would be free to leave them, taking his possessions with him.

They must decide now—such as had not pledged themselves already—for there was little time for talk. There were a hundred things to be put in hand. They must give him their support today, or he might decline it tomorrow.

Before he reached this point he was aware that the feeling had changed. They did not want a repetition of the old organizations, the old bondages, the old bewildering weight of laws and restrictions, but they were conscious of the need of leadership.

Almost all the laws that they had had to learn in their previous lives—or to suffer for their ignorance of them—had been laws to restrict or to prevent. Laws that imposed burdens or restrained activities. They might have been good or bad, or composed of both elements. Few things are absolute. But whether they had been good or bad, whether they were wise or foolish now to contemn them, the feeling was there, and it was with the sensation as of a cloud that had passed that they recognized that their new leader was more concerned to stimulate than restrain.

Seeing that he had won the mood of those to whom he spoke, he ceased quickly, avoiding the peril of the further word.

Tom Aldworth followed. He had not the gift of public speech, and his words were halting and few, but the cheers that met them did not allow his pauses to show very awkwardly. There were many in the crowd of better education, men who were shrewder and cleverer than he, but he was the one who had thought from the first rather of the general welfare than of his own advantage, and he had won a confidence which such men as Butcher could never gain.

Butcher spoke easily and adroitly. He blessed the new start which was being made, but it was in a tone of benevolence rather than respect. There were subtleties that only Martin understood, and that may have been meant for him only:

His voice did not carry well, and all that was generally recognized was that he had given his support to Martin.

It was remembered that he had held aloof from Cooper, and it was regarded as evidence that he had decided that Martin would overcome whatever opposition he might encounter.

Muriel spoke briefly. She had the kind of voice which will carry far, even in open air, without apparent effort. She spoke as she would have done to a single auditor, with the simplicity beside which any artifice is a baffled inferior.

Martin had sat unmoved in the seat of honour while receiving the fulsome praise of after-dinner speakers who had been acknowledged masters of the art of oratory, but he found it less easy to maintain the mask of indifference while Muriel, having put the simple facts of the social and economic depths to which they had fallen, expressed her confidence in his ability to transform them. "I believe God's sent him," she finished simply, "and I'm going to help him all I can."

The words did not reach more than half the audience, for attention was distracted by Claire's appearance. She came through from the back of the crowd, drawing the eyes of many men, and of all of the women. She saw a vacant chair beside that on which Helen was sitting, and walked confidently toward it.

There was a silence so absolute that it had the effect of sound. It called the attention of those whose thoughts or eyes had wandered. This was a matter which had been forgotten—to which no speaker had alluded—but which had been represented as a vital issue only three days ago.

Martin knew that he was already assured of the support of a majority of those around him, but that the extent of his triumph, the question whether the meeting could break up without a note of discord, would be decided now.

Helen saw it also, and she did not fail him.

There was a moment during which both she and Martin might have left the meeting, and none would have observed their departure.

Every eye was directed upon the advancing woman.

To those who had been with Tom on the Bellamy raid she was known already. They had known her as Martin's wife, as his comrade in the tunnel fight.

There were others who had seen her riding recklessly through the *débris* of the Larkshill Road to the rescue of Helen's child.

To most, she had been a name only, but of a mysterious quality. She was the woman had who killed Bryan in Bycroft Lane.

Had she come to make claim to Martin in this publicity? Would she challenge him to choose between herself and Helen? Were they on the threshold of some exciting drama? Was the automatic that was belted so conveniently to her hand to take a part in the argument?

Their eyes followed her till she gained the group that had risen as she approached.

They observed the meeting of the two women in a dramatic contrast.

Helen had used every resource available to maintain the standards of dress and appearance to which she had been used in the earlier days. It was by such means that she had supported Martin then, and she did not suppose that human nature had changed because the land had shifted beneath it.

So dressed, she had an aspect of delusive fragility: even of a loveliness which might have been thought to have left the world.

Claire had come straight from the landing-place. Whatever might have been the secret activity which had delayed her, it had not tended to the cleanliness of the clothes she wore.

But she had not known what might be happening in her absence. She knew that her presence had been promised at this meeting three days ago, and she had delayed for nothing:

They saw the hands of the two women meet. Helen said something, and they could hear the gay tone, though not the words, of a laughing answer.

They saw the quick movement (purposely delayed, as they could not guess, till their eyes were upon it) by which Helen adjusted her chair to make more room for the one beside it. They sat down together....

Monty Beeston had brought his bill-hook to the meeting, in the vain hope that there might be a need for its service. It was an unpopular weapon in a crowd, and it had secured him a prominent isolation.

He had watched Claire's approach in an agony of excitement, lest he should have to make election between two contending loyalties.

Now he leapt up, as he had not done since he had seen that shot that flashed obliquely across the goal-mouth from the foot of the outside-left, and rebounded from post to net, in that last minute's play which had saved his club from the ignominy of the Second Division. He leapt up, in an uncontrolled excitement, waving his weapon round his head, and burst into a raucous cheer, which was lost next moment in the noise of four hundred voices.

For the moment courage—courage and character—had triumphed. If there were discontents and reluctancies among the crowd, they were silenced by the knowledge of their minority.

But Martin knew that his real trial was to come.

They left the common while the sun was still shining. But there was a cold wind from the north. The summer days were ended.

BOOK FIVE

CHAPTER FIFTY-EIGHT

DOLL WITHLIN lay dying. She was beyond any human help available, and would have been beyond the help of all the skill of the earlier days. But she did not feel very ill. And the pain was less.

She lay gazing out of the open door with frightened eyes at the frozen pathway and the cold sea-mist upon the whitened fields beyond.

A wood-fire blazed beside the foot of the bed, and Muriel Temple sat at the farther side and tried to give comfort where no comfort was possible.

"But you don't *really* think I shall die?" came the plaintive, repeated question. "I want to live. And he told me there was no risk at all. He said he'd often done it before the flood. He said every one did it then. I'd always said I didn't want any kids.... I don't care what happens after you're dead. I don't believe anything does. I want to live.... Why don't you make him come and do *something*? I don't care what, if I don't die."

"Dr. Butcher said he can't do anything more," Muriel answered, thinking truth was best; "and, besides, the Captain has taken him."

Butcher Junior was, in fact, sitting with his hands tied behind his back, a very frightened man, under the guard of Monty Beeston's bill-hook, and knowing that nothing would give him greater pleasure than to have an excuse for using it.

"You don't really think I shall go to hell?" the dying woman began again. "It can't be very wrong if every one used to do it. He shouldn't have told me if it was. It was he did it, not me."

"I don't think you knew how wrong it was," Muriel answered gently. Who was she to say what the verdict of God would be upon this woman with the mind of a wilful child? Who had allowed the destruction of that which should have been most sacred, and could not see, even now, that it was anything serious, apart from any penalty which it brought upon her. Who was already sentenced to leave the life to which she clung so desperately.

There had been a time when she would have answered without hesitation, and her creed had not consciously changed But she had learnt that she was not God, and that His ways are past finding out, even by those who serve Him. "Shall not the Judge of all the earth do right?" Faith may answer with an assured affirmative, but even faith may falter as to what that right may be.

CHAPTER FIFTY-NINE

THERE was a very different scene in the house of "the Captain," as Martin was now universally called, where Butcher was pleading for his son's life.

Martin had declined to see him alone. Helen and Claire were present, and Jack Tolley, who was now fully employed as his secretary, and living with Madge in a house at Cowley Thorn which had been repaired for his use.

Martin had found that Jack's support was best secured by a position that enabled him to understand fully the motives that underlay his decisions, and it was a triumph of personality that he had now won an unquestioning and almost enthusiastic loyalty from this rather difficult supporter.

Butcher deserves some respect for his position, and some admiration for the self-control that he was exercising.

He was fighting for his son's life. It would have been difficult for him to find words which would have exceeded the contempt he felt for Martin's ethical standards, or the anger and hatred that raged within him. But he knew that Martin could not be moved by such expressions, and he was using every resource of his diplomacy to secure his purpose.

"I thought I'd heard it said that you didn't hold with capital punishment, even for murder."

"I've never gone that far," Martin answered, "but I should never make a law by which it would be an ordinary penalty. Murders vary so greatly in culpability. There is no crime which requires so much to be left to the discretion of those who try it, as to what the penalty, if any, should be, if the fact be proved."

"It isn't as though he'd meant to kill her. He didn't think he'd do her any harm—and you don't know that she'll die, even now."

"I'm sorry," Martin answered, "but I don't follow your reasoning. What he has done cannot possibly be made better or worse by whether she dies or lives.

"You are thinking of the foolish laws of a past time, that were less concerned with motive than precarious consequence. Laws that would even treat a murderous attempt lightly if a man couldn't shoot straight.

"But what you say is beside the point. I know he didn't mean to kill her, and I shall not deal with him any differently from how I should do if she were well. I intend to execute him because he has killed a child."

"But the child never lived at all."

"Mr. Butcher, I am sorry for you, and I want to answer patiently, but I am not a fool. Whether the child had a separate life, or to what extent, we neither of us know—nor do we know what life is. To kill life, or to prevent it, is a distinction of doubtful reality, and of no practical importance…. But you mistake me further. I am not God. I do not propose to punish your son for any wrong he has done. As you sit there, you can see that Phillips is occupied in removing daisy-roots from the lawn. I am fond of daisies. I don't like your son. But neither like nor dislike influences me in either case, nor does any question of punishment. There are reasons why they both need removal. I cannot have the idea of abortion alive among us.

"We have both lived in a time of pleasure and luxury, among people who employed others to spend their lives in their service, and who would say without shame that they bought their comfort at the cost of their children's lives. Now we live hardly, and the lives of our children are recovering their natural value.

"I would rather see half the community dead tomorrow than that the seed of those evils should take root among us."

"But there was nothing new in such practices. Intelligent people of all ages, even savages, have seen the necessity of regulating the population."

"I did not say that it was new," Martin answered patiently. "It might be difficult to discover a vice that is. The advocates of practices which were destroying the nations of Western Europe, when the waters intervened to do it more decently, would claim. the prestige of discovery and the authority of age in the same sentence. But that was only because they were weak-minded, when they were not actively vicious. The new thing was that in the absence of any government which was prepared to risk its popularity, or its existence, for the nation's welfare, such, or similar, vices had become publicly advocated, and their methods explained. The youth of the nation was urged towards them, even on the threshold of what might have been happy and natural marriages, in the endeavour to drag all down to a common level of degradation.... But we are not discussing European civilization. We have to build our own. So far as one man can, I will create a public opinion in which children shall be the honour of those who bear them, and their avoidable absence a woman's deepest shame."

"But what if, or when, the little island on which we live shall become overpopulated?"

"It is not an immediate question, and it would be as reasonable to let it influence our minds today as to commit suicide to save ourselves from the risk of dying of old age. But I can tell you what will happen if we have any success in rearing children of a sufficient vitality—they will take to the waters, to find what other lands will be open to them."

Butcher had not exhausted his arguments. He knew every plea that had been urged by a generation which had been alert for its self-called 'rights,' and impatient of the suggestion of duty, but he was fighting for a life, not an argument, and he had the sense to see that he should make no progress in such direction.

He said, "I can't agree, as you know; but I don't wish to urge anything against your judgment. If you make such a law, I should advise my son to obey it, and I should expect him to take the consequences, should he fail. But you have agreed that beliefs and practices were different in the civilization in which we were reared. Is it right to exact a penalty beyond that which would have been a legal possibility in those days, and of which my son had no warning?"

"You are mistaken. I heard something which caused me to warn him two months ago. He appears to have thought it possible that Jack's wife here, being now married to him, would not want to bear Ellis Roberts's child, or that Jack would not wish her to have it. Anyway, he gave her some hint, of which I heard, and I warned him plainly."

"There is another consideration," Butcher replied, "which you may have overlooked. My son is the only man among us who has been trained for the profession. Without him, there is no expert advice available."

"It wouldn't influence me if it were so; but, in fact, it isn't. You may not know that Hatterley has discovered about fifteen people on our north-west coast, and that one of them is an experienced doctor. I hope to get them to come here when the sea is favourable."

"Well, even so, two doctors aren't too many for all the people, here. One might die any time."

"I'm afraid one will," Martin answered, with a brutality which he regretted as soon as it was spoken, but Butcher did not appear to notice it.

He went on, "There've been a good many points of friction between us. There's the cloth now, that we were arguing about last week. You've got something to sell now. I want to save my son's life, and I'm prepared to bid high."

"I'm not prepared to deal," Martin answered, "but I'll consider all you've said—and perhaps some things that you haven't—and give you my answer tomorrow."

"Would you listen to Miss Temple?"

"I would listen to anyone. I've no reason to think she would

"I don't know, but I must try all I can. She's a religious woman. She ought to see it differently from how you do."

"Well, I believe she's with the dying girl. You can try if you like."

Butcher went out.

"I never thought I should be sorry for that man," Helen said. "Is there no other way? Of course, you know best."

"I'm sorry for the father," said Claire, "but the man needs hanging, all the same. What do you say, Jack?"

Jack Tolley assented. He remembered the poisonous whisper to his own wife. He had not been roused to any great indignation. It had been too absurd to suppose that Madge would act in such a way, or could think that he would approve it. He was not stirred to any violent emotion now, but he recognized that dirt should be cleared out. He said, "I don't see what his father's feelings have to do with it."

Martin noticed that he was getting more support than he would have expected. None of them, he thought, would have advocated such drastic action if he had not taken it, and now they were surer than he was himself that it should be carried to its extremity. They lacked the responsibility of the last decision.

CHAPTER SIXTY

DR. BUTCHER stood trembling in the uncertainty of life and death, his hands still tied, and Monty still beside him, while Martin looked at him with a contempt which he made no effort to cover. There was the same group in the room that had been round him the night before.

Muriel was not there. Butcher had seen her, and had implored her to use her influence for his son's life, and she had disconcerted him with an unexpected question, "Is he sorry for what he did?" He had answered it as he thought she would wish, but there had been a second's pause, which she understood. She knew Butcher.

She said, "I will see the Captain if you ask me again; but I don't know that I shall help you if I do. I should like you to know that before you ask."

He had looked at her in silence, and turned away.

Now Martin's voice broke the tense silence of the room. He addressed himself to the father.

"Mr. Butcher, I have thought of all you said, and I have remembered the atmosphere in which your son was trained. I don't mean that all doctors were of his character, or of his way of thinking, because that would be to malign dead men, among whom I had valued friends; but I am giving him the full benefit of the worst influences which may have acted upon him. They are considerations which may reduce his guilt, but do not supply any good reason why I should allow him to contaminate others.

"I am about to take a course which is merciful, but I wish I were sure that it is something better than moral cowardice which has led me to this decision. I do not wish to take your son's life with my own hand, and I do not wish to require of others what I am unwilling to do myself. He will have six hours to leave the district. After that, if he should be within five miles of this room at any time, or if by word or writing he should so much as mention any one of the vices of which he learnt in the old days, to any one of our people, young or old, he will die very surely, without mercy or delay.

"I should not hesitate again.

"Monty, you can loose his hands."

There was no word in reply either from father or son. The condemned man leaned his released hands on the table, as though he could not stand easily. He breathed hard, as though he had been running. His father came over to him. He put a hand under his son's arm, and led him out.

Helen said, "I think I'm glad you've let him go. He won't come here again. He's too frightened."

Claire said, "I think I'm sorry. I don't want to think such a man is alive. I can't get it out of my mind, and I know I ought to." She had the thought of her own child that was coming. She did not want any thought that should not be gracious: no thought of ignoble things. But thought is hard to control, perhaps hardest when there is conscious effort to do so. She had a feeling that it would be ended if he were dead.

Chapter Sixty-One

IT was scarcely five minutes after the two men had left that Steve Fortune was at the door. He had met Monty along the road, and asked him what the Captain's order was about Dr. Butcher. Monty, who did not like him, gave a fantastically sanguinary reply, which he would have regarded as satisfactory if he had been able to credit it.

He went on, and as he reached the door Martin came out. That was better than he had hoped. He had not expected to get past the vigilant Phillips without considerable difficulty. The Captain himself would talk to anyone, but those about him constituted a difficult barrier to surmount.

"Can I have a word with you, Captain?"

"You'd better come inside, if you've anything to say. It's too cold here."

Martin knew him to be a man of unhurried speech, and the cold was bitter. There was a sea-mist also, that lay thickly over the land, and might not lift all day. A cold, wet, penetrating mist, such as they had had many times during the past month. A new thing, and unpleasant to these English Midlanders.

He talked to Steve in the hall for a few moments, and let him go.

He went in to Helen and Claire, who were working on the provision of warmer garments for themselves and the children. There was still material available, but not much, and Butcher was known to have a quantity of uncut rolls of cloth—a very large quantity, it was believed—which he would not sell at any reasonable figure.

"I've had Steve Fortune here about Dr. Butcher," he said; "he wouldn't say what he wanted when he found I'd let him off. I half thought he meant to volunteer as executioner."

"It's never easy to tell what Steve's thinking," Helen answered. "Wasn't he fond of Doll?"

"There was some trouble about that before I came, so Tom told me, and I saw something of it myself. But there's been nothing since."

The conversation was interrupted by Muriel's entrance.

"I want to see you alone," she said to Martin.

"Quite alone?" he said, in some surprise, for there were few things which were not shared openly among those who were present.

"Yes, quite. I've promised."

"Then come into the library."

"It's about Dr. Butcher," Muriel began, as soon as the library door was closed upon them. "His father came last night, and asked me to see you, and I declined; but Doll has told me something this morning which alters it—or you may think so. Anyway, she thinks you ought to know. But she only told me on condition that I should tell no one but you; and that Will Carless should never know, under any circumstances. I've promised that, and I can say nothing unless you do the same."

"Very well, if you think I ought."

"It's this. She says the child wouldn't have been Will's. It was Steve Fortune's. She says she was sorry after it happened, and she hasn't spoken to Steve for three months. I think he bribed her with something. You know she's always been like a child for anything she could wear.

"She says she got to hate the thought of always having Steve's child, and Will not knowing. And she was dreading that it might be like Steve—you know how different they are—and every one would guess. She says she begged Dr. Butcher to do something to stop it, and he said he was afraid of you, but he gave in at last.

"I told her you ought to know, and she agreed, as long as Will never hears. They've been happy together the last three months, except for this trouble on her mind, and I suppose now she's dying—"

"I don't think it makes much difference to what I think of the doctor; and, in any case, it's too late to alter anything. I've let him go, with a warning that he'll be shot unless he keeps away."

"I can't say I'm glad," Muriel answered, "though perhaps I should be. I only brought you this tale because I knew I ought…. I don't want any man killed, but I think the children come first, and I don't think even you know how far this trouble goes…. You see, I get a good many confidences that I can't repeat…. But I can tell you this—if they spoke their real thoughts, there are about a quarter of the women who wouldn't say that Doll did anything wrong at all. There are several others who don't want children, and don't mean to have any. I don't say there are so many as there were. Some of them are beginning to see that children may be useful, and they'll be lonely later on.

"But the queer thing is that when a woman makes up her mind she won't have children, she always tries to influence others in the same way. It's like a kind of disease. They talk to younger women about how dreadful it is to have a child, and whisper ways of avoiding it, and they try to frighten them into getting rid of it, if they are expecting to have one. I suppose it's jealousy, really.

"Some of them tried it with Madge, but she was too sensible to take much notice: and they've frightened Belle Rivers till she thinks she's going to die for certain.

"You're right to try, of course; but you won't do much with some of these women. The only chance is to keep such ideas from the children. I don't know whether we can manage that.

"I'm only saying this because you should know the truth. It would have done good if you had had Dr. Butcher hanged. They won't think much of him being sent away. It will look weak—and a man that's sent away can come back."

Martin said, "I'm glad you've told me all this. I partly guessed, though I didn't know.... I knew I was wrong about Butcher. It was just cowardice, because I didn't like killing him.... And it won't make any difference to his father's enmity. As to his coming back, well, we must just wait, and see."

CHAPTER SIXTY-TWO

HELFORD GRANGE had been built about four hundred years earlier, on the ruins of a castle which had been stormed and burnt in the Barons' wars. That castle had been ancient and decaying in Lancastrian times. It was said that it had been built upon the site of a stronghold that had repelled the Mercian raiders of an earlier millennium.

The cellars of Helford Grange were of a great, but uncertain, antiquity. They were very extensive, and had been dark and ill-ventilated when Butcher had first occupied them. But he had altered that.

He had made progress in many ways during the last few months. He had enlisted the services of seven additional men, so that he now had a force of fourteen on whom he felt that he could rely.

He still used them for the systematic raiding of the deserted country, and, though he professed the creed of the peaceful trader, he had armed them, for the legitimate reason that the wild places into which they penetrated were rendered unsafe by the increasing ferocity of the dogs and cattle.

He now sat with his son in an inner cellar, which he used as his own apartment.

It was furnished simply, and without harmony of form or colour, but with articles of selected value.

The bedstead in the corner of the room was a choice example of Sheraton; the desk at which he sat was of polished oak, of ample size, and of many internal intricacies. Its papers were neatly arranged, and there was a rack of account-books above it, containing records of a thousand complicated barterings, which he entered and balanced with his own hand.

The cellar was lighted by an oil-lamp, and a faint gleam from a weed-hidden grating that opened into the side of an ancient moat.

He was writing a letter to Jerry Cooper, while his son sat waiting beside him.

"You'll have to go today," he said, as he blotted and closed it down, "and you'll have to start at once, if you're to be there before dark. But whom to send with you, I don't know. Reeves took most of the men to do that digging at Tipton. I don't think they can possibly be back for two days yet, though I sent Pollock and Sims after them as soon as the trouble started. That only makes me shorter. I've got no one fit to go now, except Slater, and he doesn't know the way properly. Besides, he wouldn't like to come back alone. It's not safe in the night."

"Couldn't he wait there till tomorrow?"

"Yes—if he got there, but he mightn't find the way before dark."

"I can't go alone. I've never been farther than Sterrington."

"We might hide you here till we get the men back. But I don't like it. Webster's hard to move when he's said anything. It won't last much longer now."

A woman pushed open the heavy oak door, without the ceremony of knocking.

"There's that Steve Fortune waitin' to see you, sir. He says it's important."

"Tell him I can't see him today…. No…. Here, Maria…. Tell him I'll see him in a minute. He may be just what we want."

He rose and followed the woman to the outer cellar, in which he had once bargained with Jerry Cooper for the arming of Rattray.

Steve stood by the door. He was not asked to sit down.

He said he wanted a smooth-haired terrier dog. He believed two or three had been seen running loose, but he couldn't get on their tracks. He'd pay well. He'd give a week's work if he could get one caught for him.

Butcher was not stirred by the offer. Dogs were hard to catch now, and his men were busy. He let Steve turn to go before he said, "You know the way to Cooper's camp, don't you?"

Yes, Steve knew that. He had spent a month, at the Captain's order, exploring the inland ways from coast to coast, and reporting the results—or as much as he had felt inclined to tell.

"I want someone to guide Dr. Butcher to Cooper's camp. I want him to start now. I'll give five yards of good cloth. It's a high price."

It certainly was a high price. So high that Steve saw that Butcher meant to settle the matter without haggling. But he was not enthusiastic. He would have to come back alone. No man would like to do that.

Butcher pointed out that he need not start his return till the next day. In the end he agreed; providing the question of the dog should be reconsidered.

Butcher arranged that he should have a meal there, and be ready to start in half an hour. He did not see the smile which quivered on the gipsy's face as he left the room—a smile that died at once, as though afraid that even the walls should see it.

CHAPTER SIXTY-THREE

IT would be entirely unfair to a great profession, which had included many of the leading men of their time, both in intellect and character, to regard Dr. Butcher as a typical example of them. He was of a constitutional cowardice, and there were not more cowards among them than in any other section of the nation: his present trouble arose from practices which would have been repudiated with indignation by the majority of his colleagues.

But it would be as entirely wrong to regard him as one who caricatured the profession to which he belonged—a profession which had been held up to public contempt only a few years before, when a doctor had first refused his evidence before a judge of assize on the ground that his professional honour pledged him to secrecy, and had then given the required information when threatened with legal penalties.

It had been held up to public ridicule when a member whom it had agreed to honour as one of its greatest and most original thinkers had informed a world of hilarious anglers that he had discovered by his researches that fishes do not learn by experience.

It is a fact that many of its weaker members had been stampeded by the chimeras of the birth-restrictioner and the psychoanalyst, or had prostituted their profession to form a lucrative practice in the service of vice or hysteria.

But Dr. Butcher was an individual, not a type.

He was a very miserable individual as he crouched beside the wood-fire which Steve was making on the frozen ground after they had wandered for several hours in search of Cooper's headquarters, and the short day was fading round them.

Steve had chosen their camp with care, at a spot where a thick hedge of holly protected them on the weather side, and he had started a fire about three yards away, so that they could be in some safety between these barriers.

He persuaded the weary man, with some difficulty, to do his share in searching for the needed wood by threatening that they would be devoured by dogs before morning should they fail to outpace the challenge of the advancing dusk.

When they sat side by side between the barriers of hedge and fire, Steve had a different tale.

He shared the food he had brought very fairly, tending his companion with an exemplary solicitude.

He drawled lamentation that the shortness of the winter day had made it impossible to finish their journey before the night had closed upon them.

He said that he would take the first watch, but that Butcher must be prepared for prompt action if he should call upon him. The dog-pack came so quickly....

"But if we keep the fire going—" said the trembling man. He was not used to such exposures, and cold and fear combined to make him shiver miserably on the frozen ground.

"It's not much good for the *dogs*," Steve drawled. "Did I say *dogs*? I shouldn't have said dogs. It might keep off the *cattle*. But dogs rather like fires. They're used to fires....

"Didn't you hear tell of how Reeves and three men with him were turned off their own fire, down south, a week ago? The dogs only drove them off, and sat round the fire to get warm.... But they caught one of Cooper's men.... They found his bones by the fire in the morning, and it wasn't near out then."

These statements may have been something more (or less) than the outcome of a strict veracity, but Butcher had no means of checking their accuracy.

He could not have slept had he tried, though mind and body were wearied by the experiences of the last two days. He could only sit and watch the face of Steve in the firelight....

The night became very dark and still. There was a mist that hid the stars. The cold was cruel.

He could see nothing now but the face of Steve, which seemed to be turned upon him all the time. He didn't speak. He just looked...and looked.

Watching Steve, and shivering with something worse than cold, he said, "I wonder what time it is."

It was a silly remark. He had one of the few watches which were still going accurately. But he must say something.

Steve spoke then. But he spoke of time differently. He said, "I suppose it might have lived eighty years. Longer than you could now. You must be near thirty. It don't seem fair somehow."

He did not appear to expect a reply. It was as though he thought aloud.

He went on, still as though he followed his own thought only. "If that had been *my* kid—but, of course, it wasn't She wasn't my girl. But if it *had* been my kid, I should have killed you *slow*."

Butcher's eyes were fixed upon him, as though fascinated, but he made no reply. He heard the slow, quiet voice, "I suppose you're not afeard of Will Carless? He didn't know, did he? No, you wouldn't have told Will. And you're not afeard of him, now you've killed his girl.... There's no call to be afeard of Will. He'd just blubber, most like, and let you go.... Now if that had been *my* kid...but we know it ain't.... I should have killed you *slow*."

The night got darker before the dawn, and Butcher slept at last, his head on a pack that he had been carrying, his body stretched before the fire, as Steve had considerately made space to allow him to do.

Steve sat looking into the fire, and when the flames flickered upward they showed that he was smiling at his own thoughts. It was a cruel smile. The man that was stretched before the fire would have slept the worse had he seen it.

The fire sank lower, but Steve did not rebuild it. It died to a glow of ash, and then to greyness.

He rose at last. He groped in the pile of wood which was beside him, and lifted a heavy log. Butcher's legs were between him and the dying fire. It was so dark that he had to feel for where they were, and pass a hand lightly along them. Then he brought the log down heavily. He heard the bone crack. His victim woke from sleep with a scream. He tried to rise, and he screamed again. He thought that the dogs had him by the leg. He called on Steve for help, but there was no answer.

CHAPTER SIXTY-FOUR

IT was midday when Steve came to Jerry Cooper's headquarters, and he had travelled hard to reach them. He said that he had camped with Dr. Butcher, and taken the first watch, and had then slept, while the doctor watched in turn, but when he waked in the morning he was alone. He had searched for hours, and had then come on, thinking that the doctor must have preceded him.

He led them back to the camp where he said that they had passed the night. The fire still burned. The camp was in a hollow thicket, between two oaks.

When he had done all that he could to assist an unsuccessful search he went home.

Four miles from home he went to look at a place where men had camped by a holly hedge. There was no one there now. But he looked farther, and found a dead man who had tried to force his way beneath a denseness of undergrowth, where he appeared to have stuck, or his strength had failed. It was a silly thing for a man to try with a broken leg.

"He must have crawled half a mile," Steve said slowly. "I'm glad I fed him. He'll do now for the dogs to finish."

CHAPTER SIXTY-FIVE

THERE was trouble with Butcher. There was nothing fresh in that. There had been trouble from the first. But he had been careful, up to now, not to press any difference to a last extremity.

273

He had been adroit to compromise, ingenious in producing such positions that Martin would see the expediency of settlement.

Only on one point—an attempt that Martin had made to establish a system of banking credits, which would have taken the place of money, and adjusted the dealings of the community by bookkeepings in the terms of the old coinage—had he definitely defeated Martin's intention.

Even in that he had not shown an open hostility. He hat merely expressed a doubt as to the practicability of the plan, and sneered at it where he could do so safely.

The fact was that his own transactions were so large a part of the commercial dealings of the community that it was impracticable to continue a currency in any form that he declined to recognize—and he could not afford to do so, even had he favoured the method in itself, for it would have revealed the extent of his transactions, and the amounts of his debits, to the interested examination of Jack Tolley, who had been appointed to keep the projected books.

But, apart from this matter, his opposition had never been pushed to extremity, and if it were a fact that those who were known to be unfriendly to the new rule had somewhat lower prices and easier credits, if there were subtle suggestions that the hardness with which Martin had driven the preparation for the winter months had not been really necessary, and that it would have been easier to have relied upon Butcher's miscellaneous resources, they had been too indefinite either for reproof or reprisal.

Yet this constant sapping had not been without its effect upon the less intelligent and more turbulent elements. And it would have been impossible, under any condition, for between two and three hundred men to be worked for three months, as Martin had done, without some discontents arising.

There had been a particular irritation at his insistence that when the majority of the men were engaged in the raiding for food and stores which he had organized in a more regular way, and carried farther afield than had been done previously, those who remained should stand to arms in a perpetual vigilance against an enemy which never came.

He had tried to obtain such supplies as would make them independent of Butcher, but he had only partly succeeded. The time had been too short, the needs too many, and it was easy for Butcher to hint that had these stores been divided or retained according to the individualism of earlier days each man to whom he spoke could easily have purchased from him directly the requirements which could not now be supplied.

Now there was friction over the cloth, of which Butcher had obtained a large supply in the earlier days; when his plunderings had been more discriminating, more farseeing, and more industrious than had been the short-distanced and spasmodic raidings of others.

Martin was determined that the cloth should be handed over without such exchanges as must render them short of other needed things before the return of the warmer weather.

It was at the acutest stage of this difference that another question had arisen, which Martin regarded as fundamental to the social order which he was endeavouring to establish.

It was in a final effort to resolve this position that Butcher came to see him one winter evening, when there was no light upon the frozen roads but that of stars and snow. Yet he found his way without difficulty, for the roads between Larkshill and Cowley Thorn had been cleared by Martin's orders before the commencement of the dangers of the early darkness, and Butcher himself had seen that the byway to Helford.

The two men met with a sense of increasing antagonism, but with a common desire to avoid an open breach—if the other would only see the necessity of giving way!

The subject of Butcher's son had never been mentioned between them since the mystery of his disappearance a month ago.

Martin had a private conviction that Steve was in some way responsible, but there was no evidence to support such a suggestion. Butcher's thoughts might move in the same direction, but he could not suppose that Martin had any connivance with it. He knew how he had himself selected Steve as his son's guide, and he knew also that Martin was not of a kind to instigate a secret assassination.

None the less, he regarded him as the primary cause of the resulting tragedy, of the nature of which there was no doubt for the bones had been identified, and were now buried in the garden of Helford Grange.

It appeared that the man must have wandered, lost and perishing from cold and hunger, till he was within a few miles of his starting-point, and then fallen a prey, either before or after death, to the wandering dog-pack. They had picked him clean, and more than one bone had been broken in their hungry teeth.

Yet, whatever hatred his mind concealed, Butcher came to compromise, as his nature was, and had Martin met him in the same way, the course of events must have been widely different, though they might have led to the same end by a longer path.

"I've come to say," he began, "that I want to work on a friendly footing, if we can. It does no good to anyone for it to be known that we can't pull together. I don't think you're fair about the cloth. If I hadn't taken my men six months ago, and dug it out, and carted it here, it's most likely that it wouldn't exist today. But I've come to say that you can fix your own price, if you'll leave me to decide who's to live in my own houses. You can't say that that isn't a fair offer."

"I'm glad you've given way about the cloth, because I couldn't have had much further patience. We'd made up what we'd got by the end of last week, and it's badly needed. But I'm sorry that I can't make a bargain about it such as you suggest.

"I can't have Pellow moving into Pollock's house, because he's got a good enough one of his own, and because I want Ringwood in there. It's convenient for what he's doing, and he's got a wife and two children and expecting another, and they're all living now in a single compartment of a railway-coach. Surely you can see that there can't be any doubt of what ought to be done."

Butcher looked unusually obstinate.

"I've promised Pellow," he said, "and I don't trust Ringwood. I don't trust him for the rent. His health's bad, and it might break down any time...."

He looked speculatively at Martin. He tried a final concession. "I'll take Ringwood if you'll tell Pellow that it's your doing, and if you'll guarantee the rent."

"Rent?" said Martin. "There won't be any rent."

"But it's my house," Butcher protested, in a genuine bewilderment. "Every one knows that. Sims has paid me rent ever since I moved out of it to go to Helford."

"Then you can move back if you like."

"I don't want to move back myself. I merely want a good tenant."

"I am sorry that these differences should arise, but I cannot allow the old system of renting houses to be re-established among us. I knew nothing of your arrangement with Sims.... Supposing, as you suggest yourself, that Ringwood couldn't pay the rent you would fix, do you suppose that I should allow you to turn him out of the house?"

Butcher hesitated in his reply. At last he said, "I can't make out whether you mean to try to abolish private ownership or not. I know it can't be done, and the attempt could only increase our difficulties; but I can't even understand what you are aiming at. You appear to allow some forms of property. Do you mean that houses are to be an exception? And, if so, how are they to be built in future, and who will be expected to do it?"

Martin answered, "It's a fair question to ask, and I'll answer it as far as I can.

"I don't propose to abolish private property, which is the natural incentive, as it is the natural reward, of individual effort. But I hope to avoid at least some of the resulting abuses which have been within our own experience.

"I am aware that I am only experimenting, and I am aware that I may find cause to modify the position which I am now taking. But regarding houses and land (the original owners or occupiers of which are no longer among us), I am willing that every man should claim the one he occupies, or the land which he is able and willing to cultivate, or otherwise use. A house or field which is left vacant may be occupied by others, and if there be more than one who desire it, I will try to decide fairly between them.

"I do not wish to take away the fair rewards of industry, nor do I suppose that we can avoid inequalities of wealth arising in future, but if we were to work together, with that object, we might do much to mitigate the resulting evils.

"Regarding houses, I do think that it may be possible to make a simple rule that the man who occupies owns. There is no communism in that. So long as he occupies house, or cultivates land, he will have protection in the ownership which he exercises. I see no reason why it should not be passed on at his death to another member of his own family, but, beyond this, I am not yet prepared to go. I see that in avoiding one difficulty we may encounter another, but I regard a system under which one man may own the homes of a thousand of his neighbours as intolerable, and I am resolved that it shall not be re-established here."

"If you allow any right of transfer, at death or otherwise," Butcher replied acutely, "it may be made conditional, and the principle of sale or letting is at once admitted."

"Possibly, though not necessarily. But, even so, the position created would be very different from that of the old landlord-and-tenant law, because there would be no right of distraint or ejection."

"It's no use having claims that you can't enforce."

"No?" said Martin. "Then how about the credits that you give, as far as I can understand, to about two hundred of our own people...? You know that there are no longer any legal means of enforcing payment of a debt, yet you continue to trade, in the assurance, I suppose, that most men are honest, or that the consequence would recoil upon themselves should they fail to maintain satisfactory business relations with you."

Butcher was silent. This was the unmentioned matter which had been at the back of his mind during the past months, and which, more even than Martin's remote responsibility for his son's death, caused him to weigh the risk of an alliance with Cooper, and the declaration of open war.

Taking his silence as no more than an admission of the force of the illustration, Martin went on.

"There is nothing really novel in that. The absence of any legal means of recovering a betting or alcoholic debt did not reduce those businesses to a universal cash basis, even under the old conditions; and it would be absurd to suggest that the betting or beer-drinking fraternities were of a higher commercial morality than the rest of the nation. But the debt of law was replaced by the debt of honour, and often received prior consideration in consequence.

"It shows that, if men had had the courage to see it, the penalizing legislation for the enforcement of legal obligations might have been swept away, with all its cruelties, all its oppressions, all its waste of forced realizations, all its endless attendant parasites, and credit trade would still have continued upon a better economic basis, and in a cleaner atmosphere."

Butcher tried to speak temperately. He had realized, as Martin spoke, that it was war between them—war which could find no ground of compromise, and could give no quarter. Really, he had always known it. Only there had been the timidity of the trader. The reluctance to take a risk until there should be no means of avoidance. But he did not want Martin to read his mind. He must have time to think.

He said, "It is a system—or a lack of system—which you propose, which appears to open the door to very great abuses. Abuses which would be inevitable."

"It would avert greater ones," Martin answered. Did this man really think that he should be an instrument for the collection of his accounts? That he was going to re-establish all the old machinery of summonses, and executions, and distraints, the accumulation of 'costs' upon the poor, the foolish, and the unfortunate the sale of their possessions to others, who might not desire them, at any price they would bring? That he would degrade some of his people to be the tools of such methods?

No. He might make many mistakes. He had much to learn. Much that might only be discoverable by the test of experiment; but there were, fortunately, some things that he had learnt already. He had been a lawyer, and that road was closed. He knew already where it led.

Almost at the same moment the realization that had come to Butcher came to him also. There could be no permanent peace between them. He must either break this man or let him break everything for which he himself was striving.

They looked at each other in a silence that became more significant as the seconds passed.

"You needn't trouble about the house. I'll tell Pellow that you want it for Ringwood," Butcher said at last.

It was a capitulation in words, but Martin did not fail to understand it. The time for compromise was over. In the future, it must be a condition of either secret or open war.

"I'm sure it will be the best way," he said coldly.

Butcher went out.

Martin passed into the next room, in which Jack was working. Helen and Claire were there also.

"Jack," he said, "who's on the patrols for the next fortnight? Are they men you can trust?"

"Mostly. Vincent's doubtful. There's no harm in him, but his wife hates you. That's always dangerous."

"Any of Butcher's men?"

"There'd be three next week. He's been keeping all his men at home lately. I meant to tell you. He says it's the cold. He let me know so that I could use them while they're about. It's just the routine. Had I better tell them they're not wanted?"

"No. But don't trust them. Set an independent patrol farther out on their nights. I don't think it's the cold. I think it's war."

He added, "You'd better let Burman know quietly tomorrow that I want Tom back at once."

Tom had been at Upper Helford a great deal during the last few weeks. He seemed to like going there. He was superintending something which was going on there with the knowledge both of Burman and Martin, but of which nothing was spoken. Last week he had taken over two men that he could trust, and they had not returned.

"I heard this afternoon that Joe Harker's been at Helford Grange twice since last week," Jack added. "Maria let it out to Betsy Parkin."

CHAPTER SIXTY-SIX

THE next day the cloth was unconditionally delivered. Butcher sent a message to Ringwood that the house which Sims had vacated was available for his occupation.

There was only one incident which showed the intention which underlay these surrenders. Pellow's forge had disappeared in the night, and his house was vacant. He took with him the two best carts and three horses.

More important, his removal left them without a smithy, or any expert worker in iron, a vocation which had recovered much of its ancient importance.

Burman came from Upper Helford, and had a conference with Martin which lasted for two hours.

After that there was a new activity. Burman's boats, four in all, including the lugger, came in twice a day, if the weather permitted, and went back loaded with many stores. Volunteers had been found to handle the boats, but they were not permitted to go ashore, and two of the boats, in which they returned, were now moored to the mainland when not in use.

The lugger, manned by Claire and Chris, ventured several times when the weather was too rough for the smaller boats. Even the winter darkness did not restrain these activities.

After a week the frost broke and there was heavy rain, but the work was not interrupted.

Then, on the second night of rain, Jack came to Martin with the report that Joe Harker had ridden over from Cooper's to Helford Grange, and returned after a long interview with Butcher.

Steve Fortune had seen him leaving Cooper's place, and other watchers had seen him at the Grange.

"I've sent Steve straight back," he concluded. "He says Pellow's there, and he's shoeing horses and repairing harness and arms as hard as he can. He's sure there's something afoot. He says Joe's not as fat as when he was with Bellamy. I suppose Cooper works him harder."

Joe Harker was an ex-jockey who had attached himself to Bellamy's gang, and had now the position in Cooper's intelligence department left vacant by the deaths of Rentoul and Reddy Teller. He was not a man of war, but he could ride, and had good eyes, and a ready wit.

"I reckon," Jack went on, "that they've got forty-seven good men that they're sure of, besides a few wasters. That's counting Butcher's fourteen. There's some I can't trust, that might go either way, and some that only care to keep clear of a row, but I've twice his number that I'd trust anywhere.

"Couldn't we strike first, and round up Butcher's lot? They wouldn't fight by themselves.

"Then we ought to be able to tackle Cooper in the same way, and get it ended."

He looked anxiously at Martin for a reply. He knew something of the plans that had been made, and he did not like them. It meant waste, which he hated. It meant a position in which the loyalty of his men might be strained severely. He thought they were in a position in which attack was the best defence.

"I don't think we can, Jack. They've given us no excuse to attack them so far, and I don't want to be the one to start a war. But it isn't only that. Suppose we attacked Butcher, and he held out at the Grange till Cooper came up? Suppose we had to besiege either of them, or first one and then the other? We couldn't do it. Think it out. We haven't even got tents, and the weather's cruel.

"Besides, the attackers always lose most heavily in such cases.

"Or suppose we found Cooper wasn't there when we arrived? You must remember he's got almost all the horses. He might be here before we could get back."

"There's the ammunition, Captain. If we took the Grange, I expect we should find some there.... And there's another thing. We shall lose more men if we seem frightened. I don't mean they'll get killed. They'll desert. I've heard some talk already."

"You must tell them to trust me, Jack. I won't alter the plans I've made. We'll have the Grange before we've done. I may see farther than they do."

He spoke confidently, but when Jack had gone he did not conceal his anxiety, even from Helen. He had thought of the problems of defending a scattered population, including some half-hearted and disloyal elements, against the trained and resolute force which he might hear at any moment was in motion against him, and he only saw one way—and that way was a hard one.

If the men's loyalty failed at such a test—well, the future was with Cooper, and not with him.

And what then would be his end? And what the fates of Claire and of Helen?

The following day Helen went over to Upper Helford, taking her children with her. She returned nest morning, having left them in Chris's charge.

She came home soaked and tired. The weather was still bad. Snow was falling, that melted as it fell, and the field-paths were deep in mud.

She found Muriel with Martin. She noticed, as she entered, that Muriel looked ill and dispirited.

"What I want to ask you," Martin was saying, "is this. Suppose you should have a message from me at any time, day or night, that Cooper is moving to attack us, could you get your people to evacuate the camp at once? I should want them to leave everything, and come just as they are—to come by Bycroft Lane, and across the park, and then by the fields over to Cowley Thorn, to be accommodated in the houses there."

"No. I don't think I could. Not at any time of night or weather. And I should need a better reason than I have yet.... Can't you find some way of peace without more fighting?"

She spoke wearily, being ill and tired. She added, "They won't like leaving all their things. How soon would they get back?"

"I can't say that," Martin answered. He was tired also, and he had hoped for readier co-operation here than he seemed likely to get. "If the women don't value their husbands, or the men their wives, more than their other possessions, they must take the consequences.... I'm not starting a war.... I believe that Cooper is preparing to attack us at the present moment. What do you suppose he wants? What sort of life do you suppose there'll be for Helen or Claire, or for yourself, if Cooper and Butcher do as they like here? And I can tell you this—most of the men who are any good won't be alive then. You can make the best of what are left."

He spoke with an irritation which arose from the unexpected nature of the opposition which he felt he was meeting, but Muriel kept both her self-control and the position which she had taken.

"I'm not refusing to help you. I'm only asking to understand. And it's no use promising something I couldn't do. Why not ask Tom?"

Helen interposed. "Tom doesn't go far from Chris these days, if he can help it." She spoke in an effort to change the tone of the conversation.

Her words drew Muriel's attention to herself. "Wherever have you been? You're wetter than I am. And you look tired out."

"I expect we're all rather tired," Helen answered. "Unless it's Claire. I left her helping to reload the boat. It's wonderful how she keeps on.... I've been to leave the children at Upper Helford."

"At Upper Helford!" The fact that Helen should have done that, and returned to take her part here, impressed Muriel with the seriousness of the position as no words from Martin would have been likely to do.

He answered her exclamation. "Yes. It's the only safe place. I should have sent every child there already, and every woman that could be sheltered, but for the effect it would have.... I'm afraid I didn't explain very patiently, but it seems to me that, if they attack us, it will be a fight that neither side can afford to lose. It will be a fight to a finish, and, I'm afraid, without much mercy on either side. You'll find that what Cooper's men will want will be the women alive and the men dead.

"Miss Temple, the real trouble's this. We're scattered over an area of several square miles, and we can't defend it. We're bound to close up, or we shall be defeated in detail. If I get all the men together, I can't force a fight where I like, because Cooper's men are mounted. Would the women like them to raid the camp while the men are away? Would the men like to leave them to such a chance...? There's one thing we do know—Cooper will have to come by the upper road if he is to make a junction with Butcher. If he has any sense—and he has that—he'll come over the heath, where the horses can move quickly. We are bound to hold Cowley Thorn, because it covers the landing-place, and, if we're beaten, Upper Helford's the only retreat we've got. Besides that, it's the only point from which we can strike back. You can guess what would happen if we were drawn into the open country in this weather.... There's another thing that we're not telling anyone, but I can trust you not to repeat it. We've scarcely any ammunition, and Butcher probably guesses that, if he doesn't know it. But we don't want it to get about yet among our own men."

Muriel said, "I expect you're right; and I'll do what I can if it comes to that. But I hope it won't."

CHAPTER SIXTY-SEVEN

JOE HARKER slipped wearily off his horse as he came up to Captain Cooper, who had seen his approach and stood waiting for his report.

Joe was two stone lighter than when he had ridden off from the scene of Bellamy's death three or four months ago to take the news to Cooper which had ended in his abortive raid. But this had been a hard ride, even for his present condition, and the weather was execrable.

"Well," said Cooper, giving his subordinate the hard gaze, devoid of geniality, which was his common regard of either friend or enemy, "what tale does he tell now?"

Martin Webster did well not to undervalue his antagonist. Cooper was a man who had not been accustomed to fail through miscalculation or lack of foresight. His plans were clear and methodical. He had fought hard for the business successes of his earlier experience, and he had learnt the value of efficiency. He had always found that the price of error must he paid, and that it is usually a high one. He was destitute of ideality or imagination, and it followed, among other consequences, that he was not unreasonably elated by success, nor depressed by failure.

We have seen him twice in retreat, and in both instances he had shown himself formidable. On both occasions he had shown the ability to judge promptly and act decisively and, by so doing, though he had known defeat, he had avoided disaster.

Had he succeeded in establishing an alliance with Martin, he would have watched for an opportunity of displacing him, but he would not have forced or contrived it. He would not have allowed the wish for that event to develop any premature or hazardous action.

Because he saw that an alliance with Butcher would alter the balance of probabilities—might, indeed, turn the scale decisively—he would not, therefore, conclude an easy bargain, or omit any precaution that he could devise for his own advantage.

"He says he's ready any time," Joe answered, "and the sooner the better."

"When does he want us to move?"

"He says, two nights after the full moon there will be two sentinels that he can trust between the Belsham Road and the common. We shall get right through to Cowley Thorn before anyone knows it.

"He says, don't make any preparations till the last minute. He doesn't want any suspicion."

"I don't need advice from him. You can go back and tell him that the deal's on, but he must come himself to arrange it. I'll see him tomorrow night, at this time, in Burchell's Hollow."

Joe looked perturbed and doubtful.

"He won't do that."

"Then the deal's off. I don't trust Butcher," he said shortly.

"He hates Captain Webster."

"He doesn't love me overmuch."

"He doesn't only hate him—he's afraid."

Cooper saw the force of that argument, but he saw also that those who advance through fear may retreat through a stronger impulse of the same quality.

"He must come himself," he said finally.

"He'll say it's a needless risk."

"Tell him I'm the best judge as to what I need. He'll come."

Cooper did not distrust Butcher particularly; he was of a kind that he could easily understand. He could be trusted—to look after himself. He was not a man to engage in a complexity of avoidable plotting, or to attempt to betray both sides at once. He was not at all likely to be in any genuine alliance with Martin. Cooper did not doubt that the invitation was serious, and sent in good faith. But he meant that Butcher should be committed as deeply as possible. He meant to prove that Butcher was prepared to take some risks to gain his co-operation. He suspected that, when it came to the actual fighting, Butcher would not be there. Well then, if he wouldn't fight, he must take his share of the risks in another way. Butcher didn't fight; he squirmed. Very well, he must squirm. He spoke his thought aloud. "If he won't fight, he'll squirm."

Joe partly followed his thought, but he didn't like the idea. It seemed a foolish risk, and needless. He was quite willing to be the intermediary of the negotiation. He felt capable, and it gave him importance. It meant a reward, to be claimed at the right time.

Besides, he didn't feel sure of persuading Butcher to take the risk. It might even lead to the end of the negotiations if both men were equally obstinate. But he knew that Cooper meant what he said, and that opposition was rarely profitable. He ventured a reminder.

"You know the warning he's had. If he's caught with us, it's most likely he'll hang him."

Captain Cooper laughed. "Why not...? But he won't be caught. If he is, he's no good to me. I don't want men who can't keep their own skins."

CHAPTER SIXTY-EIGHT

CAPTAIN COOPER and Joe were both right about Butcher's feelings—and his decision.

He didn't like going, but he went.

In fact, there was little risk. He had spies whom he could trust, for the good reason that they had little to hope for from Martin. He went and returned by night, meeting Cooper in an old saw-pit hollow, by the light of a moon that was near the full, and the whiteness of a thin snowfall that barely covered the ground in the more sheltered places.

Dimly seen, to each other as they were, each was yet conscious of the change which had taken place in the other since they had gone separate ways some months ago.

Cooper was harder, leaner, and his voice, which had always been of a metallic quality, was harsher and more dominating, easily changing into a tone of menace, and with a tendency to rise easily, which it had learnt from the controlling of others in the open air.

Butcher could not be leaner than before—was, in fact, somewhat less so, and of a more muscular quality; his difference lay in the fact that the veneer of gentility which he had worn in his stockbroking days, and which had been thinning four months ago, was now entirely lost, and his appearance and manners approximated more nearly to those of a suave and unscrupulous huckster.

The conversation was short and pointed. The weather did not invite delay, and Cooper had gained his purpose in forcing Butcher to meet him.

There was already a basis of understanding between them. Cooper was to rule, and own and control the land. Butcher was to be the monopolist of all commercial transactions.

Butcher had one new point on which he wished for an understanding. He had lost his son, and he had a natural desire to replace him with another heir. But it was a matter on which Cooper was disposed to be contemptuously complacent.

"Webster's widows?" he said. "You could have both if you liked. Only I promised one to Joe, when he brought in the first news about her. I don't believe in breaking a business promise. Of course, if she pushes into the row and gets killed, as she's the sort to do, that's her trouble.... Oh, she's like that, is she? Well, Joe'll have to nurse it when it comes.... Yes, you can have the other. More your sort, is she? Don't think I've seen that one. They're all much alike to me.... Second night after the full moon...? No, early morning's the time. No night work for me. An hour before sunrise. We shall come along the Belsham Road, and then through Larkshill, and push on straight for the railway. Why? Why, because I'm not a fool. Because, if they suspect anything, they'll look for us across the common, or up the road from Larkshill to Cowley Thorn. They'll think we shall aim first, at joining you, and lay their plans accordingly. Of course, you'll attack separately. Why not? You've only to see that they don't get between you and Helford Grange. If they're too strong, you can fall back, can't you? You'll do your part, as long as you keep them busy. Only don't lie low and do nothing, or you'll be sorry afterwards.... We couldn't keep together, anyway. My men are mounted. I've trained them more than a bit since last time. I reckon they're good for Webster's lot at two to one, and perhaps rather more than that.... Yes. That's all. There's this infernal snow coming again.... The second night after the full moon. One hour before dawn. We shall be there."

He did not know that Steve Fortune lay at the top of the bank above him, very wet and uncomfortable, but hearing every word he said, and a good deal of Butcher's replies.

But when he got back to the shelter of his own roof, and sat with John Coe, his farm-bailiff, and the one man to whom he gave some measure of trust and confidence, he said contemptuously:

"That's Butcher's idea of planning—a week beforehand; and I'll bet there'll be half a dozen that know of it by this time tomorrow. I think I could tell which night it will be, but I shan't say, even to you. It won't be the night we've arranged. That's the one thing certain."

CHAPTER SIXTY-NINE

STEVE FORTUNE brought this news to Martin nest morning.

It gave shape and definiteness to the menace under which they had been living, and stirred the preparations for defence to a redoubled activity.

Steve reported fully, including the allocation of "Webster's widows," which left no doubt of the spirit in which their opponents would use the victory, if they should obtain it.

Martin warned him not to give any hint to others of the knowledge which he had gained—a little-needed warning, for Steve was not loosely talkative. But Martin feared lest word might be carried to Butcher, which would cause their plans to be altered, even if it did not produce an immediate crisis. He wanted time. The full moon was three days ahead. He had five days.

It was a peculiarity of the position that Butcher's men were still moving freely among them—or as freely as he permitted, for he was incessantly watchful to avoid being surprised by any sudden attack that Martin might direct against him. He knew that Martin must now be aware of his enmity, but, while his men were accepted in their due turns for the patrol work, he supposed that he was not suspected of any collusion with Cooper, and relied upon the reputation for neutrality which he had gained during the earlier hostilities.

He had cautiously enlisted three or four further men whom he had known to be discontented, and who awaited his call to join him openly at Helford Grange. He had put that place into as good a state of defence as his resources permitted, and his fourteen men were well armed. He kept them from further expeditions on the pretext of adverse weather, and Martin appeared to accept this explanation, while he debated inwardly whether it would not be best to make a sudden attack upon the Grange before the date which had been fixed for Cooper's coming.

Thus there was general pretence, but little deception. There was probably no one within the district who did not move under a sense of impending catastrophe.

Of the scattered population in the woods and in isolated dwellings, some came closer in, and others disappeared into the farther wilderness, preferring to take their chances of cold and solitude, rather than to await the fury of the storm of human passions which was overshadowing them.

James Hatterley and his wife were among those who disappeared in this way, and his hollow tree was left without a tenant.

On the last night before the full moon there was a larger exodus, about twenty people, men and women, disappearing during the night, with two of the three remaining carts. They were led by a man who had been on the last expedition against the Bellamy gang, and their destination was the tunnel in which Martin and Claire had been found, which they hoped they might be able to make endurable for the remainder of the winter months.

Martin heard of these defections without regret. He had little use for the cowardly or the irresolute, and the reduction in numbers simplified the hardest part of the problem which confronted him.

On the following morning he had a message from Burman that Tom had finished the work on which he had been occupied, and hoped to return himself during the next day.

It was a needed encouragement; for, under an outer aspect of confidence, he was aware that the continued strains of work and anxiety were threatening a physical collapse, which might be fatal, not only to himself, but to all who were dependent upon him.

The secret plan which he had formed seemed more hazardous as the time approached which must test it, with the lives of all who were dearest, or who relied upon him, staked on its success.

For the first time in his life he found himself unable to obtain the sleep he needed. He was vexed by a constant neuritis, rendering the use of his left arm painful and difficult.

He found himself constantly wondering, as he looked on the faces around him, whether they would be alive in a week's time, or in what condition of misery that he had brought upon them. He saw now that he could so easily have made some compromise with Butcher which would have delayed this crisis, if it had not averted it permanently.

He watched the weather, hoping secretly for a deep snow such as would render Cooper's attack impracticable.

That afternoon he went over to Upper Helford himself to inspect what had been done, and on his return he made a public announcement that, as there was apprehension of an attack by Cooper, all women and children who were willing could be accommodated there until quieter times. He found that there was no difficulty in filling the available boats, even though it meant the abandonment of their homes to those who went, and the four boats made a loaded journey, in the course of which one was nearly swamped in the wintry sea.

For the first time for a fortnight Claire came home that evening. She reported that there was now sleeping accommodation for all the women and children who were likely to avail themselves of the protection it offered. Loft, and stable, and byre had been utilized, and some rough protection had been erected for the ejected cattle.

"I want you to take Helen back with you tomorrow," Martin said. "It's a useless risk staying here longer."

The two women looked at each other, and Helen shook her head.

Claire said, "Why shouldn't you? It's my turn to be home for a bit now."

"I didn't mean that you should stay instead," Martin interposed. "I want you both there. We don't know what may happen any moment now."

"Claire's occupied too much with the boat to look after you here," Helen answered. "I'm not going till you do."

"I don't need any looking after—and Betty can do that anyway."

"Betty's going tomorrow morning. I've arranged that with Phillips."

"I'd much rather you'd go," Martin answered; but he did not contest it further. He felt as though matters were beyond his control, and must happen as fate should lead.

He went out of the room, and Helen said, "Of course, I couldn't go and tell Betty to stay, though she was willing enough. I don't really mind, now that the babies are safe. I suppose Upper Helford really is safe, whatever happens here?"

"Oh, it's safe enough," Claire answered confidently. "Tom's put some extra barbed wire that he got from the camp along the shore side. There was a good bit there before that. I should be sorry for anyone who goes that way if he isn't wanted.... I shouldn't worry, if I were you. Martin always comes out all right in the end."

"I can't help worrying. Martin never worried before, but he does now, though he won't let people see it."

"Yes, I know that. Who wouldn't, with a plan like his? But you'll find he'll keep to it, all the same.... We shall all be glad when it's over.... I hope the weather won't get any worse.... They overloaded the boats today."

CHAPTER SEVENTY

IT was the evening of the first night after the full moon. The weather had been so rough that they had been unable to use the smaller boats, and, though Claire had made one passage in the lugger successfully, she had only taken four women, no others being willing to face the storm, and she had had so much difficulty in re-turning that she had given up the idea of a second attempt, and brought Chris up to the house with her.

She found Tom there, and Jack Tolley, taking instructions from Martin as to the procedures of the next morning, which broke off as they entered.

"I brought Chris up for the night," she said, in explanation. "There's nothing wrong, but the wind's worse than ever tonight, and there's a bad sea, and what's the use of taking the boat over empty to bring it back in the morning? There wasn't anyone but Monty and Pettifer at the landing-place when we got in."

They knew that wind and rain were the explanations of that solitude, for there was no longer any unwillingness on the part of the women to seek the safety of Upper Helford.

Feeling had changed during the last two days. It was not that there had been any open act of hostility to alarm them. There was still nothing but Pellow's empty forge, and the fact that twenty people, more or less, had fled to the inclemencies of the wilderness, and that Butcher's men had not been seen since yesterday, to give indi-cation of impending danger; but a feeling of disquiet, vague but ur-gent, had disturbed even the slowest and the most reluctant.

It was only this evening, and to the men that were now with him, that Martin had told the news that Steve had brought, fixing the attack which would be made upon them at the end of the following night, and even now he had warned them not to mention the fact to any.

"We don't want them," he said, "to change their plans because they think we suspect them. But we'll clear the railway camp com-pletely tomorrow, and we'll finish getting the women over, if the weather's at all possible."

As Claire entered he had ceased speaking, to listen to her report. It was a day lost. It meant that the complete evacuation which he had planned would be impossible tomorrow. But they must do what they could. Anyway, they would finish clearing the railway camp in the morning. The women must come to Cowley Thorn for the night, as he had first intended

They had nothing to fear for tonight—and in such weather! But Tom said he would make his way round the patrols, all the same. He would leave nothing to chance.

No man had worked harder than he during the last weeks, and none showed so little sign of fatigue, either of mind or body. He was of a disposition that works with the expenditure of a minimum of nervous force, and he was under the influence of Chris's contrasting vivacity.

"Can't I come with you?" she said eagerly, and changed to a frown of petulance at the chorus of negative which the proposal caused. It was her first night on the mainland, though she had brought the lugger to the landing-stage in Claire's company several times previously. That was the extent of her father's permission, even now that he had gained confidence in Martin, and was offering the asylum of the island to the threatened settlement, and though he was aware that she would not be likely to be far from Tom, nor to be ill-protected when he was near.

But now, under this stress of weather, Claire her out of the loneliness of the last few months to this place of excitements, and it would have been a heavenly ending to a day of storm and struggle could she have tramped six miles of rough ways in rain and wind in the company of the man with whose slower moods she could play so easily, and with the romance of shadowy danger in the darkness of the farther fields.

It was the measure of her triumphant audacity (perhaps to the judgment of a colder reason, of selfishness and ignorance also) that the gravity of those among whom she moved had no power to impress her. Even Claire's confident courage seemed to her tame, with the taint of maturity. But to Tom it was as adorable when it urged to a reckless adventure of curiosity as when it tempted and then eluded with audacious teasing.

CHAPTER SEVENTY-ONE

THAT night Martin could not rest. He had slept somewhat better than usual the night before, having arrived at that stage of his plans at which there seemed nothing more to be arranged, and it only remained to see to what issue they would lead.

After a busy morning, during which he had felt more alert and more confident in himself than had been the case for several previous days, he had yielded to Helen's urging, and taken further sleep in the afternoon.

The night found him restless, with a sense of impending evil which would not leave his mind.

He had been trained by his profession to a severity of mental discipline which did not easily rebel, nor was he accustomed to receive such rebellion complacently.

He went over all the preparations he had made, all the orders he had given, and decided that nothing had been over-looked, nothing more could be done till the morning came.

He was alone in the house with the four women. Phillips was taking his turn in the patrol work, and would not be back till three o'clock.

There was nothing in that. He had no fear of a personal attack. The doors and windows were strongly bolted and barred. It had been arranged that at any threat of danger they should retire into the kitchen, which had its own defensive preparations, and await relief. A shot would be heard in the nearer houses of Cowley Thorn, where nearly thirty of his men were barracked, and would bring help in about four minutes.

Besides, there were several reasons making the occurrence of such an attack as unlikely as its success. He thought of that possibility, and discarded it. It was not that which vexed his mind.

He sat on in the library as the hours passed, reviewing all that he had done, or failed to do, in the last four months, and wondering whether it were about to end in abortion, or would lead to the foundation of better things than had yet been reached.

If he could win now, he felt that the way ahead would rot be impossibly difficult. Doubtless, there would be blunders, disappointments, discouragements enough, but yet, if he could win this fight, he felt good hope for the future. If he could win this fight. *If*—

And if not?

It was useless—worse than useless—to dwell on such a possibility. He must not fail.

He had confidence in his own plans—he had the advantage of knowing those of his opponents. They were going to attack tomorrow night—toward dawn. That was because it was the night on which two of Butcher's men were to be on the watch between Belsham Road and...but if Cooper were going to attack as Steve reported, he would not come by the Belsham Road. Then why had he accepted Butcher's date? Simply because Butcher had proposed it.

Might he not have thought of that afterward, and changed his plans?

He heard the voices of Helen and Claire. They had not gone to bed either. Perhaps they were as restless as he. He went into the dining-room, and found them before the fire.

But they were talking of other days.

A chance reference by Helen to a school-friend, whom the had both known in Cheltenham many years earlier, had brought up reminiscences of the strange, already half-forgotten world, and they had been talking without regard to time, and in oblivion of all the anxieties which had been pressing upon him.

"I can't rest tonight," he said. "I think I'll take a ride round, as soon as Phillips returns, and see that everything's all right. I shall feel easier tomorrow, when we have cleared the camp—and Larkshill too, if we can persuade them to come."

"You can't ride tonight," Helen said. "The weather's worse rather than better. And what use could it be?"

He told them of the doubt that had entered his mind.

"If they should have seen that there can be no special advantage in tomorrow night, mightn't they alter the date, and, if so, wouldn't they make it earlier rather than later, when they heard that we're moving all the women to Upper Helford?"

"They can't make it much earlier now," Helen remarked, with some reason.

"Mightn't they decide not to attack us at all, if we must go without fighting?" Claire asked. "They get almost everything we've got, and they know that we couldn't all stay there forever."

It was one of the doubts that had been in Martin's own mind, and, if they acted in that way, he was not sure that it would help his plans. It would look rather silly if nothing happened and they had to return at last to their deserted and plundered homes. But he knew that things wouldn't be quite like that. He had one card to play which they could not guess. And, in any case, with the women in safety, he could use his men more freely. No, he didn't really fear that.

But he did want it over quickly. There was no accommodation—scarcely the barest shelter—for so many at Upper Helford. There must be discomforts, even privations, from the first. Hardened as most of them were, there might be disease if it should continue.

The crisis could not come too quickly—after tonight.

"I shouldn't think they'd be likely to do much in this weather," Claire suggested. "It wouldn't suit Butcher's rheumatism."

He was aware that he must seem unreasonable in this midnight anxiety, but it would not leave him.

A lover of the occult might have connected his disquiet with the long line of horsemen that moved very silently along a road nearly ten miles away. But there is a simpler alternative.

Was the weather really so impossible? He went to the garden door, unbarred it, and looked at the night.

It was still windy. A cold wind from the north-west. But the sky was clearing, and the moon shone on pools in which the ice was forming. It would be colder before the dawn.

He closed the door, and went back into the dining-room.

"I'll wait till Phillips comes before deciding. He won't be long now. Then perhaps I'll lie down. But there's no sense in you both sitting up as well."

But they said they did not want to sleep either. They sat and talked of old and distant things, with silent intervals, as do those who wait for the news of birth or death, or of a surgeon's work in an adjoining room.

Then Phillips came.

He had news, though it was of no certain import.

Joe Harker had ridden in about two hours ago, and was with Butcher at the Grange. His horse had been unsaddled, and it seemed probable that he was not returning.

That might mean a message that Cooper's plans had been changed. It might only mean that he was the bringer of final plans for tomorrow night.

"I wish you'd get my horse, Phillips. I'm going to take a ride round before I turn in."

Phillips was slow to move.

"I don't think I'd do that, sir. If I may say so, sir."

Phillips thought of his master first. If others wouldn't keep a good look-out for themselves, they should be the ones to suffer.

"Perhaps you wouldn't, Phillips, and you might be wiser than I. But I think I shall all the same."

Helen was silent. Sympathetically, she was feeling something of the apprehension which disturbed his mind.

Claire may have felt it also. She said, "It seems a crazy thing to do; but if you must go you'd better take my horse. She's so sure-footed in the dark."

She thought also that she was so much the swifter. Probably the best of her kind that the island held

She fetched him the automatic which she had been carrying and which had done them such good service in the tunnel fight. He would take no other weapon.

Would he take some more cartridges? There were only about a dozen left, besides those with which it was loaded. No, it didn't matter. It was unlikely that he would have any occasion to use it.

"I shall be back before it's light," he said more cheerfully, now that he had found the relief of action. "I don't suppose I shall be away more than two or three hours."

They did not guess that they would never meet in that room again.

CHAPTER SEVENTY-TWO

HE rode first to Cowley Thorn, where he was not surprised to find an alert watch, for Jack Tolley was in charge there, and he was not one who trusted to chance.

He went on to the landing-place, and found the boats well guarded.

The sea had gone down somewhat with the falling wind, though the swell was still heavy, and it seemed probable that they would be able to venture out in the morning. This was well also.

He rode westward, above the high shore facing Upper Helford.

He looked over a broad sea-channel to a cliff-shore, along which a sentry was pacing behind the hedge of wire. Like Jack, Burman left nothing to chance.

The tide was flowing out beneath him. In a few hours the hollow of Helford Brook would be bare enough for a man to walk or wade across it, as Arter had once found, though he had made little profit from the discovery.

He turned inland from there, and rode almost up to the ruined walls of Helford Grange. All here was silent and peaceful, though he thought that a faint light shone upward, probably from a cellar-grating in the side of the old moat.

Left-hand then, in a wide curve round Larkshill, and so to the approach of the railway camp across the road from which he had first ridden up to it four months ago. But he did not cross the road. He had no wish to disturb them if all were well. It came to his mind that they would be watching (if they watched at all) for mounted men, and that he would be a cause for alarm should he approach from the southward.

The moon was bright now, and there was a white frost on the fields.

He reined up, looking over the hedge into the silent road beneath him.

All was quiet.

He recognized now that it had been a foolish thing to do to come out for such a ride in the night. There was nothing left but to go home and regret the sleep he had lost, and for which he supposed that he would suffer tomorrow night, when he would be really needed.

But he was reluctant to go. Strangely reluctant to commence the return which would be a confession of the folly which had brought him out.

And while he sat silent he saw the figure of a man that came running toward him along the hedge-side.

The man was within twenty yards before he saw him, and stopped abruptly.

"I shall fire, if you move," he called out, and Will Carless knew his voice, and answered pantingly.

He came to the horse's side.

"There are about thirty men coming up the road. They must be close now. I had to come round the field so that I shouldn't be seen."

"You must leave the camp to me now. Take the field-path to Larkshill, and warn them there. Tell them to clear out to Cowley Thorn, and not to lose a second. Never mind what they leave. They're not to fight there, unless it's to give the women time to get clear."

Will Carless ran on. Martin turned his mind to his own problem. The camp was scarcely a mile away. But he could not get his horse down the bank at that point. To cross the road he must go some distance farther south, but it was the quickest way, if there, were time to do it unseen.

He rode on, his ears alert for every sound, his mind on the fact that Cooper had not only changed the night, but the direction of the attack. He was not an opponent to be regarded lightly.

He came to where the fields fell to the road-level, and the gap that he had ridden through four months ago still gave free passage.

He looked cautiously at the empty road before leaving the tall shadow of an ancient hawthorn-hedge that had grown unchecked all summer, and, though leafless now, still made a ten-foot barrier of light-proof thicket.

Something moved in the distance up the frosty centre of the moonlit road.

He turned his horse into the hedge on the farther side of the gap. He could see nothing in that position of whoever were coming up the road, but they could see nothing of him.

As they passed he would see their backs, but they would not see him, unless they should turn their heads to look—and the dark shadow of the hedge would be a good cover even then.

He waited so long that he doubted whether his sight had not misled him, and then they began to pass him, two abreast, their horses walking with muffled hoofs.

He counted them as they passed. Nearly fifty men. Seen by a better light, they might have seemed the oddest troop; that were ever assembled for a military enterprise. They were mounted on horses of very different qualities; there was no unity of clothes or accoutrements; they were armed with an extraordinary variety of weapons, ancient and modern, that a six-months' search had accumulated. But to those whose lives were staked upon defeating them, they were sufficiently formidable.

As he counted mechanically, Martin debated in his mind if he should not fire among them, and then trust to his horse's speed for safety. Would his shot be heard, and give warning? Would it stir this slow approach to a very different pace, which would hasten attack and give no time for flight? Should he not give a longer warning if he waited and rode rapidly to the camp after he had crossed the road? They might even wait till the dawn before they attacked, if they had no cause to suspect that an alarm had been given.

While he debated thus, Cooper passed him. He was disposed to fire then, but hesitated, and the chance was lost.

Perhaps it was best. He was not a practised shot, and the light might have betrayed him.

They had all passed now. Forty-seven—or forty-nine. In another moment he could cross the road—and then his horse neighed.

She may have recognized some old companion of Cooper's stable, from which she came. She may simply have resented the fact that the other horses were disappearing up the road without having been made aware of her existence, and that she was not allowed to follow.

A horse answered, and she neighed again.

Martin abandoned concealment and pushed out into the road.

It may have been a mistake. It is possible that there might have been no disposition to inquire into what was no more than a horse's neigh from a roadside field. But his first thought was for the warning of the camp; and if he were to be chased, he wished to be on the right side of the road.

But he found that he could not leave the road at this point on the farther side. There was an awkward ditch, and a high hedge beyond it. He did not know what the chance might be to the south, but he knew that, a little farther on, if he should ride toward the camp, there would be no obstacle whatever. Road and waste-land had no division of hedge or ditch or wall to impede him.

He turned his horse to follow the invading troop, and as he did so he became aware that Cooper was leaving nothing to chance. He was sending two of his men back to investigate the shadowy figure on the road behind him.

It was at that moment that the depression which had been weighing upon him, and against which he had been fighting for several days, was suddenly lifted. He trotted confidently forward, the automatic concealed against his horse's neck.

Cooper had pulled his horse to the side of the road, and was looking back to see what happened.

Observing a single horseman, who rode forward to meet his men, he did not suspect an enemy, but he thought that messenger from Butcher had been sent to intercept him with news of some unexpected development.

He rode back also.

Martin quickened his pace. The men were near, and there was still this obstructing hedge on his right. If he could pass them and get up to the man behind—who he felt sure was Cooper—the way of escape was clear.

He edged his horse across the road to the right.

The two men met him.

"Is Captain Cooper here?" he demanded. "I want to speak to your Captain."

The men were strangers to him, and he to them. They were puzzled, but this was not like the approach of an enemy. They gave him way, and turned their horses to follow.

He quickened pace as he passed them.

Cooper saw that they had allowed him passage, and was confirmed in his previous opinion.

He called to Martin to halt as he approached, and turned his own horse across the road to stay him.

"I am Captain Cooper," he called out. "What have you brought?"

"This for you," he answered curtly. He remembered the remark about "Webster's widows," and as he spoke he lifted his hand and fired.

But he should have fired without speaking. The tone, rather than the words, gave a warning to Cooper's mind, so that he swerved somewhat, with a quick instinct of danger, just as the shot came.

The bullet, which might have found a deadlier lodging, struck his bridle-arm just as he pulled on the rein, and the jerk caused the horse to rear.

Doing this, it took the next bullet in its own chest, and horse and man came down in a heap together.

Martin turned his own horse as the second bullet was fired, and made off, at a rapid pace, over the waste land that lay between the road and the canal-ditch. There was some half-hearted pursuit by slower riders from a force which he had rendered leaderless for the moment, and who were unfamiliar with the way he was going. There were some random shots. But the suddenness of the event, and the covering night, gave him sufficient advantage to make retreat seem easy.

His real danger was that the chestnut should stumble on the rough waste-strewn ground, but she justified Claire's confidence in her, and hen he rode into a camp which had been roused already to activity by the firing, he was alone and unpursued.

CHAPTER SEVENTY-THREE

MARTIN'S attack upon Captain Cooper had succeeded by its unexpectedness, as an audacity may often do. Among its major consequences must be counted the restoration of the cool and tenacious attitude with which he was accustomed to face a conflict, but which had faltered under the working and waiting strains of the previous days. It had succeeded also in causing disorder, and a delay which was of vital importance. It had not killed Jerry Cooper, nor inflicted any disabling injury.

He had a bad fall and a bleeding arm. The fall shook him for a time, and the arm must be bound up; but he was not of a disposition to be lightly turned from his purpose, nor to give undue regard to a physical disability.

Within fifteen minutes he felt himself fit to continue, and issued his orders accordingly, without losing time even to curse the men who had let Martin pass them. His horse was dead, and he was content to take an inferior and quieter animal from one of his men, such as could be safely ridden with only one arm in working order.

Then, preferring speed to any further attempt at secrecy, he ordered John Coe to ride on with twenty men to attack Larkshill, while he advanced upon the railway camp with the remainder of the force.

It was arranged that Butcher should advance at the first sign of dawn upon the defenders of Cowley Thorn, either to capture it, if the resistance should be sufficiently feeble, thus cutting off the line of retreat to Upper Helford, or at least to hold them engaged until Cooper should have completed his own part of the programme, and could effect a junction with him.

Cooper was well informed of the condition of those upon whom these attacks were to be delivered. He knew that the women had been partly evacuated. He supposed that Martin's plan was to place them in security while he continued to operate upon the mainland with most of the men. By attacking before this evacuation was complete, he hoped to capture some of the women. But that object was subordinate; for their fate must ultimately depend upon the result of the fighting, as it had done since the world began. It might be an actual disadvantage to be encumbered by them till the conflict was over. But he aimed to demoralize his opponents with a confused disaster, while they were themselves so embarrassed, and before they could complete their dispositions for unimpeded battle.

It was good strategy enough; and though he could not know that it was part of Martin's own plan that he should appear to be driven back, with all his force, upon Upper Helford, the energy of his attack, and the earlier date that he had selected, might easily transform a tactical retreat into a real disaster.

The experiences of the next few hours were blurred in the minds of those who fought or fled from Larkshill and the railway camp to the doubtful refuge of Cowley Thorn. If their memories held any clear impressions, these were rather of the events of the later hours of the group of women round the boats that waited the slow rising of the indifferent tide, while the noise of battle and pursuit pressed closer; and of the embarkation at last, the while the remnant of the little guarding force fought hand-to-hand with the horsemen who had dismounted to reach them among the fallen larches. Or, it might be, of that longer wait for the tide to fall again, so that those who had defended Cowley Thorn could retreat over the hollow of Helford Brook to the security of the barbed-wired cliff of Upper Helford—a wait under a fire from their assailants to which they could make little reply, because there were few, except Jack Tolley, who had any cartridges left.

It was here that Helen and Claire had waited, with a distracted Betty, who had good cause to believe that Phillips hat perished in the house, in which they had delayed too long. For they had been reluctant to leave it in Martin's absence, and the advance of Butcher's men had left them scanty time for flight to the protection of the houses in Cowley Thorn; which Martin had chosen as the first line of defence at that point. And even then Phillips had obstinately remained to test the quality of the defences which his ingenuity had provided, and had found them of such avail that Reeves, in impatience of the unexpected delay which this resistance caused, had ordered his men to set fire to the house, which the more frugal-minded Butcher was too late to prevent when he came up, and observed the folly which his lieutenant had committed.

For Butcher had intended that house for his own occupation, as he had intended Helen for his own wife. But now dense columns of yellow smoke rose upright in the frosty air—an omen, as it seemed to many on either side, that Martin's reign was over.

But Phillips was not dead. He had not anticipated the event with accuracy, but he had known that a siege cannot long be sustained without a sufficient supply of water for the garrison, and he now owed his safety to the fact that he had filled a large hogshead with water in the cellar to which he retreated, the temperature of which never rose above a tepid warmth as he crouched within it.

It was mainly due to Jack Tolley that the final retreat to Upper Helford was achieved without loss or disorder. The few women who had retreated in this direction, and who had not been taken off in the boats in consequence, were first transferred to the other side by means of the horses, as soon as the tide had fallen sufficiently. Martin had returned Claire's horse to her after he had united his retreating bands on the heath between Cowley Thorn and the sea; and with the two others indifferently ridden, but fastened to her own bridle on either hand, she had forded the falling channel three times before the water was low enough for pedestrian passage.

Then, when the time came that the fighting force could retreat across the lessening water, Jack Tolley had volunteered to hold back pursuit with his single rifle, and had proved equal to the occasion.

It was just before that time that Cooper had endeavoured to combine his own force with Butcher's in a third charge, which he felt sure, if it could once reach its object, would decide the issue; but he found his men, and Butcher's even more so, were of little heart to attempt it.

Butcher's force had already suffered somewhat severely, being the first to encounter the prepared line of defence at Cowley Thorn, and as they wished to remain alive to enjoy the fruits of victory, they received his suggestion without enthusiasm. They had twice been driven back with loss: if their opponents were prepared to retreat without further fighting they had no objection to offer.

Cooper asked contemptuously if they would follow his leading, to which they agreed, but disconcerted him somewhat by inquiring from whom they were to take orders if he were

It was Jack Tolley's rifle that was responsible for this question. In the charges that they had made already, they had learnt that the first man to break from cover was hit immediately.

Slater, groaning on the frozen ground, with a broken knee-cap, and Prescott, still wiping the blood from his eyes as it ran down from where a bullet had scored his forehead, were the more fortunate examples of this experience.

Cooper was not a professor of heroics: he was a practical business man. He said no more about the leading of charges.

So they watched and waited till three riderless horses appeared at the cliff-top, and ran loose over the heather, when, correctly supposing this to indicate that their enemies were retreating across the hollow, and would provide an easy mark for the bullets of those above them, they made another attempt to advance, on which a single shot came from the gorse-bushes that lined the edge of the cliff, and Reeves, who was somewhat in advance of the others, pitched forward awkwardly, and lay still; on which his companions retreated too hastily for a second shot to be necessary—for Jack shot with economy.

Seeing the effect of his bullet, he judged it to be an excellent time at which to slip down the cliff and follow his companions to safety, leaving his opponents to a half-hour of further waiting, before they ventured to investigate whether he might still be there.

CHAPTER SEVENTY-FOUR

CAPTAIN COOPER looked across at the cliff-front of Upper Helford, and down at the intervening hollow into which the tide was flowing.

He considered that it would be passable during the night, and that the moon would still be good.

He was pleasantly aware of victory, though he was not elated beyond reason.

In the course of one day's fighting against an unmounted but larger force, which had been worse disciplined, worse armed, and (he thought) worse handled than his own, he had captured the railway camp, the ruins of the mining village of Larkshill, and the larger and more populated Cowley Thorn—the latter with the assistance of Butcher's force, augmented by desertions to over twenty men, and which Butcher had commanded with some discretion as to his own location, but with a businesslike ability which had increased Cooper's respect, if not his liking, for his ally.

He had his own list of dead and wounded—John Coe among the former—to consider, but he reckoned that the retreating force had suffered at least as heavily. He had counted seven who lay dead upon the captured territory—John Pettifer among them, who had fought one-handed at that last defence of the waiting boats (for Muriel's amateur surgery, and Dr. Butcher's subsequent efforts, had made a poor job of the broken wrist), until a sword-point took him under the ribs as he stumbled against a fallen bough, Monty's bill-hook being interposed too late to turn the blade, though it went on to avenge it with a slash on the swordsman's thigh which would mean a halting future; and Will Carless also, who fell with a bullet in the neck at the first rush of Coe's troop into Larkshill, he having delayed to give warning to houses which had been already vacated.

Besides these, they had captured about a dozen more or less seriously wounded men—for there had been no possibility of the retreating force carrying them over the Helford hollow—concerning the fate of whom Cooper frowned uncertainly.

He had no scruples one way or other, but he would rather be the ruler of fifty men than of thirty. He must see how they talked in the morning.

But they had taken no women, though men had searched in the thickets of Cowley Wood for Belle Rivers till the darkness stayed them—Belle Rivers, always fearful of danger, who had refused the risk of the storm of yesterday, and now crouched shivering under a low-branched holly—and they might have taken Mary Willetts had they looked for her and desired to do so; for that sensible woman, having always avoided giving countenance to any disorderly proceedings such as may bring you into discredit with the surrounding gentry, had remained quietly in her lodge, and no one had called to disturb her.

Cooper looked thoughtfully at the last retreat of the man that he was resolved to break, and calculated the chances of one bold thrust, which would end the fighting and make his gains complete.

But he knew that his men were exhausted with the efforts of the day. They had been in motion most of the previous night, on which point they were at a disadvantage, for most of their opponents had been able to sleep till dawn.

Still, there was exhaustion on both sides. He was half inclined—but it might be difficult to arouse his men to a further effort.

The sky was clear. There was little wind. It would be very cold before morning.

Perhaps his own physical condition decided the argument. He had not slept for forty-eight hours. He had taken a wound, and he had lost blood. He was not fit to lead such an attack, and he felt that it would not be successful unless he did so. John Coe was dead. So was Reeves. Butcher? Not he!

There was no sense in risking a failure. He was aware of his own losses. He was doubtful whether he could muster more than thirty men (besides Butcher's) who would be fit for the enterprise.

No. They should sleep tonight, and let their opponents' spirits sink as they reflected on the desperation of their condition.... He could do with some sleep himself.

CHAPTER SEVENTY-FIVE

CLAIRE came to Martin with the news that Belle Rivers was not to be found among the women. She had not been in any of the boats. Ted Rivers wanted to go back to find her. Might she take him in the lugger? Chris would come also, and the boy, Ned. It would be safe enough, for who would watch the deserted landing-place?

Martin did not think it safe, but he would not refuse if Claire wished to do it.

Belle had been in the frightened group of women who had fled up Bycroft Lane. She had been with them as they crossed the fields toward Cowley Thorn, and when they turned to take the field-path to the landing-place. She had been missing after the first sharp skirmish with the pursuing horsemen at the edge of Cowley Wood.

"Ned thinks she probably lost her nerve and hid in the wood," Claire added in explanation. "She'll be almost out of her mind if she's alone there—and you know her baby's due in about two months, and the cold will be cruel."

"Yes," Martin admitted, "we ought to try. I suppose no one else could manage the boat in the dark? But, of course, you'll stay in it with Chris, and Ted and the lad can go and look. If you think you're seen you must come back at once, and they must hide on the land. It mayn't make many hours' difference."

"Oh, there's no real danger," she answered lightly. "They'll all be as tired as we are. They won't look where they're expecting no one to come. But I'll take this, if I may." The pistol changed hands once again. "It has a busy life between us," she laughed, as she went out.

There were about forty men in the dim-lit kitchen of the farm-house of Upper Helford.

The lamp shone on the deal table in the centre, and the men stood crowding in the shadows of the large, low-ceilinged room.

They were as many as it would hold, and they were the men whom Jack had picked as most fit in physique and courage for the part which they would be required to take.

They were wearied men, conscious of good fighting done, and of a momentary respite in the security they had reached. Confident also in their leader, and with the comforting knowledge of a meal just eaten, which had been ready on their arrival. But they were dispirited by the sense of defeat, and knowing no hope for the future but by returning to the attack of those before whom they had fled today.

Martin stood with his back to a great fire, so that his face was in shadow. He was conscious of a controlled excitement, and of a great weariness which made that control difficult, but he knew that he must not relax until this struggle should be over.

His voice, when he spoke, had the confident coolness which it had held all day.

"I want you all to have a good sleep now, and then to be ready at about two hours before dawn, when we hope to give Mr. Butcher an unexpected visit. There is something which has been in preparation a good many weeks, but it has been necessary to keep it quiet, and it has not been mentioned by anyone, except on this island.

"Some of you know that Helford Grange is a very old building—how old it is hard to say—and it is probable that there has been a farmhouse here for about an equal period.

"There have been ancient tales of a passage below the ground that connected the two, and of uses to which it was put, but it had never been discovered in modern times, and most people had ceased to believe in it.

"Well, some months ago Miss Burman discovered this passage or, at least, one end of it.

It was followed underground for some distance, and was then found to have fallen in.

"That wasn't surprising. The wonder was that it remained at all, after what's happened. But the land between here and Helford Grange hasn't changed relatively not much, if at all—and it seemed worth investigating.

"Tom Aldworth took it in hand, and didn't think the falls need be very serious. Then I sent over Smith and Gilkes, who, as most of you know, were used to such work in the mines, and the end is that we've got the passage sufficiently cleared and repaired, and we know where it opens, and how it opens, into one of Butcher's cellars, which is too full of goods for him to find out we're coming before we're there.

"I think you'd better get some sleep now. You'll sleep rough tonight, though everything possible's been done, thanks to Mr. Burman, and our other friends that came over first, and we've most of us known what it is to sleep on worse than straw in the last six months. But if you all do your parts, as I know you will, I think we shall be back in our own homes by this time tomorrow."

There was no cheer as he finished, but a murmur that was half a chuckle and half a growl. There was none too dense to see how different would be the position if Butcher's gang should be surprised asleep in the fancied security of his own cellars, nor the effect of the capture of Helford Grange, with all its stores.

Confidence was renewed in the most despondent, and wound and bruise were forgotten as they discussed this new development.

CHAPTER SEVENTY-SIX

IT was three hours before the first light of the winter dawn when Martin came through the outer door into the farmhouse kitchen, where a great fire was still burning.

He had been round the sleepy sentries, and changed them twice already, for his mind had been vexed by a fear that there might be some traitor among them who would carry news of the plan which he had disclosed, and that the men who trusted him might be led into a death-trap in consequence. But there was only one way back to the mainland for anyone who was not prepared to swim for half a mile in the wintry sea, and he had seen that the cliff-top was well patrolled.

Claire was by the fire as he entered, and Helen, who had risen from a late attempt at rest, was with her. They had Belle Rivers wrapped in blankets before the fire, and were feeding her with warm milk. She lay white and half-conscious, and talked deliriously at times, but Claire spoke hopefully.

"I think she'll come round now, but we were afraid before. She's not been fully conscious since we found her, and she was so cold in the boat."

"How are things looking ashore?" Martin asked.

"They're dead quiet. You ought to have a walk-over if you go now. We could have sung hymns if we'd wanted. There's no sign of life anywhere. We shouldn't have found her if we hadn't shouted right up to Cowley Wood. She must have known Ted's voice, for she answered, and crawled out from under a tree, though she didn't seem to know us when we got up. I think she fainted when she knew we'd found her."

"Then you didn't stay in the boat?"

"No. Chris stayed. It didn't need two."

"It was a foolish risk to take. If they'd caught you—"

"Chris's risk. Not mine. But I can't argue now. I could sleep standing." She thought of that narrow channel into which they had run the lugger in the dark, with the wind behind them. When they got back with their burden there had been scarcely enough water to turn the boat, and they had had to pole it out for a hundred yards, more or less. Certainly the one who stayed in the boat had not been the least exposed to the risk of capture. A lug-sail may be very useful for beating into the wind, but even it won't take a boat down a narrow channel in the wind's teeth.

She added, "But the little devil nearly killed us all coming back. She steered us the short cut that we can't take very safely even when the tide's full and we've got light to see where we're going. We grounded once, and shipped about half a ton of water, and then we slid clear. I don't know what the keel looks like.... I suppose she thought Belle couldn't stand much more.... I'm sorry for Tom."

"Why?" said Tom, who came in at the moment, and had not heard the preceding words.

"I'm sorry for anyone that Chris marries."

"Who said I was going to marry Chris?"

"No one. You're not. She'll marry you—if she likes the way you kill Cooper."

"Kill Cooper?"

"Yes. Or someone else. If you don't know what I mean, I'm too tired to explain. I'm just going to sleep, and you don't seem to have waked up." She turned to Martin, returning the pistol as she did so. "Your turn now. You'll find a bullet missing. I had to shoot Joe Harker.... Yes, we had a few words, and it seemed necessary.... No, no one heard us. No one came, anyway. He was just spying round, after his own style. Looking for Belle, I expect.... No. I tell you it's all as dead as a church.... But I'm going to bed now. Helen dear, you'd better come too. Betsy Parkin can look after Belle now. *Noblesse oblige* is all right, but you overdo it.... Besides, I want your help. Joe wasn't the only one who got shot, and I'm afraid I'm a bit messy.... I thought that would fetch you."

She was in the passage with the last words, and Helen followed her as Chris came in at the outer door.

"Claire hurt?" she exclaimed, in reply to Martin's question.

"No, I don't think so. She was all right in the boat. She shot Joe Harker. She says they ran into each other in the dark and got the shock of their lives. Joe got his pistol out first and told her to come along or he'd shoot, and she said she wouldn't and did.... Yes, two. But they didn't seem to wake anyone. Lucky for us they didn't. We were stuck in that channel as tight as sardines for half an hour after that.... But I'm sure she's not much hurt."

Reassured on that point, Martin turned to Tom. He was going to rouse the men now, and they would start in about twenty minutes. Food was ready to be taken in to them in the large barn where they were sleeping. Martha Barnes was seeing to that.

Tom had been underground, and reported that all was well. Martin went out to rouse the men, and left him alone with Chris, and Belle Rivers asleep or unconscious before the fire.

It was ten minutes later that Helen re-entered the kitchen. She found them standing some distance apart, and in the attitudes of those who are waiting idly for something to happen. It may seem a reasonable deduction that they had found the time pass slowly, but reasonable deductions are sometimes

"Is Claire really hurt?" Chris asked, with something as nearly approaching anxiety as she had ever been known to show. She was eager for the romance of life, but her romantic requirement was a world in which you hurt your very numerous enemies, not one in which they hurt you or your friends in unpleasant places. She had been startled to hear of the death of John Pettifer, whom she had learnt to know and like as Monty's companion at the landing-place, but she was still inclined to assume the immunity of her closer friends.

"No," Helen answered. "She's asleep now. The shot must have just grazed her side. She says Joe shot first, when he saw her drawing her pistol."

Burman came in as they talked. He wore the wide-brimmed hat and leggings, and had the shot-gun under his arm, as when he had first introduced himself in Stacey Dobson's library.

"You won't mind a volunteer?" he asked, as Martin came in from outside at the same moment. Martin assented, thanking him for the help he offered. He had given the hospitality of Upper Helford, and ungrudging help in food and shelter and service, on the sole condition that his own freedom remained, and that neither he nor his were to be considered under Martin's authority.

Then the men began to file into the kitchen, and Tom put himself at their head, with Smith and Gilkes, and led the way to the cellar.

The others followed in single file, Jack Tolley, and Burman, and Burke, who had given good evidence of strength and courage during the previous day, being next behind them. Steve Fortune was in the first ten, his imagination already uneasy at the idea of this subterranean transit. He would willingly have been farther back, and there were those farther back, including Davy Barnes, who would gladly have been further forward. Last of all, an indignant Monty ended the line, Tom having considered that the unpopularity of his bill-hook, and his own impetuosity, would have a good effect in the prevention of a straggling rear.

CHAPTER SEVENTY-SEVEN

IT was a natural assumption from Claire's experience that Cooper was neglecting to keep a sufficient watch, and it had a degree of truth, though the inference may have done less than justice to his own abilities of leadership.

The end of the day had found him with about thirty very weary men who were without any serious injury as a result of the day's fighting, and about two-thirds of that number of wounded on his hands, including those that his opponents had left behind them.

He had no help from Butcher, who withdrew his own men to Helford Grange immediately the day's operations were over. He slept them all within his own doors, as he had done for several previous days, and was more concerned for the strength of his bars than with any ulterior watchfulness. It was not reasonable to expect attack from the inside, or to take precautions against such an eventuality.

Captain Cooper had these wearied men on his hands, and about fifty horses. It says something for the discipline that he maintained that he was able to get them together when the short winter twilight was approaching, to allot their sleeping-quarters to his satisfaction, to find food and accommodation for the horses, and to insist that the wounded men should be conveyed to warmth and shelter, and receive such rough attentions as the exigencies of the occasion permitted.

He did not anticipate any attack during the night, yet he set two of the most reliable of his men to share the task of watching his own side of the Helford hollow; and he chose four others to divide the duty, two after two, of patrolling the outskirts of Cowley Thorn.

Of these last, one of the two who were to take the second watch was Joe Harker, whom he rightly judged to have done something less than his share in the operations of the day.

Joe, who was quite fresh, having slept all afternoon, wrapped in a horse-cloth, among the gorse-bushes, commenced his vigil by wandering into Cowley Wood in search of the woman who was said to have bolted into its cover, with a result which we already know; and the other sentry, after half an hour of what he considered to be an utterly useless vigilance, found a straw-lined corner sufficiently comfortable to enable him to complete the rest he needed.

He had been enjoying this sleep for about ten minutes when Joe and Claire made comparison of their shooting abilities, and it would have required a good deal more to rouse him than the sound of two pistol-shots something over a quarter of a mile away.

Yet he slept uneasily as the night passed, having a dormant fear that he might fail to wake before his comrades should be astir, and his fault discovered, and it was about an hour before dawn that he intruded upon the rest of his captain, as he had been instructed to do under such circumstances, with a tale that he had heard shots in the direction of Helford Grange.

Captain Cooper yawned, and got up reluctantly. He was heavy with sleep, and his wounded arm throbbed painfully. It sounded an unlikely tale. Yet he came into the road to do his own listening.

The night was very still, the stars were bright, the cold was bitter.

He stood listening for some time. He had good ears. He thought he heard a fox bark in the distance. Besides that—nothing. He yawned again, and went back to sleep.

The sentry, having given proof of his vigilance and received no thanks, felt that he had earned a further rest, and took it; but not for long, being waked again by the sound of shots which were too near to be doubtful.

He looked out from his refuge to see a group of his comrades standing unarmed, in a sleepy bewilderment, already in the hands of their enemies, whose rifles menaced them, and to observe that some resistance was being offered farther along the road, where a house stood from which shots were being exchanged with those by whom it was surrounded.

He was a prudent man, and one who could estimate the probabilities of such a position very easily. He went home.

Arriving there, on the back of a horse which he had been prompt enough to secure without observation, he had no scruple in providing for his requirements from Cooper's stores with the liberality which the severity of the season suggested, and disappeared into the wilderness, with Nance Weston for company.

His subsequent experiences might not be uninteresting, for he was a man of character, and adventures found them, but they would be out of place here. We must watch him ride away, and for the time forget him.

Seventeen men, who were less fortunate than he, stood in a group on the main road in Cowley Thorn. Their hands were tied, and half a dozen men who stood round them with loaded rifles made the idea of escape unpopular.

Martin surveyed them with embarrassment, and Burman, who stood beside him, with unconcealed disfavour.

They were an unsavoury group. The countenances of most of them illustrated the attractive candour with which Nature is accustomed to own her errors. They were not improved by the fact that they had not washed for two days, more or less, and that those who were without the usual straggle of beard had not shaved for a similar or longer period.

"You won't keep this scum?" said Burman bluntly.

"I don't see what else I can do," Martin answered. The prospect was far from pleasing. It was made worse by the fact that there were a dozen men at Helford Grange, including Butcher himself, who had surrendered in the same way. The surprise had been almost too great, the success too complete, to please him.

Cooper, sleeping with a well-bolted door, and with eight of his best men in the same house, was still offering resistance, and Martin, not wishing to sacrifice life without necessity, had withdrawn his own men somewhat (now better weaponed than before by the capture of Butcher's arsenal), to give him time to think it over..

"You'll be sorry if you do," Burman persisted. He was a farmer, and he regarded them with a professional eye. They were poor stock. Poor stock, not worth its keep. The fool hopes the impossible, and goes on feeding. The wise man kills it off.

"Well," he said, "I shall close Helford again if you do. You must face your own troubles. I'll have no vermin there."

Martin was silent. He knew he spoke sense. He had paid heavily more than once before for the hesitation which now troubled his mind. But he knew also that he could never give an order to shoot men in cold blood. He had no jail, even had he been disposed to confine them. What could he do except give them life for a promised loyalty, and hope for the best?

"They've been badly led," he said. It was the best excuse he could think of, but he knew that most of them had chosen their leader, and many would have been better pleased with a worse one.

"You'll be keeping their leader next, like you have Butcher. What'll be the change when the fighting's over?"

"I don't think they'll fight again," Martin answered. What was the use of talking?

"No. A shot in the back's more likely."

Well, if so, it was a risk that had to be taken. He couldn't refuse quarter to men who yielded without a blow. "And now here he comes," said Burman.

Captain Cooper was walking down the road, with his hands raised over his head. He had decided that he could gain nothing by a prolonged resistance, and he might lose much.

He had been impressed, also, by the fact that the first of his men who had shown his head had been shot through it by Jack Tolley's rifle. He had learned to face facts.

"You can name your price," he said, as he came up to Martin. "I give you best."

Burman brought his shot-gun to his shoulder, and fired both barrels.

Cooper collapsed on the road. He lay on his face, and the blood spread out on both sides, over the frozen road.

Burman turned to Martin.

"I'm not under your orders, Captain Webster. We bargained that. But I've done what you couldn't do, and you'll thank me later. I'd rather it had been that cur Butcher, but he'll be no trouble alone. I expect he's finished pricing the tea." He paused a moment as Martin did not reply, and then said: "Friends still?" and held out his hand.

Martin hesitated, and then took it.

"There's some things has to be done, though we mayn't like doing them," Burman added. "It's all in Joshua. I suppose you'll save the rest now. If I knew how long you'll live I could tell how long you'll be sorry. But I shan't interfere again."

CHAPTER SEVENTY-EIGHT

THE morning sun was still low, shining from a clear sky upon a frozen world, and there was little stir of life at Upper Helford, except among those that anxiety did not allow to rest, when Steve Fortune came back to the farmhouse door with a note from Martin to Helen to say that all was well and that the women could return to their homes as quickly as the necessary arrangements could be completed. He added that there were about twenty men more or less seriously wounded who were in urgent need of attention.

His own men were tired, and he still required their services in many ways; could Helen send some of the women, many of whom, having crossed by the boats in the earlier days, should be fit to come at once, to undertake such duties? As the need was urgent, Steve would guide any of them by the underground passage who might be willing to come that way.

Helen only delayed to give the good news to Chris, and went to find Muriel.

It could not be said of either of them that they were fit for further exertion, but it was not a call to be disregarded.

"Claire's asleep, and I wouldn't wake her. She's done her share," Helen explained, "and Chris will get the best crews she can together for the boats from the men that are still here, and take as many as they will hold. I expect they'll all want to get home at once now. But it'll be about three hours before they can start. I don't suppose many of the women will be willing to go the underground way unless we do it."

Muriel said, "You look worn out, and I'm afraid I'm too tired to be much good when we get there, but I'll come if you really think it will make that difference…. I'm glad it's all over. There ought to be better times now."

They went together to enlist the help that was needed.

It was scarcely an hour later that Steve, with about a dozen women behind him, led them through a passage which, now that he knew it, was no longer fearful.

The passage sloped down for a long distance, and then became level. It was damp and cold, and very dimly lit by a series of lamps which Tom and his fellow-workers had fitted to the roof.

Muriel had the dog with her. He went on for a short distance gaily enough, and then whined, and hung back till Steve called him, when he ran on without further protest.

They were less than half-way through when Helen noticed that Muriel was falling behind, and went back to her.

She had stopped beneath the light of one of the lamps, and seated herself on a piece of timber which had been brought for repairing the tunnel and left unused.

It had been about there that the falls had been worst, and the repairs most extensive.

"I'm afraid I'm too tired to come on just yet, but please don't wait. I shall be all right in a few minutes."

"You don't look tired: you look ill."

"I'm not as strong as I was, and I've done a good deal since yesterday. But I don't want you to wait. There'll be so much to be done…. I'll come on when I've rested."

"You're not fit to do anything more."

"If I don't feel better I'll go back."

"I think someone ought to be with you."

"No, please, Helen. You'll be needed there. I should be wretched if I felt I were keeping you. And there's really no need at all. And—there are times when we all like to be alone."

The last plea was not easily to be ignored, especially by one of Helen's training and temperament. She went on reluctantly.

Muriel had spoken no more than the truth in saying that she wanted to be alone.

She had worked beyond her strength, and the stresses of the last two days had produced an emotional exhaustion beyond the experience of those who had reacted with a simpler selfishness.

She was aware now, too vividly aware, of the misery of those who were wounded, and were so unlikely to be well tended—of the thirst, the cold, the pain…. But she could do no more. She had fallen out of the ranks. After she had rested awhile she would go back. "His little ones at home." If God would not use her further, even that must be taken patiently…. But she did not want to think. She was too tired. She only wanted to rest. Above all, she had not wanted to talk. She was glad Helen had gone. But Helen always understood, though her own feelings were so carefully covered… And the pain was coming again—that came so often now….

It could only have been for a few moments, for there can be many thoughts in a little space, and Helen's steps had not died in the distance, when a spray of water fell on Muriel's hand, and did not cease.

She looked up and saw a tiny jet that shot out from the opposite wall, beneath the lamp. A very thin jet, but coming out very strongly. Did it mean that the sea was breaking in?

She forgot the pain she was feeling, in a panic instinct of flight.

Then with the thought there came to her the memory of a tale that she had read in childhood of someone—was it boy or man?—who had saved a dyke in Holland through which the seas were breaking by inserting his arm in the hole by which the water had commenced to enter. It might have been nothing more than a tale.

She stood irresolute. If she ran after those who had gone before, she could give them warning, and they would hasten. Surely she could do a more certain good in that way, and her own life would have no better chance than the others. She knew suddenly that she did not want to die. She had been fighting against death all these months. Striving to ignore the pain: to persuade herself that it was less intense, or less frequent. Praying for miracles. Had there not even been a vague, unquietened hope that it was not too late—that out of this strange chaos to which the world had fallen might come the things that she had never known—love, children, home? She did not want to die.

The pause of uncertainty was no longer than a footstep takes; but every thought and action that her life had known, every faith and doubt, every valour and weakness, were in the scales that trembled to the decision that she was taking. Then she had crossed the tunnel, and her hand was pressed upon the cold clay soil from which that jet of water burst.

And as she did this, fear left her mind. It faltered back for a moment as the thought came that if the pressure of her hand could prevent the passage of the water entirely, it might not get worse, and, if she could endure long enough, help would be sure to come. Hope came at the thought, and fear re-entered with it.

But the hope died quickly. She saw that it could not be. Her hand could do no more than check, it could not staunch, the flow.

She began to doubt whether her efforts could really make much difference, whether they would be sufficient to save those who were still such a short distance ahead, so unconscious of the danger behind them.

And seeing this, she saw also that it did not matter. She saw the high purpose of life, which overshadows its eternal frustration, its reiterated futility.

In those few minutes that she stood there, how much she knew, and thought, and remembered! Death might be near, but life triumphed....

The water was spraying out from each side of the pressed palm, and between her fingers. It was deadly cold, numbing her hand. She moved it for a second, thinking to improve its position, and a stream as from a hosepipe shot out across the tunnel. She was able to push her hand into the hole, and, for a moment, she stayed it. Surely they would be safe by now!

The light flickered, and went out. She was in a darkness such as the earth's surface can never know.... There came to her a vision of that Whitsunday morning when she had wakened to sunlight, and fresh air, and to a shadow of death, which she had fought, and then accepted with the words of an earlier confidence. "*To be with Christ, which is far better.*"

The rush of water was too strong for her arm to contend against it. She thought that it was breaking in at other points also. Surely they must be safe by now! She gave up the useless effort.

She did not know that she spoke aloud in the darkness, "*which is far better.*"

The confident words died, and the ocean-floor fell in.

CHAPTER SEVENTY-NINE

IT was nearly midday before Martin was able to relinquish control to the hands of others almost as tired as he, and to return with Helen to Upper Helford—for his own home was in ashes—for the rest he needed.

They went in the returning boats, and he slept heavily for a few hours, and then waked with a stiff and aching body, but with a mind alert and restless, so that he rose, and went out, and walked for a time upon the northern cliffs, which looked upon an ocean that showed no limit.

He saw that for the moment the fight was won.

Whether for good or evil, he had become the ruler of this little land, this isolated tribe, and he could do with them what he would.

By one stroke of successful strategy, by the accident of that discovered passage, he had made a name which would be a tradition of greatness long after he had ceased to be. But he did not know that. He saw less, and he saw farther.

He saw the futility of all endeavour. He might rule with an old wisdom, or a new foolishness, but he would die, and his will with him, and even that which he had sown in wisdom might be brought by others to a foolish flower.

Was it not even too much to hope that the present isolation would continue?

Might not all the coercions of the old civilization be existing still?

Might not any morning bring the sight of smoke-trailed funnels, and the black menace of the lifted guns?

There would be no use in weapons. As the curse of European civilization smote the islands of the Pacific in an earlier century, so, if it came here, must it smite, remorseless in its penetration, until they should have become the customers of its vices once again.

Surely, if belief could be in any personal devil, he had been the whisperer in the ears of the laboratory workers, guiding them in successive centuries to the invention of black powder and of a hundred subsequent more fiendish evils, steeling their hearts by the appeals of greed or vanity to put their knowledge into the hands of their fellows. Even Dante might have failed to imagine a sufficient hell for such as they.

He remembered that terrible bureaucratic slavery which the waters covered, when every man had been compelled to walk; the same road at the same pace as his neighbours; when he could not take pleasure, or work, for his own gain or his fellows' good, but at the licensed times; when he could not find a corner of England so remote that he could build a home to his own liking without the interference and restraint of others; when he could not teach his own child in his own way, but it must be raped from him to be patterned in the common mould.

There was no hope but in isolation....

He became aware that the wind was colder, and that the night was falling around him. *"The night cometh, when no man can work."* The words entered his mind as a warning, and as an unescapable doom. What use was there in thought and anxious effort in a world in which the night was always approaching.

His influence might be good or evil, but it would pass like a shadow, like an impression in water. The water might give way very easily to the moving hand, but it would close as easily behind it, and what would be altered? And the hand was Life, the water Time. Was it not a wiser rule to accept the inevitable end, and not to exhaust its brevity with a useless effort? *"The night cometh, when no man can work."*

And then the thought came that these were the words of one who had the gift of putting the deepest wisdom into a simplicity of words, and that he had used them to a directly opposite argument.

It was because of that approaching darkness that the labour should neither be delayed nor stinted. Taking no anxious thought for the morrow, the day's work must be done as best we may, because the darkness is so certain—and so near.

The new order of life which he was striving to build with such partial success, with such inevitable errors, might disappear tomorrow, but what he did today would have become a fact unchangeable, the significance of which was beyond his seeing.

The night moved round the earth. It followed daylight men are followed by the overtaking feet of death, but there was no finality in its triumph.

For behind it followed forever the indifferent dawn.

www.ingramcontent.com/pod-product-compliance
Lightning Source LLC
Chambersburg PA
CBHW050556260626
47157CB00002B/589